DREAM WEAVER

A Mystic Beach Fantasy Rockstar Romance

Aislinn Archer

Mystic Beach Press

Paperback edition ISBN: 979-8-9862117-2-5

Kindle edition ASIN: B09X51WN5T

This book is a work of fiction. The names, characters, places, and incidents are products of the writer's imagination or have been used fictitiously and are not to be construed as real. Any resemblance to persons, living or dead, actual events, locales, or organizations is entirely coincidental.

While every effort has been made to ensure errors have been eradicated from this book, we are only human. If you find a typo, missing word or other error, please email the author directly at Aislinn@AislinnArcher.com so she can fix it as quickly as possible. Thank you!

Content Warning

A content review for this book, and others in the series, is available on the author's website at AislinnArcher.com. If you have any concerns about whether you might find the content of this work disturbing, please take a few moments to check the content review on the website and do not read if you think you might find any of the content disturbing. The recommended reading age for this work is 18 or older.

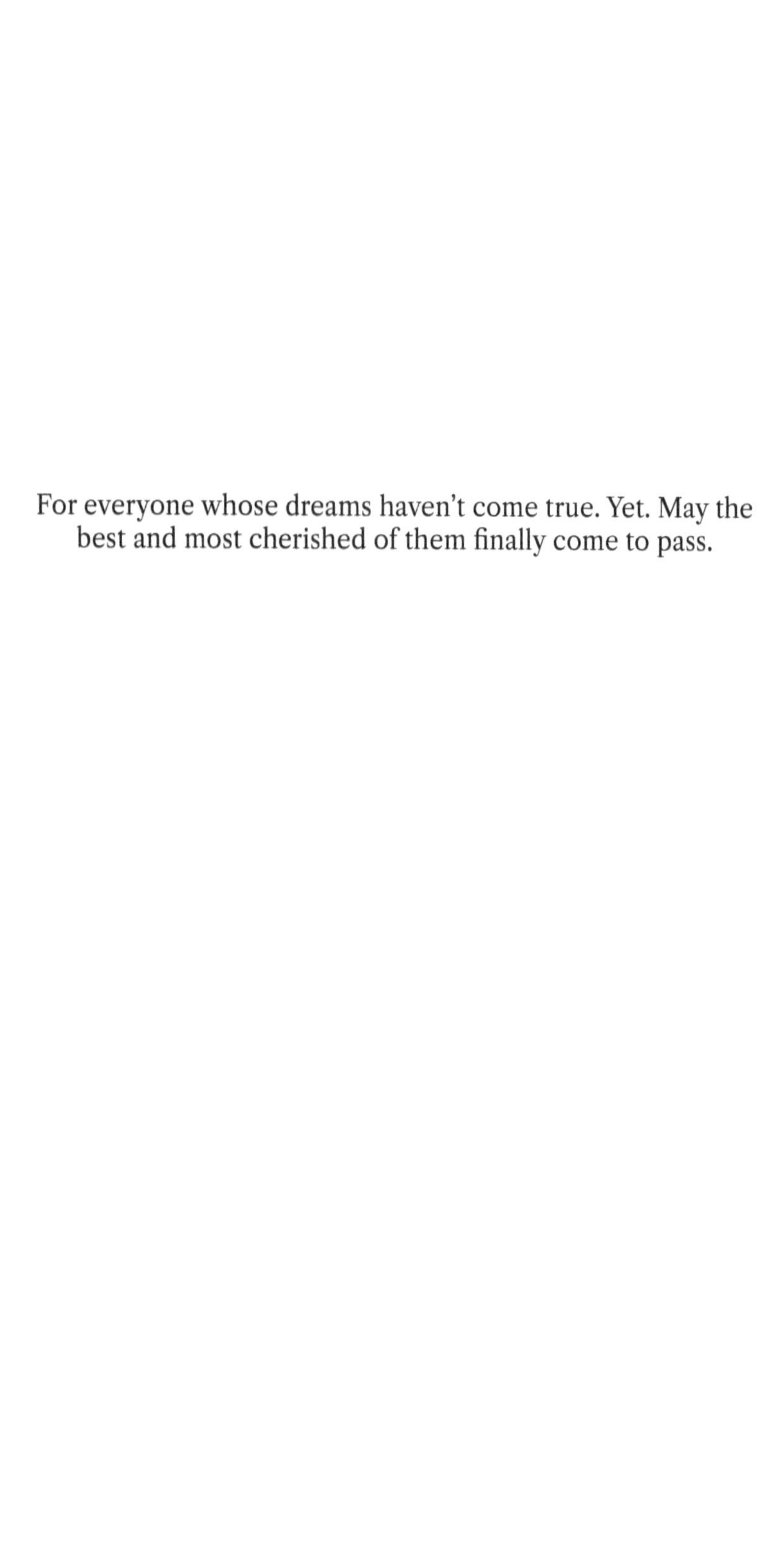

For everyone whose dreams haven't come true. Yet. May the best and most cherished of them finally come to pass.

CONTENTS

PROLOGUE

Two and a half years ago

There's an insistent knock at my door. I haven't even sat down after getting back from my birthday dinner — 27 is supposed to be a banner year, right? My friends took me out to the new restaurant right next to my shop, where my new friend Callie is the chef. The other ladies — Amber the jewelsmith and Siobhan the tattoo artist, my other business neighbors — just dropped me off, still wheedling me to come out for drinks and dancing as I got out of the car.

"It's too late for trick-or-treat, kids! The candy was gone hours ago!" I announce, knowing that, at this hour, it's just the girls come back to try to change my mind about going out. "Seriously — I told you. I don't drink," I tell them loudly as I head to the door. "And I'm not up for dance—"

I swing the door back open, expecting to see the pair laughing at my determination to stay home. That's not what I see.

"Happy birthday, Bridge."

Hunter holds his arms out, a miraculous presence, like the gods have left me a birthday present on my front porch, minus the bow. I throw myself at him, my best friend of more than twenty years, bawling like a baby, soaking his T-shirt in seconds.

"I've missed you, Bridge. A lot. Let's never do that again," he says into my hair. He takes a deep breath and sighs. "I really am sorry. So, so sorry."

For nearly two years now, that's what I've needed to hear — but more than that... to know he really meant it, on a deeper level than just the words. I couldn't take him at his word when he'd called two weeks after that horrible night in New York and said he was sorry he'd let me become the butt of a joke. Because I knew then that it wouldn't change a thing if I didn't draw a line on our friendship, even if we had been best friends for basically our entire lives. In all those years, I'd never been able to stay mad at him, and it's been hard, building a life without him. But it was necessary. For both of us.

I needed him to do more than acknowledge that he'd screwed up and he'd hurt me. I needed to know that that mattered to him, that he'd really try to do better. And I needed him to pull my best friend of two decades out of the bullshit of the rockstar lifestyle and his tortured past so I wasn't stuck with the same asshole I'd met that horrible night. I wanted my best friend back. And this time, I couldn't be the one doing all the work to pull us back together.

"I missed you, too, Hunter." I sniffle. "But I can't keep doing this. I respect myself too much to accept being treated like that. By anyone."

"I never wanted to hurt you." He looks deep in my eyes, his own so full of regret that it tears at my heart. "I fucked up big-time. And I know it. When you stayed away, and I realized you might never come back..." He sighs, his breath catching on the way out. "I heard what you said that night I called. Really heard it. You kicked me in the ass that night. No — the balls. It felt like you'd clocked me in the nuts and left me gasping on the floor. And you didn't leave me much choice but to sit with it, absorb it and hold myself accountable for what I did, what I'd become. I've spent the last two years soul-searching. Trying to find a way to be better. For me and for you. Trying to think of a way to make it up to you, show you I've changed."

"And...?"

"I'm not sure I *can* make it up to you. That's how badly I messed up. I know that. I'm honestly not sure I can ever fix the damage I did to you, to us. And, knowing that, I finally decided maybe I should just come and try. Actually show you I've changed, even if I'm not perfect. Show you that I've tried to become the grown-up version of your best friend, the best friend you deserve, not just the one you ended up with because my band got an album deal. I decided I'd just have to try to make it up to you, however I can, starting with a long-overdue apology from the core of my heart."

I pause to absorb his words, the emotions naked on his face. This familiar face, changed in our two years apart — older, his scruff grown out to a short beard, his hair longer, his emerald eyes haunted in a way that reminds me of the day I found out he'd been essentially homeless for a year, and also of... of a troubled man sitting on a beach in a dream I'd once had...

As the moments tick by, tension, fear, dread creep into his expression, alongside that regret. But he waits for me to respond. Maybe he really has grown in the past two years. And that image of the man on the beach... the one I've never been able to forget...

"Apology accepted." A wave of relief spreads across his face. "But the jury's still out on revised-rockstar Hunter. You're going to have to prove to me that it's my friend inside there, not that jerk who kept showing up in his place."

"I know. I don't blame you for being skeptical. I know I still have a long way to go to fix what I did. If I ever can."

I nod, accepting his honest self-appraisal. Time will tell whether he can prove to us both that the old Hunter is back.

"Come catch me up..."

He plays it down, maybe out of sensitivity to what happened that night in New York, but what he tells me of the last two years of his life is impressive. Sold-out shows at Madison Square Garden with aMUSEd, and in Paris, Sydney, Tokyo, Rio... A Best New Artist award for aMUSEd, and Song of the Year, the award for writing the best new song, for Hunter himself.

If he's seeing someone, he doesn't tell me, and I find it a relief.

I tell him about the shop, my ever-increasing clientele for healing and spiritual counseling, the friends I've made among my fellow business owners, far more of them Pagan or witches and such than odds would account for, since we're a pretty small minority. It's like something about Mystic Beach just draws people here.

And now it's brought Hunter home to me. Just for a few days this time, until he has to go back to the tour. But he's here, and this time, it feels like my best friend — my real best friend — is coming back. To Mystic Beach, and to me.

CHAPTER 1

CALL ME

Brighid
Present

"I can't believe you're actually going to be here! And for what? A month? Two?"

"Maybe three," Hunter says, angling his tablet so it's not cutting off the top of his head on my screen. "The label booked the studio exclusively for the whole summer so we had time to finish writing and record the full album. We're there until we're done."

"Wow... Three whole months — maybe," I correct myself, smiling back at him when he grins over the qualifier, "of time when I can actually hug my best friend, go out to dinner with him and see that pretty face across something other than a phone screen! Whatever am I going to do with this luxury!"

He chuckles.

"Enjoy it — because as soon as we're done with the album, we move on to tour prep and then four months on the road, and then on to Europe," he warns. "I've missed you," he says, his expression momentarily more somber. "How long has it been since we've actually seen each other in person?" His memory is notoriously lousy. We sometimes joke about me being supplemental brain space for him...

"One year, three months," I pause to count on my fingers as I do the math, "and 12… no — 13 days." *…And six hours, 42 minutes and… checking my watch… 28… 29… 30… seconds*, I continue in my head. Best not to let him know I know down to the second exactly how long it has been. It's not like I've been keeping track as our days apart drift by… *Nope. Not at all.*

But, seriously, after the incident at the release party for their first album, four years ago now, Hunter and I hadn't spoken to each other for even longer than that. I'd always trusted him to have my back, just like I had his, and he always had. Until that day he hadn't. And that's before we get to the other complicating factors.

I'd always felt like I didn't quite belong in that rockstar world of his — not one of "the beautiful people," not talented like that, preferring to stay home and watch a movie over going out and partying. And what had happened that night had cemented that my place was here, in Mystic Beach, running my shop and, eventually, making some new friends. So that's what I did.

When he came back into my life after that wakeup call nearly two years prior, it was like we'd never been apart. Nearly. I was stronger, a little more self-assured, a little more equal in our friendship. And that was why I'd done it. For his part, he'd found his way back to the old Hunter, mostly. He was more self-aware, more observant of his impact on others, more reflective than he'd been when we were younger. Still a giant goofball, and still loving the spotlight almost as much as the music. But more mature in the ways that counted. He'd proved to me that day — and since — that, like me, he'd grown in that time we'd been apart.

Something else had changed in his time away — he truly is a rockstar now, and it was his rockstar life he returned to a few days after he showed up on my doorstep on my 27th birthday. But he started coming to visit me, for a few days or a week, whenever he had some downtime. We spent a lot of that time curled up on my couch together, binge-watching Star Wars movies or the "Doctor Who" episodes he'd missed amidst the hectic tour schedule the band now maintains. And sometimes we watched "The Princess Bride," or, more often, "Some Kind of Wonderful," even though parts of that story still hit very close to home for us. We both love that movie, the dynamic between the main characters. Even if the best-friends-to-lovers narrative isn't one our own story has followed.

With his grueling recording, touring and promotional schedule, I haven't seen nearly enough of him these last two years, though we usually talk a couple times a month. At least a text or two, just checking in. He's been a very busy boy ever since his career took off. Almost overnight, it seemed, he went from local kid playing his guitar on the beach to full-on rockstar, complete with a limos-luxury-hotels-and-lingerie-models lifestyle. And almost since the day he signed his record deal, the gossip sites have been filled with photos of Hunter with various tall, slender model types — blondes, brunettes, even a redhead or two. Eventually, I stopped looking. It wasn't my business who he was dating, even if he seemed to be going out of his way to cling to the overdone rockstar-model relationship cliché.

Not that I'm jealous. Nope. Not at all. The sarcastic voice in my head peeks in long enough to roll its eyes. I stick a mental tongue out at it. Nope. Not jealous. Not at all...

But now he's coming here, to Mystic Beach, for a couple months.

"I wish I could get back there more often, but it's been a rush of publicity events, charity concerts, writing with the guys so we had something to bring with us into the studio for the next album. Even our 'downtime' is crazy busy, and it's not like I can fly in to Georgetown once or twice a week on the corporate jet the label lets us use for official travel."

"I know... demands of the life of a rockstar and all that." I sigh. "Living in New York, touring, Rolling Stone photo shoots, hot- and cold-running groupies, champagne and caviar in the private dining rooms at the best restaurants atop the best hotels, with the waitresses slipping you their phone numbers and you slipping them something else... Such a hardship," I rib him good-naturedly, despite the underlying sentiment being somewhat true. Not that I'd tell him that.

"Hey — that's not true! You know I won't eat fish eggs!" he objects, if only to that one thing. "That cultural unit in eighth grade proved that. Yuck!"

We both chuckle at the memory... Mrs. Taylor's social studies class, which she liked to sprinkle liberally with hands-on cultural experiences from a different country each month. She'd brought in some inexpensive caviar for the Russian unit, to go along with the blinis that Margot Marsden (or, more likely, her mother or their housekeeper) made, and the reception had been pretty evenly split. Personally, I hadn't minded the caviar, even if I wouldn't have gone out of my way to have it again. But Hunter hadn't made it past the first bite.

"That chocolate mousse of yours from the French unit, though — now *that* I could have every day and never get tired of it..." he moans sensually, sending a shiver down my spine while also instantly warming up areas contiguous thereto. *Down, girl! Can't let yourself get turned on by him... even if he is the sexiest thing you've ever seen, along with being your best friend.*

"Of course not — you're a chocoholic! I don't even have to imagine what your 'sex face' looks like, because it's your default expression whenever chocolate lava cake is on the dessert menu," I tease.

"Darn right! Whoever invented that stuff deserves a Nobel Prize in sensory delight." He moans again, setting off another flush, both on my cheeks and in those areas farther south.

"Are you blushing or is that some weird video filter?" he jokes.

"Hot flash," I toss back at him.

"We're not even 30. You're not having hot flashes. Not that I want to know when you are, either. I draw the bestie line at the 'woman stuff.' You know that."

"Yup, so no mentioning the impending invasion by The Red Menace."

He claps his hand over his mouth, gagging.

"No — not that! TMI! Ack!" he jokes.

"Anyway — I've got a ton of stuff to do to get ready for your arrival... I've arranged things with Molly so I can take a week off after you get here, so we should have some time to catch up before we're both swamped with work again. Speaking of which... my lunch break is almost over..."

"And you've got to get back to the shop. Got it. I'll see you Tuesday, maybe Wednesday. I'm still waiting for them to finalize the schedule," he says.

"Well, let me know. We can do dinner if you get in early enough."

His expression gets serious for a moment. I wait.

"I really have missed you, Bridge. A lot."

"Me, too."

He ends the video call, and I'm left sighing, full of mixed emotions — excitement that he's actually going to be here, warm fuzzies that we'll get a chance to just hang out for the first time in a long time, and a well-worn wistfulness that no matter how much I love him — and not just as a friend — for reasons I can't quite understand, he's never going to be mine.

Chapter 2

Video Killed the Radio Star

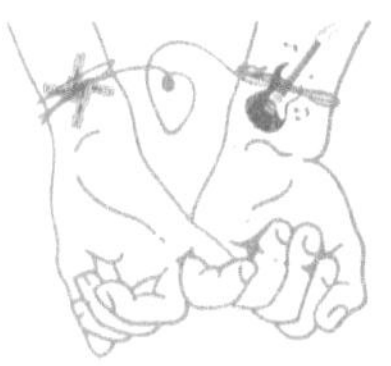

Hunter
A few days later

"What the fuck, Billy? A reality show? While we're in the studio and nominally on vacation? I mean, seriously — what the fuck?"

"Orders from on high," our manager explains with a supplicating gesture. As if I won't be pissed off about this just because he's not personally responsible.

The rest of the guys are carefully avoiding making eye contact with either of us, which is harder than it might seem, since we're all sitting in adjacent seats on a small private jet 45,000 feet in the air and I'm so hot about this I'm straight-up shouting.

"The media-relations rep from Siren's Song just called and told me it was already set up and that you were going to do it, and I quote, 'Whether he's inclined to be agreeable about it or not.' And, under the terms of your contract with the label, they can direct you to take part in promotional appearances as needed, with no specific guidelines as to what constitutes a promotional appearance."

"Remind me to have an actual contracts attorney double-check our next contract for shit like this," I tell him, exasperated that I appear to be on the hook for this nonsense.

"Will do. In another two years," he says wryly.

Great. Just great. Two more years of being obligated to do stupid shit like this "show."

"And why me and not one of the other guys? Or all of us? It's not like we're not all single right now."

"Hey — don't throw us under the bus!" our drummer, Rhys, objects from the other side of the aisle.

"You've only got yourself to blame for that, pal — you're the one known for simultaneously dating multiple models and influencers," Billy tells me.

I start to protest that I've changed, but Billy has no idea what my private life is like now. We've been on tour for so long, he just assumes that other than me refusing to have anything to do with the groupies, things are status quo. Apparently, the label does, too.

"Maybe limit yourself to serial monogamy, groupies and a waitress or two, like the others do, and you won't be high on their list for a celebrity dating show," he suggests.

Rhys snickers, not making much of an effort to be quiet about it.

"Laugh it up, fuzzball," I growl back at him. "You're not exactly known for your quiet lifestyle either."

"Hey — I stick with the occasional groupie or after-dinner waitress. And I'm not going near anyone whose idea of a job title is 'influencer' — 'Holly *Hard*wood,'" he cough/chuckles. "That's totally on you. It's the price you pay for dating girls with millions of followers on social media."

Yeah, that life decision is really coming back to bite me in the ass, even if I haven't actually been out with anyone since before the tour started. Now, I had my reasons for how I've conducted my personal life since all of this started. But fuck me if that hasn't turned out to be exactly the thing that will turn my life into a blazing dumpster fire, even after things have changed, after *I've* changed. I don't need Brighid to read my tarot cards to see disaster coming. Not that I could ask her about this anyway, since she's half the reason I made that decision in the first place.

"So what exactly is entailed in this 'show'? I can't possibly expect they'll just follow me around on a couple of dates, right? That would be too close to actual reality."

"No. You'll wish it was that simple. The concept here is that you, as the eligible single rockstar dating multiple beautiful high-profile women at the same time — including Holly

*Har*wood," he corrects, glaring at Rhys, "are going to have to finally pick one to call your girlfriend."

"Tell me you didn't just say that."

"I wish I could."

"I repeat... *What the ever-loving fuck*, Billy? How is this even a concept for a show? This is just messing around with my personal life, and I sure as hell am *not* 'inclined to be agreeable about it.'" Especially not when they're digging up women I've been dodging for the better part of two years. Especially when that includes Holly, who's been angling to lock me down in a relationship for even longer than that.

"I don't know what to tell you, Hunter. It wasn't my idea. Don't shoot the messenger. The good news is they're going to award your appearance fees to the charity of your choice, and you'll get a chance to talk that up, too. It'll be great exposure for you, the charity and the band."

Now, that's promising, even if the rest of this is a disaster in the making. I could easily match any amount of money the network is offering to the charity, but the exposure from talking up my favorite mental-health awareness non-profit on a national and international scale is something money can't buy. It'll spur both awareness and donations from viewers, maybe get people who need it some real help.

"You should be glad this is the first thing they've asked you to do that you find objectionable," Billy adds, drawing my attention back to the nightmare he's just dropped in my lap.

Yeah. Glad. Thrilled. Oh, boy! What have I gotten myself into?

More importantly, how am I going to explain this to Brighid? Who I just the other day promised I would finally be spending time with? Oh, just fuck me...

"**H**ey, Hunt — give me just a second to finish up with this customer."

"That'll be $225, Mrs. Lowell. ... Let me get you your change... Oh! Well, thanks! That's really not necessary. ... Well, if you insist. Have a good day!"

"What the fuck did she buy that cost $225? And did she just tell you to keep the change?" I ask Brighid, incredulous, since I can't see anything but the shop ceiling right now over our FaceTime call.

She chuckles.

"She bought a big amethyst geode from my special display stock. She's been eyeing it for months. And I threw in a tarot reading for free, so I kind of earned that extra $75."

"Remind me to invest my royalties in crystals and tarot readings," I joke.

"*Ethically-sourced* crystals. And you know as well as I do that things have changed here in Mystic Beach while you've been gone," she reminds me. "I've had a huge uptick in customers in the last year or two for some reason, and these days, most of the full-time residents are wealthy retirees from big cities along the East Coast, or part-timers with second homes big enough to accommodate kids, grandkids, nieces, nephews, cousins, business associates, and their dogs... Man... I still want a dog," she digresses. "Shouldn't selling a $225 hunk of rock entitle me to a dog? But then, I'd have to have time to spend with a dog... The life of a self-employed entrepreneur, I guess."

"You could make it a shop dog," I suggest. "Customers love a friendly fuzzball greeting them! Just ask Rhys!"

"I heard that!" Rhys yells from the back of the plane, where he's now playing Texas Hold'em with Declan, David and Alex — our lead singer, our bass player (also Declan's brother) and our keyboard player, in that order.

Kier, our lead guitarist, is napping with his noise-canceling AirPods in, which is a good thing, because Billy is pacing back and forth in the aisle next to him, arguing loudly with some promoter about our greenroom requirements for a private gig months from now.

"No, Sunkist is not acceptable. No, not Crush! Fanta only! It's right there in the riders! ... Well, get a copy you didn't spill coffee on, then. Geez!" (The orange soda is for me. At least he has my back on the beverage front.)

"Maybe," Bridge replies, pulling me back to the conversation about her wanting a dog.

She's been wanting one since we were kids. Her parents actually got her a golden retriever for her 12th birthday, but a few months later her dad decided it was too much work and gave it away. She came home from school one day and the dog was just gone, no warning. She ran straight over to my house, devastated, and cried on me for hours, until she fell asleep in my arms. She never really forgave her parents for that. And I don't blame her. Not that I'm any model for positive parental relations...

I don't have time for a dog, either. With our touring schedule, he'd spend more time with a dog-sitter than with me.

Besides, one stray hair on my sofa, and I'd never hear the end of it. Holly would go straight to her Insta and post about the horrors of an inconsiderate boyfriend. Not that I'm really her boyfriend. Or anyone's. At least until this reality show nonsense is done, apparently. And even then, the "winner" isn't going to be getting anything more from me than they already do. Fucking "reality" TV...

"Hey, Bridge — I was calling for a reason..."

"Oh? What's up? Other than you, on a fancy plane," she jokes.

"Billy just dropped a bomb on me. It seems the label arranged for me to be on some ridiculous reality TV show, where all the girls I've dated recently compete for the title of 'girlfriend.'"

"Oh. I see."

Her voice gets tight. I can tell this is triggering for her. Exactly what I'd been afraid of. And it gets worse.

"They want to film it immediately, while we're down there at the beach."

"Oh. OK..." She pauses. "So you're not going to have time to hang out? I mean, I know you were already busy in the studio and with those gigs to test out your new material..."

Her disappointment carries across in her voice. Not that I need to hear her to know she's upset. We've just got this connection to each other. We generally know instantly when something's wrong with the other one.

"No — I'm going to make 'us time' a priority. I promised you we'd get some quality time together after all my time on the road, and I meant it. We'll just have to work around a couple hours of filming here and there. And we won't get heavy into studio time for at least another week or two, maybe more. Declan and David are still finalizing their new songs."

"Well, that sounds workable. I mean, I can change my days off if I need to. Molly's flexible."

"That shouldn't be necessary, hon. We'll make it work. It's all good."

"OK. Can't wait to see you!"

"We'll be on the ground in less than an hour. Did you want to do dinner tonight?"

"That would be great. Molly's already coming in to cover me. I assume I'm picking your pampered ass up?"

"If you would. Do you know where the studio is?"

"I do!" she says. "My friend Rory — well, she's my friend Lyric's best friend, so we've become friends, too — she works for that new local newspaper, the one that started after we left for D.C., and she did a whole story about the studio. It sounds amazing! I can't wait to see who else shows up to record there!"

"This live-in setup is awesome. Somebody should have done this before our last album — 24/7 access to the studio, individual rooms for each of us and just a few steps to the beach, plus all the touristy things, which I know the guys will all love. Alex is already talking about 'The Culinary Coastline,' and Rhys has been chatting up his dark-ride fanatics group about the old Haunted Mansion ride at the amusement park."

"Clearly, you get why I moved back here to start up my shop," she says. "We've got all the benefits of a vacation town during the summer, with stuff still going on in the fall and spring, and a quiet winter. Though less quiet than it used to be. Which isn't a bad thing. I missed the D.C. cultural scene almost as much as I've missed you."

"Well, you'll see me here in less than two hours."

"Can't wait!"

"Me, either."

I'm grinning like an idiot as I hang up. I'm really looking forward to spending time with my best friend. So much that I can almost forget about the impending torture of this reality show. Almost. Because with a complicated relationship like ours, there's a decent chance that anything involving my dating life is going to be an issue for at least one of us. But Brighid and I have always had each other's backs, and challenging times have only brought us closer together. A stupid reality show can't change that.

CHAPTER 3

LOVEFOOL

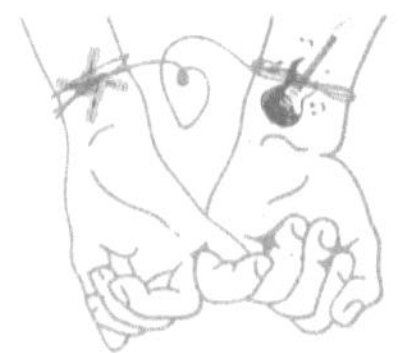

Brighid

The waitress makes sure to lean across Hunter to place his glass on the far side of the table. Even with the table tucked away in a corner and Hunter with that ridiculous WTF — sorry, I mean WFT — cap on to hide his hair, he's been recognized.

I should be used to this by now, this completely unsubtle offering to Hunter of things that are not on the menu. It's almost comical how predictable it is. There's about an 86.5 percent chance she'll give him her number along with the check.

"Thanks so much!" he enthuses, beaming at her as if she'd done something particularly clever and not just put two cups on the table without spilling them. She batts her eyelashes at him in confirmation before sauntering away with a little more hip sway than strictly called for.

"*You* are an incorrigible flirt." I shake my head at him with affectionate dismay. This is not the first time I've noticed it. But it is the first time I've voiced that thought aloud, to him.

"Who? Me?"

The incredulousness in his expression appears genuine. I've surprised him.

"Yes, you. You flirt with anything that moves. Young, old, single, married, blonde, brunette, redhead, female, male, non-binary, human, feline, canine... Doesn't matter. You flirt with them all... Well, except me, that is."

In the back of my head, I've just realized that fact. And I have to wonder why that is. What is it about me that this born flirting machine makes an exception for me? He thinks I'm delightful, but he doesn't flirt with me. Something to ponder later, maybe...

He rolls his eyes at me, and then smiles indulgently.

"That's because I love you."

My heart splutters for a split second. I like how those words sound coming out of his mouth, but I also know better.

"But you're not *in* love with me..." I supply automatically. "Yeah, yeah... I know..." I roll my eyes right back at him.

"Seriously, though — you really think I flirt with everyone? Even guys?"

"Well, it's not the same kind of flirting with guys. It's bromance flirting — you want to be liked, you want to be engaging, entrancing... And when someone new walks into the room, you turn on that 100-watt charm and go to town. I doubt most of the guys are going to drop trou and beg you to take them up against a wall..." I suppress a physical response to that imagery. Is it hot in here? Maybe I really am having hot flashes. "The girls and the dogs, on the other hand..."

He cracks up.

"OK — I get it. You're jealous," he declares.

Oh, I don't think so, mister. Gotta nip this in the bud.

"Now, wait a minute. We've talked about this... I am not—"

"Yeah, you are — you're jealous of my flirting skills. You just can't stand that you can't meet the bar I set for making waves with the ladies."

I throw my napkin at him, cracking up myself.

Gods, I've missed this.

I grab my drink to ward off a coughing fit from laughing so hard. A paper straw wrapper nails me right between the eyes.

"You..."

He's looking at me so innocently, you'd swear his eyes had little stars pinging in the corners. Just innocently sitting there, drinking his own drink through a now-paperless straw.

"What?" he asks, unable to disguise the cheesy grin breaking out across his face. I roll my eyes at him again.

Yeah. I've missed this. Us. A lot...

CHAPTER 4

ALIVE

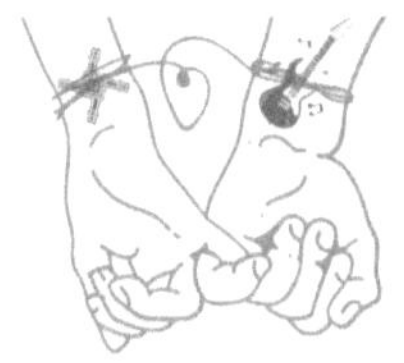

Brighid

I can't remember the last time I saw aMUSEd live.

Actually, that's a lie. I remember it precisely. But it sounds better if I say I can't remember the last time. Because it's been a long time. Years and years. And that's kind of the point. There was a day when I rarely missed a gig. There was a day when I rarely missed a rehearsal, either. And in those days, the guys were playing venues like the one they'll perform at this week — the little bayside restaurant and bar that usually has a full house on the weekends in the summer. Meaning about 500 people, tops. As opposed to 20,000, which is a pretty normal size of crowd for them these days.

So, yeah. Things have changed.

And this is a throwback for them, and for me. Pretty much no one else who's at this week's gig will have ever seen them in a venue this small. But we're not going to get a normal aMUSEd show, nor any of the other times the guys play out this summer. There will be no Top 40 hits, no deep cuts from their first album or even B-sides from an EP single recorded before they were signed to a full album deal.

Nope — this will be something almost no one has seen in more than six years: Six of the most talented and sought-after musicians on the planet, playing only covers and a few never-before-heard originals. And, for the most part, no one in the audience will be aware it's a big award-winning act they're enjoying. And that's the entire point.

We locals tend to leave our celebrity visitors largely alone, except selfies with Dave Grohl when he shows up in Rehoboth. But he's like the world's nicest guy. Something about being the major summer vacation destination for a significant portion of D.C. keeps everyone pretty blasé about our big-name visitors. Which is another reason the guys have come here. And, according to Rory's article, one reason the studio exists here at all.

The guys want some downtime to just enjoy themselves, plus a chance to try out their new material without concerns about bootlegs, security, paparazzi, music reporters, label execs, groupies and the pressure to churn out another mega-hit or five. So, they'll work on their new material, in the studio and live, and get to relax when they're not working. It's the best of both worlds, for them and for one local friend who's missed her bestie while he's been touring the world.

Have I said I'm *really* looking forward to this?

So, you may ask — how does one of the hottest bands in the world perform at a tiny little venue in tiny little Delaware and not end up swamped with fans?

Easy — they perform incognito.

Hunter said the label made arrangements with the owner of the bar for the guys to take a short mid-week slot. Which would normally bring fans in in droves. But not when the band in question doesn't use their real name, nor even the same name twice. Hunter said they expect they can pull off at least six or eight gigs, one every week or two, before word really gets out. And by then they expect to have most of their originals ready. For now, the focus in preparing for this first gig is on which cover songs to do.

"So, we've got the three new ones ready to go. What else goes on the setlist?" Alex asks from the chair at the desk in the control room of the studio, which is located on the ground floor of this massive beach house.

"You've got to put 'Here Comes the Sun' on there," I suggest. "It's where you started, right here in Mystic Beach. It's got a lot of sentimental value, and not just for Hunter."

My best friend gives me a warm smile from his spot on the floor at my feet, knowing I remember that day just as well and as fondly as he does — the day when I kidnapped his beloved green PRS guitar to draw him out of his grief and my house, and back to his music. The day when the core of aMUSEd was formed.

"Brilliant idea," Alex says, giving me a nod of approval.

"Who's singing it?" David asks.

All eyes turn to Declan, and I prepare for the diva fits of old, but he's surprisingly neutral about it. Maybe Hunt and I aren't the only ones who've grown up a little in the past few years.

"Hunt can have it. He sang it that day, with some help," he allows.

"Done," Alex says, writing it down on a sheet of paper. "What else?"

"We need to come out strong, show the audience what we can do, get them going so they'll be paying more attention to the music than to who's performing it," Declan says. "I need to go outside the box of aMUSEd's vocals, show them something they haven't heard before."

"Zeppelin? STP?"

"Queen. We'll take a page from Freddy's book — show them we're going to rock their socks off and get them singing along before they know what's hit them."

"Awesome. Done."

"I want some '70s," Rhys says. "And a six-minute drum solo."

"Rhys!" "No!" "Not happening!" It's a chorus of protest from the other guys.

"Seriously, guys — what's wrong with six minutes of rhythmic perfection?"

"Nothing, Rhys. It just can't be six minutes straight of only drums," Dave says. "How about we pull out some '70s funk? Something with a bassline to go along with the drums, give them some melody to dance to?"

"And bridge it into some Chili Peppers!" Alex adds with enthusiasm. "There's that great keyboard intro..."

A chorus of nods all around. Compromise found.

"You know what I'm going to suggest," David adds after a minute of silence.

"The Fixx," Alex says with a nod. "I can handle the synths on my end. I've got all my girls with me." He writes it down.

"I want to lean hard on the blues," Kieran adds from beside me. "I hardly ever get to go full-bore blues with our songs."

"What do you have in mind?" Alex asks.

"Arc Angles."

'Oooh..." Hunter intones, clearly excited at the prospect. "Two strong guitar parts. Some smooth, gritty vocals for Declan to show off his range. Harmonies for the rest of us. Man, I wish they'd stayed together..." he says wistfully. "Dylan's lucky Charlie Sexton's still willing to tour as his guitarist sometimes. He could be doing solo projects and producing 24/7."

"Done," Alex adds.

"And I want to try something crazy," Kieran adds. "We'll never get to do it for real as aMUSEd..."

We all wait.

"Bag-rock."

My delighted squeal is lost amid the grumbling from the other guys. I know I don't get a vote, but this idea is just too exciting.

"We don't have a piper, Kier. How are we going to pull that off?" Alex asks.

"I'll translate the bagpipe and fiddle parts to electric guitar, and you can cover the drones and any overlap on keys."

"I did like that Seven Nations song you were playing the other day."

Kieran looks over and winks at me. "Told you they'd go for it someday," he says. "It was Brighid's idea, way back when..." he volunteers.

"She's always had excellent, extraordinary, exquisite—" Hunter says.

"You said 'ecstatic' last time," I interrupt.

"So I did. I also said 'erotic' last time." He looks at me meaningfully, and I turn bright red, remembering that playful conversation that pushed up against the line of his determination that we were just friends.

Alex clears his throat. "Yes, well... Brighid's taste aside... You think we can really pull off a Celtic-rock song?"

"I'm sure of it," Kieran says. "I'll start the arrangement as soon as we're done with the list. If it doesn't work, we can pull it off the setlist."

"Done."

I excuse myself to let them wrangle the details without me being the seventh wheel in the room, and to grab some air out on the first-floor deck, overlooking the ocean. The only thing better than living where I do would be living where I could look out my windows and see nothing but ocean. But I love my old house, and I wouldn't want the added risk of being right on the beach when the inevitable nor'easter roars through. As it stands, the six feet of elevation a forward-thinking builder had gone with a hundred years ago has been a saving grace.

The guys will have to add at least a handful more songs to their list, since they're starting off with three originals, and all the rest will be covers. Every show, they'll swap some covers out for their latest completed songs. In the meantime, Hunter, thankfully, will get to do some Beatles for his mom, who would have been so proud to have watched him come back home and perform at a place that's been here since she was young.

The key for them to do these incognito gigs is that they're doing things low-key. No roadies. No band-hired sound engineer — just the house engineer. No security outside of the norm for the venue. All the trappings of the million-selling rock band are being set aside, as much because they draw attention as because the guys want to take a break from the pressures of being rockstars.

The fly in the vasoline here is that the reality TV show that's followed Hunter down here — bringing four high-profile models/influencers with them — wants to film the girls at an aMUSEd gig, so they've also got a camera crew that's going to have to stay unobtrusive. I'm not sure how they're keeping the girlfriends from posting on social media when publicity is their bread and butter, but Hunter said something about non-disclosure agreements.

So, when the afternoon of their first incognito gig arrives, I pick up Hunter and his equipment at the studio, and we unload it at the bar. Shades of ten years ago. With the house engineer and bar staff keeping an eye on things, we go back and start hauling the rest of their equipment in loads.

Alex's keyboards and Rhys' drum kit are the biggest hassle, but thankfully, they're both guarding their instruments like prized pets as we drop them off and go back for David with his selection of Spector basses and Kieran and his Fender "guitarsenal." I'm not sure Hunter's wise to bring his distinctive blue PRS Dragon guitar out for this gig, though its dragon design is pretty prominently inked on his left arm now. He said he may not play it, but he's bringing it, along with the green PRS his mom gave him and that's inked permanently on his right arm, along with aMUSEd's muse logo.

As the clock slides past five and the equipment is basically set up, with a cursory soundcheck only, the guys join me at a bayfront table and have dinner, leaving plenty of time to enjoy the view, the local seafood and some relaxed conversation before they have to be up and active for two hours.

David apparently had a little run-in earlier with the house engineer, and he's been distracted ever since. But the others are asking for recommendations for places to visit. "Hunt keeps telling me they're calling this area 'The Culinary Coastline' now," Alex says. "Where should I go to explore that?"

"A friend of mine has a café downtown, basically next to my shop. It's called Castalia. She makes the most amazing food. People have said it's almost magical how good it is," I tell him. "Start there. I'm sure she'll give you some other ideas if you ask. She respects people with a deep interest in food, even if they don't cook professionally."

"Alex almost *could* cook professionally," David notes. "He's gotten that good."

"That's awesome! I'll definitely mention to her that you'll be stopping by, then, if you like, Alex."

"Sounds great."

"Hunter said you two used to ride the Haunted Mansion all the time when you were kids," Rhys says. "That thing is legendary. Classic dark ride."

"It really is. It's not high-tech — no 3D, no modern effects, but it's so fun, nostalgic. Makes you feel like a kid even when you ride it as an adult."

"That's got my name all over it," Rhys says. "You know..." He looks thoughtful. "I wonder if they'd take a sponsorship, like actually put my name on it."

"Rhys!"

"What? It's not like I'm not famous enough to have my name on something! Maybe they call it 'The Madman's Haunted Mansion...'"

I roll my eyes and let it drop.

"I just want to go out and have some fun," Declan says. "Where's good for dancing around here these days?"

"That's still Ocean City, Declan. All the other towns are pretty quiet, comparatively speaking. But are you sure that's a good idea? Somebody's sure to spot you out at a club full of people."

"Gotta blow off some steam," he says. "If somebody recognizes me... Well, that's not exactly new, is it?"

Hunter and I exchange a look, but Declan doesn't seem displeased at the idea of being recognized, even if I think it's a recipe for disaster with them trying to fly under the radar down here — and with no security. But no one has ever been able to get Declan to do anything other than what Declan wants to do, so I shrug it off. It's his problem to deal with if it blows up in their faces.

"I'm going to need some new ink soon," Kieran says, predictably.

"Do you have any bare skin left at this point?"

"A little. We've been on the road a long time. I haven't gotten any in a while. I'm overdue."

"There's a shop in downtown Mystic Beach. A friend of mine owns it. She's unbelievably good, especially with anything related to music. She did the piece on my back."

"Wait. You're inked now?" Hunter is surprised. I may have forgotten to mention it when I got my first tattoo a couple years ago. Or I may have kind of, sort of, waited for this moment, when he'd realize I'd done it and hadn't told him. Turnabout is fair play, right? And he got inked the first time without telling me. So now we're even. In that, at least.

He grabs my arm and turns me around, as if he expects to be able to suddenly see the tattoo that wasn't obvious before.

"It's on my lower back." And I'm not flashing everyone to show it to him, even if it's driving him crazy, which he kind of looks like it is.

"It's not Hunt's name, is it?" Alex teases. I know he's teasing. I'm not sure I'm entirely comfortable with it, but I know he's just teasing.

"I'm too unique to get the same tattoo a thousand other women already have, Alex."

"Oooh... Burn!" Rhys says, erupting in laughter. "She's got you there, Hunt!"

Hunter has the grace to blush.

"He's actually been very good this last tour," Alex notes. His expression gets thoughtful. "Actually... I don't remember seeing him with any groupies since the tour started."

"Me, either," Dave says.

"I can't think of a single time I did, either," Kieran adds.

"Hey — I offered to share a few times. He turned me down." Now, that I expected from Declan. Well — the sharing part. Not the part where Hunter hadn't taken him up on it.

"I didn't even see him with any of his girlfriends this tour," Alex adds, still sounding thoughtful.

"I had better things to do," Hunter explains vaguely, looking away and seeming even more embarrassed than he did after my jibe about all the women with his name engraved in their skin. Is it possible...?

But the waitstaff arrive with our entrees, and we're all distracted by some pretty amazing food. It's not Castalia-level fine-dining, but it's probably some of the freshest seafood these guys have seen since this last tour started, and the chatter takes a back seat to some appreciative moans and comments.

While the other guys now have some ideas on what to do with their free time,Hunter and I have plans for pretty much all his free time this week, between meals out, movie marathons, beach time and showing him how things have changed here. And just generally catching up. I'm looking forward to that even more than I am to tonight's gig. We'll have to see how this reality show impacts those plans. Hopefully, not too much.

Soon, it's time for the guys to get ready to go on, and they leave me for their dressing room — the one "rockstar" privilege they're indulging in here, though it's more a practical thing than a luxury. Hunter drops a kiss on my head on his way out, and I give his hand a squeeze for good luck.

I'm still waiting for the slice of key lime pie that Hunter talked me into ordering while I wait for them to go on when a tall woman with dark blonde hair sits down at the table with me. And says nothing. Just sits. I'm looking at her, confused, when two other women — one with ink-black hair and the other with mahogany brown hair — approach and greet her with air kisses and an energetic gab-fest that's already grating on my nerves, even before they, too, sit down without saying a word to me.

The last time the guys played a place this small, I was the designated table-holder so they had a place to come sit when they took a break or finished up, and Hunter didn't say a word otherwise before he left the table. So I've assumed that role again now.

Having done this dozens of times, I'm used to sitting alone at a table with a lot of empty chairs. Sometimes people ask if they can join you, and you have to break it to them that hardworking musicians who are about to entertain them will want to get off their feet and have a drink when they're done. So, having people just sit without saying a word, let alone asking, is problematic. And I'm not good at confronting people when they're being rude. I end up either saying nothing or going overboard and coming off as a bitch. So, this is not a comfortable moment for me.

"I'm sorry — this table is taken. The band is sitting here."

The first woman looks down her nose at me — literally — gives what can only be described as a "dainty" snort, and laughs.

And now I know I'm dealing with a crazy woman.

I look around to see where the bouncers are located, just in case, with the bartender taking notice of my scan and raising an eyebrow, as if to ask if he needs to intervene. He knows I'm here with the band and that this is their table. I reply with a gentle shrug, hoping he'll give me a minute to try diplomacy before he sends in reinforcements.

"I'll have to ask you to find another table, ladies. The band is sitting at this one," I say more loudly, addressing all three of them.

"I'm right where I'm supposed to be," the crazy woman informs me, apparently quite serious about that. "I'm the guitar player's girlfriend."

Oh. No. Hunter's rotating squad of models has arrived. I should have known.

"I see... I presume you're one of the women here for the reality show?"

"I'm his girlfriend," she reiterates. "Holly. Surely you know who I am. You're his little assistant, right? We'll have four apple-tinis. Grace is powdering her nose."

"Hunter doesn't have an assistant. And I'm not the waitress. I'm his best friend."

She laughs heartily at that.

"Right... Like he'd give *you* the time of day. I've never even seen you before, and I've been going out with him for years.

Francesca, Sophie — have either of you ever seen Hunter with this frump?"

I look down at what I'm wearing and wonder when my new sundress became frumpy. Must have been about five minutes ago.

"Never, Holly. You think she's a groupie trying to meet the band? Maybe she just took over their table after they went backstage," the brunette replies, seeming genuinely concerned that she may now be sitting with riffraff.

"What do you think, Grace?" she asks to the space behind me. I turn around to find a redhead approaching the table, wrinkling her nose in distaste. "Should we have security remove the groupie?"

Before Grace can answer, I make it clear I've had my fill.

"I am *not* a groupie — Holly, is it? Let's start over. I'm Brighid," I say, holding out my hand, which hangs empty in the air before I give up and put it back in my lap. "I've been Hunter's best friend since we were 6. I live here, where he grew up."

"Now I know she's a groupie! Hunter's not from this backwater little town. He's from D.C."

"You've been 'seeing' him for years, and you don't even know where he lived the first 17 years of his life?" I don't think Hunter's ever hidden where he was from. Why she's unaware of it, I don't know. But it doesn't say good things about her or her "relationship" with Hunter. My dislike has gelled as she's moved from rude to willfully ignorant. "He moved to D.C. and lived with Declan and David and their parents after high school. And it was Northern Virginia, actually — not D.C. Which I would know, since I was there with them until they went to New York."

"And clearly, Hunter didn't want to drag your oversized ass with him to a place like New York," she replies. "If that's even true."

The other three join her in laughter.

I take a deep breath and close my eyes, trying to remain calm.

"We're still waiting for our apple-tinis," Holly reminds me, as if I was a forgetful assistant or a lousy waitress.

"I can see that. You may find them easier to get if you walk up to the bar and ask. Or you can wait until the waitress comes back with my dessert."

"Dessert! Oh, honey — you shouldn't be eating dessert. You shouldn't be eating at all, really. You could probably go a year or two without eating and spending every day exercising and still not get rid of all that blubber."

It's at this point that I start making appeals to the divine. Surely I haven't offended any gods sufficiently lately that I'm being punished like this. I decide to go for humor.

"I'm actually amazed by people who lose weight with exercise," I comment, calling on one of my favorite little memes for support. "When I exercise, nothing happens. My DNA seems to thinks I'm still a European peasant. So it's like, 'Oh! Are we running from the English again, lass? Dinnae ye worry: we'll keep ye plump as a partridge to outlast the murderous bastards!'"

If we weren't sitting next to the bay, I'd be sure I was hearing crickets. I'd say seagulls instead, but it's dead silent, and that's the last thing seagulls are.

"Did you just make a fat joke on yourself?" Holly asks, laughing. "Girls — did you hear that? She made a fat joke, about herself! She couldn't even wait for us to do it for her!"

"Listen, whoever you are... whatever you think you are to Hunter..." I start.

"Ladies! I see you've arrived!" Hunter says loudly from several table lengths away. He's giving me the hairy eyeball, as if pleading with me to ignore whatever they've said and let him handle things. Hey — more power to him. If I hadn't been waiting so eagerly for this show, I'd have already gone backstage to find him, or maybe straight home. And I don't like the idea of being driven away when he was looking forward to me seeing him perform for the first time in a long time.

I note that he hasn't actually welcomed any of them. He merely observed that they're here. And I'm reminded how much he was dreading this whole reality-show thing. I'm not sure he even likes any of these women as people. But Hunter's "relationships" have always baffled me.

I notice a video camera pointed at him from outside the deck. I tap him on the arm and nod in that direction.

"I see it, Bridge. It's fine. Just ignore it. You haven't signed any releases. They can't include you in any footage they put in the show."

I have to admit I'm relieved about that. Especially since I don't know how much of Holly & Co.'s insult-fest the camera might have caught before he arrived. For that matter, I'm not sure how much of it *he* caught. It's not like him to let someone insult me. Especially after the one time he did.

"Ladies, I would like to introduce you to my friend Brighid. She grew up with me here. And she's been kind enough to hold the table for me and the guys while we're getting ready and on stage."

Their expressions don't change. At all. And I'm not sure whether that's an issue with their emotional spectrum or with too many doses of botulism injected into their faces.

"Did you get your pie yet, Bridge?" he asks sweetly, smiling at me.

"Not yet. I think the other 'ladies' here were hoping the waitress would return and take their drink order soon. Or sooner," I suggest. I'm hoping he'll pick up on my wording and not only get a waitress back here to appease his pussy posse but recognize that my stilted use of the word means I am *not* considering any of these females "ladies" — not by his definition or society's, let alone the respected position the term indicates for me. These are no ladies.

"Gotcha," he says, reading me clearly without further explanation, as he so often does. "I'll send the waitress back over for your drink orders, and, hopefully, she'll have your dessert, too, Bridge. Order me that chocolate lava cake for when we're done, will you, please?"

I smile back at him. He's working hard to smooth the waters, even if it's a pointless pursuit with these four dumped in my lap. And he's put me back on familiar footing by asking me to order him his favorite dessert.

"Will do. Have a good gig. I'll be right here," I emphasize, letting the women know that I'm not going anywhere, and promising both Hunter and myself that I'll stick around, if at all possible. It's already a close thing.

Hunter waves and heads backstage. A minute later, the waitress returns with my pie, ready to take some drink orders. I contemplate asking her to bring me something strong, but I have to drive myself home tonight, and I really did swear off alcohol after that frat party. If any night was going to tempt me to reverse that decision, it's tonight. But I hold fast and soothe myself with pie. It's not as good as Callie's, but it's still quite good. I eat in silence, as Hunter's lukewarm response to them and acknowledgment of me seems to have rendered the models mute and of sour mien.

I can already tell that this is going to be a long week. And that's not counting the weeks afterward when at least some of these four will still be hanging around. I resolve to avoid any future filming. Let them enjoy the cameras while I give them *and* the TV audience a wide berth.

In the meantime, I'm going to enjoy my pie and the chance to see Hunter perform, just like the old days.

Chapter 5

Live & Let Die

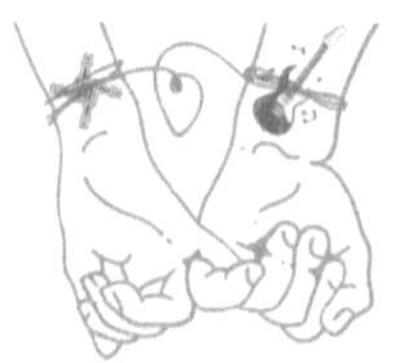

Brighid

"**G**reetings, ladies and gents! We are Rock & Grohl, and we're here to 'amuse' you," Declan says, in a comparatively low-key introduction for the band. Declan's playing with fire with the aMUSEd reference and that band name, but I guess with a brother named Dave in the band, that was kind of a given.

And if there was any question, despite that low-key intro, what attitude aMUSEd was taking into this gig, they answer it — definitively — with their first song, right out of the gates. Rhys puts that big kit of his to use with a thumping bass drum, while Hunter, Dave, Kieran and Alex intersperse it with claps that pull the audience to participate before they've even realized what they were doing. And then, Declan makes them a promise for the evening: "We Will Rock You." It's a promise they will keep.

The song puts Declan's world-class vocals straight to the forefront. No one will ever be Freddie Mercury's match, as a frontman or a rock singer, but Declan's making his bid for a spot in the top ten, supported by vocals from Hunter, Dave and Rhys that bring the audience into the song for that chorus that nearly everyone knows.

Then Kieran slices through the percussion with the blazing guitar, before they go a cappella for the intro to "Fat Bottomed Girls." This song has always made me a bit uncomfortable, even if my posterior isn't especially ample. But it's a great, fun song, and they take the audience for a ride that leaves some in the audience already wanting to take them home, ample posteriors or not.

Holly leans over halfway through the song, and I brace myself.

"They didn't even have to dedicate this one to you! It's already clear who it was meant for," she says with a chuckle.

I want to correct her, point out that the song is actually an ode to big butts that Brian May wrote just for Freddie, but I'm not in the mood to get close enough to her to make myself heard, nor to shout the information at her. I just roll my eyes and watch the boys kill it.

They don't pause for applause. But I kind of wish they had, so I could have conceivably excused myself to go to... the restroom, home, Mars... pretty much anywhere but here, next to Horrible Holly. Because the next song on the set list is "Brick House," with a little more Rob Zombie informing it than the original Commodores version. Declan's growl is on full display, as are Holly's claws, because she's cracking right up and leading her model mob in the guffaws at my expense.

Hunter looks over and smiles at me, but his smile falters when he sees the girlfriends laughing and me carefully ignoring them.

And I can ignore them, because again she's missed the point — it's a song of admiration for the woman of Amazonian proportions. "Never be ashamed of your size, Ellie," Mom had always told me. "There are women who'd kill to have that hourglass figure." OK, I was a little bigger than the idealized 36-24-36 in the song, but that was a lot closer to my shape than Holly & Co.'s. And I was tall enough to carry it off, even if I'd been targeted by other kids over my weight before my 13th birthday.

Besides, the song is great, and the guys own it. Dave appears to be in heaven, with the band getting about as funky as I've ever seen them. Until they move on to "Higher Ground," with a version that owes as much to the Stevie Wonder original as it does to the Red Hot Chili Peppers' version. Again, Dave is showing everyone what he can do when let loose on one of his Spectors, and that's impressive, though he seems to be concerned about his in-ear monitor mix, based on how focused he is on the engineer.

I quirk an eyebrow at Hunter and nod toward Dave and the engineer, who's a petite dark-haired girl with big eyes and apparently not a fan of Dave's, based on their earlier interaction. But surely she's too much of a pro to mess with his mix. She's certainly doing him justice in the house mix. Hunter shrugs, and I chalk it up to a personality conflict.

It hasn't taken Dave out of his bass-player's headspace, because he's all over that bass line. And he stays in Flea mode when they shift over to RHCPs' "Dark Necessities," with that great funky bass guitar part that pops in right after Alex's keyboards get their time to shine.

Declan owns the entire audience when he goes Chris Cornell for what has long been one of his favorites to cover, "Spoonman." That lets Dave continue with a strong bass line, while Kieran rips into the guitar solo and Hunter's all over the distinctive riffs in his rhythm guitar parts, all before Rhys shows off with the song's solo drum break. Then they all come back together, showing their strength as a cohesive unit.

It's an unexpected selection next, with the blues-rock sounds of Arc Angels' "Crave and Wonder," which features two stellar guitarists, just as aMUSEd has, and lets Declan do the gritty Charlie Sexton verses before the rest of the band joins in for some exquisite harmonies on the choruses.

The next one I don't recognize, but it has that aMUSEd feel to it — hard, almost grungy, but very danceable, calling the audience to get on their feet and participate in the show. There's no need tonight, though, because they'd already pulled all those people into the experience and they're ready to keep going, even if they don't know the song.

I'm keeping my eyes and ears on the audience to gauge their response to this new material, and they seem to be getting into it pretty quickly. "They sound kind of like aMUSEd," someone behind me bellows. "The singer definitely is cut from the same mold," their tablemate shouts back. I hate to tell them, but they broke the mold and stomped it to pieces when they made Declan Carter. He's lucky they haven't put two and two together and started livestreaming to every social media site on the planet.

The next song starts off keyboard-heavy, and I'm getting a very un-aMUSEd '80s vibe when I suddenly recognize the tune. Dave had asked for some '80s covers, but there's no way this was a Dave request. It's Flesh for Lulu's "I Go Crazy" from the "Some Kind of Wonderful" soundtrack. I look over at Hunter, and he's grinning from ear to ear. I blow him a kiss in appreciation, because this one is clearly for me. Maybe he did actually miss me while he's been away...

And I know the song instantly when I hear the signature guitar line from his mom's favorite, "Here Comes the Sun," and he's taking over lead vocals from Declan, who pauses for a drink during the verses — a move that seems necessary once Hunter's guitar fades and they launch into another new song that has that aMUSEd signature sound and demands a good bit from Declan. But based on the audience reaction, they may have another hit single on their hands.

Dave finally gets his own '80s request in with "Saved by Zero" from The Fixx, which also lets Alex show off his skills. Then Kieran and Hunter get to float the funky guitar part over that ethereal synth base.

Kieran shifts into a crunchy guitar that quickly yields the forefront to a wailing lead part that sounds decidedly bagpipe-inspired, with Alex covering the droning undertone of the instrument. No one else in the audience is likely to recognize "Up to Me" by Seven Nations, but the fact that they included it at all is a testament to Kieran's skill at transmuting the traditional instrument in the rock setting. He catches my eye and winks, as we're the only two people in the room who really know the song, but the audience is still surprisingly into it. Who knew? Well, I guess Kieran did!

Another aMUSEd original seems to be pushing the envelope on the guys remaining anonymous when I hear Declan's name from the people right behind me who'd taken note of his vocal resemblance to... well, himself. I can't tell if they've figured it out. But there's a phone being held up to record now, and I sit up as high as I can, shifting my chair back when I do it, blocking at least some of the person's shot. I feel a little guilty, but it's better for everyone if as little of this as possible gets spread around in the social media age. The sooner they're recognized, the sooner the anonymous gigs will have to stop.

But, if the response to the three new originals tonight is any indication, aMUSEd will have another platinum album hanging on the guys' walls very soon.

Whether they sense they're pushing their luck or just ready to take a break, the guys thank everyone and head backstage again. I have a sneaking suspicion that if I leave the table I'll find my chair has disappeared when I come back, so I sit and wait.

The restaurant has a DJ playing in the inside bar now, and people have started to move in there. Francesca seems to be inclined to join them, urging Sophie and Grace to go with her, but Holly fixes them with a glare and warns, "I'd hate to have Hunter come back to the table and find that there's only one girl waiting for him, with the cameras rolling."

Though I presume she's intentionally omitted me from the "girls" who'd be waiting for him, her warning seems to have immediate effect, with the three women sitting back down, if with some reluctance. Holly smiles smugly and then smirks at me.

"Oh! You're still here! I didn't notice you there. Which seems kind of hard to do with the amount of space you take up, but some people just fade into the background. Why don't you make yourself useful and go get us some refills?" she suggests before turning around to talk to the others and ignoring me entirely. *Deep breath, Bridge. Deep breath.*

"What was with that tired '80s song right before the one Hunter sang?" she says, apparently to the other women, though she's said it loud enough I think half the remaining people on the deck heard her. I'm sure aMUSEd's publicist would love to hear that she'd been knocking the band's set and hadn't had a positive word to say. I'm set to tell her that when there's a voice behind me.

"It's a song that requires excellent taste to appreciate, Holly," Hunter tells her. I try not to smile. "One that's got a lot of sentimental value for me, which is why *I* suggested we play it." He looks over at me and smiles before dropping another kiss on top of my head.

"What'd you think, Bridge? I really value your opinion on these things," he says, appearing determined to take Holly down a peg and defend me. She huffs in annoyance.

"The audience loved all of it. Even the covers they didn't recognize, and they didn't so much as take a step toward the bar when you were doing the originals."

"And what did *you* think of them?"

"Well, first, thank you for that 'tired '80s song.' It meant a lot." He reaches around my shoulders to give me a hug. I brace myself to be tackled to the ground by an angry Holly, but she might break a nail, so I appear to be safe. "The originals were all amazing. Maybe a little more polish needed on that last one. The second one is your next hit single."

"Exactly what we were all thinking. Thanks for confirming that. You have always had... excellent taste in music." He smirks at the nod to our long-ago conversation about my musical taste. I smile for that alone.

"Come sit down over here, Hunter," Holly insists.

But Hunter pulls an empty chair from the next table over and sits down next to me at the end of the table.

"Did you order my chocolate lava cake?" And, with perfect timing, the waitress drops it in front of him, handing him two spoons.

"What do you say, Bridge? How's your chocolate tooth today?" he asks me, offering me a spoon.

"Well, my sweet-tooth has been assuaged by that key lime pie you twisted my arm into getting... But I've got just enough of a chocolate tooth left for one bite, if you're eager to share," I tell him, taking the proffered spoon. "I know you — you go first," I add, since he could consume the entire dessert in about 30 seconds flat. He digs in, and — yup, there it is, the orgasmic sex face he always makes for chocolate lava cake, or chocolate mousse.

"Ooh, that's good..." he says, drawing the word out. "Have a taste."

I move to grab a spoonful for myself, but he's already scooped one up on his spoon and is holding it out in front of my mouth. I hesitate, sensing this is a performance being put on for the girlfriends' benefit, but he nods, insisting. So, I let him put the spoonful of decadent dessert in my mouth and then draw the spoon out slowly, almost erotically. *You are a bad, bad boy, Hunter.*

"Good?" he asks.

"Delicious," I reply, playing along by drawing that word out and then licking my lips. His eyes catch the movement, and he leans in again.

"You missed a spot," he says, swiping his thumb over my bottom lip and then putting it in his mouth. It's a loaded gesture for us, but one that seems intended to be reassuring to me, as well as irritating to Holly. I resist the temptation to smirk and smile happily at him instead. If nothing else, he's proven we're still partners-in-crime.

"I'd offer you all some, ladies, but I know you don't eat dessert," he tells the women, proceeding to devour the remaining cake in about 20 seconds. He swipes a finger across the thin layer of sauce remaining on the plate, bringing it to his mouth, but at the last second he diverts and uses it to tap my lower lip. My brain stops working, but my mouth instinctively opens to lick his finger clean.

Four women are staring at us. Their expressions range between disbelief and livid. Holly looks like she'd turn me instantly into embers if she could. Just then, the camera guy moves, and all of us seem to remember at once that this is being filmed, even if they can't use my portions.

"Hey, Bridge — I'm kind of tired after all that. Do you think you could drive me home?"

"You can't leave, Hunter! They're supposed to be filming me — us — here with you," Holly reminds him.

"Oh, I think they got enough footage of you all sitting here watching me perform, including that 'tired '80s song.' And you might want to give 'Fat Bottomed Girls' and 'Brick House' another listen sometime. It could be educational. I'm going to call it a night, ladies. Long day ahead tomorrow with the show shooting. The guys are going to handle load-out without me," he says. "Ready to go home, Bridge? The tab's been taken care of."

"Sure," I say, though I'm not the least little bit sure this is a good idea. I get that he's irked about the reality show, but at this rate, I may need to invest in some flame-proof underwear while they're shooting. Worst-case, it could help keep things from igniting down south if he's going to keep pulling stunts like that one with the chocolate cake.

Whoa. I don't think he realizes the pure sexual wattage he wields.

CHAPTER 6

NO EXCUSES

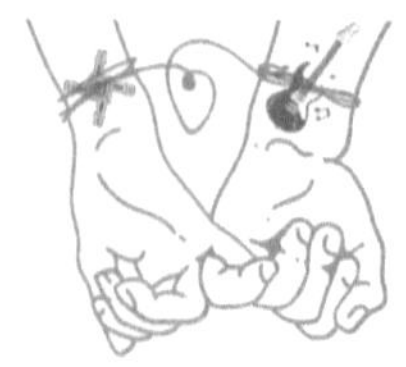

"**I**'m really sorry about that, Bridge. I'll talk to them tomorrow, make sure it doesn't happen again."

"It's OK, Hunt. It wasn't your fault. Just let it go. I can stand up for myself these days. I just didn't want to make a scene if I could avoid it."

He gives me a scrutinizing look from the other side of my sofa, as if he doesn't quite believe me, that I wasn't really bothered by the mean-girl squad he's imported to Mystic Beach with him, willingly or not.

"They're not used to dealing with normal people. Their world is all about cattiness and who's on top."

I raise an eyebrow at him, causing him to re-consider his wording.

"I meant in their social hierarchy... not..." Again, that blush that steals across his face. It's not something I've seen on him often since that day he arrived at my little loft apartment to apologize for having let me walk in on him having sex with groupies twice in one night. Which really wasn't his fault, anyway. But he was still embarrassed about it. I've seen him deeply apologetic about other things in the intervening years, but not embarrassed.

Again, I ask myself whether there's something more going on with him than just him finding his way back to the old Hunter, or some version thereof.

"Hunt... What Alex said — about you and the groupies..."

"I've just been busy with — focused on — other things, Bridge. Trying to write some songs. I've got a reputation to live up to, with that Song of the Year award on the mantle in my apartment, mocking me. This dry spell has been going on too long."

The explanation doesn't quite ring true with me, as well as I know him. But I don't call him on it. I know it's been a couple years since he's written any new songs, and that wears on him. I wish I could make that easier for him, but he's been on the road so long, it's no wonder he's struggling to bring a creative spark into his work again. This vacation, working or not, is long overdue for him.

I lean over and give him a hug, and he pulls me over next to him, tucking my head under his chin.

"I missed you, Bridge. I know I've said it a couple times lately, but I really have. I want you to know that."

"Well, I've missed you too, Hunt. You know that. But you're here now."

"I don't like that I've left you alone here for so long. This tour just went on and on and on..."

"I haven't been alone."

He pulls back away from me, scrutinizing.

"You haven't said anything about Tyler in a while. I kind of assumed something happened there but you didn't want to talk about it."

"It didn't work out. It's fine. Really," I emphasize when he gives me a skeptical look. "I've got other friends here."

"Other male friends? Boyfriends?"

"Hunter..." I don't want to talk to him about this. There's too many buttons we push for each other, where we're the only people who can even see, let alone reach, those buttons.

"You can't blame me for asking," he says. "I want to make sure you've got someone looking after you like you deserve, someone caring for you, especially when I've been gone for so long, out of touch with you too often."

I don't tell him that I've gotten used to it, to the radio silence that happens when a tour gets busy. Over the years, I've learned how it goes. It's one of the reasons I've focused on building my life here, my business, friendships, even if they're not the kind of friendships it seems he'd rather hear that I have. I can't tell if he's feeling sorry for me, that I don't have a boyfriend, especially while he has a handful of girlfriends, or if he still just wants to be assured that I'm not focusing my romantic interests on him.

"I have enough people in my life to keep me content. That's all you need to know."

His expression is wounded, that I'm not sharing with him, I guess.

"That's fair," he eventually says. "I'm sorry if I'm prying. I really do just want the best for you, want you to have someone who deserves you."

"It's OK. I get it. It's just... It's not a focus for me. I'm focused on my business. I've made a lot of good friends among my fellow business owners downtown. We all take care of each other."

"It's not the same thing, Bridge. You deserve to have someone who loves you, who's focused on your needs."

He's said this to me before, including that night at the Telltale Signs concert in D.C., where we both dumped a lot of emotional baggage on each other, and not without leaving some wounds behind for each of us. That's one of the reasons I'd rather not get into this with him. Because my feelings haven't changed — not my feelings for him and not my feelings about his persistent efforts to foist me onto some other guy, like I'm a problem he wants off his hands. The thing that has changed is whether I hold out any hope he'll change his mind about us. I know he won't. And I've learned to be OK with that. Mostly. Most of the time, anyway.

"You should have someone like that, too, Hunt," I say, turning the script on him.

"I'm not so sure about that. I don't think it's in the cards for me. I don't think it ever has been."

I snuggle back down into him, not sure what to say. He thinks he doesn't deserve to have that. He's wrong. But that's what he thinks. Nothing I've ever said to the contrary has stuck with him. I sigh, and we sit there quietly together for a while, each wrapped up in our own thoughts.

"So what's this about a tattoo? You got inked and you didn't even tell me?"

"I feel like I've heard that line before, and it was me saying it..." I tell him with some serious side-eye.

"Oh. Yeah. I guess I kind of earned that."

"You did."

"But you've seen mine now. You've seen all my ink at this point." I have. He doesn't have a ton, not like Kieran, but he's got a few significant pieces on his arms and shoulders. "You going to leave me in the dark?"

"It'd serve you right if I did."

"Agreed. But I still want to see."

I throw caution to the wind.

"Fine. But it's low on my back." I sit up and turn my back to him, reaching for the zipper at the back of my sundress. I have a sudden flashback to the time when he zipped up a similar sundress, having gotten an unplanned eyeful of a tipsy me in a compromising position with an opportunistic frat boy. But this is very different, even if I'm having a similar problem getting my fingers to grip the zipper pull.

"Let me." His voice is too close, his mouth too close to my ear as he sits up and brushes my hand aside. I shudder and then wiggle a little to hide the unavoidable reaction to his touch as he slides the zipper pull downward.

The dress loosens as he drags it farther and farther downward.

I wasn't kidding — the tattoo is low on my back. It's not in "tramp-stamp" territory, even if those are making a comeback, according to Siobhan and her recent spate of clients. But the bottom of the design sits a couple inches below my waist, so by the time he's bared it all to his view, there's a large expanse of naked skin staring back at him.

I can feel him hesitate before he reaches out to touch it, the callused skin of his fingertips grazing along the outline of the kneeling priestess, her robes, the candle flame she tends. My breath escapes in a shuddering sigh. Can he not feel this tension? The electric energy between us when he touches me?

"Beautiful..." he says quietly, reverently. And I can't tell if the reverence is for me or for the priestess inked into my skin. I'm probably deluding myself to think it could be for me, but I find the mere idea that he'd treat this design with such reverence to be more than I could hope for.

He's always respected my beliefs, even if he doesn't understand them, and Brighid — the goddess, not me — has always seemed to have a soft spot for him, poet that he is, after a fashion, with his songwriting. But there have only been a few times when the two of them seemed to truly connect —

especially that odd moment when he was looking at the statue of Her in my loft apartment, and I could have sworn...

"It's beautiful work," he says, drawing me out of my ruminations. "Your friend did this, you said? She's very talented."

His fingers trace back around the design before he lays his palm against it. Now I straight-up shiver.

"Bridge..."

Music erupts from the coffee table next to us, where both our phones sit.

"That's Dave..."

He quickly zips my dress back up and grabs for the phone.

"Yeah, Dave — what's up? ... Oh, shit... Yeah — sorry. I wasn't even thinking about that. Those girls just... and Bridge... Yeah. We'll be right there." He hangs up.

"We need to get the equipment back to the studio. Sorry — I was just so pissed about how they were treating you... I didn't even think about the guys needing your car for load-out. They're packed up and ready to go. I can just take your car, if you want to stay here. I can bring it back when we're done."

"No, that's OK. I'm wide awake." Especially after having his hands on me like that. Probably better that I get some air and shake off whatever this feeling is with a little manual labor. "Let's go."

The next day

"I 'm really sorry, Brighid. I know you had plans with Hunter today."

"It's fine, Molly. He had a shoot for this reality show they're doing. No reason I couldn't come in to deal with this."

"If you're sure."

"I am. It's fine. I still have some things I have to do for clients myself. It'll be a while before you'll be up to speed on all the herbal remedies."

I weigh a scoop of nettles and add them to the other herbs in the bag.

"You'll want a bit of honey with this blend, Mrs. Lowell. Clover honey would be nice with this flavor profile, if you have it. But there's a slight bitterness to this tea that the honey will compensate for."

"Thank you so much Brighid, dear. I wish I hadn't needed to call you in on your day off, but my knee is acting up, and I have Zumba in the morning."

"It's not a problem. I'm happy to help. My plans for the day kind of fell through anyway, so it's not an imposition."

"You're such a sweet girl."

"Thank you, Mrs. Lowell. Did you need anything else today?"

The seaglass chime over the door jingles.

"No, dear. That's all for today. Unless you have some more big pieces of rose quartz that aren't out on display."

"I'm afraid you got all the big pieces last time you were in, Mrs. Lowell. I have some more on order, but I'm down to just some pebbles right now."

"Ooh! Hunter! Look at this! This is exactly what I've been needing to cleanse my chakras. That shop in New York didn't have any and said it would be months to get it in!"

I look up slowly from the counter, having a very good idea of what I'm going to see.

Hunter's actually making very good use of his well-practiced apologetic expression.

"Hi, Bridge… Uh… Sophie saw the crystals in the window and just had to come in."

I look behind him, spotting not one, but two camerapersons with their cameras hoisted on their shoulders, and an audio tech with a microphone on a boom. Awesome.

"Keep the change, dear. For the extra trouble," Mrs. Lowell tells me, handing me way too much money and then making a surprisingly hasty exit on that arthritic knee. I'm tempted to complain about her abandoning me to the wolves of reality TV, but she's a smart cookie and got out while the getting was good. Would that that was an option for me.

"Hi, Hunter. Hello again, Sophie."

"Oh! It's you! Hunter's assistant!"

I grit my teeth.

"Sophie! She's my friend, not my assistant. I don't have an assistant. You should know that. This is Brighid, and this is her shop."

"Do you want me to handle her?" Molly whispers urgently in my ear. I'm a little concerned about what she means by "handle her," based on the tone of her question. Hunter might have one less girlfriend to eliminate if I set Molly loose, I think.

"No, I've got it. But thanks..."

"Wait — don't I know you? Aren't you Logan's girlfriend?" Hunter is scrutinizing Molly.

I turn to look at her, because that's news to me. She looks a little embarrassed.

"It's kind of new," she explains, shrugging. "We've kept it kind of quiet."

"I see..."

"It didn't look all that quiet when I came into the shop the other night..."

Oh, Hunter... No subtlety.

"Molly, why don't you go take care of that new shipment of pattern books. I'll take care of Hunter and his... friend."

Molly looks relieved.

"Sure thing, Brighid." She heads off around the corner.

"Hunter... You shouldn't embarrass her like that. She hadn't even said a word to me about seeing Logan. But I guess that's a thing?"

"Based on what was going on when I walked in the other night, I'd definitely say they are a thing."

"I'm glad. Logan's sweet. He'll be good for her."

"Things looked more spicy than sweet when I walked in. Though she did say something about doughnuts on her way out..." His expression is both speculative and less-than-innocent. Not that Hunter's been innocent for a long while, of course. Nor, for that matter, have I.

His knowing eyes catch mine, and there's something...

"So — about the crystal..." Sophie interrupts, seeming a little put out.

"Sorry. Yes — that's a nice piece of selenite. You said you wanted something for cleansing chakras?"

"My guru said I should find the largest piece I could get and take a nice hot bath with it, regularly."

"No!" OK, that came out louder than I meant it to. Hunter and Sophie both look startled. "Sorry — just don't ever get selenite wet. It's a form of gypsum, which dissolves pretty easily in water."

"I thought that was the point of bathing with it, like a bath-bomb."

I close my eyes and take a deep breath before I speak. Who is this guru of hers, and how much is he charging to advise her to waste money — and nice crystals — like that?

"A piece that size normally runs at least a hundred dollars — two or three hundred if it's ethically sourced, like that one." She shrugs.

"That's one expensive bath-bomb," Hunter puts in.

"If you want something you can use in a bath, you can try plain sea salt — or a pretty Himalayan pink salt, if you want some warm and caring vibes. Salt will do double-duty as an exfoliant, and it's grounding, which will help with cleansing any negative energies — you can visualize it all washing down the drain when you're done. And if you want to bathe with crystals, even something as simple and inexpensive as quartz can work just fine. Or, ideally, you can get a set of crystals — one for each chakra — and use them to cleanse and retune your energies as needed, since each one should really be dealt with separately."

"I don't know... Guru Gary said I should get a big piece of selenite and take a bath with it."

Guru Gary?

"How's this: I'll put together a kit for you. A set of crystals suitable for a bath-based cleansing ritual, and a bag of herbs you can put into your bath with them. I can do that for less than fifty dollars, and you'll have the crystals to use again next time you need them."

"It doesn't sound very... elevated," she says, wrinkling her nose.

"Bridge knows what she's talking about," Hunter advises. "She's had training in healing and counseling, and she's been running this shop successfully for years. Her clients trust her."

I give him a grateful smile, as much for getting her to go along with the idea as for the respect he's just openly given to me.

"If you say so, Hunter," Sophie says. "But I'm going to ask Guru Gary about all of this when I get back to civilization."

I swallow a chuckle and start putting together her kit.

"This isn't going in the show, is it?" I whisper to him as I pass by him to get to the baskets of smaller crystals.

"Unlikely. Maybe just some of the video of her with the big crystal. I'm sure someone will do a voiceover explaining its use as a sacred dildo or something..."

I sputter with laughter, and he and I exchange a grin.

"Let's do dinner tonight," he suggests as I start adding herbs to a muslin bag.

"Don't you have plans with one of your girlfriends?"

"I'll blow it off."

"You can't do that."

"I can."

"Let me put it this way — the sooner you get this show over with, the sooner we can spend some time together without having to deal with a whole group of girlfriends. Unless... Are you keeping the 'winner' here with you once you've picked her?" I ask tentatively.

"I don't know what I'm doing," he admits with a sigh. "None of this was my idea."

"I'm pretty sure dating all these women at once was originally your idea, and your idea alone."

Again, that blush of embarrassment.

"Listen, Bridge... I..."

"Are you ready to go now, Hunter? I'm getting bored," Sophie whines from her spot in front of the cameras.

"Yes — we're all done here," I reply, gathering up the items I pulled together for her and putting them in a recycled-paper gift bag, which I then hand to her.

She looks expectantly at Hunter, who sighs and then gets out his wallet to pay for the purchase. I give him a shove toward the door.

"Pay me later."

"I owe you one, Bridge."

"Several, by my count," I reply, heaving a sigh of relief when Sophie, Hunter and their camera crew have left and the door is firmly closed behind them.

"So... should I get out the cedar incense?" Molly asks from around the corner.

"Please... I think a serious cleansing is exactly what this shop needs after that."

CHAPTER 7

YOU'RE MY BEST FRIEND

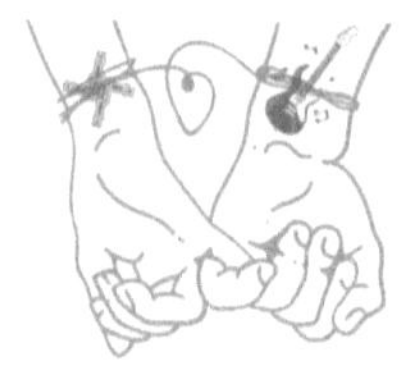

Brighid
The next day

I'm more than an hour earlier arriving at the studio than Hunter had suggested. I was hoping to get a peek at the guys recording, or at least practicing. But the reality show crew has taken over the house, and when I get there, I've barely got time to say hi to him before they pull him into the living room to go over the plan for today's shoot.

It's interesting, watching him interact with people in his professional mode. I'm used to seeing him backstage at a show, but I haven't been to a promotional event in years. Not since the big party when they released their first album. Which I'd still prefer to forget.

He's polite, friendly, but firm in what he's telling them. He doesn't seem thrilled with whatever they've got on the agenda. After some debating back and forth, they seem to be in agreement, and he passes back by me, dropping a kiss on my head and saying, "Here we go" with a shake of his head as they whisk him away to do wardrobe and makeup in his room on the second floor of this massive compound.

I'm left to stand idly around, watching the crew scurry, setting up lights and testing their equipment. I haven't seen any of his bandmates, except Alex, who came up from the studio to do a quick cameo the producers want to insert in the show.

"He really would be better off if he'd just pick you," Alex says suddenly.

My heart must be naked in my eyes, because he seems to register what he just said and immediately withdraws the comment.

"I'm sorry — it's really not my place to say that."

"You're not the first one who's said it," I acknowledge. "Nearly everyone who knows the two of us has said it at one point or another, in one way or another. And I don't disagree. But you know this is long-trodden ground between the two of us — and he's made it pretty clear that he's just not interested in me that way."

Alex frowns and looks at his feet, but says nothing.

"It's a pretty painful topic for both of us at this point," I admit. "So we generally don't talk about it anymore, except for the occasional joke... Well, he makes the occasional joke... But mostly we just pretend it was never an issue. Please," I plead, "don't say anything like that in front of him. I don't want to upset things again..."

He looks at me for a long moment, regret and even a bit of compassion in his expression.

"I'm sorry — for saying that, and for your situation," he says, pausing for a moment before taking out his wallet and handing me a business card with his cell number on it. "Just in case," he explains. I haven't had Alex's number for years, and I've never needed it. That he's giving it to me now is concerning.

"You really are good for him — I meant that," he says. "I think he'd be much better off if you were in his life more." He turns, walking away with a shake of his head.

"You and me both," I mutter quietly to myself, with a sigh. "You and me both."

"He's never kissed you, has he?"

It's worded as a question, but it has the ring of a statement, as if the answer is a foregone conclusion.

Yes, big-boned Brighid, with the forgettable figure and, apparently, a face only a mother could love... how could the hot rockstar have ever possibly considered her attractive enough to even contemplate kissing her?

Nevermind that he never has.

It's the assumption that's painful.

I turn to face the producer, whom Hunter introduced to me as Marcia, and I pause before I answer, pondering how to let her know the question was insulting, and that it didn't go over my head that it was meant that way. It's not like I haven't heard that kind of thing a thousand times in the two decades and change I've known Hunter.

"We're friends," I state definitively. "We've been friends since we were 6."

"No exploratory teenage makeout sessions? No kiss goodnight after an eighth-grade dance?"

"No. We're *friends*," I reply, stretching out the word to make sure she has had a chance to absorb it. Nevermind that I've heard him say the same thing hundreds of times and have always come away mildly offended.

"Good! You're perfect!"

"What?"

"Come with me. You're going to be on TV!"

"Uh... No. No, I'm not."

"Sure you are. You're going to stand in for our sick contestant."

"I'm what?"

"You're going to be the fourth woman in this little game we have set up for Hunter."

"What kind of game?"

"Just a cute little challenge. We're calling it 'Kiss and Tell'!"

"That sounds very, very wrong. And that's *before* you got to the part where you said you've lost your mind and decided I'm taking part in said game."

"No — really. You're perfect for this! You're single, right?"

Again, she's asking a question but she's really not. I'm even wearing a ring on my left ring finger, and still she assumes I'm single. Nevermind that I so, so, *so* am...

"Yes. Not that it's any of your business."

"We need a single girl who Hunter's never kissed to add to the mix today. One of the girlfriends has a cold. We don't want to get Hunter sick! You'll do."

"I'll do what?"

"Kiss him."

My jaw moves, but words do not come out. She cannot have just said that. After all these years of wanting to do just that and having to restrain myself from doing it, she thinks I'm going to go on national TV and kiss my best friend?

"I don't think you're understanding the concept of *friend*," I say, drawing out the word again, like I'm not sure she speaks the same language I do.

"Sure I do! You all are chummy! You know each other well, trust each other, can laugh together... all that good stuff. So you're perfect for this."

"I'm still missing the part where my being his friend means I'm supposed to kiss him. Presumably, you mean on the lips, like 'more than friends.'"

"Oh, sure! Of course! That's the whole point of the game! Hunter's going be blindfolded, and he'll get a kiss from each of the four contestants, and for each kiss he correctly guesses which contestant it is, he wins more money for his charity, the one that's getting all his appearance fees for this show. You want to make sure he can get as big a donation as possible, right?"

I'm still trying to process what she's asking me to do. But I know Hunter's charity of choice is a mental-health non-profit, and it's a cause I believe in strongly as well, and there's no way I could make a donation anywhere near as large as what she has to be talking about here. Hunter lives on a financial scale now that I can barely comprehend, let alone match.

"Can't you just postpone this 'game' until the fourth girl is well?"

"No time. We're on a schedule. A production day lost — especially when we're already set up to shoot, with a full crew here — is costly. My bosses won't allow it. I've been told to find someone to fill in. Besides, throwing in a fifth possibility adds to the challenge and the drama. The audience will eat this up!"

"I can understand that, but why me? Aren't there other women on set? Why don't *you* do it?"

She scoffs.

"I'm going to be directing everything. I can't be on camera. Too much to do! And the only other women on my crew here are married. And the network won't let us use a married woman for something like this. Not to mention that every member of my crew has a job to do. So, it's you, today, now, or Hunter loses some of his charity money. You don't want to be responsible for that, do you?"

I get the impression that she knows full well that I can't refuse anything where Hunter's concerned. He's my weak spot. Especially when it comes to something that hits as close to home for him as mental-health advocacy.

I'm silent, pondering what she's asking of me.

"I suppose we could go find his bandmate who was here a minute ago... Alex, was it?"

"And do what?"

"Have Alex stand in, since you don't want to."

"Hunter likes *women*," I explain to her, again like she's just learning English. Heck — I understand Irish better than she seems to get what I'm telling her. "*Alex* likes women. Alex is his co-worker. You don't think that's going to cause issues?"

"I don't know what these rockstars get up to in their dressing rooms..." she drawls, implying something that I know is not the case but that she knows full well would make great tabloid fodder. Especially with video evidence to go with it. She'd guarantee a few million more people watching her show, and she'd do it at Hunter's, and Alex's, and the band's expense.

She's got me fenced into a corner, and she knows it.

"What are you going to tell Hunter? He can't guess correctly if he thinks those four women are the only possibilities."

"We'll just tell him we've pulled in someone who was on-set. He doesn't know all my crew. He won't think anything of it. He'll just have a fifth possibility of 'the unknown woman' to add to the list. We won't even tell him which of the other four isn't participating."

Other than the possible personal fallout for me, she seems to have this all sorted out. It makes logical sense. I can't really think of a good excuse not to do it, not without making it clear to everyone on this set that there's a reason I won't kiss Hunter, and I don't want to see speculation about the two of us taking root in a Hollywood production crew.

Bringing in Alex is a non-starter, and she knows it.

In my head, I hear the snap of a trap closing over my foot. I'm stuck. And Hunter's just going to have to get over it.

Marcia knows she's won. I haven't said a word in agreement, and she's already full of greedy glee, like a hungry shark catching sight of a baby seal.

She shoves a stack of papers in my hand, along with a pen.

"Here — sign these. We've got to get you straight into hair and makeup, and do something about your wardrobe."

She looks me up and down with an expression that blends skepticism with distaste.

Five minutes later, I'm being swept into the hair and makeup room. And her (apparently married) crew members begin turning me from "natural beauty," as they put it — plainly aiming to keep me cooperative — to something closer resembling the glamour girl they would expect to put on TV. If by "closely resembling" one meant the difference between a couture gown and a knockoff prom dress from one of those online sites...

They manage to find some five-inch heels in my size amongst the wardrobe — "I think we had a larger pair in here in case we had a drag segment," the wardrobe assistant yells from the depths of a trunk full of accessories. The shoes are gorgeous, but I'm a barefoot beach girl by nature and I haven't worn anything other than sandals on my feet in years.

Trying to make sure I can even safely take a single step in them, I mince along, and I'm still wobbly all the way. Compared to the other girls, who are all models (of course, because who else would Hunter date?) and for whom five-inch heels are like comfy slippers, I feel extraordinarily awkward, and that's on top of the awkward situation I somehow find myself in.

I'm walking a few steps out into the hallway, holding onto the walls for balance, when I realize the other three "contestants" are all waiting out there, like spectators at the coliseum of old, expecting to see something horrifying yet thrilling.

Holly whispers something, and there's a less-quiet tittering amongst the group that I try to ignore. It's like the hallway in high school all over again, with the cheerleaders enjoying themselves at my expense. At least that's something I'm used to.

Unlike these heels, which choose that moment to catch on the threshold between the rooms. The laughter becomes open when I nearly trip, before catching myself on the doorframe.

I sigh.

"Can't I just wear my own shoes?"

"Oh, honey, you don't want to do that," the wardrobe assistant advises. "They'll have him blindfolded, and he'll be hearing a pin drop in that room. They can't have one of you four not wearing heels. It'd be a dead giveaway.

"What if we all go barefoot?"

There's a roar of laughter from the hallway. What was I thinking? These women wear five-inch heels with bikinis and lingerie. I blush straight through the heavy makeup.

"They're wearing three-inch heels today. The five-inch heels come close to making up the height difference between you and them. I'd have gone for six if I had a pair that'd fit you... You really are big-boned, aren't you?" she marvels. (Thanks, Dad. The only thing you gave me that I haven't gotten rid of after all these years... Even my old name is long gone.)

"Built like an Amazon, my mother used to say."

"Huh. She wasn't wrong there..."

Thanks? I think?

"Anyway... without the heels, you're three inches shorter than the shortest of them, and that would give it away, too. So, heels it is. You just need some practice walking. How long has it been since you've worn heels?"

"The homecoming dance our sophomore year of high school. And those were only about two inches at most."

"No wonder you're so out of practice. Not even senior prom? College graduation?"

"I didn't go to prom. Either year. And I never finished college. I was running my own business by then."

"You go, girl!" she cheers. I suspect she'd have cheered louder if I was managing to walk in these shoes without wobbling all over the place.

She ushers me back to the makeup chair, where they take down the messy bun I have my hair in. They spritz and brush, curl and spray, until my hair becomes loose beachy waves trailing down my back.

They couldn't find any clothes in my size in the wardrobe, of course, since I'm more size 16 than size 2. Instead, they take what I'm already wearing and "jazz it up," as the wardrobe assistant explains, shortening my full, ankle-length skirt by rolling it up and adding a designer belt. The sleeves of my favorite peasant top get pulled down, revealing the shoulders I always thought were my best feature.

But I'm shocked to see an almost indecent amount of cleavage when I look at the finished results in the mirror. That waitress could take lessons from these people. She might've gotten Hunter to take her number...

The lipstick they've put on me is too bright, the smoky eyeshadow more than I'd consider appropriate for daytime. The false eyelashes frame my eyes surprisingly nicely, but I keep looking up at them, giving me a weird, distracted look.

"Why do I need to be made up when he won't even be seeing us for this little game of yours?" I ask Marcia, who's peeked in to see the transformation.

"Because you'll be on camera. This little instant makeover isn't for his benefit. He's got plenty of... more conventional..." she prevaricates in what must pass for tact in L.A. "women to choose from already. We just need another warm body, and you were here and single, and we're on a schedule," she confirms, accepting the results with a sharp nod.

"Really, this is for you," she adds with a note of indulgent confidentiality "— you wouldn't want to look like a plump little partridge next to these elegant swans, would you? How embarrassing would that be?"

She chuckles and walks away. It may be the most ridiculously transparent backhanded compliment I've ever gotten. And I've gotten a lot.

"Is this what he really likes?" I wonder quietly to myself. Looking in the mirror, I realize I've been rendered nearly unrecognizable, and then I take in the glamorous women behind me, hovering in the doorway. "Stick-thin women with big boobs, made up to within an inch of their lives?"

"Honey, that's what they *all* like," the wardrobe assistant assures me. "But you polish up nicely. You should wear your hair down more often. It suits you," she adds with a smile, before gesturing for me to head out to the living room, where the cameras are set up.

I take a deep breath, close my eyes and pray for courage, picturing my spine straight and tall, like a well-crafted sword, and my mind as sharp as a well-honed blade.

I set off down the hallway.

I can do this.

CHAPTER 8

A KISS BEFORE DYING

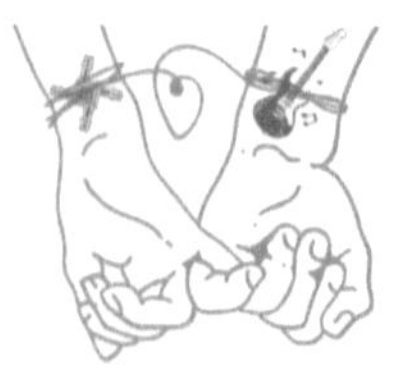

Brighid

I can't do this.

This is a bad idea. Like, colossally, epically, volcano-earthquake-tsunami-raining sharks-rolled-into-one disaster-movie bad. With zombies. Fast zombies. I know it. I can feel it. It doesn't take a star chart to see catastrophe on the horizon.

I can't deny that I've wanted to kiss Hunter for more than a decade, but doing it in front of a bunch of strangers, in front of cameras... not what I had in mind. And with our history, he may not appreciate finding out after the fact that he's locking lips with his best friend, I now realize.

But the alternative is worse. The guys would never stop ribbing him about tonsil hockey with Alex, and they have to work together. Surely, if he and I can share a bed, we can handle a brief kiss without things getting too awkward. All for a good cause, right?

Here goes nothing...

They advise a blindfolded Hunter that they've thrown a ringer into the contest and removed one of his dates, to avoid getting him sick and to make it more of a challenge for him. "One of the girls on the set," they tell him when he asks where they found the extra body. "Don't worry. She's signed the NDA."

The four of us are already lined up on the other side of the room, with Holly first, at her own rather loud insistence, and me last. Holly struts across the room, walking confidently up to Hunter, wrapping her arms around him like an octopus in heat (do octopuses even have heat?), and kissing him so aggressively that my lips hurt in sympathy. Having provided him with a complete, yet utterly unique dental checkup and a complimentary tonsillectomy, she pulls back slowly and looks at him expectantly.

"Can you identify this girlfriend, Hunter?" the host asks.

"Easy," he says. "That was Holly. There's no mistaking that kiss for anyone else."

Holly preens, clearly proud of herself for being so memorable.

I narrowly avoid rolling my eyes.

"And our next girlfriend..."

The second woman clicks her way across the wood floor, lays her arms loosely around Hunter's neck, running her fingers down the skin below his ears.

"Let's watch the hands, ladies. Kisses only."

Lady No. 2 starts to protest the obvious favoritism for Holly but goes silent at a censoring look from the host. She leans back in and licks Hunter's top lip, diving in face-first for some sloppy making out, then grabbing his bottom lip between her teeth and drawing it out as she pulls away.

"Hunter? Which girlfriend is this?"

"Hmmm... I'm going to guess it's Francesca. She's got that... edge... to her," he replies, rubbing his lip, which is red from her little nibble. (Is she so hungry that she needs to gnaw on him for sustenance?)

Francesca gives a self-satisfied grin that quickly shifts into a predatory smirk as she opens her mouth to speak.

"No talking until the end, ladies, please," the host admonishes.

"No. 3, please give Hunter your kiss."

The russet-haired swimsuit model from this year's big cover sashays over to Hunter, running her hand up his back, under his suit jacket, and then down again, loosely grabbing his butt, before she lays one on him like he was a drowning man and she was the only one in the room equipped to provide oxygen.

Hunter rubs his hand along his chin as she pulls away, pondering.

"Hunter? Which girlfriend was that? Do you want to make a guess?"

"Well, I'm pretty certain the first two were Holly and Francesca. That leaves Grace and Sophie... And you've taken one of them out of the running? So, this could be Grace, Sophie or your ringer, right?"

"We can't confirm who is or isn't left after your guesses, Hunter. But, yes, one of your original four is not here and has been replaced with someone you definitely haven't kissed before."

"OK... Then I'm going to say that was probably Grace. But I'll need to kiss the fourth lucky lady before I'll make that my final answer," he adds with a chuckle, that legendary charm of his on full blast with the cameras on him, despite his stated objections to the whole idea of this show.

The swimsuit model looks irritated that Hunter couldn't immediately identify her, but plasters a smile on her face and walks back to the lineup, her heels clicking sharply. I absently worry about the finish on the floor...

"No. 4, please give Hunter your kiss."

For half a second I freeze, until Holly gives me a shove. I stumble half a step before I recover, already blushing madly. I do my best impression of the confident strides these professional ...walkers have demonstrated. Somehow, I manage not to fall, and in only slightly more time than it took them, I'm across the room, standing in front of Hunter.

Wow, this is awkward...

The host gives me the hairy eyeball, gesturing at Hunter, and I know I can't delay any further, lest it give away the game.

I raise my hand gently to the side of his face, wrapping the other around his neck to pull him down to me. Even with my shoes raising me up five inches (unlike the extra-tall model types) and him in his dress shoes, I still have an extra inch or so of height difference to overcome.

One last deep breath, and I brush my lips lightly along his, then nudge his upper lip with my bottom one. He opens to me willingly, exploratorily, and takes control of the kiss with a sweep of his lips across mine that is less tentative than my own was.

His hands reach up and tangle in my hair, callused fingers grasping the back of my head and angling me where he wants me. He licks at my lips in invitation and I whimper just a tiny bit, probably only audible to my own ears (I hope), and I open up for him, tongue eagerly tangling with his now, as the adrenaline hits my bloodstream... And suddenly the two of us are the only people in the room... in the world...

He presses his mouth into mine, our tongues dancing together in a sensuous tango, making me momentarily wonder what it would be like to actually dance with this man — another on my list of wishes where Hunter is concerned... and then I wonder what it would be like to dance with him between the sheets... sensual, instinctive, connected... This kiss is all of those things and more. And we're both lost in it, in each other, as his arms wrap around me and he inhales some oxygen from the heated air around us...

And instantly freezes. Pulls away. Takes in a deep shuddering breath that seems half in shock and half intended to confirm the scent is one he recognized.

"Brighid..." he exhales my name, and somehow, over the blood rushing through my ears, I can hear quiet surprise erupting around me... but I am hardwired to this man, and I know he's not uttering my name in sensual delight, but in shock as he struggles to process what has just happened. Confusion, disapproval... horror?

He reaches up for the blindfold, and I see just a glimpse of the naked emotion in his bright green eyes as he pushes it out of the way. I'm not sure what else to call the sweeping emotion that strikes *me* at that moment, except perhaps... terror.

Regardless of the name I put to it, my fight-or-flight response falls decidedly, decisively, in favor of flight, and I drop those five-inch heels behind me like Cinderella escaping the ball, only considerably less elegantly, as I half trip out of the first shoe and leave the second standing in place, wobbling like a drunken domino.

"Bridge!" he shouts after me as I run toward the front hall table where I had dropped my keys and purse, quickly snatching them up.

"Oh, let her go, Hunter!" I hear Holly plead dismissively through the slowly closing door behind me, "She was never supposed to be here in the first place... frumpy little hippie..."

I careen barefoot down the precisely 263 steps to the ground and my car. (How the heck did a shoeless princess manage such a smooth escape? Damned fairytales. Setting such high expectations...)

I stop for just a second when I reach the car door and exhale my dismay. Well, if the producer thought I'd embarrass myself on national television by not wearing makeup, she had no idea what the reality of me in high heels would be. Awesome.

I quickly put the car into reverse and pull off the most efficient three-point turn I've ever made (and Hunter knows better than anyone that I got a perfect score on my driver's test).

I get clear of the driveway just in time to see Hunter rushing down the steps. A handsome prince with no shoe clue to retrieve. But then this prince doesn't exactly need a clue to find me. He knows exactly who I am, where I live. But, somehow, I doubt he'll be eagerly anticipating a romantic reunion, no matter how easily he finds me.

Chapter 9

Kiss Me Deadly

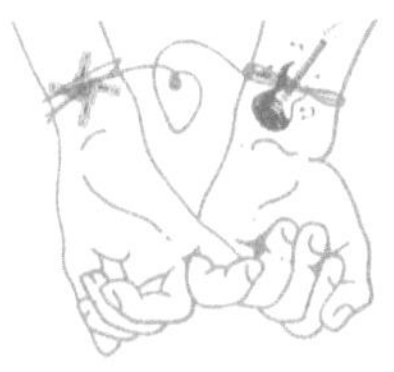

Hunter

I can't believe it.

Brighid.

How did she get roped into this mess? I'm determined to find out. I suspect the producer of this reality nightmare knew exactly what she was doing when she sent Sophie packing with her "cold" and pulled Brighid into this little "game" in Sophie's place.

Brighid.

Wow.

My brain is trying to process the simple fact that I just unknowingly kissed my best friend, and then trying to deal with the undeniable knowledge that I liked it. A lot.

Man, that woman can kiss. What would she be like in bed, if she kisses like that? Like every erotic fantasy I've ever had, come to life right in my hands... in the form of my — platonic — best friend.

I run my hand over my face, trying to wake myself up from what has to be the most fucked-up daydream I've ever had.

My dick doesn't seem to care about the platonic part of "platonic best friend." It definitely didn't care about "platonic" when I had my tongue in Brighid's mouth and my fingers wrapped up in her hair. Thank Brighid's "Mother of twelve gods" that I didn't pull her against me any sooner than I did, or there would have been no denying exactly where "Hunter's arrow" — damn those gossip sites and their clickbait stories about my sex life — was aimed.

Geez... What a mess... and one no one but me can clean up.

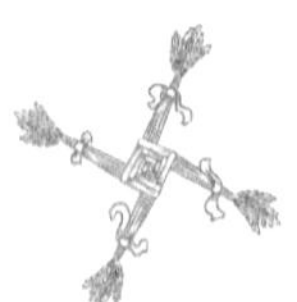

I know she thinks she's supremely subtle, but Bridge and I are, as she's often said, hardwired to each other. There's not much that one of us thinks or feels that the other one isn't instantly aware of. So I've known pretty much from the start that my best friend had feelings for me that went beyond friendship.

I've done my best to gently discourage her over the years, breaking eye contact when it got too intense between us, making it clear when I was interested in other girls, encouraging her to date the few guys I thought were good enough for her. Which would not have included me.

Don't get me wrong — I would never lay a hand on a woman that she didn't want on her. Not that that's really been a problem... But I can't deny that, to teenage me, part of the appeal of being in a band — even before there *was* a band — was how many women I expected to someday throw themselves at my feet. And like any horny teenage boy dreaming of becoming a rockstar, I thought more in terms of the quantity of my relationships than the quality.

And Brighid — she's quality.

There's only one guy she's ever told me about who I'd have said treated her good enough that I'd have been able to watch them together without wanting to rip his arms off. That Tyler dude... She refused to tell me the other night, other than to say it didn't work out, so I'm not sure what happened with him. She just stopped talking about him while we were on the European leg of our tour. But everything she said about him until then had made it seem like he was perfect for her — respectful, caring, funny, smart, and an artist, which, right behind musician, I know is a major box on Brighid's checklist for her ideal man.

And, honestly, I was relieved when she first told me she was seeing him, because it took her focus off me, and because I worried about her here, all alone. Her "circle" girls all look after her, look after each other. And I know that the "three Brighids" especially — my Brighid, the healer, and then the poet and the smith, as she described them, (it's some kind of sacred conjunction or something...) — they take care of each other. But that's different from having someone, a boyfriend, to care for her, to treat her how she deserves to be treated. Tyler seemed like that guy.

Me, not so much, as I zoomed around the world, most recently not seeing her for more than a year, not speaking to her for weeks at a time as the tour schedule got nuts, dodging commitment to any woman like it was an Olympic sport.

But then she just stopped talking about him, and I got worried that she'd dumped him because he wasn't... well... me. That's not my ego talking. I've still got a healthy ego, but that's one of the things I've really worked on in recent years. I'm still a fuck-up. I know I'm not good enough for her. I always did. But I also know her ideal man is... well... me. I'm not sure she'd give *any* guy a real chance, even if he was another blonde, green-eyed guitar player with a geeky sense of humor. Because he wouldn't be me.

But I don't want her to be alone, especially when I can't be here. So, yes, I've encouraged her to date. Maybe a little overzealously. I want her to have that experience of having someone she can have fun with, who'll love her and take care of her and... yeah, do all the things I'd do if I was here, but better and... more. More other stuff. Yeah, *that* stuff. I don't want her feeling bad about the fact that I've refused to go there — yes, *there* — with her.

So I dodged the issue as long as I could, trying to avoid hurting her feelings. It really *is* a case of "it's not you, it's me," but she'd never have seen it that way. All those delicious curves — she'd have blamed her weight or some other perceived flaw, and not me and my womanizing ways or my hangups about relationships.

I didn't invite her up to New York when I was home, because I knew we get photographed together and I didn't want to see her ripped apart on social media by all of the jealous fangirls who'd see her as a threat to their nonexistent chances with noncommittal me. It was either that or stay in the entire time she was there, and I couldn't see how she could come visit one of the country's greatest tourist destinations and just stay inside my apartment, not without it seeming like I was ashamed of her. So I just didn't invite her. And she didn't ask more than once or twice... and that was before the incident at our first album release party.

I'd reformed my ways since then, but some things haven't changed. I still love women. Maybe not in the commitment sense, but I love looking at them, being touched by them and touching them in return, and especially making them come. God, I love that. Even with thinner or more athletic women, I love that extra bit of softness, the roundness, the curves, the things that make them female. And I honestly don't care about their shape or size, so long as there's physical chemistry.

But I'd made two decisions after the incident with Bridge walking in on me the groupies. First, no more groupies, though it'd taken me a while to put that into practice. And, second, I could never be with anyone who reminded me of Brighid. Especially if there was a chance she'd see them with me, at a gig or, since we got popular, in photos. I couldn't risk letting myself think of her even for a nanosecond in that context, and I also couldn't risk making her wonder why I'd sleep with a woman who looked kind of like her but wouldn't sleep with *her*. That seemed like the only thing worse than letting her think I was a shallow asshole.

So — I know it's a cliché, but I'd gone out of my way over the years to date models, at least publicly. (I'm not sure dating lingerie and swimsuit models was a better option, but it made sense in my head at the time, and it was easy, because rockstars and models just naturally go together, apparently.) But the real reason was that I didn't want one curvy girl photographed with me at a club in NYC to make Brighid wonder what was wrong with her that some other woman who looked kind of like her was attractive to me and she wasn't.

Because, man, was she ever. And Dave's phone call the other night came not a moment too soon, with my hand on her bare back...

I just never dared to let myself think that I'd ever be good for her. She deserved the best. She'd been there for me when I was at my worst, and she'd never judged me — not until that night I nearly lost her for good. And I totally deserved that. Heck —

I needed her judgment for that. Fucking up that badly forced me to reevaluate everything in my life. It wasn't just an act of self-protection when she'd cut me off, it was my best friend rescuing me from myself. I can't say I've been perfect since then, but I've tried — really hard — to be the person I want Brighid to see when she looks at me.

When she'd admitted to me, at 15, that she had feelings for me that went beyond friendship, I'd shut her down. I'd all but literally put my hands over my ears and gone, "La-la-la-la-la — I can't hear you!" Since then, I'd made excuses about plans with the band, I told her I thought of her like a sister, which wasn't strictly true either... I'd told her I was flattered, especially because she was so wonderful, but that while I loved her dearly, I wasn't *in love* with her.

That didn't go over too well. I wanted her to hear that she was loved, and all she heard was that she wasn't good enough for me to have fallen for her romantically, or even just sexually.

And from then on, I avoided telling her I loved her. I wanted her to hear it, but I knew she'd either hear the words and hold out hope that I'd come around and fall in love with her — which I didn't want to encourage — or she'd only hear the "but..." part and it would negate the other half of the sentiment.

Sometimes, she still told me she loved me, and I knew it held double meaning for her.

"I know," I'd reply.

After a while, she'd gotten me a Star Wars T-shirt with the Han Solo quote on it, and it seemed like she'd gotten past the hurt and could look at it with some humor. She didn't get the matching Princess Leia T-shirt for herself. I guess it was still too sore of a subject for that.

Actually, I know it was. After we'd discussed our relationship a couple dozen times in the next few years, I'd lost my temper with her — see, not good enough for her! — and when she said she understood, I told her with a chuckle that I hoped she'd finally, after all this time, gotten the message that I wasn't interested in her that way.

I meant it as a joke. But one look at her face, and I realized I'd spoken a harsh truth that had hurt her. She didn't say much the rest of the night, through dinner, until we were waiting for dessert.

"Are you OK?" I asked her, kind of afraid to hear her answer.

She paused and seemed to be thinking.

"Not really," she said, finally.

"I'm really sorry. I know that wasn't cool, even if it was honest."

"I don't ever want you to feel you can't be honest with me," she said. "I usually know when you're hiding something anyway," she added with a grin that lifted my heart a little to see on her face again. "But I need to make a deal with you..."

"O...K..." I said hesitantly.

"You can resent my feelings for you or you can make jokes about the situation — but you can't do both. Pick one or the other. I can't deal with the turns back and forth between the two. We can either accept the situation good-naturedly and move on, or you can stay uncomfortable with it and we just won't talk about it."

"That sounds fair," I agreed. "So, should I start replying, 'As you wish' whenever you tell me to do something?" I added with a grin.

She laughed and elbowed me in the ribs.

"We are such a pair of geeks!"

"We are."

I don't think either of us thought at that moment that the issue of our relationship would never come up again. But I think we'd reached a point of detente where a comfortable respect for our disparate views on the subject was enough for us to move forward, together.

This, today, with that kiss — it was not detente. It wasn't comfortable for either of us, and the lack of respect shown to my best friend today, on camera and off, while not my fault, was still my responsibility. And, in retrospect, pulling her into my little dessert display the other day was probably over the line, too. But things had been so comfortable between us for a while now... I just didn't think. No — my circus, my monkeys, and I'll clean up this elephant-sized pile of shit, whatever it takes.

I return to the living room, where the production crew is packing up and carefully avoiding making eye contact with me.

"Marcia, we need to talk. Now."

I gesture to the library they'd been using for hair and makeup, not waiting for the producer to confirm she's coming with me.

"Hunter, I'm sorry if you're upset about what happened..." she begins the moment we clear the doorway.

"If *I'm* upset? *If* I'm *upset?* Wow. You really are clueless. *Brighid* is upset. I'm *livid*. You've recorded the last second of footage you'll get from me — unless you immediately delete any footage in which Brighid appears."

"She signed the legal waivers. She signed the NDA! We have every right to use that footage how we see fit! And you're also under contract — so don't think you can just refuse to cooperate and this all goes away. We've spent a serious chunk of change on this production already — equipment, crew, flying your girlfriends down here to this backwater town, putting them up in accommodations that meet their very expensive requirements... If you think you can just back out because your little — heh — or, rather, your not-so-little 'friend' got her feelings hurt, you've lost your mind, and you'll be losing a chunk of your tour earnings if you don't complete this shoot."

"Let's see what the label and the lawyers have to say about that."

"You really have no clue, do you? The *label* pushed this project through. The *label* demanded you be a part of it — *not* aMUSEd — *you* specifically! They're not going to take your side in this little diva fit of yours!"

This makes no sense. Why would Siren's Song have insisted that I, and not any of the other guys, participate in this farce? Would they have been on board with using Brighid like this if they'd known it would happen? I'm going to find out, and anyone getting in my way will find out exactly the lengths I'd go to to protect my Brighid.

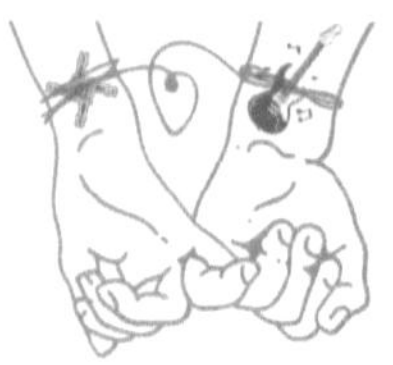

Hunter

"**C**ome on, Hunter. It was all in good fun!" Holly wheedles in my ear, her hand gripping my arm. "It was just a joke! I figured you'd do a double-take and we'd all laugh, and it'd make for some amusing viral footage."

"You figured? You? You were the one who set this up, who set Brighid up?"

"I may have mentioned to Marcia that you had a female best friend who lived here and that I thought it would be amusing to see what would happen if you were to accidentally kiss her," she drawls. "It really *was* pretty funny. Surely, you can see that in hindsight. You froze, and she ran right out of her shoes! It was priceless!"

"This is what you find amusing, Holly? Humiliating an innocent girl who was just trying to do me, and a charity I care a great deal about, a favor? How old are you, 12?"

She scoffs. "You saw how ridiculous she was, wobbling on those heels with her absurd boho clothes. You've got four — well, three — models here who would look perfectly in place on your arm on the red carpet at the Grammys, and you've got that silly little Stevie Nicks wannabe who weighs more than two of us put together, hanging on you like seaweed..."

Holly isn't really looking at me, or she'd see my expression turning from irritation to anger, and she'd stop.

"What do you care about her and her feelings?" she continues, oblivious. "Why would you bother? She's nobody. You've got me! I'm here, and happy to indulge any whim you may have, Hunter!" she adds, in a tone she seems to think is seductive.

"You really *are* a narcissist, Holly... Brighid is my best friend. She's a caring, authentic, devoted woman who's been there for me whenever I've needed her. She doesn't care about my fame or money or how many followers I have or who's retweeting me, or any of the shallow crap that you spend all your time and energy on! Brighid is real, and she's important to me. And if what's important to me means so little to you, I think that proves that *you* are the one who doesn't belong here. So pack up and get out! And tell your pet producer to lose today's footage, or I'll make sure you regret having ever laid eyes on Brighid, or me."

"Really, Hunter — you're blowing this out of all proportion! We're good together, a golden couple shining in the limelight of the social scene. You need me!"

"What I need is to never see or hear you ever again. Take the hint, Holly, or we'll see how 10 million aMUSEd followers feel about a shallow, conniving snake in sequins trying to take advantage of their favorite band for her own public profile. You know — the band's millions of fans who so love our *authenticity?*"

"You wouldn't dare!"

"Try me. Seriously — try me. I don't think you'll like what you see... any more than I like what I'm seeing right now. Get out!"

"You'll regret this, Hunter!"

"Out! Now!" I corral her toward the door, where she splutters and grabs for her ridiculously giant designer bag.

"I need to call a car."

"Do it from the driveway. And then keep walking. Away. Far away."

I slam the door behind her. I'm now alone, the crew all gone, the girls all gone, no sign of my bandmates. I pick up my phone. Brighid hasn't even responded to the text I sent her earlier today to confirm our plans. It's marked as read but no reply. That worries me, but I need to clean up things on this end before I can go to her and settle things between us.

I call our manager.

"Billy, I need something handled. Today. Right now. There's some footage from today's filming that cannot see the light of day. Ever. I need it scrubbed from existence."

"Geez, Hunter! What did you do this time? Or should I ask *who* you did this time? I thought this show was going to be PG-13. What the heck did you and those girls get up to in front of those cameras?"

"It's nothing like that," I growl. "They took advantage of Brighid for a cheap gimmick. I need that footage burned, with prejudice."

"So ask the producer to delete it!"

"I did. She refused. Said the label was behind this whole thing and I didn't have any leverage to get rid of what she thinks will be an audience driver for the show. Is the label really behind this whole thing?"

"I know the order came down directly from Marina Matthews' office."

I curse to myself, but loud enough that I know he hears.

"I don't know if it was her PR head or the lady herself," he continues, "but I doubt either of them would want embarrassing footage of you guys being aired, let alone a potential lawsuit from a bystander who wasn't fully on board with whatever happened."

"Can you make a call and get this sorted? Get them to strongarm the production crew into deleting the footage from today?"

"I don't know, but I can try."

"Let me know either way."

"Will do. I'll make the call right now."

"Thanks, man. I owe you."

"All part of the job, Hunter."

We hang up, and I start to formulate a plan to mend fences with my Bridge. I don't like leaving her alone after that scene, but I can't go talk to her until I've got a handle on things.

Hunter: *I'm sorry about today. Please tell me you're OK. I'm doing damage-control here, but as soon as I've got things sorted out, I'm coming over. We need to talk about what happened.*

I pause for a second before I hit Send and add, "*As you wish...*"

The text sends but doesn't show as delivered. She may have turned off her phone. Not a good sign.

My phone rings. Thank god!

"Bridge — I'm so sorry!"

"This isn't Miss Weaver, Mr. Graves. It's Marina Matthews."

"Oh, Ms. Matthews — I wasn't expecting you to get involved in this, let alone call me yourself. I'm sorry for the trouble."

"I'm the one who needs to apologize, Mr. Graves. This entire thing has gotten out of hand. What should have been a simple publicity appearance has caused chaos and pain for innocent bystanders, including your Miss Weaver. Miss Harwood's voracious appetite for self-promotion has had wider-reaching consequences than were expected. I take it you are not with Miss Weaver at present?" she asks.

"No, she ran out of here like her hair was on fire. Not that I blame her. I was hoping to have the issue of the footage resolved before I went to go see her."

"I can promise you that Ms. Douglas is at this moment being severely chastised, by both her superiors and their attorneys. You won't have to worry about her using that footage. Her career is hanging by a thread after that stunt."

"Wow. That was fast. Thank you for taking care of it so quickly. I appreciate it."

"It was a mess of my own making, Mr. Graves. I clean up my messes, on the rare occasion I make them. Unfortunately, I'm afraid the situation with Miss Weaver is something only you and she can sort out. I regret that I've put you in that position. Please offer her my sincere personal apologies for my role in this debacle. If she wishes to pursue legal action against any of the miscreants, I'll happily support her in that endeavor, though I am confident things on the production end have been resolved."

"Thank you again. I'll be sure to let her know."

"Take care with that girl, Mr. Graves. She's special. More so than you yet understand, I think. Take care of her."

"I haven't always done a good job of that," I admit. "But that changes today."

"Good. You're capable of far more than you give yourself credit for, Hunter. Listen to your friend when she tells you that. Don't wait until it's too late."

She hangs up, and I sit there for a moment, stunned. First Siren's Song CEO Marina Matthews gets personally involved in my messy personal life. Then she offers me advice with veiled suggestions of knowledge she should not reasonably have. Odd.

But now it's time to start the hard part. I have some deep shoveling ahead...

CHAPTER 11

KNOCKIN' ON HEAVEN'S DOOR

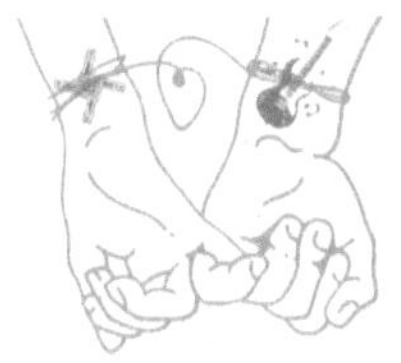

Brighid

I'm sitting on the sofa in my living room, in the corner farthest from the front door, back to the wall, with my knees tucked up in front of me like a protective barrier. I haven't even bothered changing out of my clothes — the ones I'd put on planning to go out with Hunter tonight that were then haphazardly transformed...

I'm so stunned by what happened that I can't even bring myself to cry. It was bad enough I let them talk me into getting made up like that — and high heels, just to make it even worse — and letting them record me for national television. Then, Hunter's reaction...

I shudder. That stiffening of his entire body when he realized. That look on his face. I'm going to have that seared into my memory for at least several lifetimes. Ugh.

Friends for all these years, and a lot of embarrassing moments, but this tops them all, by like a mile. When he's rejected me in the past, I've always reminded myself that his girlfriends come and go, but there is always him and me. That's never changed, no matter how things have fallen out between us. We even survived nearly two years apart, and then came right back together, best friends forever, but better — healthier. But now I wonder if this will be the faux pas he finally can't forgive. Especially with video of the moment of infamy to remind him over and over exactly what happened. Not to mention Holly, who I'm sure will be reminding him of it every chance she gets.

If the universe is merciful, Hunter will be tied up with the show, his girlfriends and band stuff until the shock has faded. Maybe he'll go out drinking with the guys and be able to laugh it off in a couple of days. Good thing I had Molly lined up to cover the shop. I can hide out here, in comfy clothes, dip into my stash of strawberry cheesecake ice cream, play sad songs and watch Hallmark movies until I can bear to show my face again. Did I say ugh?

There's a knock at the door. I don't move. And now it's more like pounding. Like really demanding pounding. And I'm pretty sure I know who it is.

"Brighid! Open this door! Right now! We need to talk!"

Welp, so much for the idea of Hunter getting drunk and forgetting all about what happened. What I did...

I can't face him yet. I can't even look in a mirror at this point, especially with my face still all made up, looking totally unlike me and entirely like the fool who thought she could be in the same room with a bunch of models and somehow not make an idiot out of herself.

Every once in a while I forget I'm awkward Brighid and do something a normal human would pull off just fine. And then I remember I *am* Brighid, because I totally did a ridiculous Brighid thing that made sense in the moment and that anyone else could have gotten away with — and instead I'm in the center of a self-created disaster. Like right now.

Safer for everyone if I sit right here in silence and wait for Hunter to give up and go away.

"Bridge! I'm not going away! You can let me in, or I can let myself in!"

And I suddenly remember that Hunter knows exactly where my spare key is. But he's never here, so maybe he won't even remember it's there. If I'm lucky, he'll have forgotten whe...

I hear the door locks rattling.

Nope! Man, my luck sucks today. Time for another offering to several gods of chance. But it's too late for today, apparently.

"Bridge!" Hunter bellows from the doorway. There's a thunk of something falling on the hardwood floor. Probably my last shred of dignity. "Bridge! Answer me! Where are you?"

Maybe if I don't move, he'll miss me curled in on myself in my quiet little corner. Surely, if I think small, I'll magically shrink to the size of a house-cat and he'll look right over top of...

"There you are! Brighid! What are you doing?"

He marches across the living room. I'm still pretending to be a house-cat. I stop short of meowing in response. Thankfully.

But he's not fooled. He plunks himself down on the sofa next to me. I don't move. I don't even look at him. Maybe this is like T-rex and if I freeze he won't notice me.

He's quiet, and for an instant I think maybe it actually worked. And then he sighs.

"Oh, Bridge..."

He puts his arm around my shoulders, his hand on the side of my face, and pulls me over against his chest.

"Are you OK? Talk to me..."

I'm silent as my mouth moves but I can't think what to say to him. I turn my face into his shoulder and heave a sigh of my own.

When I can bring myself to speak, I say the only thing I can think of.

"I'm sorry, Hunter. I'm really, really sorry. I'm so, so sorry."

"Brighid — you're not the Doctor, and I'm not mad at you," he says quickly, lifting my face up so he can look at me. "I was worried about you. If anything, I'm angry with Holly, and the producers. They never should have gotten you involved. It's bad enough they're messing with my love life — I won't let them drag you into this craziness. I signed up for this — well, not for *this*, but for this life. You didn't. I'm sorry they thought this was even an option, let alone a good idea."

He grabs my shoulders and turns me to face him.

"I want you to know — I took care of this. I called the label, and Marina Matthews herself told me she'd taken care of it. The producer got a dressing-down, and the footage they shot with you is being destroyed. Ms. Matthews even wanted me to apologize to you on her behalf for having had any part in what happened, even if none of us could have predicted they'd try a cheap stunt like this."

"I'm sorry for all the mess, Hunter. I should have found another way. I should have told them to reschedule..."

"It's OK, Brighid. I'm sure they said what they needed to to get you to cooperate."

"I'm still sorry. I know you weren't fond of this show idea to begin with, and now I've just made a disaster of it."

"Come here, you..." he says, wrapping me in a bear hug and dropping a kiss on the top of my head before tucking me under his chin. It feels like old times, comforting each other with simple physical affection. I've missed this, too.

We sit that way, in peaceful silence, for a long while. It's gotten dark outside, and with no lights on in the house, it feels like we're the only two people in the universe, and that's fine with me.

After a while, Hunter clears his throat.

"I have to ask, Bridge — Whatever possessed you to let them talk you into doing that?"

Possessed is right.

Hunter seems incredulous.

"They were talking about your charity losing out on a bunch of money. And then they talked about sneaking in Alex or one of the guys on the crew if I didn't fill in. I knew you wouldn't be happy about that. Unless there's something you want to tell me?" I joke.

Hunter guffaws.

"No, no surprises there. I mean, you've known me for almost 25 years. Have I ever tripped your gaydar?"

"Not once. Not for a moment. But I don't know what you and the guys get up to on tour — public sex, sharing women, whatever backstage is like *now*, as opposed to how it was years ago — it's not too much of a stretch that the guy who's joined you and a groupie might enjoy... spreading the wealth, as it were..."

Not that I'd judge. Some small part of me might even prefer Hunter was gay. But never for an instant have I ever pictured the scenario I now have in my head. Thanks, Marcia.

"Uhh... No. At least not with me. What the other guys get up to is their business. But I avoid having sex with groupies these days. Too much opportunity for things to go wrong."

"No — instead you keep a steady rotation of girlfriends..." I tease him with a laugh. Even though it doesn't really make me feel like laughing. I've had a lot of time to think about this since I first confessed to him years ago how I felt about him. Part of me wants him happy and settled down, not worrying about groupies. And part of me suspects that he will never be completely happy... well, with anyone but me.

"A rotation that is going to be whittled down to just one, on national television, apparently, with me having no say in the matter." He growls in frustration. "Bridge — we need to talk about this. About today. About that kiss."

"Hey — I saved you from sucking face with Alex! Would you rather I hadn't?"

He pauses way too long in responding.

Great. Given a choice between me and Alex, he's got to think about it. And it seems like maybe he'd pick Alex.

No blow to my self-confidence there... Nope.

"Bridge — we've talked about this. You're an amazing girl — an amazing woman. My best friend. I just can't be with you, no matter what you've seen, no matter how you feel. I won't risk us for that. You need to find somebody who's good for you, better for you than I am. You've seen what my life is like — I mean, after today, how could you possibly want any part of that life? The paparazzi, the social media, the narcissism, the... Holly."

He chuckles.

"She's pretty horrible," I admit.

"I'm sorry about that, Bridge. I had a talk with her, and I made it clear that you are very important to me and that being anything less than respectful to you is unacceptable."

"Did you boot her ass to the curb?" I joke.

"As a matter of fact..."

"You didn't!"

"I did."

"What about the show? She's going to roast you alive on her social media channels."

"Probably. But she's signed an NDA regarding the production, so she's going to have to be very careful if she does it."

"Well, that's something."

"I know I probably stepped over the line the other night over dessert. That wasn't fair to you. And I'm sorry about that. This whole reality show thing has me on edge, and I was lashing out at the girls after I saw how they were treating you, and I didn't think how it might feel for you, playing along with me on that. So, I'm really sorry if that was uncomfortable for you."

"Oh, no! It wasn't a problem. I knew you were putting on a show for them. We make a good team."

"Yeah. We do." He squeezes me around the shoulders again.

It gets quiet for a minute.

"Bridge..."

Uh-oh. I can feel it coming.

"That kiss... it can't happen again. I really don't want things to get confused between us. I don't want to give you reason to hope I'll change my mind. I just can't."

"I know," I admit with a sigh. "It's OK. I get it. You don't think of me like that."

"Bridge — don't do that."

"What?"

"I know you very well."

"Better than anyone."

"And I know what's going through your head when you say that. You're thinking, 'If he's not interested in me, if he can't love me, how could anyone?'"

I tear up. He does really know me that well.

"Well, so far, the evidence seems to support that."

"You've had boyfriends. You'll have more."

"Heh... A couple of dates doesn't make anyone my boyfriend, really, even if I sleep with them."

I stop myself before I admit to him that the relationship he thinks I had with the amazing "Tyler" was as fictitious as "Tyler" himself. He'd been so concerned that I wasn't dating, like I was mooning over him and not even trying to date. Which was half-true. I wasn't dating. But it wasn't because of Hunter. At least not entirely. I was just busy with the shop, and, honestly, once I'd seen what I'd seen in those visions, pretty much every guy had a hard time measuring up, even the one...

But I couldn't tell him that, so "Tyler" was born.

"And apparently, my kissing skills are lacking, judging by today..."

He gives me a hard look I can feel even in the near-pitch dark.

"I would not say that. At all."

I turn to him, trying to read his expression in the little bit of light filtering in the window from the distant streetlights. What is he telling me? Is this a pity compliment? Or maybe — is it even possible? — maybe I wasn't the only one who felt chemistry in that kiss...

Now I know what he meant about confusing me.

"Any guy would be lucky to have you. And I'm not just saying that because you're my best friend. You're a treasure, Bridge.

And you should be treated like a treasure. Don't let anyone, any guy, treat you like anything less than that. Including me."

"You're such a romantic..." I observe with a wry laugh. "You're going to make some girl very happy someday."

"It's really not in the cards for me."

"Going to live the rockstar lifestyle until you're 92 and having to pry the old ladies off your wheelchair in the nursing home?"

"Maybe 72..." he suggests with a chuckle. "By the time I'm in that home for aging rockstars, you'll be sitting in that rocking chair next to me, wiping the drool off my chin and reminding me of the lyrics to my own songs."

I scoff.

"More likely I'll be down the hall, watching Hallmark movies while you're surrounded by a dozen ladies in their own wheelchairs, just waiting for talent night so they can throw their granny panties at you."

"If they can get them off without help."

We both laugh out loud at that image.

Dropping another kiss on my head, he says, "So — 'Some Kind of Wonderful'?"

"Always."

"Popcorn?"

"In the pantry. Popper's out on the counter. Butter on the fridge door. I'll get the drinks."

"Orange Fanta?"

"What else? I laid in a supply before you got here."

"See — you're amazing."

"You only love me for my taste in movies and my ability to stockpile your favorite foods."

"Not true. You do a mean tarot reading, too."

I smack him on the shoulder and head off to grab our sodas.

But part of my brain is still digesting all the things that happened today — including that kiss — and all the things he said, including yet another polite rejection. I still can't get that image out of my mind — Hunter frozen in shock, dismay, at having kissed me like that.

After the heat of that kiss, the chemistry I felt in it, regardless of what he may have said to make me feel better, he not only didn't feel it himself, he was repelled by it. There's no getting around that. And no matter what kind, flattering things he said to me afterward, no matter how he explains it away, I can't help being hurt by that.

I'm starting to wonder if he's been right all along — maybe in the back of my mind I've been holding out hope that he'd change his mind. And maybe us being so close has kept me from moving on with someone who isn't repulsed by the idea of kissing me, someone who's in my own league, someone who actually finds me attractive and really wants to be with me.

Because Hunter's made it very clear that he doesn't — not any of those things. And maybe I've got to finally take that to heart and move on, get back to that balance we'd started to get after our time apart. And if I'm going do that, maybe I've got to put some space back between us.

CHAPTER 12

WAKE ME UP

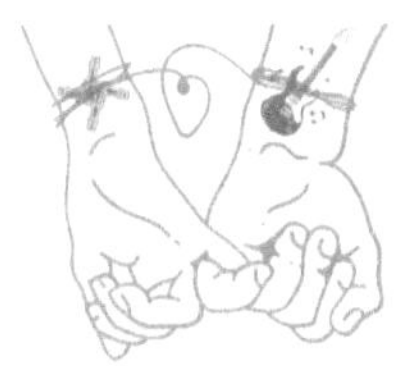

Hunter

I wake up in the same position I've woken up in so often in my life — with Brighid in my arms, sleeping softly against my chest.

We snuggled up under a blanket last night to watch the movie — which we've watched together at least a couple times a year since we were teenagers, even if we had to do it via chat in the last year or two while I was on tour — and, of course, we fell asleep before it was over.

It turns out emotional turmoil, followed by damage-control, and then more emotional triage, is pretty darn exhausting.

I think back to the movie plot and wonder if maybe Brighid identifies with Watts a little too much, hoping for the same kind of happy ending with her best friend as Watts got with the long-oblivious Keith.

That first kiss of theirs... the totally contrived "prove to us both that you can deliver a killer kiss to a girl by kissing your best friend" kiss — it was hot when we were teenagers, and it's still hot. The chemistry between those two characters was just off the charts, despite Keith still being "stupid" at that point. (Yes, he really was. Tomboy or otherwise, Watts was a hottie, and he had to be blind not to have noticed that.)

And watching it again with Bridge last night, in the wake of our own contrived first kiss...

I can lie to her. Mislead her. Over this one thing. I have to. Because it's for her own good.

And I hope she really listened when I told her she was a treasure and that she deserved a great guy. She does.

I know my reaction to our surprise kiss yesterday was a blow to her ego, which can't really stand to take many more, after all the teasing she's had over the years and what Holly just put her through. Not to mention me. So I really hope she got what I was trying to tell her.

But I have to admit it, just to myself — watching the movie with her last night, the closeness and loyalty between those two friends, which we'd always both identified with... and then watching that steamy kiss... The same thing happened to me that's happened every time we've watched it since we were 13.

That tension of arousal, needing to shift things around to keep from imprinting my zipper on my dick... watching her watch it and seeing her pupils dilate and her breath catch and her heartbeat speed up... Last night, it was all that, overlaid with the very fresh memory of that same kind of heated, electric chemistry in the kiss I experienced that afternoon with my own best friend...

And as I watched Brighid watching that kiss on the screen last night, I couldn't help noticing her heart racing and the flush in her cheeks as the same heat I was feeling hit her. I found myself wondering if her heart raced like that when we'd kissed, if her cheeks were flushed with arousal when she was pressed up against me, if she felt the electric interchange of energy across our skin. Had it made her wet, just like it made me hard?

And I was hard all over again, sitting there next to my best friend, threatening to bust through my fly, not so much because of the kiss on the screen but because of Brighid herself. My own amazing and — I admit it, at least to myself — utterly enchanting best friend.

Have I been just as stupid as Keith, but for far longer?

I tell her I won't cross that line with her, that I can't do it, but all I can think about now is that kiss we shared yesterday — if unknowingly on my part — and how it blew Holly's octopus impression and Francesca's little dominance display completely out of the water.

If it had been anyone other than my best friend delivering that undeniably hot kiss...

But it *was* her. And now I'm stuck wondering if it's my response to that kiss, to our chemistry together, that's wrong, or if it's my determination to not get into a relationship — especially not one with Brighid — that needs to be reevaluated.

Have I been as colossally stupid as I think I have?

I need some time, some space, to think. Somewhere where Brighid's soft skin and beguiling scent isn't influencing my thoughts, or making me hard to the point of distraction.

I slide Brighid's head gently off my chest, cushioning it with the blanket, and pull my arm slowly out from behind her neck. She says she's a light sleeper, but I've managed to disentangle myself from her without waking her often enough to know it's possible when she's sleeping soundly, which she seems to be now.

I let myself quietly out — avoiding tripping over her shoes, which I brought back with me and left by the door last night — and I replace the spare key where I found it. There are a few people out on the street already this morning, and I find a spot on Brighid's porch where I'm less likely to be seen so I can wait in peace for the Lyft driver to get here.

I didn't even grab my ball cap and sunglasses when I ran out to check on Brighid, and I don't want to risk getting spotted coming out of Brighid's house early in the morning. She doesn't need the gossip following her around in this small town, let alone the exposure if the gossip sites were to start speculating about our relationship.

I mean — *I* don't even know what our relationship is right now, thanks to yesterday's rearranging of everything I thought I knew. I'm going to need some time to sort that out. And the whole point of yesterday's damage-control efforts was to keep from tossing Brighid to the wolves of the tabloids and social media.

I'm lucky enough to get a driver in short order and even luckier to get one who isn't the talkative type, since I'm not sure I could hold a conversation right now with all that's spinning around in my head. Five minutes later and — part of the beauty of a small town — I'm back at the studio compound. Dave's surfboard is gone from under the house, but the rest of the guys are probably still asleep, knowing them.

I come up the stairs quietly. I can get a couple more hours of sleep and then join the guys in the studio when they're all up.

Or not.

"What the fuck? Holly? Do I even want to know how you got in here, or why you'd think I wanted to see you after yesterday?"

"Oh, you want to see me. Trust me."

This can't be good.

CHAPTER 13

BLACKMAIL

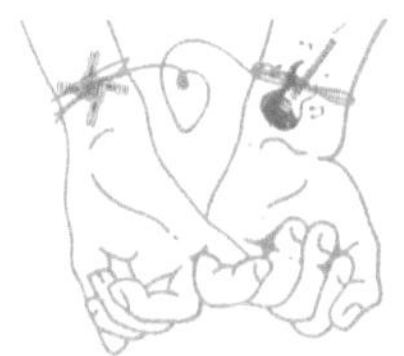

Hunter

Holly's expression is smug, and she cuts right to the chase. "I have the video from yesterday,"

"It was erased. Try again."

"They may have erased the original, but a little birdie sent me a copy before that happened. You really should be more careful about who you piss off, Hunter."

"There is no way Marcia gave you that video. They threatened to fire her already for having pulled that stunt. Marina Matthews called me personally and told me that."

"Well, Marina Matthews doesn't have the power she thinks she has, then. Because I have that video. And unless you want poor, sweet not-so-little 'bestie' to be the laughingstock of the internet, you're going to do what I tell you for a change."

I'm still not sure I believe she has the video. She could be trying to bluff her way through this attempt to gain the upper hand, since I've been dodging her every time I got back from a tour.

"If you've got it, prove it."

"My pleasure," she says, with a feral look that suggests canary feathers should be sticking out from between her lips.

Uh-oh...

She holds out her phone toward me, hitting the play button on a video. A video I instantly recognize as raw footage from at least two cameras from yesterday's shoot. On the screen, I see Brighid freeze when she's called up for her turn. Holly shoves her from behind, and she wobbles slightly as she crosses the room on those high heels she left behind like Cinderella yesterday.

But as I watch the video of her approaching me, what catches me about the footage isn't her barefoot-girl awkwardness in heels, nor the uncharacteristically made-up face on my friend who hardly ever wears anything more than lip pencil and a dash of mascara.

No, what hits me about her is her expression as she gets nearer and nearer to the blindfolded me. After nearly 25 years, I can read Bridge like a book, and I can see the emotions naked on her painted face.

A hint of pure terror as she seems to be silently imploring me (or her gods) for me not to react badly to what she's about to do. (Oops.) But right underneath, there's an earnest, deeply caring expression that is such a sharp contrast to the way Holly is looking at me right now that Holly's objectively model-perfect face actually turns my stomach.

It's like Brighid is standing there telling the entire world that she loves me, with just a look, and doing it in spite of the pressure of the cameras and the production crew and the other girls, and in spite of her obvious fear of my potential response.

The me on the screen can't see her, can't see that expression, can't see her tentatively reaching her hand out toward my face like it's a treasure she's sought her entire life and can't believe she's about to have in her grasp.

And suddenly, watching this thing that's already happened, I not only accept that Brighid's love for me is that strong — something I've always avoided acknowledging, even to myself — but that it strengthens her, rather than weakening her. She's said before that I'm her weakness. But that's not what I'm seeing written on her face. I already knew she'd do just about anything for me, but now I can see why.

No one has ever looked at me like that... Ever. No adoring fan, no backstage groupie, no girlfriend, and especially not Holly. Brighid sees down to the very deepest parts of my soul, and looking at me, preparing to kiss me for the first time ever, she transparently adores all of me, flaws and all, even after I've rejected her. It's pure unconditional love.

Maybe you can get that from a parent — goodness knows I barely had a chance to learn that with my mom and certainly never got it from my dad — but I don't recall having ever seen it quite so strongly directed at me.

And now Brighid is cradling my cheek, and I can remember that gentle, sensuous touch... How did I not realize it was my Brighid? Fuck. I *am* stupid.

On the screen, she reaches up and pulls me down to her, and brushes her lips across mine, and I'm back in that moment, feeling that connection with this mystery woman, her soft sweetness instantly pulling me in to the kiss, so I'm no longer caring about this stupid game, all thought of anyone else even being in the room vacating my mind entirely.

Her lips open, and I take her up on the invitation immediately, wanting to learn this mouth like I know my chords — intimately and with utter certainty that they will be there when I need them. My hands dive into her hair, pulling her face harder against my own, devouring her just as eagerly as she's devouring me.

My senses are on fire, then and now, as I simultaneously watch the scene unfold from the camera's view and remember how every millisecond of the experience felt — lightning racing though my nerves, heat burning outward from where our mouths meet and dance together, and all the blood in my body making a mad dash straight for my cock.

I'm standing here watching myself kiss my lifelong — platonic — best friend and all I can see is two people with incredible hot, sensual, *sexual,* chemistry that is so unbelievably erotic that I'm already highly aroused just watching it, and I was there when it happened!

I am officially stupid.

Then, I watch myself go stiff as I detect the faint scent of Brighid's distinctive perfume, pulling out of her arms, pulling away, and I want to shout a warning to that other me: No! Don't stop. Don't push her away. Don't scare her away.

But as I push the blindfold off my eyes, the shock on my face is clear, and I can still hear my mind yelling, "No! No no no." I'd sworn I wouldn't cross that line with her, of anyone in the world, not her. And to find I'd been tricked into doing so just cut me instantly to the bone.

It was a risk I had refused to take for more than a decade, and in one moment, that had been thrown out the window, and I was terrified what that would mean, for me, for her, for us.

And my damn stupid ass — every bit of that fear was there for Brighid to see, to feel. That expression she'd approached me with, begging me not to react badly, and I'd done exactly what *she'd* feared. And she'd done exactly what any sensitive human — let alone a woman bullied and rejected so often in her life — would do.

She ran.

And that's all on me. Holly and Marcia set this up. But it was my thoughtless reaction that hurt her. And it was my reaction and her resulting response that was captured permanently on this video. Video that Holly had and clearly planned to use against us both.

Whatever Holly asks in exchange for not sending that video out to her 10 million-plus followers, I will do. Whatever I need to do to protect Brighid — whose only mistake had been to trust a conniving bitch and a ratings-hungry TV producer — I will do.

"What do you want, Holly?"

"You."

"You can't have me. Not anymore. We're done."

"Unless you want your flighty friend to go viral across every social media site in the world with the tap of a button, you're going to act like we're together. In fact, you're going to declare the competition over, send the other three girls home, and be very conspicuous about enjoying your newfound commitment to your true love — me."

"Why do you even want this, Holly? You can't be getting off that much on the idea of keeping me when I'm unwilling. I don't care if people would think we're officially together — at this point, you repulse me. So much ugly, so much rot in your soul. I couldn't get it up for you if my life depended on it."

"Well, it's a good thing then that it doesn't. But Brighid's does, unless you want a horde of paparazzi on her doorstep by tomorrow afternoon. Never fear, though, after the way you've treated me since I arrived, ignoring me in favor of that lumpy, frumpy hippie-chick, I wouldn't want you back for real either. What I *do* want is the publicity that being publicly declared your only girlfriend will give me, on top of the buzz from the show, especially once it's announced it's come to an end sooner than planned, now that you've found the one woman you want to be with." She beams at me, like on some level she actually believes that could really happen.

"My follower count is going to explode! More followers means more promotional contracts, more perks, more influence — and my entire brand lives or dies by influence. 'Rockstar girlfriend' will go right in my bio now, and I'll forever be known as the woman who bagged 'The Hunter.' See — it's perfect! And don't pretend you won't like some positive publicity yourself," she tells me. "No more Mister No-Commitment! The ladies will think you've settled down and are ready to do the marriage-and-kids thing. You'll be more in demand than Declan is! Enjoy it! Get your PR people to play it up! You really don't have any choice in the matter, so you might as well get the benefits."

I'm dumbstruck. She's thought all of this out. She's holding Brighid's reputation, her privacy, maybe even her business — her whole life — in her hands, along with that phone.

"One more thing, Hunter: If this little fiction of ours is going to be believed, you can't tell anyone — not a soul! — and you can't be seen with your little playmate anymore. No Francesca, no Grace, no Sophie, and especially no Brighid." She smirks at me. "You smell like her perfume, by the way — just in case you thought you got away with spending the night with her..."

I grimace. It's not like I did anything other than watch a movie and sleep... But Holly would never believe that. I knew she was self-serving, but I realize now that she's also too underhanded to believe anyone else could ever act honorably.

"I'm going to be watching, just in case you're tempted," she adds, just to make it clear how screwed I am. "You step one foot near her, call her, say anything about this in a text, I'll know, and I'll release the video."

I make a sudden grab for the phone, knowing that it's a long shot that she hasn't uploaded the video to the cloud already. She sees it coming and snatches it away.

"Fuck!" I roar.

"It wouldn't do you any good anyway, Hunter. I've got backups on two separate sites. And you try anything stupid like that again and I'll just go ahead and send it out. At least then I'll have the satisfaction of seeing both of you going viral looking like fools."

I scrub my hands over my face, trying to think of any way out of this trap she's set for me. But it looks like she's going to get away with it, slithering free like the viper she is.

My phone pings with a message received.

"That's just so you'll remember what's at stake if you don't follow the plan," she spits at me. The video attachment preview makes it clear what she's sent me.

True to form, she cackles malevolently and turns on her heel, walking triumphantly out the door.

The sound is a far cry from my real-life witch's sweet laugh. Which I now desperately want to hear, because I know it would lift my spirits, which are about as low as I can remember them being since I messed up so badly with Brighid at our first album release party and I thought she was done with me.

And what am I going to do about Brighid? The only positive I can take from that video not being erased was that I got a chance to see from the outside what happened between me and Brighid.

I really hurt her. Badly. That look on her face when I pulled away... I won't ever forget that now that I've seen it. That she still seemed to forgive me for it doesn't diminish the damage done. It just emphasizes how unconditionally she loves me, that she didn't toss my ass permanently to the curb last night instead opting for a movie and a couch cuddle.

And I can't forget other parts of that video, either — nor do I want to... The unfathomable love on her face, her gentle touch, her sweet lips on mine, the megawatt electric connection when we came together, the pure eroticism of watching us together, without the blinders of my self-imposed restrictions. Restrictions that it now seems hurt her, rather than protecting her from getting hurt.

Yes, I'm the king of stupid. And now I've got so much more to lose. I have to find a way to protect Brighid without destroying us in the process.

To quote my... friend? Maybe more-than-friend? — I'm not sure what to call her even inside my own head anymore. — "Mother of twelve gods!"

Chapter 14

A Rock & a Hard Place

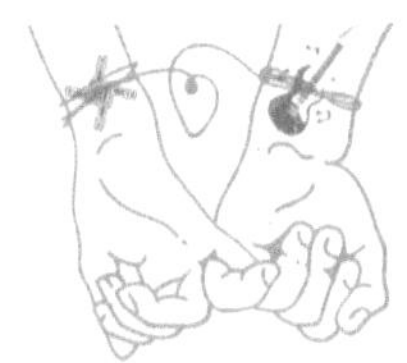

Hunter
Four days later

The last several days have not been my best. By a long shot. Brighid isn't speaking to me. And I'm not sure if that's because she's decided she's too hurt by my reaction to that kiss to even deal with me after all, or if it's because I canceled our plans for the foreseeable future, telling her I had to be in the studio with the guys and deal with the end of the show filming before I could hang out with her again.

Yeah, I know. Lame. Especially when she took time off so we could spend time together after the tour.

At first, I just couldn't think what else to tell her while I followed Holly's mandate to stay away from her and say nothing about the blackmail to anyone. So far, Holly's kept up her side of the bargain, and I've just gone along for the ride.

Or it could maybe be that Bridge has seen some of Holly's social media posts with photos of us out and about, and she knows I canceled on her to go out with Holly, with photos documenting us out for breakfast, lunch, dinner and afternoon snacks in an array of nice restaurants. (There are a lot more now than there were when I was a kid. Alex is in heaven, and keeps trying to join us, but what would I tell him to explain the stilted conversation between me and Holly?).

So, we're constantly being seen in restaurants, but Holly never eats more than a few bites, filling up on protein bars before we even go out. I always hated that about her. What a waste of the chef's time and effort! But when I mention it, she says she can't eat too much or she won't be able to get the cosmetics and clothing endorsement deals she's aiming for with her ever-increasing influencer profile. And she's taken more than a few potshots at Brighid in the process, saying if she ate any more she'd look like her. (In my book, that's a good thing, especially considering their polar-opposite attitudes. One of them has a healthy relationship with food. The other... is Holly.)

Holly's got photos of us riding the carousel at the amusement park on the boardwalk in Rehoboth. (Rhys tagged along and just rode the Haunted Mansion over and over again.) I look like a brooding asshole in half of the photos, because what grown man wants to be stuck on a merry-go-round with a woman he hates? Holly said it was fine, that it's good for my rockstar "cred." Declan complained that I'm stealing his signature attitude.

And she's got photos of us on the beach, though David keeps trying to shoo her away from his surfing area, even though he mostly just sits on the beach and stares out at the ocean. (No idea what's up with that... Even when the surf is flat, he's still a constant presence on our little strip of private beach. Maybe he's aiming to take up Declan's asshole mantle if I don't?) And Holly's got photos of us out clubbing at night. I'm more than a little drunk in more than a few of those shots. It's the only way I can tolerate Holly long enough to satisfy her demand that we be seen out together. (Can you blame me?)

The band *is* getting in some studio time. We arrived with three songs basically written and nearly ready to record, but we'll need a dozen or so before we can pull together an album. David and Declan both seem distracted, and since they are our primary songwriters, it's slow going on that front. But this was also supposed to double as a vacation, so I guess they're entitled. In the meantime, we're finalizing the song arrangements in preparation for Malcom Fisher, our producer, to join us for actual recording.

And when we're not in the studio, I've been trying to get the stupid TV show wrapped up so I can get the traitorous Marcia and her crew out of the house. (I was being honest when I told Bridge that part.) They're talking about using it as a mid-season replacement, which would mean it would air within a few weeks of wrapping. The turnaround time on these reality shows is insanely short, it turns out. They're basically editing as they go. That's probably why the networks love them so much — cheap to produce and sensational enough to draw viewers even when they won't admit they watch them.

And that means I've already taped the scenes where I send Francesca, Sophie and Grace home. None of them seemed to be very broken up about it. I got the impression Holly had a hand in that, like all of this. And the crew has been accompanying Holly and me on our outings — I refuse to call them "dates" — so they have footage of our supposed love story to wrap up the series.

We're supposed to go out dancing tonight, but I've just about had my fill. I'm thinking about going AWOL so there's no "date" and nothing to shoot. The more I think about it, the better that idea sounds. Especially when I finish off Kieran's bottle of Jameson, then dig out his backup bottle and cuddle up with it like I'd prefer to be doing with Brighid.

Eventually, I get tired of the four walls of the bedroom and head out onto the beach, bottle in hand. I'm going to walk out. Literally. Holly and the camera crew can come find me if they want. I tie my shoelaces together, toss them over my shoulder and hit the road... Well, the sand. Ha!

I give Davey a salute as I walk past him on the beach. He blinks at me in surprise.

"Where ya headed there, Hunt?"

"I'm taking my friend here for a walk," I tell him, showing off the bottle like it's my lovely date for the evening. Which it is.

"Uh... OK. Be careful, there. You don't want to get in trouble for having that..."

"No law against public consumption in Delaware!" I inform him brightly. I knew there had to be a good reason to come home for this little vacation! Woot!

I amble down the beach toward town, ignoring the "Private Beach — No Trespassing" signs (the private beach is ours, right?) and taking a slug of whiskey here and there, as it strikes my fancy. It's getting dark out, and people are out on the boardwalk, eating, playing, shopping, even listening to a little concert at the bandstand.

At least a few of them are looking at me. I'm not sure if it's because I'm already a little wobbly, walking along with my bottle, or if it's because they recognize me. But it's making me uncomfortable, reminding me that I've got a camera crew and a fake girlfriend/extortionist who are probably back at the house, wondering where the fuck I am. Yeah! That thought cheers me up, actually.

I grab my phone out of my pocket, and sure enough, there's eleven texts from Holly and five more from Marcia. Each is increasingly shrill, and that makes me smile more than it should. I don't even look at the voicemail count.

I may end up paying for this little rebellion later, but if I don't get some time away from Holly and that fucking film crew, I'm going to lose it. I can't even go hang out with Ellie — oops... Bridgie... Bridge... my bombshell blonde bestie. Ha! I crack myself up.

But thinking about my bestie, and my critical-level frustration over having my hands tied like this when I need my best friend... Heck —*want* that blonde bombshell... I remember that first time she tried to kiss me, on the playground at school when we were like 7 or something. Even as close as we've been, on some level I've been dodging her almost the entire time I've known her. Maybe it just became a habit — something I didn't think about beyond eventually setting boundaries I thought would keep us both safe. And I did a shit job of that, anyway...

If I could turn back time right now, would I do it differently with hindsight? Would I have let that little girl kiss me?

Nah... probably not. Girls had cooties back then. Heh.

But I do want that innocence back, back from before I noticed how my dad treated my mom, with all the insults and emotional arrows, before Mom decided it was too much to take. And before I let my guilt over that and my fear of turning into my dad affect how I treated Brighid.

Our old school is just a few blocks from the beach, and while I'm dodging the crowds downtown, I find my feet taking me in that direction. I wonder if the school, if that playground, still looks the same. I wonder if a 7-year-old boy ran away from a 7-year-old girl last month and whether the two of them will end up together in ten years or twenty, happy and so glad they were friends from the start.

As I reach the school, I note that there's been an addition to one side, with more classrooms, it looks like. I walk around the back, to the playground, and realize the playground has changed, too. It's all safety-focused now, with more things on the ground, no bare metal chains on the swings, a smooth plastic curlicue slide. And there's a climbing wall we didn't have back then. Cool! I would have loved that. Bridge would have loved that. I miss my Bridge... I've been missing her for a while now, actually. I should really have told her that more...

The playground is no longer surrounded by a 4-foot fence with an easy-to-open gate. The fence is easily 6 feet now, and the gate is padlocked with a heavy chain. I couldn't get through that even if I'd had bolt-cutters in my hand instead of a mighty fine bottle of whiskey. Speaking of which...

After another solid swig from the bottle, that fence looks very climbable. I size it up, holding my feet up against the openings in the chainlink. I can do this! No kids' playground is going to keep out Hunter Graves! Sticking the bottle in the waistband of my shorts and dropping my shoes on the ground, I start climbing. Way easier with no shoes on, by the way, though it's kind of uncomfortable.

I manage to get to the top and I throw a leg over, spilling some of my Jameson in the process. Alcohol abuse! I giggle to myself. I grab the bottle to hold it upright again. Gotta keep my date safe! Mom always told me to be a gentleman!

Before I let the pain of that thought hit me, my phone buzzes yet again in my pocket, as I sit atop the fence, and I look down at my hands — one holding the bottle and the other the top of the fence — and decide to keep ignoring it. Fuck Holly! And fuck Marcia! Marcia, Marcia Marcia! Ha!

I slide my other leg over the top of the fence and start working my way down, one-handed, while I clench the bottle in the other. I drop the last couple of feet a little less gracefully than I'd pictured it — 7.6 out of 10 possible points. Gonna have to do better if I want a medal! Even if that Russian judge is clearly biased!

But the bottle has been preserved intact, if a good bit emptier, and that still seems like a good reason to celebrate! I wander over to the swings, squeezing my ass into the kid-sized seat, and I do something somewhere between swinging and twirling — until it starts to make me want to puke. Then I just sit there, drinking my Jameson.

After a while, I'm picturing me and that little blonde girl on the playground that used to be here, and I'm kind of wishing I'd let her kiss me. Then, and when we were 15, and in the almost 15 years since then, and especially in the last week.

Stupid, stupid Hunter.

I smack myself on the forehead. Harder than I meant to. Ow.

Would I have ended up where I am if I *had* done any of that? Would I have three platinum albums and a handful of Top 40 singles, my Song of the Year award? Would I have used my first big check to buy my Dragon guitar — the limited-edition one I'd been drooling over, at 10 times the price, when Mom got me my green PRS, which itself was something no 15-year-old should ever reasonably have been given? And that's one less tattoo I might have, since I got that same dragon design on my left arm to match the muse and green guitar on the right.

Would I be playing to tens of thousands of people most nights of the year if I'd kissed Brighid, even once? Would I be writing and recording music with some of the best musicians on the planet? Would I have had my pick of groupies, and then of the hottest models in New York City? (That's sounding like less of a good thing than it did a couple weeks ago.)

On the other hand (models — or one particular model — aside), would I have paparazzi following me around? Reporters digging into my personal life and potentially into my best friend's? Would I be getting blackmailed by the evilest bitch to ever post a duckface selfie to Instagram? Probably not.

And, really — Bridge has always been my biggest supporter, my biggest fan. I wonder what might have happened if I'd had her right by my side for the entire ride. Would she have been a partner who helped me reach even higher heights?

I look up at the top of the swingset half expecting I'll see the two of us projected on the sky, enjoying our good fortune together in this alternative reality, and I instantly decide looking up was a bad idea. I may have done a little too much making out with my date for the night. Hmm...

Would hypothetical Bridge and I have broken up over groupies sneaking themselves into my hotel rooms or too much time away from each other when I was on the road? Would we still be friends at all? Losing my best friend is the possibility that's terrified me from Day 1 of my climb from aspiring teen guitarist to rockstar. But what has it cost me to ensure that would never happen because I'd crossed that line?

Brighid was all I had at some of the lowest points in my life. I couldn't risk that, risk her, risk *us*. But now that I'm staring losing her in the face once again — whether from Holly's machinations or my own stupid mistakes — I realize I've ended up there anyway, minus maybe 15 years of having somebody look at me like Brighid looked at me the other day. Like she's probably always looked at me — but I just never really noticed, never let myself notice.

It's like a lightning strike in my brain. I have to fix things with Brighid. We'll figure out how to deal with Holly. Together. But I'm not losing my best friend over this, and I'm not going to give up what could be my one real chance at happiness — not without a fight, not anymore.

I pry my butt out of the swing, taking what's left of Kieran's whiskey with me.

Getting back up this side of the fence is a little more challenging now, but I'm nimble. Usually. I manage to get up to the top again and throw a leg back onto the other side. I sit there for a minute, getting my bearings before I attempt the climb back down — gotta show that Russian judge what I'm made of!

Like clockwork, my phone buzzes in my pocket again. Do I not get reception on this playground unless I'm 6 feet up in the air on a giant metal post? But this could be Brighid. I hope it's Brighid. It's probably not Brighid. 'Cause she's mad at me. But it could be.

I weigh my priorities and decide to go for the phone. Because it could be Brighid calling me. I can't let go of the bottle, because, hello — broken glass bad for small children! So I bobble the bottle neck between a couple fingers and use the rest to hold on to the top of the fence. I reach for my pocket and manage to get my phone out without wobbling too badly.

Fucking Holly!

I'm tempted to hurl the phone across the parking lot, but I decide to just decline the call so I can go ahead and get back on the ground now, before anything goes wrong. I throw my other leg back over the fence, my Jameson-addled brain realizing a moment too late that I'm now holding my phone in one hand and the bottle in the other and not so much the fence anymore.

I hit the ground with a crunch, and then it's lights-out for Hunter. Oops.

CHAPTER 15

SOMEBODY'S GOING TO EMERGENCY

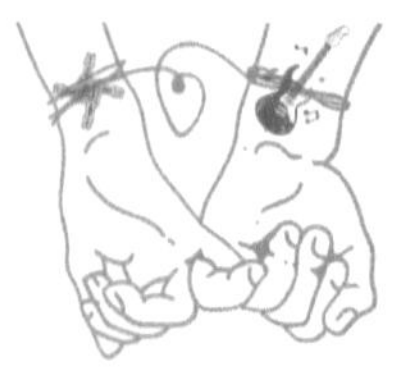

Hunter

"**I**s he OK?"

"It doesn't look like anything's broken... except the phone screen and the bottle, of course. He's got a bump on his head, though I think that might be from the bottle landing on top of him before it hit the pavement," replies a voice I don't recognize. "And I'm not sure about the left arm and hand. He definitely landed on that. It's just a question of whether it's a minor break, a strain, a sprain or just some bruising."

"Fucking shit!" someone yells from far too close to my pounding head. "Fucking idiot guitar player falling drunk off his ass and onto his fretting hand!"

Yeah, that's Declan all right...

"Ow!"

And that's me, trying to move my left hand, which appears to be in the grip of a very amused paramedic. Ow. That hurts, and that's not good. The pain in my hand makes the pounding in my head feel a little less like someone whacked me with a baseball bat. Or a bottle of Jameson, apparently. That someone being me.

They may have whacked my *hand* with a baseball bat, though. They, again, being me.

"And here he comes! Back to the land of the living! How'd that walk with your buddy Jameson go for you, Hunt?"

That's David. Hey — I managed to get him off the beach for what seems like the first time since we got here! Go me!

"Hi, guys!" Ow. Don't talk that loud. "What happened?"

"It appears that you got sloshed on my last bottle of whiskey, ya eejit, and then, for some reason known only to yerself, tried to climb a fence at a playground."

That's Kieran. He's Irish, in case you didn't realize that from his colorful vernacular. He only sounds like that when he's pissed off, or pissed, and he can't be the latter, since I've drunk all his Jameson.

"Oh, yeah..." It's coming back to me now. I was rushing to get back out of the fence to... I think about it for a minute.

"Brighid!"

"She's not here, man," Alex puts in. "But you're lucky she was looking for you — she kept calling us, saying she was worried something had happened to you. That chick really is psychic, isn't she?"

"Something like that," I reply offhandedly, wondering what the full story is. "Where's Rhys? And how did you all get here?"

"Well, your girl there was panicked and kept begging us to check and make sure you were OK. She even called Holly like four or five times. Not that Holly gave her the time of day. She was already pissed off because you skipped out on your date and let her get stood up with the cameras rolling. And because I gave Brighid her number."

Alex chuckles like he enjoyed that a little too much. I can't say I don't, too.

"Anyway — Dave said you'd been pretty far gone when you headed out and that you took the bottle with you. I still had the finder app set up on my phone from the tour, so after we didn't hear from you for a couple hours and Brighid was still freaking out, I used it to locate your phone — which is pretty smashed up, by the way. You're lucky the GPS locater was still working, or we wouldn't have found you."

"And Rhys?"

"Trying to keep Holly distracted from the fact that we all took off after we said we didn't know where you were, so that she and the camera crew didn't end up following us here."

"How's that working for him?"

"Not great. He's threatened to drown her in her own cosmetics at least twice now. I'm not sure how much longer he can..."

"Oh! My! God! You poor thing!"

"And here's Holly!" Declan announces, way too loudly.

Fuck.

"And her camera crew!" he adds, just as loudly.

Mother of twelve gods! Could this get any worse?

"Did anyone let Brighid know I'm OK?"

"I'll uh... do that next," Alex says hurriedly. I want to object — Brighid should never be an afterthought for anyone.

"We need to get him in the ambulance and to the hospital," the paramedic puts in, apparently no more eager to be on a reality show than I am. "He needs his head checked and that arm X-rayed to see if there are any breaks."

I shudder at the possibility. We've got songs to write and record, gigs to test them out at... Declan's right to be pissed at me. We've got some time, but not enough to rehab a broken hand up to performing standards.

"Yes, honey, he's alive and mostly intact. Though I wouldn't blame you if you wanted to make him slightly less intact after all this." Alex is clearly on the phone with Brighid. *Honey?* But I can't think of anything to say to her right now. There's too much to say and I'm not sure any of it will make this situation better.

"Ohhhh! My poor Hunter! Is he going to be OK? Is his hand mangled? Will he be able to play ever again?"

That's Holly, who has apparently decided that playing the distraught girlfriend and starting rumors of the premature demise of my career is the way to go with today's reality TV performance. Because she's flanked by two cameras. As I look over at her, she starts literally wringing her hands. I narrowly restrain myself from rolling my eyes in full view of the cameras.

She pushes the paramedic aside and starts peppering my head with kisses.

"Fucking stop, Holly! I've got a fucking bump on my fucking head and you're fucking making it worse! Fuck!"

The sentiment is honest, though I had just enough presence of mind to toss in as many F-bombs as I could, hoping it'll deter the producers from using this footage in their show.

She looks back to make sure the cameras aren't on her in this moment and glares at me when she sees she's clear. I nearly chuckle. But ow.

I climb onto the gurney at the paramedic's insistence and get pushed into the back of the ambulance. The paramedic goes to close the door behind me, but Holly sticks her hand in the door and pulls it back open.

"I'm his girlfriend! I'm coming with him!" she yells, not only too loudly for my pounding head but too loudly to be anything other than a transparent play for the cameras. A model she may be, but an actress she is not.

The ambulance doors shutting sound like the bars of a jail cell locking closed behind me.

CHAPTER 16

BROKEN WINGS

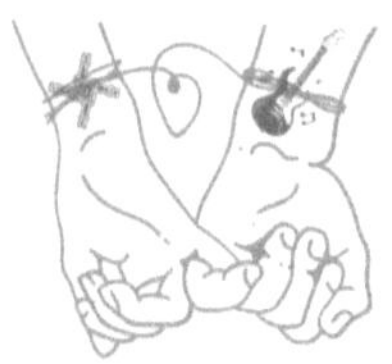

Brighid

I'm pacing rapidly around my living room when Alex finally calls me back with news.

"Is he...?"

"Yes, honey, he's alive and mostly intact. Though I wouldn't blame you if you wanted to make him slightly less intact after all this."

"What the heck happened, Alex?" I demand. "Where was he?"

"I'll let him explain that to you himself," Alex demurs.

He promises to call me back when they know which hospital he's going to.

I return to my pacing. My pretty rug is never going to forgive me.

A half-hour later, my phone rings and I've answered it before it rings twice.

"They took him to the hospital about 20 minutes ago, just to check him over," Alex says, thankfully oblivious to the fact that I'm fully ready to tear his bejeweled arms off for making me wait this long for news.

"I'll be there in 10 minutes."

I grab my purse and keys and am out the door mere moments later.

I *knew* something had happened to him. I just *knew* it! I shouldn't be surprised. But, frankly, this last week and all the drama of it has scrambled my sense of how he feels about anything, and I don't really trust my instincts anymore where he's concerned. Even after a single kiss, things have gotten complicated, just like he always warned me they would if we were more than just friends.

That thought sends a shiver through me. I didn't want to think he could be right about that. I've seen too much of us in my visions of the past to think that we wouldn't work together here and now. But this last week has borne out that fear, and I'm not sure how to fix it.

I was walking on the beach earlier when a flock of twenty-seven pelicans flew overhead. They're often associated with nurturing, to the point of self-sacrifice, as well as with safety — but also with the ferrying of the souls of the dead to the afterlife — and I've never seen them en masse like that, usually just one or a few at a time. But this was twenty-seven of them — three times three times three. The omen could have meant anything, or nothing, but instinct told me to check on Hunter, no matter how awkward things were between us right now. He might have needed me, and I couldn't have lived with myself if I hadn't been there for him, despite how complicated things have become.

When I didn't get any answer from him on his phone, I called Alex, whose effort to make sure I had his number makes me wonder if he has a bit of prescience himself. But that's for another day.

Alex didn't know where Hunter was. He checked with the rest of the guys, and none of them knew where he was either, but David had said he'd seen him walking along the beach, tipsy and still drinking. I immediately worried that he'd fallen into the water, unconscious, and could have drowned. Hunter swims like a fish, as do most of us who grew up at the beach, but drunk? I'd had that one close call all those years ago with doing stupid things while drunk, and I just wasn't a big fan of alcohol. But this had me on high alert.

I knew Hunter was supposed to be finishing up shooting the TV show with Holly. She'd tagged him on roughly 353,012 social media posts in the last few days.

I'd tried to ignore it. But I missed him. Watching him out at restaurants, dancing, going to the amusement park like we did when we were kids... I can't say it didn't hurt, especially in the wake of yet another rejection, and doubly so when he was spending time with Holly while making excuses to me about skipping out on our plans.

I had pulled that pain close, to remind me that I was playing with fire where he was concerned. It hadn't dissuaded my heart from loving him, any more than his rejections had. I was stuck with it, and he was stuck with me, until he told me he wanted me gone. Which it seemed like maybe he had this week. So I just kept to myself.

Until today. Until something, or Someone, told me to check on him.

I spent a panicked evening waiting for someone to call me back with word. I knew I was being a pain, that they thought I was freaking out for no reason, and Holly had just plain shut me down after Alex gave me her number just to get me off his back. She hadn't been nice about it, either. But I hadn't expected her to. Hunter was just more important.

"Where Hunter is isn't any of your business, you silly groupie," she said before she hung up on me. The first time.

"Holly — I just want to make sure he's OK. What does it cost you to tell me if he's with you and he's OK?" I demanded the second time.

"It costs me nothing, but seeing it eat you alive that he's mine and you can't get to him — that's priceless."

I only barely get up the courage to call back after that one.

"Stop calling me! You are just pathetic! Hunter would call you if he wanted to talk to you. This is pretty shamelessly stalkerish behavior for someone who's just a pity-fuck for a star like Hunter."

That was all I could take. He'd never even slept with me, and she'd made it clear that if a miracle occurred and he ever did, it would be out of pity and nothing more. I knew he was out of my league now, but until that moment I hadn't fully realized just how far out of my league he was. And I'd gotten nowhere with getting her to tell me if he was OK.

There's an odd place between "I knew it" and "I told you so" where anyone who has a gift of Knowing can trip themselves up. You don't want to gloat that you were right. You also don't want to appear to be asserting provable prescience when most of the time it can't be proven at all. But you want people to take you seriously when you're certain of something and have a decent track record to suggest they should take you seriously.

So as I'm driving over to the hospital at slightly above the posted speed limit, I'm reminding myself not to say anything that could come off as "I told you so!" Even though I did. Hunter has come to trust my instincts, even though he remains skeptical. His bandmates — I'm sure they already think I'm a kook, even without me pointing out I was right.

I rush into the ER waiting room and spot Alex. He points me back to the ER treatment area just as the door opens to let out another patient. I never beat Hunter at our playground races, but I dart through that doorway before anyone can stop me.

I immediately spot Hunter walking down the hallway, a nurse walking behind him with a wheelchair that he clearly is supposed to be in, and her expression tells me he's not exactly complying with hospital policy.

I see Holly behind him and part of me enjoys the glare she levels on me. *Told you!* I tell her in my head. And I give myself that one. She's earned it. In my mind's eye, I stick my tongue out at her, too.

And Hunter — he walks right up to me, smiling his winning, flirtatious Hunter smile, and I don't even absorb the fact that he's aiming it at me, for once.

"Do you have any idea how much you worried me?" I shake him hard by the shoulders, avoiding the brace he now has on his left forearm and hand. "I was going out of my mind!"

"Apparently," he snarks pleasantly, seeming a little drunk.

I glare at him.

"Don't ever do that to me again!" I snarl back, grabbing him by his chin, his short beard brushing against my fingertips as I stare directly into those green eyes, making sure he absorbs my words. I catch myself then and let my hands slide down his ink-covered upper arms, whose patterns I know like the back of my own hand. My forehead drops to his chest, my eyes closed as I pull myself back together, inch by hard-won inch. I take a deep breath and sigh.

"Sorry," I say solemnly. "I really shouldn't have done that. You don't owe me anything — any explanations, any heads-ups, any check-ins, anything. So, I'm sorry," I say again, looking up at him but with only a glancing bit of eye contact.

"Don't be sorry," he replies, grabbing my hand and holding it against his chest in a dramatic gesture I suspect is fueled by whiskey, based on the smell of things. "You were worried. I get it. I'm sorry to have worried you. Next time I decide to fall off a fence, I'll make sure to let you know ahead of time."

He chuckles, giving me a rueful grin.

I stare at him, the wheels in my brain running at full speed with a dialogue only I hear. He's giving me permission to worry about him, because he knows I'll do it regardless. He's cutting me a break because he knows he hurt me and he's now predisposed to be kind to compensate for it. He's defusing the scene I'm in the middle of creating, because he doesn't want to make more of a spectacle of us and he doesn't want to upset Holly, who looks oddly at loose ends with no camera crew following her around in this restricted area of the hospital, where I've now barged in.

I can feel the pain leeching into my expression as that realization hits me, until surely my eyes are nearly drowning in it. My breath catches.

"No. You don't have to do that," I tell him quietly, shaking my head, glancing at Holly, who seems to now be addressing the lack of a TV camera on her by starting a livestream in which she's telling her followers about the harrowing accident her boyfriend the rockstar guitar player had tonight and how he narrowly escaped a certainly career-ending injury, though his prognosis is still in doubt.

My eyebrows go up in silent inquiry, and he shakes his head subtly, telling me she's exactly as full of shit as I think she is, at least as far as his injury goes. He points at his head, and I can't decide if he's drawing my attention to that big bruise on his forehead or making the universal "crazy" sign in reference to Holly.

But in that moment, it seems like the girlfriend part of her statement is right on the money, and I have to consciously cede the partner role I've so often assumed with him in the past, to a woman who clearly hates me and would like nothing more than to further humiliate me. And he *is* her boyfriend. So she's got every right to get territorial about this.

"I'm really, genuinely sorry," I tell him, keeping my voice low to avoid being overheard by her livestream audience. "I have no right. I have no right to worry, no right to be upset, no right to expect you to keep me in the loop of your life."

Unconsciously mirroring how he pulled away from me after that kiss, I pull my hand free of his, taking half a step away from him.

"I'm not the girlfriend. I'm not *your* girlfriend," I say earnestly, my voice threatening to break. "I can't expect you to think of me when things are going off the rails for you. You've got somebody else to think of. And it's only right that you would forget about me."

"Listen, Bridge... You..."

I shake my head, tuning out the interruption.

"Tell Holly I'm sorry about all the crazy calls," I continue. "I'm sorry I bothered her. It won't happen again. ... I promise."

Taking a quick last look at him, I turn quickly and rush blindly down the hall, hoping desperately to reach the privacy of my car before the threatening tears escape and pour down my cheeks.

"Brighid! Wait!" I hear him call out behind me.

"Sir — you can't leave until the doctor checks the fit on your brace and addresses that concussion..." I hear the nurse warn as the heavy door to the ER shuts behind me.

I sprint across the driveway — probably the fastest I've ever run for any reason — garnering startled looks from the EMTs who were clustered around the ambulances. But, honestly, I barely notice their stares as I rush for the parking garage entrance and stab repeatedly at the elevator call button, as if my frenzied motions would make the darned thing get there faster. Fourth floor... third floor...

With a small cry, I tear myself from the uncooperative elevator door and race up the stairway, my heart pounding as much from fear that Hunter will find me and hold me accountable for my crazed behavior as from the unplanned flight up the steps to the fourth floor, where my car is parked.

I throw myself at the stairwell door, the pressure plate barely getting it unlatched before my full weight hits it. That's going to bruise. But the bruises on my heart are of far more imminent concern right now.

How could I have been so stupid?

I fumble for my keys.

He was taken, belonged to someone else. Not mine. Nevermind that we have this connection, a history. It's insignificant against the draw of a new face and a pair of long legs, just like all those girls in high school. I know him well enough to know that.

I manage to fit key to lock, stumbling as I all but dive into the driver's seat, my mind racing at a hundred miles per hour even while the car remains firmly parked...

And now I've ruined the friendship between us. There was no question of that. If I hadn't crossed the line with that kiss — a line he'd so firmly drawn between us over and over again — I'd done it with this little display of over-the-top concern, both when he was missing and again when I'd confirmed he was safe. I'd revealed the full depths of my feelings for him. A blind man could have seen it. Goodness knows the entire population of the emergency room had, including his bandmates and his *girlfriend*...

A sob wracks my chest as I put the key in the ignition and slam the car into reverse, pulling out of the parking space at a speed that alarms the couple just coming off the elevator. No, it's not him. Flee... just flee...

My tears are flowing freely now as I navigate the seemingly endless spiral down to the ground floor, dreading that he might still find me and complete my mortification.

Today I'd made myself just another girl futilely throwing myself at the hot rockstar, and the best I can hope for from him now, from any of them, is pity. And I refuse to be pitied. I had lost my dignity irrevocably in making that scene, and I know that in their minds I'll forever be that girl.

No. It might be like cutting off my own arm, but I am done. No more gigs. No more photos or comments on the band's social media. Unfollow. Unlike. Delete his number from my phone. Kiss my best friend and our history goodbye. Minus the actual kissing, of course.

I gasp for air as I choke down another sob at the mere thought of that. But no, the temptation to contact him would be too great. He has a life, and I refuse to interfere. I'll just have to pull the shreds of my self-respect together and delete his contact info as soon as I get home, back inside my house, with walls and a solid door between me and the pain waiting outside. The pain inside — that I'll have to live with. That'll be right there with me, a constant companion inside the walls of my home, and inside my mind and my heart, my soul.

Pulling out of the garage, I race past the ER entrance again, briefly sending the car airborne over that mountain of a speed bump. Fifteen mph in a 10. I'll feel guilty about that later. No time now.

I glance in the rearview mirror as the drive unfurls behind me, spotting a familiar form rushing out the doors just as I stop at the stop sign. My wheels spin for just a moment as I accelerate across the blessedly empty crossroad and out onto the now-quiet street that would take me home.

In that moment, my walls collapse, and tears stream freely down my cheeks, moments of stark quiet interspaced with wracking sobs as I drive the familiar route home, to safety.

I grab my purse and race for the front door, stopping only to grab that traitorous spare key and bring it safely inside. I dump everything on the table in the foyer and feel relief only when the front door is once again shut and locked behind me, the deadbolt locked and the safety latch thrown, grateful for another small barrier between me and the world that has left me raw and in pain.

I climb the stairs only barely aware of the steps under my feet, numbness beginning to creep over me like a blanket of fog over rocks, softening the blow of the uncharted emotional territory that I find myself in so suddenly. A whisper of relief as I absorb it — He is OK. If nothing else, Hunter is OK. Nothing else matters, in the end. All the rest, I'll deal with later.

I let the fatigue of so many hours of worry over him, and the hours of emotional turmoil, this past week and since, wash over me, succumbing to the lure of unconsciousness.

CHAPTER 17

LEARNING TO FLY

Brighid
A few days later

Hunter has been trying to talk to me. I've lost count of the text messages and voicemails. And he's come over to the house at least a few times. The first time, he went to my old key-hiding spot and cursed up a blue streak when he realized I'd removed it.

I'd entrusted it early that morning to my neighbor, who's far more difficult a guardian to overcome than a sculpture of a Japanese water goddess.

He pounded on the door and begged me to let him in again. But I put my noise-canceling earphones in (thanks for the 29th birthday present, Hunter — they came in handy!) and listened to some guided meditations until I was certain he had gone.

Next, he left notes tucked in my screen doors, front and back, but I'd already decided not to go out for a while, and I knew he'd be waiting to see if I read his notes. So I didn't. I spotted him outside the house at least once after that, peering at his notes from afar to see if they'd moved or if I was still holed up in my safe space.

Being here by myself for a few days gave me time to calm down and go over, methodically, what had happened in the last couple weeks and in the prior 15 years.

The emotional storm that carried me home from the hospital that night was long overdue. It had built up over the course of 15 years, with me always tamping it back down or finding ways to shed it briefly and Hunter always ducking away like it was a hot potato someone had just randomly chucked at his head. Not safe to handle until it had cooled down, even though I was inevitably left holding onto the thing with scorched fingers. And here I am again, dealing with the fallout of his refusal to face what's between us head-on. So it boiled over. And now I've taken the lid off and moved the pot off the heat.

I'm not sure if that's a mixed metaphor when it all involves cooking of one sort or another. But this stew we've had going for more than a decade is just about done, one way or another. I'm just hoping it satisfies, rather than giving us both a case of food poisoning.

It's not that I don't want to talk to Hunter. I do. I want desperately to hear his voice as he sits next to me on the sofa again. But I can't trust myself around him. I have to find some degree of self-control and dignity — two things I hadn't realized I'd lost until they were long gone, and publicly at that. I need him to respect me, to acknowledge my strength even though I haven't exactly demonstrated it lately. But it's there, and it's gotten us both through some very rough patches.

I'm also not sure exactly what his intentions are. He had made it pretty clear after the kiss incident that he was going to redraw that line of his, keeping me within carefully contained parameters that he found weren't of risk to one or both of us.

And it's clear that he's with Holly now, with the other girls nowhere to be seen and so many social media posts tagging him that I've stopped letting myself even use the apps anymore. And she was at the hospital with him, marking her territory through livestreams and selfies, whether I was there to see it in person or not.

I didn't let myself read all of his texts. The first day or so, I ignored them all until the notifications weren't visible anymore. A day or two later, at which point I'd hoped he had given up and would leave me to lick my wounds in peace, another one popped up, and I'd read it before I realized what I was doing.

Hunter: *I am not with Holly.*

Hunter: *I never wanted to be. Not since that kiss.*

Hunter: *Bridge — Please talk to me. I need to explain what really happened.*

Hunter: *I miss my best friend, Brighid. I love you.*

That one struck home. He'd stopped telling me he loved me a long time ago, with very rare slips. I understood why. But that still hurt. A lot. That he was saying it to me now, in writing, where it would be a lot harder to take back... It meant something — to me, and, I suspected, to him.

What if he was telling me the truth about Holly? Goodness knows she had some serious issues with honesty and pettiness, not to mention being shallow and selfish. Maybe she had somehow manipulated Hunter and made their relationship appear more concrete than it actually was.

I can't think of a time when Hunter had ever flat-out lied to me. He'd occasionally misled me, usually for my own good, or at least what he perceived as my own good. And on the rare occasion I had seen him lie to someone else, he got caught. He was a lousy liar. Maybe it was because he knew I'd see right through him, as easily as we read each other most of the time, but he hadn't ever truly lied to me. And, honestly, I was inclined to believe he was telling me the truth now.

I'd come to realize while we were apart that Hunter's choice of relationships had more to do with his father's abusive behavior than it did Hunter himself. The way his father had treated his mother, his mistresses, Hunter himself. The way he'd encouraged Hunter to sleep around, even at 16... But I hadn't ever talked to Hunt himself about it. He'd always been so resistant to seeing a therapist to help him deal with his past trauma, or even to talking with me about it in detail. I knew just enough to despise Howard Graves more than anyone on the planet. And to know that Hunter's patterns were well-established, even if he didn't realize how they'd come to be.

Hunt had only ever been with shallow women, in even shallower relationships, and nothing had shown me that was going to change. So while I might be inclined to believe him when he said he wasn't with Holly now, I wasn't going to let myself read into what he was telling me with that text and get my hopes up that he'd somehow come around to the idea of us being more than just friends.

But I was intrigued. I have to admit that. So, when the phone rang a week after I'd seen him at the hospital, I picked up.

"Bridge — don't hang up on me! Please!" he begged, even before I'd had the chance to say, "Hello."

I let the silence lag.

"Bridge?"

"I'm here, Hunter."

"Thank god. I've been trying to talk to you."

"I know. I wasn't up to doing that. I don't think I really am now, either."

"But you are."

"For the moment." My tone is harsher than I intended. I'm not sure if I'm more angry with him for putting me in this position or me for letting him, or with Holly for... well, being Holly, based on what little interaction I've had with her.

"I don't know what to say, Bridge. Things aren't what they look like."

"It looks like, despite all of our plans for when you came back, you've been enjoying yourself on all-day outings with your girlfriend instead."

"It's definitely not what it looks like, if it looks like that," he says, his tone suggesting there's a lot more to that story, and what's there doesn't make him happy. My heart clenches. Is there something going on that's bothering him that much? Should I be worried?

And I catch myself. Why am I worrying about Hunter? Why am I worrying about what it means that he's been plastered all over social media, Holly hanging on his arm? She's his girlfriend, clearly, despite his protest. Why shouldn't he be out in public with her? And why is he trying to imply that he's not happy about that? It's not like he doesn't have free will. He could be going out with Sophie or Grace or Francesca instead, or pick up some random girl on the boardwalk. Or he could be here with me. No one's got a gun to his head. That he's implying otherwise makes me angry. With him, and with myself for my weakness where he's concerned. This is not the woman I want to be, not the woman I've grown to be. "Goddesses bend. They don't fold." It was a lesson I'd been taught long ago. And I can't fall back into that origami habit with him. Not again.

"There's more going on than I can talk about right now."

"Right, the NDAs... Well, let me know when you're no longer prevented from telling the world — or your supposed best friend — what's actually going on. Sounds like it's an interesting story."

And I hang up.

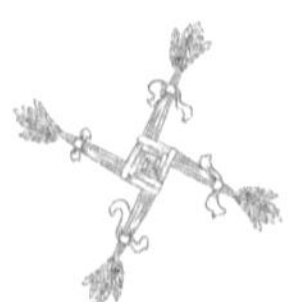

It's been a week since I last talked to Hunter. My first instinct that night at the hospital had been to promise myself I'd cut Hunter off, cut me off from him, for both of our sakes. I can't handle another moment of humiliation in front of him or his friends, and I no longer feel like even he knows what he wants from me, which leaves the whole situation ripe for misunderstanding, unreasonable expectations and false hope. And I can't do that to either one of us. At minimum, we both need some time and space, some equilibrium. I know it, and if he wasn't so contrary, I suspect he would admit it, too.

Our relationship had gotten unbalanced a long time ago and has only slid more and more out of balance as the years have gone on. There had been that correction after the incident at the band's album release party, and Hunter had emerged from our time apart more like his old self than I'd seen him in years, and far more mature. And I'd found a pool of self-confidence I'd lacked in our earlier years, even if it had seemingly run dry lately. But true balance was something we'd never achieved. We usually pretended it hadn't, but the explosion of his career had exponentially expanded that gulf between our lives. He's a bonafide rockstar now, with all the glamorous trimmings and perks thereof. I'm a small-town business owner with practical concerns and one big personal dream that had been placed out of my reach long ago. Maybe it's time to just give up hope that I'll get a happy ending there and just focus on the things I can control, like my business. That's my real strength.

And that's why I decided to go back to work tomorrow. Molly had agreed to give me more time off if I wanted it, but I'm reaching the end of the time I'd originally asked to have off, and

I don't see any point in extending it when the reason I'd planned for it — Hunter's visit — has gone so far awry.

It's time to get back to practical things and let go of rockstar-scale dreams. The only question is whether the rockstar in question will allow me to do that without a fight. Because I'm feeling too battered and bruised by the last few weeks to believe I could fight him on anything, though I'll certainly try. Hunter himself has always been my greatest weakness, so I already know going forward that it's going to be an uphill battle not caving in to him.

But if balance is our problem, I can't let him continue to put his heavyweight rockstar charisma-machine thumb on the scale in favor of what works for him but not for me. It's time we interact as equals. If we can't find a way to do that, then maybe it would be better if we didn't interact at all.

That thought hurts beyond measure, so, hopefully, it won't come to that.

CHAPTER 18

MEETING OF THE WATERS

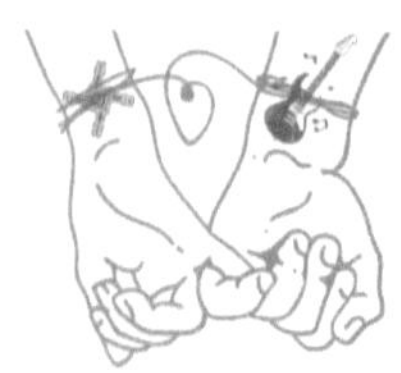

Hunter
The next day

I've been standing outside Brighid's shop for the better part of 20 minutes, trying to get up the courage to go in.

"I need her help in a professional capacity," I tell myself.

Not untrue. But an excuse not even I believe.

I have to see her, talk to her, clear the air. Having decided Holly isn't really watching me and deciding to say "Screw it" and let the chips fall where they may in the unlikely circumstance she actually is, I've tried calling Brighid, texting her — and other than that one call a week after the hospital, when she hung up on me, she's ignored every overture. My attempt to stage a repeat invasion of her house using the spare key was thwarted, as the key is no longer there.

I can only be glad that my histrionics on discovering that went ignored. How the gossip sites would have loved that!

"aMUSEd Guitarist is Not Amused!"

"Hunter Misses His Mark!"

"Graves Digs His Own Grave!"

"Pro Musician is Tone-Deaf and Off-Key in Emotional Performance!"

I was tempted to roll up with a boombox lifted over my head, playing my own music, but I doubted she (or her neighbors) would find that endearing. At least not in her current mood. It didn't work in that movie, anyway.

Meanwhile, she hadn't left the house in more than week, at least that I could tell — not to go in to the shop, nor out for groceries nor, it looked like, even out for her usual walks on the beach. Her car hadn't moved an inch, and the notes I left in her doorways, front and back, remained wedged between the storm doors and the frames, exactly where I left them.

Until today.

I've been here long enough, standing out of the view of the shop window and (I hope) of the general public, to have an idea how many customers she has in the shop, which is due to close within the hour. It's a narrow window, trying to time my entrance between when her customers are all gone and when she'll lock another door that I don't have a key to.

I don't plan on giving her any choice about talking to me right now. This is too important. To both of us.

By my count, there's now just one person left in there, other than Brighid and Molly.

"Did you want me to lock up behind me? You've had a long day." Molly calls back inside from the open front door.

"I've got it! We're almost done here. Have a great night!" I hear Brighid say from somewhere deeper inside the shop. My heart trips at hearing her voice after wanting to hear it so badly these last few days.

"You, too!" Molly replies, letting the door shut behind her and heading down the sidewalk toward Logan's music shop.

I can't wait any longer. I quietly open the door again, trying not to jingle the little seaglass windchimes she has over the door as her shop bell.

"I'll be right with you!" she calls out, clearly in the back room, where she keeps "the good stuff," as she calls it — the things only a witch or Pagan would be looking for. It's also the space where she does the occasional tarot reading and any spiritual counseling her clients or acquaintances may need. The woman got certified in pastoral counseling, so she's serious about being there for the people who need her.

Her remaining customer appears to be back in the back with her, so I wait in the front of the shop, toying with the contents of a big basket of polished rocks marked "Fill a bag for $5!" The little velveteen bags hold too much to make it a profitable offering for her, but she says it brings the customers in so they can get used to the shop, including kids who just like rocks.

I like rocks. Not like *she* likes rocks, but the smooth, cool stones and the gentle clacking they make when I run my hand through them are soothing, taking my mind off the stress of this impending conversation.

"Thanks so much, Brighid!" a grandmotherly woman much shorter than Brighid's 5-foot-8 says as she clears the heavy curtain that conceals the back room. "What do I owe you?"

Without even looking up, I can feel Brighid enter the front of the shop and spot me standing there. Oh, boy... Yeah. She's not happy. I'm still not sure exactly where I stand with her now. That night at the hospital, she seemed to rapidly and randomly fluctuate between relieved, caring, angry with me, hurt, defensive and angry with herself, and she didn't seem much less angry on the phone, even though she picked up. Before she hung up. Things really *have* gotten complicated.

"Not a thing, dear!" she says brightly to the woman. "Just stop back in when you want some more of your tea. And I should have that apophyllite crystal for you late next week — ethically sourced, as usual!"

Heading to the front door, the woman gives me an appraising glance before replying. I smile back warmly, hoping those flirting skills Brighid credits me with do the job and disarm the woman's scrutiny.

"I'll see you then! Have a good week, Lady!" the woman says to Brighid, with a knowing smile. A little too knowing. But what else should I expect in here? Witches...

"You can leave now, too, Hunter. I need to lock up."

"I just got here. And you're open for another seventeen minutes. It says so right on the door. And I'm here as a client."

She raises an eyebrow at me.

"It's my shop, and I say when it's closed. Besides, clients usually make appointments so I know when I need to be available."

Even though she's not cooperating with me, I like this self-assured business owner side of her. She's showing the self-confidence I always thought she should have.

"Did *she* have an appointment?" I inquire, nodding toward the door where her last client just exited.

"It was an emergency consult," Brighid replies. "Is this an emergency?" she asks, gesturing in my general direction.

"In fact, it is. I've got an injury that I need some help with. It's interfering with my work."

Her frown deepens for a moment, but then I see my friend peer out from that wall she seems to have erected around herself and she softens, gesturing for me to come farther into the shop. She walks past me and locks the door, flipping the door sign to "Closed."

"Have a seat," she tells me, pointing to the stool next to the counter.

I grab it with my good hand and pull it between my legs to sit down. Her eyes follow the movement, and she blushes instantly when our eyes meet, caught looking at my crotch, which is suddenly tight under her gaze. It's an odd sensation when connected to my best friend, but it isn't as uncomfortable as it once was...

With a sigh, she crosses the room to me, taking my injured hand gently into hers to examine it.

"What did the doctor say?"

"A sprain, they said. 'RICE,' as usual. Wear the brace as much as possible. Go see an orthopedist if it doesn't feel better in a week or so. It's been ten days, and it still hurts too much to play. I've got to lay down tracks in a few days if I don't want to put us behind, and we've got another test gig Thursday."

She carefully removes the brace and prods the tendons in the back of my hand. It's uncomfortable but not really painful, since I'm not moving it.

"You haven't been icing it enough," she quickly declares, "and you've been using it when you should have given it at least a week of rest from playing."

"How'd you know?"

She gives me a knowing look, full of irritation.

"I know you. You don't do what you're told. In fact, you usually do the opposite. And nothing stops you from playing, even if playing now will make playing again later harder."

I grin at her sheepishly.

"Yeah..."

"It won't be back to normal in a few days if you keep this up."

"I can't wait any longer for it to heal. I need your help. Your special brand of help."

"Ah — so *now* you want my help... *Her* help," she scoffs, glancing upward. "*Now* you're willing to believe in something you can't see and that science can't verify..."

She scrutinizes me, clearly skeptical that the skeptic has really come this far around.

"I figured it couldn't hurt... It can't hurt, right?"

She laughs.

"No, I'm not going to cut it off or hit it with a hammer..." she says.

"As tempting as that might be," she mutters loudly enough that I know she wanted me to hear. "Are you sure this isn't just an excuse to come in and talk to me?"

"I can neither confirm nor deny that hypothesis," I reply with a smile, turning on the charm. "But, seriously, it hurts," I admit, "and I can't play up to my usual standards, and I don't have time to just wait it out. So, could you — both of you — give me a hand here?"

"Ha! Give you a hand! Good one," she says. She sighs and then smiles, seeming almost unwilling to grant me even that much. "Herself likes a good pun. It makes for amusing poetry, which She's fond of, as you well know..."

All the times she's talked about the other Brighid, the goddess, run through my mind.

She pauses, appearing as if she's listening to a far-off voice. From what she's told me over the years, she probably is.

"She'll accept one quality pun as a token in trade for one healing bath. She says *my* fee is up to me."

"And what are your services going to cost me?"

She ponders for a moment.

"One favor. As yet to be determined."

"I can live with that."

"OK. Give me a minute to gather a few things, and then we'll get started."

"Goddesses bend. They don't fold. Not even to *him*. I am *not* origami," I hear her mutter to herself as she heads into the back room. Is she going to change her mind? Send me packing with a sore hand and my hopes dashed?

But she returns with a modestly-sized hammered-copper cauldron, into which she dumps spoonfuls of dried herbs from her array of offerings. She grabs a jar from beneath the counter and pours the contents in with the herbs.

At my questioning glance, she says, "It's just water. Blessed by Herself on Brighnassadh. But still good old H_2O."

"I trust you," I tell her. Her expression suggests she wants to believe me but doesn't know if she can extend the same level of trust to me anymore.

She sets the cauldron's flat bottom on top of a hot plate and plugs it in.

"What?" she asks as I quirk an eyebrow at her modern take on a cauldron fire. "I can't exactly dump a bunch of logs on the floor and start a raging bonfire in here, can I?"

"I didn't say anything," I reply innocently.

After a few minutes, she breaks the silence, her curiosity clearly getting the better of her.

"No Holly today?" There's a bitter tone to her question. But it gives me the opening I've been hoping for for more than a week.

"I meant it, Bridge. I'm not with Holly, or anyone else. Things have changed. *I've* changed. And I'm done with all of that. None of it was what I wanted. What I want — what I *need* — is something... some*one*... different."

Her skeptical expression yields to one that suggests she's intrigued. But she says nothing. Does she believe me? Is she willing to trust that I'm telling her the truth? Does she get what I'm trying to tell her?

Ten minutes of silence and some stirring later, the water is steaming and she turns off the burner. She grabs an insulated mug from under the counter and opens up the top, then dumps the contents into the cauldron with the rest.

"Ice water," she explains, preemptively. "It's literally my ice water I was drinking today. I assume you don't want to wait for it to cool down naturally?"

"I'm in a hurry to get my hand back in working order. I'm not in a hurry to leave," I reply, my words chosen carefully for what they imply.

She looks deep into my eyes, searching for something, and there's a sensation of discomfort for us both, as has been the case since we were kids, whenever we connected so strongly in that way. But this time, the tension in the room ramps up, and it's not the electric jolt of direct eye contact between us, but the simmering heat of something else.

She breaks away to give the cauldron another stir and dips a fingertip gingerly into the contents.

"It's quite warm, but not scalding. You're well past the 72-hour period for just using ice to reduce swelling. The heat will loosen things up, open your pores to let the herbs soak in and encourage blood flow to speed the healing. Here — give me that," she says, gesturing at my injured hand.

She pulls a piece of cloth from her purse and wraps it around, murmuring quietly to herself and igniting my senses as she caresses my hand through the fabric before guiding it gently into the cauldron.

She's right — it's very warm. The warmth makes me relax for the first time since I arrived at the shop, and I inhale the light floral-herbal scent from the water. It blends pleasantly with Brighid's own fragrance, also made from her herbs.

Tension becomes peace and then back again as she gently rubs the back of my injured hand under the surface of the warm water, careful, in her usual way, not to cause me more pain than I'm already in but massaging vigorously enough to get the blood flowing through my hand.

However, that's not the only place my blood is flowing. The shock of kissing her, despite years of good intentions, has worn off, and an evening of drunken ruminating has left me with a new perspective. That familiar scent of hers — sandalwood and something floral, overlaying a sweetness that's all Brighid — rekindles the raw chemistry that enraptured us both in that moment when the cameras disappeared from our awareness and it was just the two of us.

My free hand moves to her face without a thought directing it, caressing her cheek. She freezes for a moment, avoiding eye contact, and I steer her head toward me, forcing her to look at me. Her jaw loosens, her lips parting slightly, and that's all the invitation I need to try this again — my way.

I pull my injured hand from hers, sliding it out of the cloth wrapping and then out of the warm water, then tracing the other side of her face with damp fingers. She leans into my touch, her eyes sliding shut in a gesture that suggests both surrender and safety.

"Brighid, I want to kiss you — really kiss you. But I need to know that you want this. Can I kiss you again? Putting the past aside, is this something you want? Now? Not some childhood crush being indulged, but the two of us, adults, deciding this is something we both want?"

She peers up at me, as if she's searching for the answer to that question and all mysteries of the universe, and expects to find them in my eyes. She nods tentatively.

I lean forward and brush my lips across hers — our real first kiss, with both of us exquisitely aware of exactly what is happening between us. But with that hardwired connection of ours, I can sense that her body has shifted from finding peace in my touch to stiff, and I pull back, looking deep in her violet eyes. For just an instant she glances away from me, toward the stairs that lead to her stockroom above the main shop.

"Don't run. Not again," I tell her as I see the urge to flee flicker through her eyes. "You're braver than that, Bridge... You wouldn't be here..." — I gesture to the shop around us — "*We* wouldn't be here if you weren't brave. You built this all by yourself, with no safety net — not your father and not me. You built it despite the potential dangers of having this kind of business where not everyone would understand what you were about. That proves you're brave. And this is me — Hunter, your best friend. So stop running from me, here and now. Please," I plead.

She swallows deeply, placing her hand over mine where it still rests on her cheek.

"You've always been my safety net, Hunter, whether you realized it or not. That's why this is so scary. Everything I've ever wanted is being dangled in front of me, and I know it could all come crashing down if I make one wrong move and accidentally sever that safety net I've come to rely upon."

"I'm not going anywhere, Bridge. If you don't want this, it won't happen. Either way, we're still friends. We'll always be friends. I may not have been the best friend sometimes, but I want to make up for that. And I want to see what this is between us now that the blinders I put on my own damn self have been removed. Do you feel it? This thing between us? This pull?" I ask her, hoping it's not just me now, that I haven't ruined things by waiting too long.

"Of course I do, you idiot," she says, with the same affectionate irritation she usually has in her voice when she calls me out on my shit. "I've always felt it. Why do you think I kept trying, kept waiting? I know people think I'm pathetic, following you around like a lovesick puppy, but not one of them has seen what I've seen. Not one of them knows how it is between us or how it has been before." She grabs hold of my good hand with both of hers. "I know, Hunter. I've always known. The question has been whether you'd ever wake up to it, and if so, when — whether you'd wake up before it was too late."

"It's got my attention now. *You've* got my attention now, Brighid."

I grab her face between my hands and look into her eyes, this time seeing the unbelievable strength that's gotten her to this point in her life, and with me. My rock and my touchstone. I'm beginning to see exactly how much strength she's needed to hold on for this long to her certainty in me, in us. She may seem fragile, but she's adamantium inside.

"It's about time," she replies with a chuckle.

"Yes, it is. Sorry I was late," I apologize with a grin. "Let me make it up to you..."

And with that, I take her mouth with mine, picking back up where we were before I took off that blindfold. I give myself over to those lush lips and gentle hands, which are suddenly no longer quite so gentle with me.

Given free rein to touch me as she's been wanting, I experience my witchy woman unrestrained for the first time, and I'm nearly overwhelmed by her passion as she pulls me hard against her chest, as if she's trying to meld us together. And I'm all for it. I grab her luscious ass and make it clear what she's doing to me, rocking my erection into her center.

She moans, and once again the world disappears in a flurry of hands, mouths, tongues. Whatever we can taste and touch is fair game now, and I plan on fully and deeply exploring this new dynamic between us.

CHAPTER 19

PRELUDE TO THE DREAM

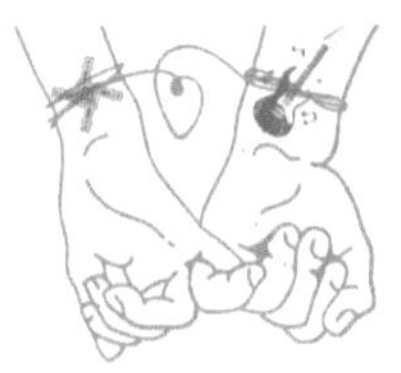

Brighid

A small part of my brain can't believe this is real. Surely, it's another vision, and I'm actually sitting at my spinning wheel while my mind flies free once again.

But the sensation of the rough pads of Hunter's callused fingertips brushing up the sensitive skin of my bare back, under my shirt, grounds me in the moment. We've been platonic friends for years, but it's like he already knows where my most sensitive spots, my little personal erogenous zones, are and just how to stimulate them for the greatest effect. Either that or this is just how we are together, now that we've erased that line of his, setting us free to be more, to be what we could be with no rules, and no fears, keeping us apart.

It's a literal dream come true for me, one fifteen years and more in the making. And I quickly lose myself in it.

Hunter slides his hands across my shoulders, pushing the wide neckline of my top aside to bare them to his view. He's seen my bare shoulders before, of course, but with this new perspective, he seems to be drawn to them, caressing them with his hands and lips, like he's learning a new map by touch alone.

I'm not unfamiliar with his body either, and I've had a lot longer to consider exactly how hot this man is, with his lithe muscles laid out across that tall frame, broad shoulders, well-muscled arms, a decent set of abs, all speaking to time spent performing, rather than just in the gym.

These arms have held me as I've fallen asleep more times than I can count, and I can't help wondering now how they'll feel when they're there not just to comfort but to arouse and delight.

All those times when I woke up with our legs entangled and his cock poking me in the ass... how will it feel when he's inside me, part of me, part of a whole made up of our two parts.

Emboldened, I reach down and rub my hand along the part in question, and he moans into my mouth, his hips swinging forward to trap my hand between his already substantial erection and the soft cleft where it seems like it was always meant to be.

He chuckles, and I look tentatively up at him, wondering if I've made a fool of myself yet again. Maybe he didn't mean to let things go that far this fast. Maybe my comparative inexperience has revealed itself to the legendary ladies' man who's had more women on some nights than I've had men in my entire life. All of those women undoubtedly more expert in the way they touch him.

"Bridge — back here with me, please... get out of your own head. Or I can make you..."

He could make me do almost anything at a time like this, but his tongue tracing its way up my throat is all that's needed to serve the purpose behind his threat. My head falls back to give him access, and because I'm too far lost in the sensations he's delivering to even keep it from falling.

Now it's me who's moaning, right into his mouth as he reclaims that while pressing himself hard against me, his hand on my ass as he pulls me forward to meet him. He grabs my trapped hand and uses his own to guide it in an exploration of one of the few parts of him I've never seen, no matter how many times I've surreptitiously looked or accidentally felt in very different contexts.

Together, his hand and mine stroke along his length, through the fabric of his fly, and he rhythmically pushes into my touch, now panting slightly, right along with me.

"Part of me has wanted you to do that for a long time," he breathes huskily into my ear. "Even if I didn't let myself admit it."

"And I've wanted to do it for a long time, as you know all too well," I reply with slight chuckle. "We've spent an awful lot of nights in the same bed for two people who've never officially touched each other on some pretty pertinent body parts."

"Well, I wouldn't say I've never touched you with my cock before, Brighid. I remember quite a few mornings, and nights, when I had to think of geometry homework, laps around the soccer field and chord progressions to keep from waking you up with my cock jabbing your butt cheeks. Chord progressions, by the way, do very little to take my mind off those curves of yours. It actually made it worse on a few occasions."

We both laugh at that, but I have a confession to make that really can only be made in this moment.

"I have to tell you something, Hunter... I, uh... I didn't sleep through all those times when you were poking me in the ass. Remember when I told you I'm a light sleeper? That was me trying to hint that I knew you were aroused sometimes when we were sleeping together, without saying it openly."

My eyes drop to avoid his.

"I really wanted you to tell me it was me who made you hard, not biology or a dream or thinking of some other girl. But I was afraid if I mentioned it at all, you'd have refused to share a bed with me again."

"I probably would have," he admits, and my heart sinks. But he grabs my chin and pulls our eyes back to each other again. "Not because I wouldn't have wanted to sleep with you anymore, but because I would have been too embarrassed that you knew what you did to me. And, later, because I'd ruled out the possibility of us."

"Yeah. Well, you're stupid. I always knew... always knew you were stupid," I tell him.

His eyes widen in surprise as he recognizes the words we've heard so many times. His face is rapt upon mine, and I suddenly feel like a connection has snapped back into place, like we've finally arrived at the place we'd always been headed.

"Why didn't you tell me?" he says, continuing the dialogue, his expression earnest and belying the context of our complicated past.

"I did. Repeatedly. You didn't want to know," I say, deviating from the script.

"I never asked," he acknowledges.

"Thereby proving what I always knew."

"You were stupid" — "I was stupid," we say simultaneously, our smiles mollifying the insult and setting aside the tension of that complicated past.

"But not anymore," he adds, grabbing my leg and wrapping it around his hip. (Flexible yoga girl for the win!)

He attacks my mouth with fervor now, and I give the same back to him. I've waited a long time to do this, and I'm not holding back anymore.

He rolls his hips against me, proving instantly that he's not going to hold himself back any longer either. I let out a long moan and reach for his waist, grabbing hold of that top button on the road to glory.

Hunter grabs my wrist and stops me, though, and for a moment I think he's going to call things to a halt, saying it's too fast and suggesting we slow things down out of some feeling of obligation to my sensibilities.

I look up at him, frustrated and prepared to argue.

"Soon, Bridge. But not here."

He nods toward the front of the shop, and I suddenly realize that a glass door and display windows only partially blocked by merchandise are probably not the best backdrop for sex. Especially when one of you is a celebrity whose sex life is already the fodder of TV and tabloids.

I sigh heavily.

"Well, it was fun while it lasted."

He grabs my arm as I start to turn and move away.

"The fun's not over. Not by a long shot. It's time to take this home."

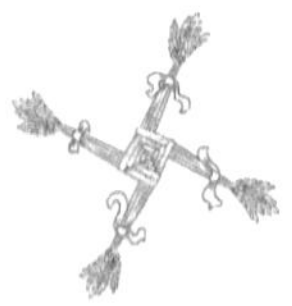

I'm fumbling with my keys at the front door, in such a rush that I can't get the right key matched up with this lock.

It doesn't help that Hunter is literally right behind me, so close that, once again — if for just the first time with real meaning — his hard cock is pressed between my ass cheeks. He rocks forward against me, his hands reaching around me to take the keys, and I rock back against him right as he puts the key to the lock. He drops the keys to the floor.

"Not nice, Bridge," he growls as I turn to face him.

"Turnabout is fair play!" I singsong back at him before dipping down to grab the keyring again.

This time, I manage to get the right key inserted into the lock (no symbolism there, eh?) and get the door open so we can finally get inside and away from potentially prying eyes.

I drop my purse to the floor and go to shut the door behind us, but Hunter's already done it. He presses me back against it, using his hips to hold me in place while he firmly locks the deadbolt and safety latch.

"You're going to have to give me a spare key," he says, his voice low and predatory.

"You'll have to earn it!" I reply cheekily, ducking under his arm and making a dash for the stairs.

I make it to about a yard from the bottom step — which means not far at all — before Hunter catches me around the waist and drags me back to him, running his hands over my breasts and setting me moaning again.

I stand there with his hands around me, leaning back against his solid form, and just enjoy the sensation of having him here, our bodies touching and our minds caught up with each other at a level beyond even what we've shared for nearly 25 years.

His hands slide down to bracket my waist for a moment before he grabs my wrist and pulls me toward the stairs, leading me up to my bedroom.

I've owned this house (well, what portions of it the bank doesn't still own) for six years. And while he's been gone on tour and in New York for much of that time, this is not the first time Hunter has been in my bedroom, nor will it be the first time he's been in this bed with me.

But this is uncharted territory between us, and having him pull me by my hand across the threshold has special meaning. For both of us, if I can judge by his suddenly serious demeanor and the extra time he takes drawing me across that distance.

It feels almost sacred, and while that's a sensation I've always associated with him, it was only ever in my head. Until now. Feeling it for real, with my hand in his as we approach the bed — the moment feels heavy, as if it has import that carries beyond this moment or this day, and the anticipation makes the air feel thick, like wading into the soft surf on a flat day and being buffeted by the current.

Everything slows down, like time wants desperately to stop but must nonetheless march forward, because that's what time does. It's inevitable, inexorable — both the progression of time and this progression of things between us two.

I look up at Hunter, only to find that he, too, seems to be feeling the import of this moment between us. He leads me to the foot of the bed and sits me down there before dropping to kneel in front of me. He picks up my hand once again and brings it slowly to his mouth, placing a gentle kiss on the back of it. He keeps hold of it but drops it down to my lap, a noticeable beat elapsing before he speaks.

"Brighid... We've probably already gone too far to ever go back, but I want you to be sure about this. We can stop here if you want. Nothing will change with our friendship, nothing important. I want this — I want *you*," he says, drawing out the words as if he needs to be sure I'm understanding.

I lean back to look at him from a greater distance. What I see in front of me is impossible to describe with words. Maybe a song could do it, maybe some form of art, but a dictionary does not contain enough words, nor even letters, to properly convey who this man is to me. Nothing I could say about him would ever be enough.

The words I do have, inadequate as they are for him: My best friend, my oldest friend, the man I've loved for nearly a quarter-century and been *in love* with for more than half of that...

He's my biggest source of frustration in life and the biggest source of my heartache, but he's also my safe place, my greatest supporter and advocate, my sometimes partner-in-crime, my greatest treasure, my most erotic fantasy, all rolled into one, and now my dearest dream come to life.

I pull him to me, cradling his face in my hand and looking so deep into those pools of emerald green that I see both of us looking back at me, spread across time and space and being, both infinite and perfect.

"Make love to me, Hunter."

"As you wish."

Chapter 20

Sexual Healing

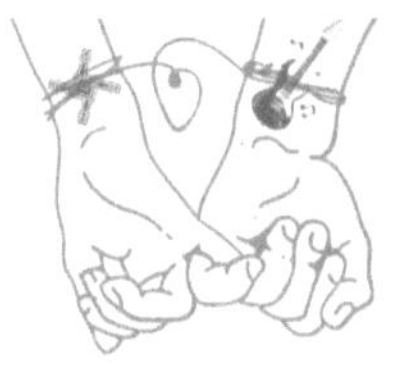

Brighid

Hunter presses his lips to mine, gently, then more insistently, with his hand wrapped around the nape of my neck, pulling us together. His fingers lace themselves through my hair, gripping the back of my head as he angles my head the way he wants it and then uses his lips to nudge mine open, licking at them until I open my mouth, welcoming him inside.

It's unreal, and on some level I don't trust it, because as many times as I've seen "us" do something like this, kiss like this, none of that was real. Whether dream or vision or wishful thinking, as real as it was in that moment, the instant whatever it was left me, the instant I awoke back to this current reality, everything that Hunter and I shared became no more than an illusion, because I was the only one who had seen it and felt it and carried it with me.

Will it happen again, after whatever we do here now? Will I wake up tomorrow and find out that Hunter doesn't remember or understand it? Will I be left feeling like I must have lost my mind, because something I know was real turns out to not be real as far as anyone else — as far as Hunter — is concerned?

"Bridge — what is it? What's going on in your head?" Hunter asks me, for the moment tangible and real and, as far as I can tell, entirely concrete and immutable. A fact, not a fantasy.

"This all feels a little unreal to me," I admit.

"Why? I'm here," he assures me, lifting my hand and placing it over his heart. "Breathing, heart beating, flesh and bone... sprained hand and all," he adds with a chuckle. "I'm not going anywhere. I promise."

And I want to believe him, but there have been so many promises that never came to pass, no matter how good the intentions when they were made.

He grabs for my cheek again, and I realize my gaze has broken from his, full of the fear to hope. He steers me back into that riveting degree of eye contact we so often have and so often have had to break.

"Bridge. It's me. It's Hunter. I am here, with you. I want to be here, with you. I want to make love to you. And unless you change your mind and tell me to stop, I am *going* to make love to you. Right here and now. Do you trust me? Do you trust that this is real? That we're real?"

His eyes are entreating, begging me to let go of my doubts and trust that, after all these years, we can be something different for each other. Lovers and *not* just friends. And I desperately want to believe that. But my conviction that this was how we were always meant to be is now coming back to haunt me, because I've been told so many times that it would not happen, *could* not happen. Now, faced with the reality of it right on my doorstep, my belief falters.

I reach out to touch his face, and it's solid in my hand, my fingertips feeling the smooth texture of his skin, the soft fuzz of his beard, the warmth of his flesh. I slide it back to his neck, feeling his heartbeat pulsing under my fingers, and it finally feels real.

"We're real. We're here and now," I say, reassuring us both, I think. "We're us. This is us. This has always been us."

"Yes, it has. It's time. Past time. Now."

Our lips reclaim each other, my mouth welcoming him inside now without hesitation or fear. He pushes me back onto the bed, lying on top of me, his hardness prodding my center. My hips roll up against his, and he matches the movement, our breath quickening together. My legs fall apart, and he settles between them. My breasts press into his chest, and he moves his hand up to thumb my nipple through my shirt. I pull back out of our kiss to look at him above me.

"What?" he asks, his winning Hunter smile sparking my own.

"You really are here, aren't you? In my bed, lying on top of me, kissing me in a very much not-friendlike manner..."

"And touching your breast. On purpose — just in case that was in question based on past situations. And enjoying that, and all the rest of this, quite a lot. Yes, that's happening."

"And now I'm going to pull us even further out of this very sexy headspace and be practical, Hunter..." I take a deep breath, because this is a question I've asked him a couple times in the past, but never in this context, never in anything even vaguely like this context. "When's the last time you were tested?"

He blinks. Hard.

"About a month ago. Which is pretty much the norm. Everything's negative, Bridge. Always has been. I've been a bit of a slut in my life, but I'm a conscientious one."

"I wasn't implying you were a slut... No slut-shaming in my house, nor in my head. People need to own their sexuality, whatever that means for them. And I know you better than to think you're irresponsible about such things. I just wanted to make sure you were up-to-date on things, since I have no idea when you were last with Holly, or anyone."

"It's been longer than you'd think, Bridge. A lot longer. The last test was just routine. I don't have sex without condoms. Ever. Too much risk with... well, pretty much everyone. Holly included. I don't want to let a minute of carefree behavior result in some heavy-duty worries. So, condoms — always. I haven't ever had sex without one."

"Wow. OK. Very conscientious, then..." He waits for me to complete the thought I very obviously haven't finished expressing.

"I'll say it again: What?"

"I'm on birth control. Just in case. But — pretty obviously — it's been a long time since I've been with anyone. I haven't been tested in years, but it was well after the last time I had sex."

"How long has it been, Bridge?"

"About four years."

"'Wow' back at you. How did you survive that?" he adds with a grin.

"Lots and lots of 'self-care,'" I admit.

"I see... So, your sex drive is..."

"Very high. Just... self-sustaining..."

"And these 'self-care' sessions... would they involve fantasizing about men? Men doing certain types of things to you?"

"Frequently."

"And would these be generic men? Jason Momoa? Certain rockstars, perhaps?"

"Hey — there is basically no one on this planet who doesn't find Jason Momoa attractive. I don't even like all the muscles, but the big kid inside the serious actor, the family man? He's delightful. And he plays bass!"

"I'm not sure I like this ode to fucking bass-playing Jason Momoa while I'm lying on top of you."

"Hey — you were the one who brought him up!"

"In the context of your fantasies, my dear. The ones that make you hot when you're pleasuring yourself. Alone. Wishing someone was doing those things to you."

"I cannot confirm or deny the presence of Jason Momoa in my fantasies. My very respectful fantasies..."

"Bridge..." he says with a warning tone.

"As to certain rockstars... Just one."

"So help me, if you say Sting..."

"Well, he's got that whole tantric yoga thing going..."

"Bridge..."

I can't help myself. I giggle.

"I do still think Eric Stoltz is cute."

"Oh, you are asking for it now..." The mock-threatening tone continues.

"You know — if I'd spent the last 15-plus years fantasizing about sex with my platonic best friend, that would be pretty creepy. But there's this certain guitar player..."

A smile grows on his face.

"And he's got this great... Irish accent."

"Oh, you're going to pay for that!" he says before diving at me with tickling fingers. I'm laughing before he even touches me, and I keep giggling until his fingers switch from tickling to stroking my sides, slowly approaching my breasts, and then I'm no longer out of breath from laughing but panting in desire.

"Hunter..."

"Hmm?"

"We kind of got off-topic."

"What was the topic?"

"Practicalities."

"Right. And four years?'"

"Yes, so I know I'm clean. And I'm on birth control. And you're clean..."

"I like where this is going. A lot."

"So, you maybe want to..."

"Make love to you for the first time, skin on skin, with nothing between us?"

"I think I'd like that."

"I think I'd *love* that."

His eyes are intense now, even more than usual. It feels like he's devouring me, body and soul, and I like that, too.

"Do you want me to say, 'As you wish' again?" he asks, phrasing it as a joke, but his tone is anything but.

"I want *you*. Period."

"You have me. And you'll have more of me here very soon..." he promises, pushing up my skirt along the side of my thigh.

My eyes close as I just enjoy the sensation of his sensuous touch on skin he's never touched like this before. All the times we've touched each other, never like this. I want to savor every tiny little pulse of nerves, the smallest little movement... No fantasy could ever match the reality of having him here, now, doing the things he's doing to me.

He slides off to the side of me, now drawing his hand up my hip, over my waist, across my ribs. He grabs my breast and squeezes it lightly, lowering his lips to capture my nipple through the thin fabric of my shirt and sucking it to a hard point.

"Off," he orders, raising me up until he can pull my shirt off over my head. His lips dive immediately for my collarbone, nuzzling that little spot between shoulder and neck that sends my pulse skyrocketing. My breath hitches and my breasts heave, drawing his attention back to them. He caresses the side of one through the lacy cami while reaching his fingers for the nipple of the other, pinching it and giving it a little twist, and my head drops back.

This is everything I've ever enjoyed about sex, only exponentially better, because it's Hunter who's doing it to me.

He pulls my breasts above the top of the cami, devouring them with his eyes, and I start to blush from the attention.

"So beautiful... Just perfect..." he murmurs before taking one into his mouth, sucking hard and flicking the nipple with his tongue before releasing it with a pop.

The look on his face is predatory, and I swallow hard, waiting to see what he'll do next. When he moves, it's to pull the cami up over my head, leaving my chest bare. But that look remains on his face as he slides back off the bed. He reaches over his head and pulls his own shirt off, and for the first time in my life, I'm a hundred percent allowed to look at Hunter with his shirt off and think of him in a sexual context. His expression confirms that he's completely fine with that.

I smile, simply because I've been freed from the constraints that have kept my thoughts and feelings and actions contained for fifteen years.

"Acres and acres, and it's all mine!" I gleefully incant, not even recalling where I first heard that line.

"A time like this, and you're quoting Looney Tunes?"

"Of course *you* know where that's from," I say. "I didn't even remember."

"From this moment on, my job is to make you forget *everything* but what I'm doing to you. And my name, because you're going to want to be screaming that soon. I'll remind you of your own name when we're done," he says.

Wow. He's even sexier than I thought he was... Is that even possible?

"I want to yank your skirt straight off of you," he says, and in my mind's eye, I'm seeing it happen, and I'm all for it. "But..." he waves his left hand.

"Oh! I totally forgot! How's it feeling?"

"Better, but not enough that I want to risk yanking anything..."

"I could probably help with that..."

"You can help with all *yanking* I need done from this moment onward," he says. It takes me a second, but I get the double entendre.

"You are a bad, bad man..."

"I'm a nice man."

"No, you're not... You're—"

He grabs the back of my neck pulling me forward into a torrid kiss.

"Don't you dare say anything about a power coupling..." he warns.

"What? Would we even be us if we didn't incorporate geeky dialogue in our lovemaking?"

"Probably not... but I have other 'power-coupling'-related things in mind right now."

"Oh," I say as he recaptures my mouth, leaving me panting when he finally breaks the kiss again.

"Skirt. Off," he orders.

I scoot to the end of the bed and quickly slide off my skirt, glad at this moment for my preference for lacy panties. Still self-conscious, I scoot back onto the bed. He's watching me closely.

"I haven't seen you naked before... not since that last joint bath we had... which we will now have to re-create in an entirely different context, now that I think of it..." he drawls.

I've never been so glad to have that giant antique bathtub.

"All those nights we slept in the same bed, always with our clothes on. What a shame..." he laments. "Time to fix that oversight."

This time, he does yank — wrapping his good arm around my knees and pulling me back to the edge of the bed. He kneels down and begins to peel my panties down my hips, oh so slowly, before pulling them off entirely. Leaving me truly naked to his view. I have a momentary impulse to pull a blanket over me... something... anything...

In all my fantasies about what it might be like to be with him like this, I glossed over this moment of truth, when he'd see me with not a stitch of clothing to hide the imperfections, the bumps and dimples, the jiggly bits... all the things the women he's always slept with didn't have, never had to worry about. And no matter how sexy and seductive I've felt at certain moments in my life, it all deserts me here, leaving me feeling vulnerable like I've never felt before. The gauntlet of the high-school hallway had nothing on this for scary. Because if this whole thing between us is going to go awry, it's right now.

I'm so nervous in the silence, in his frozen posture, that I'm on the verge of tears. He's not saying anything, not doing anything... Is it that bad? It's been four years since anyone's seen me naked. While being wanted then was a boost to my self-esteem, a model, plus-sized or otherwise, I am not. I look up at him, trying to read the expression in his eyes, terrified of what I might find there. But it's not disappointment or anything like that. It's... like he's just uncovered a buried treasure and is so stunned by the shine of the gems and coins that he has to stop to take it in. Maybe I'm reading him wrong, though… I have to be.

Finally, his hands move, reaching for my inner thighs and pulling each leg, gently but firmly, to one side. There's truly nowhere to hide now, because my pussy is bare in front of him. His eyes have moved to mine, and I'm not sure what he's seeing there. Likely something between terror and lust.

"Mine," he says. "All mine."

And with that, his mouth drops straight between my legs, taking a long swipe with his tongue through the length of my slit. His eyes remain on my own, and I'm seeing in them something I can only call adoration. I want to hedge that conclusion, but he closes his eyes, seeming to be enjoying his exploration with his lips and tongue, and moments later, I am quickly approaching his goal of forgetting everything I know, including my own name.

"Oh, gods… Hunter… that feels… so good," I tell him. See — I still remember *his* name. Whoa— nope. Forgot that, too. Wow.

It's been a while since somebody did this to me, but I don't remember it feeling like this, like my entire awareness has focused itself in that particular piece of real estate and is just enjoying being the center of attention of a very rapt audience. A devoted worshiper at the temple. There's that name…*Hunter Graves* is licking my clit. Wow.

I open my eyes and look down at him, finding that he's looking back up at me, and the sight makes me shudder. I've wanted this so much, for so long, and it's so much better than anything I ever thought it could be. And it's not what he's doing to me that makes it that way so much as it is his expression… hunger, delight, caring, like more than anything he wants to give me pleasure, like my pleasure is his own.

And with that thought, he slides a finger inside me. I throw my head back, barely able to stand the added sensation.

"So wet…"

My eyes press closed again, until he slides his finger back out again… and slides it back in with a second. He starts up a slow, building rhythm before sucking my clit into his mouth, and my thighs jump, instinctively trying to close around him. I moan.

"More… more, please…" I urge him, and he curls his fingers inside me, pressing on that little textured pad inside. My hips push up, pressing his mouth harder into my mound. He lays his forearm across my hips, pressing me down into the bed, and the restraint ratchets everything up another notch. The tension begins to build inside me, his fingers stroking it into full bloom, his lips and tongue teasing it to a new height.

My hands reach for his head... This beautiful head of my beautiful Hunter... A gods-given miracle that he's touching me like this, after waiting and hoping for so long. My fingers tangle in those dark gold strands, half seeking to guide him to where his attention is most needed and half just to touch him, to feel him under my fingers as he brings me ever closer...

"Gods... that... there... oh, yes... Gods, Hunter..."

He flicks my clit with his tongue and increases the speed and roughness with which his fingers move inside me, pleasuring me with an intuitiveness that I would never dream any man would have and yet if one did, it would be Hunter, who knows me so well, but who is just now beginning to learn me in this way.

I'm approaching my peak, and I'm torn between wanting this tension to explode and wanting the feeling to go on forever. And then Hunter takes the choice out of my hands, grazing my clit with his teeth and pressing hard into that one spot inside me with his fingers, and my hips fight his hold and my back bends, and I'm grasping hard at his head, pressing his mouth to me as he continues licking and sucking on me, the quick movements of his fingers drawing everything out until I'm not sure I can take anymore. As the contractions finally begin to subside, he uses his mouth to milk the last pulse of ecstasy from me before sliding his fingers out of me.

I loosen my grip on his head, and he looks up at me again, taking another swipe of his tongue from my opening to the top of my slit, watching closely as the stimulation sends my hips rocketing up against him once again. He smiles mischievously and does it again, and I know I've unleashed a monster by letting him see how sensitive I am down there after my orgasm. He runs his thumbs around my lower lips and pulls them gently apart, using the improved vantage point to aim his tongue directly at my clit. I'm ready to object when he flicks it quickly back and forth over that ultra-sensitive spot, and the stimulation sends me over again.

"Oh! Gods! Hunter! My gods... Oh..." It's a long string of gibberish after that as he returns to licking and sucking me through this second peak, using his good hand to hold my hips in place until the spasms begin to slow once more. Looking up at me with a still-hungry expression on his face, he prods my clit with his tongue, yielding another rush of my hips upward.

"No... no more... please..." I beg him. "Can't... Too much..." I'm panting as the waves subside within me.

"I'm going to give you a triple one of these days, Brighid Weaver..." he promises.

That may be his long-range plan, but in the short term, he sticks his fingers in his mouth to lick them clean, holding eye contact with me the entire time until my eyes roll up, unable to take watching the overtly sexual display a moment longer. Then, he again swipes his tongue up my slit from bottom to top, licking me clean, too.

I have melted entirely. Boneless and now part of the mattress. He leans up across me to kiss me with that glorious mouth of his, and I taste him and me, blended together, pleasure-filled and hunger sated, but knowing this is just the beginning.

"You are very... very... good at that," I tell him as he lies down on his side next to me, looking over at what must be a very sated-looking Brighid.

"Did it live up to your fantasies?"

"Yes, and other things," I tell him, retaining only enough brain processing power not to directly refer to my visions.

"Bridge..."

"Hmm?" I reply absently.

"I want to be inside you."

Oh. And now things are stirring down below once again. *Really? You told him your libido was strong, but this is a little ridiculous. You can barely move!*

Hunter runs his hand over my chest, dragging his guitar-roughed fingers across my nipples, and my chest rises, pushing them into his hand. Apparently, I *can* still move.

"Bridge... I want to come inside you."

"Oh. Gods."

"You said that before. When you were coming all over my tongue."

"I'm going to come without you even touching me if you keep that up..."

"Sounds like an experiment worth attempting," he says with a seductive drawl before attacking my mouth, licking at my tongue until I'm returning the kiss with equal passion.

After a minute, I break off the kiss myself.

"Hunter..."

"Yes, Bridge..."

"I want you to be inside me, come inside me... I want that. I've wanted that a long time. And I want it now. Right now."

He looks in my eyes again, and I notice there's no pressure to look away. The intensity between us — so often to the point of discomfort — seems to have transmuted into something not just comfortable but utterly desirable. I could look in his eyes like this forever.

He presses a sweet kiss to my lips.

"How did I ever go this long without doing that?"

"The kiss?"

"All of it," he replies. "Should have kissed you fifteen years ago, and every day since. Should have locked lips with you that day in the dorm and let everyone know you were mine, for real. Should have filled you up and made you scream my name the first time you told me you wanted me."

"Then do it now."

"I'll have to take off these clothes... Because... Nothing between us, Bridge. Nothing."

I shudder, and I reach for his waistband again, channeling the confidence of my former self as she undressed her husband, caressing him through the fabric before unbuttoning and unzipping them. He lies back on his back, leaving it up to me to undress him. Naked Brighid is self-conscious again with his attention free to roam over my entire body. But I set that aside and grab his shorts, pulling them off after he lifts up to let them slide over his hips.

How many times has he been in my bed — this one included — clad only in his boxer briefs? Countless times. And yet this one, of all those times, is the one that's special. The one that has so much added meaning.

"Come here, Brighid."

He gestures me up his body, and I assume a position that's as familiar as lying here by myself in this bed — tucked under his arm, with my head on his chest. His fingers trail along the tattoo on my lower back, tracing the long hair of the Brigidine priestess Siobhan inked there for me a few years ago, the flame of the candle she holds in her hands, the knotwork detailing of her robes. The comfortable familiarity of lying in his arms like this undermines any sense of self-consciousness from my lack of clothing. He presses a kiss to the top of my head before capturing my hand in his and pulling it down, toward the waistband of his underwear. Our hands slide below, and Hunter wraps my hand around his cock, which is steel wrapped in velvet.

"This is for you. In a few moments, it's going to be inside you, making you feel even better than I just did with my mouth, and then I'm going to come inside you, filling you up to overflowing with me."

My hand grasps his cock firmly, purely instinctively, and my hips jump forward of their own will.

"I want that. I want you."

"I'm all yours, Brighid."

This time it's *me* attacking *his* mouth, opening both of us to each other, wrestling his tongue with my own. My hand strokes along his cock, two sets of hips now moving with instinctive rhythm, seeking each other but still separate for the moment.

I pull back and take a deep breath to regain my focus, and then I pull his underwear down and off his legs. He's as beautifully formed as the tight-fitting boxer briefs had hinted... had hinted at me for years, while I pretended not to hear.

My hands are drawn back to him like an electrical force pulls between them and his cock. I stroke him up and down a few times, watching, fascinated, as a drop of pre-cum trickles from his head. His breathing has become shallow and rapid, and I look up at his face to see what his expression is. It's restrained ecstasy, and I don't want it to stay restrained any longer.

"Bridge..."

"Yes?"

"If you keep that up, you'll have to wait a while longer before I can use it on you."

"Oh." I smile and chuckle. "I suppose you could go ahead and do that now..." I purr. "Just to avoid any unnecessary delays,

I mean. I could always finish my little exploration later, after you're done with that."

"I think that sounds like an excellent plan."

Hunter pushes me onto my back, running his hand up my side and looking at me with a sense of wonder. He takes one of my nipples in his mouth, flicking it until it's hard again, while the other one is kneaded and caressed, heightening the sensation. He nudges my lips open with his own, presaging what is to come by invading my mouth with his tongue, which meets with mine and begins a dance of exquisite, primal beauty.

He shifts to lie on top of me once again, this time with nothing between us except longing and lust. I can feel his hard shaft between my legs, nudging and prodding. He reaches between us and slides it along my slit, stimulating my clit and covering himself in the liquid evidence of my arousal. His mouth is again upon mine, and we're sipping at each other, tasting and taunting with tongues, lips and teeth.

"Brighid — look at me," he urges, and my eyes pop open, seeing those green orbs of his looking back at me, into me, inside me, and my breath staggers. There's no urge to break the contact. Just soul-deep longing, wanting, connection. And he places the tip of himself at my entrance, nudging at my opening, before sinking slowly inside me. I maintain the eye contact until he's seated fully within me, and the sensation, of being filled, caressed from inside, overwhelms me and I let my eyes fall closed again.

When he pulls back, I look down, and there's just enough space between us with his hips lifted back to see where we're joined.

"Watch, Brighid... That's me, inside you, fucking you, making love to you," he says as he pushes back inside me again. I'm lost in the sensation of Hunter and I becoming one, and I look back up to see his face locked in an expression of deep concentration, as if he, too, is savoring every second of this long-overdue joining.

I pull his head down, his lips upon mine, and the dance of our tongues above mirrors the progressing dance between our hips below. He rocks his hips against me, pulling nearly fully out of me before pressing back inside. We eat at each other's mouths, as my hips begin to push back against him, my arms wrapping around his back, caressing the skin there.

"Oh, god, Bridge... You feel so good... So glad this is you, this first time completely naked, no barriers, nothing separating us... Want you so bad..."

The rhythm of our hips working against each other continues to speed up, becomes harder, rougher, and I moan as a sharp thrust from his cock hits deep inside me, causing my inner muscles to clench and flutter around him. He moans in response, small grunts marking his efforts as he plunges in and out of me.

His mouth leaves mine and drops to the side of my neck, pressing small kisses there, until he sucks the flesh between his lips and presses down hard, and I know he's marking me... marking me as his... it's a flashing sign that reads, "Hunter was here. This is his." My head is thrown back, exposing my neck to a barrage of his kisses, and he marks me again, and again, while his hips continue to smack against mine, an ever-growing symphony of flesh against flesh, pleasure on top of pleasure.

I want to scream with it, so full of pleasure, so full of him, so full of my glorious Hunter, that it feels like it all has to overflow in a rush of ecstasy. But my words are lost to the sheer primal nature of what we're doing to each other. I can feel that tension beginning to rise again within me, stronger, more pervasive, threatening to explode.

"Hunter... so close... so... Ahhh... so..." I manage to get out, each utterance punctuated by the slap of skin on skin, and my legs wrap around Hunter's hips, trying to pull him even farther within me, even though he's already powering inside to the hilt, bumping against my cervix, causing me to jump with each thrust.

"Nearly there, Bridge... Just hold on... nearly there..."

His hips are bucking wildly now, pounding me into the bed, and I'm grasping him to my chest, my mouth open, my eyes raised to the heavens, and the wave within me breaks, crashing down onto the shore below with an elemental inevitability.

"Aahhhh," I'm singing, meaningless and utterly meaningful all at once. "Hunter! Gods! Hunter!" I cry.

My muscles grasping at his cock inside me... my cries of ecstasy...

"I'm coming, Bridge. Coming! God. Coming inside you. God. Oh, god!" he thrusts inside me a few more times, and it feels like he's trying to climb inside me, and I'm happy to let him, happy to have him here with me, inside me, one with me. My best friend. My love. My soulmate. My Hunter...

He collapses on top of me, his arms giving out, but still filling me inside, and the ecstasy pulses between us as we both lay panting together. Quiet, sated, time passing unmeasured... Somehow, I'm the first one of us to find words again that aren't orgasmic utterances.

"That was..."

"Yeah."

"Yeah."

"Should have done that a decade ago... longer..."

"I'm not sure I could have handled that. I think I might have spontaneously combusted if we had."

"I'm not sure I'm not still going to," he says with a chuckle, placing a kiss on my shoulder. "I... uh... marked you up a little."

"I remember. And I'll be remembering for a few more days, I suspect."

"Sorry about that."

"For gods' sakes, never apologize about that. I liked it."

"I liked doing it."

"Well, that works out, then."

"We're going to have a mess when I pull out."

"Good."

"Good?"

"Good. I like having you in me, like having you spilling down my thighs, leaving a bit of yourself behind so I can remember you were really there."

"I was really there, Bridge. I still am," he says, looking me in the eye again and rubbing his thumb along my cheek. He rolls his hips against mine in reminder. "Nothing between us. Naked. My cum inside you. Me inside you."

I shudder.

"You really like that, don't you... Being claimed, marked, reminders left behind."

"Seems to be how I'm built. Though it's been rare that anyone's wanted to do it."

"I wanted to do it. I *really* wanted to do it." He licks a streak up my neck, over several of the little welts. "I kind of want to do it some more..."

I moan.

"Does that make you hot? Are you getting wet all over again?"

"We could find out..."

"Sounds like a plan... Just gotta do one thing first."

"What?"

"This," he says, pulling out from inside me, releasing our combined fluids down my thighs.

"Ohhhh," is all I can think to say.

Hunter reaches down to slide his fingers through the slickness before running his thumb over my clit again. My hips pop up, and he slides two fingers back inside me. My muscles clasp at them, just like they did his cock such a short time ago.

"You're ready to go again, aren't you?"

"Always. The question is whether you are."

"You tell me," he says, pulling my hand back to his crotch, where I find his cock rising once again. "Both of us seem to have very strong sex drives. Oh, this is going to be fun..." he adds with a smirk.

CHAPTER 21

IF YOU COULD ONLY SEE

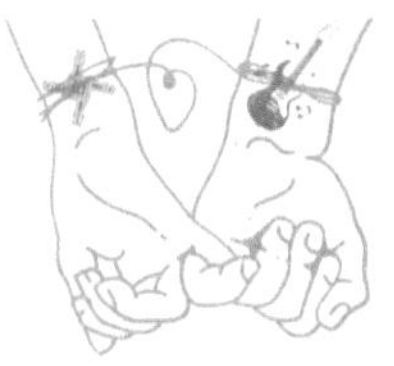

Hunter

I wake to the sound of Brighid at her spinning wheel in an alcove off the bedroom. It's almost like the sound of a needle spinning in the center of a well-worn vinyl record that's been left too long — softly percussive over a soothing shushing sound. It's a sound I associate with Brighid and Brighid alone.

The bedroom is dark, cloaked in room-darkening curtains — the same ones Brighid had in her dorm room during college. They were a nod to my semi-nocturnal schedule, proof that we shared her bed often enough that she wanted to ensure I got enough sleep, even if my hours weren't necessarily the same as hers, or even consistent.

But in front of Brighid, the sun streams through a window, flickering over her fair skin and blonde hair as the big oak tree outside the window filters the light through its leaves. Her beautiful soft shoulders are nearly bare beneath a lacy blue knee-length chemise that reveals the swell of her breasts. The window is ajar, and a slight breeze introduces the tang of salt air into the room. It's familiar and soothing, a scent I missed in the city, though I'm only now, in Brighid's bed, realizing it was an absence I had noted on some unconscious level.

She sits in a comfortable chair at her wheel, her bare feet pressing rhythmically on the pedals as her fingers guide the wool fibers into place. She's talked to me before about how hypnotic the work is, sending her into a state of deep relaxation and taking her mind off everything but the sounds and sensations of spinning yarn. (Fabric-string, I correct myself. It'll forever be fabric-string to me...)

Brighid had devoted herself to learning to spin and weave after my mom died. And she treated it as needed therapy after her own mother passed. Now, it's like a religious ritual for her. I wonder what has driven her to her wheel this morning. But I suspect I already know.

Things changed for us both last night. After nearly 25 years of friendship, now we're something more... And it's exactly as scary as I feared it would be. And exactly as glorious as I dreamt it might be when I allowed myself to consider it at all.

I lie back down on the cool pillow behind me, looking up at the ceiling overhead. Brighid is too focused on her spinning to have noticed yet that I'm awake. It's one of the few times when she doesn't feel me looking at her the moment she's in view. And it's a reprieve I welcome as I try to put things into perspective in my own head.

Was this wise? There are so many ways it could go wrong, from expectations set too high to the challenges of being a touring musician in a relationship, the paparazzi and public scrutiny, or even just getting bored with each other. What do you do when you get bored in a romantic relationship with your best friend?

And that's before we get to my long-ago decision not to ever get into *any* committed relationship. Especially not with my best friend.

The risk of becoming my father, incapable of monogamy, fidelity, putting the needs of someone he supposedly loved above his own... and the gaping emotional wounds he inflicted on my mother, driving her to her death. And my own guilt that I didn't sense how much she needed me that night and instead sought solace for my own pain in Brighid's arms.

And then there's the risk of hurting Brighid, who I have loved since we were kids, but who has been too precious to me for me to let myself see where that love was leading me all along.

I glance over at her now, the view across my bare chest, down my legs, naked underneath the cool sheets of her bed — having, for the first time ever, slept naked in Brighid's bed, my arms wrapped around her much as they always have, but nothing between us this night except what we feel for each other and the deep, unavoidable attraction she's been laboring under for more than a decade and that I have let weigh us both down in denying it.

And still the wheel spins, the gentle susurration lulling me into sleep again as I watch her at her task.

When I wake again, Brighid is still spinning away. It's dark out now, and I've been asleep long enough that she's changed into a long white nightgown, just a hint of her rosy nipples showing through the thin fabric. My mouth is drawn instantly to them. She's pulled the ankle-length skirt up past her knees, leaving her long legs free to work the spinning wheel.

She quietly hums a tune as she works, the song weaving together in harmony with the sound of her spinning wheel. It's a melody I cherish all the more because it's my own, played for her this afternoon, a gift given to her with my return to our home after a long day working the sheep. My penny whistle now rests abandoned in the empty chair by Brighid's spinning wheel, and it's her lovely voice that brings the song from her mind to my ear — now a treat for me in turn.

It's as mesmerizing watching the firelight flicker across her milky skin as it is watching her spin fibers into yarn, and my fingers yearn to play a song of their own over her flesh. I pull the warm woolen sheet from my naked body and cross the room to her, my cock already rising to attention, called by the lure of her feminine curves.

I approach her silently from behind, wrapping my arms around her and under her breasts, brushing the nipples with my thumbs through the fabric of her gown. She releases the wool and slides her arms back along mine, bringing her hands up over my own as I squeeze those beautiful globes that so perfectly fill my palms.

"I knew you were awake," she says in a low, seductive tone.

I tweak her nipples between my thumb and forefinger.

"I'm not the only one," I reply with a sly smile.

"Mmm..." she hums, enjoying the gentle torment of my hands, the sound tickling my chin where it rests next to her elegant neck.

With one hand, I pull her warmly hued tresses away from her ear, running my tongue along the gentle slope before nipping the fleshy round lobe. She gives a sharp intake of breath, and a shiver runs down her spine.

"You and my nipples aren't the only ones who are awake and paying attention," she cautions me. I look in the direction her chin points me, and sure enough, a pair of brown eyes is looking right at us from under shaggy brown fur.

"Crógan," I lament. "Mind yourself. My Lady and I are engaged in pleasurable pursuits. Pursuits that I would rather you didn't interrupt."

Brighid chuckles, the warm sound stirring an answering heat in me, and I take half a step back from her chair to make room for a swiftly growing erection that I'd much rather have rubbing up against her ass than the wooden chair.

The dog puts his head down on his front paws.

I grab Brighid's left hand in mine and pull her up to standing, then spin her around to face me, the chemise once again covering her legs — a tragedy I intend to remedy in short order.

I tug her hard against me, and her peaked nipples rub against my chest through the thin fabric. I pull them into my hands again, massaging, twisting the tips until they're as hard as my dick below.

Brighid's breath is coming in short pants now. I pull the chemise up her legs with one hand while the other continues to work her nipple. Beneath the hint of sandalwood and tuberose from her softening hand cream, I can detect the scent of her arousal — that musky fragrance that's uniquely hers, uniquely that of my incredibly sexy wife, and one of my favorite scents in all the world.

Still tweaking her right nipple in one hand, I plunge my other hand between her bared legs, sliding my fingers up through her slick folds. My thumb rubs lightly over that little button of delight at the apex of her thighs, and her knees begin to buckle.

I smile in satisfaction, relishing that even the smallest touch makes her melt in my hands.

I pull the chemise over her head, leaving her naked before me in the firelight. The warm light reflects over her sensuous curves, picking up the russet tones of the light covering of hair over her mound. I pull her arms over her head, grasping her wrists with one hand, and she gasps in surprise before the adrenaline hits her bloodstream and her skin flushes for me.

I growl, powerfully drawn to her but restraining myself mentally, and her physically. I drag her against me again, taking her lips with brusque heat. I thrust my tongue between her lips, and she moans, opening her mouth to me and tangling her tongue with mine. We suck at each other's tongues, teeth and lips, devouring each other as if starved for some essence that only the other can give.

When we finally pull apart, we're both panting heavily, as much in anticipation as from this small but intense exertion. Our eyes meet, and the air between us is instantly aflame. I can feel her excitement, and it feeds my own, which reflects back to her and is magnified, setting up a swarming cycle between us where our arousal explodes on an exponential scale.

I spin her around again and pull her back against my chest, her wrists still imprisoned in my left hand. My right hand drifts slowly down along her waist, grazing her belly before dropping down to her mound, which I cup in my hand, pulling her ass sharply against my hard length.

She gasps, throwing her head back along my neck, and I dip my mouth to the crook of her neck, sucking the flesh into my mouth and against my teeth, marking her as mine. She revels in it, her mouth hanging open as she goes a little limp against me. I run my tongue up her neck... once, twice, savoring the salty flavor of her skin as the heat between us goes liquid.

I grab her by the waist and use her upraised arms to steer her to the bed. I push her forward, her chest crushed to the mattress by my hand firmly pressed against her back. I let go of her hands, and they fall alongside her head, preserving a small space for her to breathe, which she's going to need.

I grab her around her waist, pulling her legs standing up straight to raise her ass in the air in front of me and make it clear that she should keep it there, giving me free access to her most intimate parts. She moans again, and I reach down between her thighs, finding her dripping.

"Is that for me?" I ask her huskily, my mouth next to her ear. She shudders, and I laugh, delighted by her neediness and eagerly anticipating satisfying her every need, and my own.

I brush my fingers across her clit again, spreading her arousal there and causing her to spasm against me. Her moist cleft beckons me, and I can restrain myself no longer. I line myself up against her opening and push straight in, giving her no time to anticipate, but she takes me willingly into her, moaning into the mattress and wiggling her ass against my thighs.

I slide my rough hand up her spine, wrapping my hand around the back of her neck. She quiets instantly, calmed under the power of my control over her, and eagerly awaiting whatever I choose to give her.

I pull back out of her clenching warmth, slowly, inch by inch, torturing us both just a little in pursuit of a higher goal. She hisses at the sensation, turning her head to the side so she can see me out of the corner of her eye. This is no battle of wills. My dominion over her in this moment is entirely with her consent, solely in service of her pleasure, and of mine in giving it to her.

I slam back into her, our flesh smacking together so delightfully that I pause right there to land a sharp smack to her butt cheek. She gasps out in sensory overload as I rub my work-roughened palm over the reddened flesh. I chuckle quietly at her response before slowly pulling back once again. She's holding her breath, anticipating my next move, whether it will be to smack her on the ass again or to plunge deep inside her.

I do both.

She cries out in sheer pleasure, and her spine goes soft as she stretches her hands out in front of her before clenching them tightly into fists and turning her face forward, her eyes closing and isolating her with the sensations I'm giving her.

With her attention fully focused on what I'm doing to her, I begin moving in and out of her grasping warmth, gradually increasing the speed with which I'm pounding myself into her. Her pleasure ramps up in time with me, moans turning to whimpers, which become a soft keening as I reach under her and drag my fingers through her folds, gathering her moisture on my fingertips.

I give her another smack on the ass, and she's babbling almost incoherently between every thrust. I transfer her lubrication from my fingers to the puckered hole before me before slowly pressing the tip of my thumb against the ring of muscle. She cries out, calling my name on rush of sound that starts as a moan and ends as a scream.

"Yes! Oh, yes! More! Give me more!"

I press my thumb slowly inside her while keeping up my steady assault on her pussy. Each time I plunge my cock into her, the force of my hips slamming against her presses my thumb farther inside her, until there's no more left to feed into her. I drop my other hand again to gather moisture from her slit and slather it over her where she's impaled on my thumb.

I begin to work it in and out of her in time with my cock pounding into her, the force of my thrusts pushing her across the bed in tiny increments as legs gone languid from pleasure fail her and her weight falls fully upon the bed. I give her another smack, rubbing the resulting pink mark on her pale flesh with a gentle touch before diving again to her slit from around the front, where this time I grip that little bundle of nerves between my outstretched fingers, pressing on either side and sliding them back and forth across and around it, in time with my ever-faster thrusts inside her heat.

I can't hold out much longer, and I want her to come with me this time.

I can feel the tension inside her starting to build, as surely as if was my own, and with this intense connection between us, it essentially is my own.

As she reaches higher and faster, nearing her peak, I let myself go, plunging freely into her, barely able to maintain any sense of rhythm as I continue to fuck her ass with my thumb and her pussy with my cock, and rubbing her clit with my fingers until she suddenly tenses up around me, front and back, and a rolling wave of spasms shudders through her, kicking off my own explosion of pleasure.

I spill inside her with a tortured cry, continuing to work her clit between my fingers as she rides out her orgasm, clenching my dick inside her, her other hole tightening its grip rhythmically on my thumb, pulse after pulse, until she goes limp and I collapse on top of her.

After a few moments, she reaches behind her, brushing her hand across my back where I still lay on top of her. I smile into the soft skin of her bare shoulder and press a kiss there before sliding to the side and wrapping her in my arms, spooned up against her, my front to her back, my hand between her dewy breasts and my nose trucked amongst the strands of her sunrise-tinged red-gold hair, inhaling her unforgettable scent deep into my lungs as we drift off to sleep, limbs intertwined as surely as our hearts and souls.

CHAPTER 22

WHITE LIGHTNING

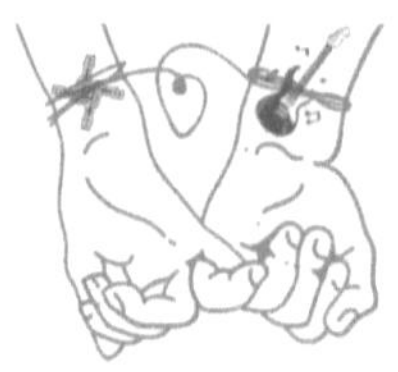

Hunter

I rise to consciousness again when the bed dips beside me, Brighid sliding smoothly under the sheets, where I remain happily naked. Her blue chemise is soft against my back, and I sigh in pleasure as she rubs her breasts against me, hugging me to her before sliding her hand down to what instantly shifts from half-erect cock to rock-hard rod.

I realize an instant later that I've already come recently, very recently, and not inside Brighid, as I did when we came together last night in the wake of her work on my injured arm. The sheet beneath me is damp. I've come all over myself in my sleep, like a teenager dreaming about his first crush...

That thought stops me in my tracks.

If I'm honest with myself, Brighid was my first crush. And now, more than fifteen years later, I've finally gotten my head out of my ass and made love to her — something I've never really done with anyone, no matter how many women I've had sex with.

And it was incredible.

Our deep connection with each other magnified every sensation, from the touch of skin on skin to the delight we found in giving each other pleasure. The memory grabs me by the balls, while Brighid herself, here and now, has her hand wrapped around my cock.

She lacks anywhere near the amount of experience that I've had during my rockstar odyssey, but she seems to innately sense what I like and does it without having to think about it or even say a word.

I turn over to look at her. Tracing my hand up her cheek and drowning instantly in those violet eyes. I press a soft, sensuous kiss to her lips.

"Good morning, you..."

"Hi," she replies, almost shyly, the quick glance away and slight reddening of her cheeks confirming that she's having a hard time adapting to our new circumstances.

I grasp her upper arm with my left hand, giving her a squeeze to reassure her that it's all going to be OK.

And it doesn't hurt. My hand... doesn't hurt.

I look down at it, incredulous.

"It's better?" she asks.

"It doesn't hurt. At all. Literally. Not a twinge."

"Good." She smiles at me, looking pleased. "She likes you. Poet, musician — basically the same thing as far as She's concerned. She even likes your horrible puns."

Brighid chuckles.

"My puns are not horrible. They're delightfully punny... You know you love them."

She smiles quietly, which I take as agreement.

"So, She decided to give me a hand, after all," I muse.

"It would seem so," she replies, still unaccountably shy. "Just make sure to take it easy. You didn't follow instructions before, and you made it worse."

"That seems to be a thing with me," I mutter to myself before nodding my assent. She smiles.

"Did you sleep well?" she inquires.

"I did," I confirm. "I slept next to this gorgeous woman who wore me out with all these amazing curves and made me feel amazing in the process."

"That sounds wonderful."

"It is." I clasp her hand to me. "And I hope it's something we'll both keep getting to enjoy."

"Hmmm," she replies noncommittally. Not wanting to push her too hard, I decide to drop the subject, for now.

"Why'd you change? I've been lying here in bed with no clothes on, and you've already had two different outfits on today."

"I just put on my chemise earlier when I wanted to spend some time at the spinning wheel. I can take it back off if you don't like it," she suggests playfully, and I like to see her warming up again.

"No — I mean the white one... the long chemise... gown... shift — whatever you call it — the one you had on before."

There's a long pause.

"I don't have a white gown, shift, or chemise, at the moment," she says slowly.

"But — I saw you working at the spinning wheel earlier, wearing white. That one was longer, and you had it pulled up around your knees as you worked. The firelight reflected off of it."

Her gaze evades mine.

"Bridge? What is it? I like both, if that's what you're worried about. You look beautiful in both."

"Hunter — I don't have a white gown or chemise. Not anywhere in this house... I used to have one... A long time ago," she continues slowly.

"Maybe that's what I was remembering," I suggest.

"Maybe..." she replies, now seeming preoccupied, even more than before. Her lascivious intent in grabbing my dick just a few minutes ago seems to have been forgotten. I'll have to remedy that.

I grab her by her knees and slide her down the bed under me, her chemise riding up against the sheets.

"No panties?" I leer at her. "You naughty girl... Do you know what happens to naughty girls?"

She shakes her head, but I can see she already knows what I'm going to say.

"They get spanked," I tell her, flipping her over on her stomach and, before she can react, landing my palm on that luscious ass of hers. Just hard enough to smart and leave a beautiful imprint from my hand.

She moans.

"You like that, huh?" My face takes on an evil grin. "I'll have to use that against you later. But now..."

I slide my hand between her legs, finding that she's already wet for me. My cock is fully erect now, ready and willing. But that, too, can wait.

She moans as my fingers trace through her slickness.

I place a soft kiss on the red mark on her ass, and she moans again, louder and longer.

I can't stand it anymore.

I flip her back over, onto her back, and slide her knees apart and out to the side.

"Hunter..." she moans.

"Shhh. I just woke up. I'm hungry after a *long* and *hard* night," I drawl, palming my cock for emphasis. Her eyes are on me, and she whimpers at my words. "I need sustenance."

She gasps as my mouth falls onto her slit, and the gasp becomes a whimper when my tongue finds her opening and licks firmly along the track to her most sensitive spot. Her thighs close around my head, and I press her hips into the mattress to keep her where I want her. Forget breakfast. This is the feast I'm craving.

I begin with a most intimate kiss to her lower lips, mimicking our passionate kisses last night. My saliva soon mixes with her inner juices, and I lap up every drop. Her hips are wiggling beneath me as I plunge my tongue inside her, and she grabs my hair, steering my mouth where she wants it most. I oblige, following her wordless demands from hole to clit and back again.

"More, Hunter!" She urges. "Please!"

I fuck her with my tongue, my hand sliding down from her belly to massage her clit as I do so. Her hips lift from the mattress, bucking against my face as I devour her.

Beneath me, my cock is a solid rod, not so patiently waiting his turn to plunge into her warm depths. Soon, I promise.

She's panting above me now, the tension rising in her as her juices run down my chin, urging me on. I circle her opening, pressing against it from every angle, while I continue to massage her clit. She moans long and loud, driving me to a fever pitch.

She's so responsive. How did I never see this tempting sexpot underneath the loving friend, not in all the years we have known each other, all the times we shared a bed? How did I not understand that I held the key to unleashing her innermost desires and that the result would be so glorious for us both?

She grips my head tighter, pressing my mouth to her, and I can tell she's nearly there. I lap at her opening and run my tongue up her slit to her clit, moving my hand down now. At the same moment, I drive two fingers into her, tapping on that sensitive pad of flesh on her internal wall, and suck her clit into my mouth, flicking it with my tongue as I pull at it with my lips.

She spasms beneath me, silently screaming, as if no word or sound can convey the ecstasy she is feeling. I nearly come myself, just from watching the expression on her face. Exquisite. Just exquisite.

As she comes down from her high, she looks down at me and smiles lustfully.

"Hunter. Come here."

She pulls me up her body until our faces align. How am I just now noticing that she's the perfect height for me? Not too short, not so tall that I feel like we don't fit. She fits perfectly in my arms, standing, cuddling or...

She looks at me for a moment, almost incredulous. Then she proceeds to lick my chin, cleaning her juices from my face as if it was the sweetest and juiciest fruit she'd ever known. She licks around my mouth in the same manner before fastening her lips to mine, nibbling and sucking like she's now the one who's starving... for me.

I feel her hand reach between us, and she sweeps it over my cock before dropping farther down and squeezing my balls lightly. I nearly come on her hand, right there, just from that. My hips slam forward, and that's all the permission she needs, pulling my cock up to her slit, leading me firmly to her opening and then using her other hand encourage me to press my hips forward, impaling her on my dick.

Still sensitive from her orgasm, she cries out at the penetration. I give her just a moment to adjust to having me inside her, and then I begin with a steady rhythm to fuck her, hips mashing against hers, twisting just a little to press against her clit with each thrust.

I'm so aroused that I know I have very little time to see to her pleasure before I take my own. But she's right there with me, our eyes locked onto each other until I have to close mine to focus for just a moment. When I open them again, her face is alive with... joy? ecstasy? love? There's too much there to process, let alone find a word for it.

Her muscles flex inside her, clamping down on my cock, and I'm gone, stroking quickly in and out of her as my hips move of their own accord. Her legs wrap around my waist and she screams out her pleasure, her thighs locked in place while a firm rhythmic massage pulls at my cock.

I shoot inside her, filling her to overflowing and leaving us both a dripping, heaving, heated puddle, recovering from our participation in this long-overdue dance.

CHAPTER 23

DEJA VOODOO

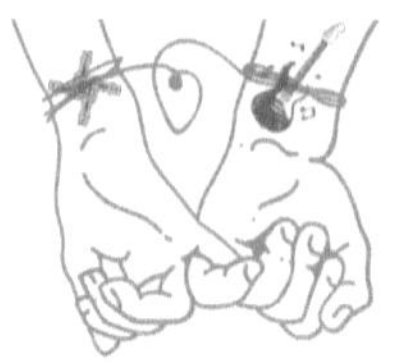

Brighid

Hunter and I lay in bed, sated and comfortable in each other's arms in a way we've never really experienced before.

I dot his chest with kisses as he runs his hand up and down from the taper of my waist to the fullness of my hips and back again. His lips press against the top of my head, dropping his own kiss there.

It's sweet and quiet and beautiful, and everything I wanted when I first told him I loved him as more than a friend. Our innocent puppy-pile sleepovers have completed their transformation, through friendly comfort to less-innocent hints of what might be, to torrid sex and now to this — pure, simple post-coital happiness.

I wonder what he's thinking, and I nearly ask him. But my insecurities have started to rear their ugly head again, and I know what I'm wanting to hear from him boils down to reassurance that he enjoyed this as much as I did and wants it to continue, that he's not disappointed in my body, so different from that of his past girlfriends.

I not two days ago promised myself I'd reset the balance in our relationship, but this wasn't exactly what I envisioned when I made that decision. Hunter seems to have swept all the pieces off the table, and now there's no sense of how things are supposed to be. Is this the beginning of balance? Or are we going to fall back into unhealthy patterns that could be further complicated by sex?

Me trotting out my worries about how he feels about me, my body and what was mind-blowing sex for me — it's the first ingredient in a recipe that puts me back on the defensive, and I'm determined not to go there. I was strong when he came to the shop yesterday. He worked for it, for me to give him a chance, and he made it my choice whether we'd go beyond that, never assuming that my past feelings would make that an automatic yes.

In the moment, I took the power I had and treated us as equals. And he'd responded by doing the same. I'm not going to give that up just to reinforce my weak spots. Time will tell how this new — dare I call it a relationship? — works between us. And I'm not going to rush him with requests for reassurance. Let's let this be what it's going to be.

But in the quiet, my eyes wander to my blue chemise laying on the floor, where it landed after Hunter stripped it off me the last time we made love.

I try to avoid replaying his words in my head — him asking about the flowing white nightgown, talking about seeing me in the firelight... in my bedroom here, which has no fireplace... but it keeps coming to the surface of my brain. He was confused, and I know that feeling well — not entirely because him asking about it confused me, but because I've been in that position myself.

Fourteen years ago, I drifted off to sleep next to him and awoke to find myself with him in a distant past that was at that moment our present. I had seen us together — partners, lovers, husband and wife — and it had felt just as real as the existence I was living when I had closed my eyes.

So real, in fact, that waking up once again, a 15-year-old girl sitting next to her 15-year-old best friend, I had been beyond confused. Things were the same and yet they were different. Dream — vision — overlapped with reality and left a confusing double image.

I'd initially chalked it up to a vivid imagination and wishful thinking of a girl with a crush. But it always seemed like more, and that ate at me, until I eventually confessed to Hunter what I'd seen, and how I felt about it and him, only to realize that while he believed I believed it and still didn't think I'd lost touch with reality, neither did he credit what I'd seen as the truth.

And I'd spent the last decade and change with that vision — the many visions I'd had of us together in the distant past — stuck in my head, while he went on with his rockstar-to-be life with me as his platonic best friend, his biggest supporter, and occasionally uncomfortable unrequited admirer. What I'd seen meant nearly nothing to him, and at some points, nearly everything to me. And I always had to hide that.

But that question today about the white gown — it had struck me to the core. Coming from anyone else, any other lover, it would have been innocuous, dismissed as a dream. But what he'd described sounded hauntingly familiar, to the point where it sent a shiver down my spine.

The part of me that had eventually accepted that Hunter would never believe, would never act on what I knew in my soul to be true — that part of me refuses to credit that he might have had his own vision of that shared past, even though *I* was the one sitting at the spinning wheel.

But back when we were 15, it was his song that had drawn me into that first vision of the past, and it seems a perfect parallel that perhaps my spinning had done the same to him, especially in the wake of this seismic shift in our relationship.

Was he starting on some level to notice the parallels, the common elements of our lives then and now? I don't dare hope. And I don't dare burden this tiny seed of a romantic relationship with him, after all these years, with the heavy weight of that past life.

And I once more resolve not to mention it again until he does himself.

CHAPTER 24

BLACK DOG

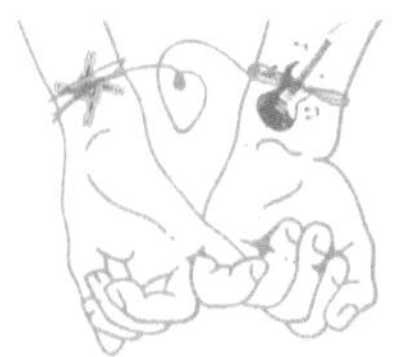

Hunter

I'm not sure I've ever woken up with a woman in bed with me after a night of hot sex and wanted to spend the day in bed with her, just lying there together.

But today — with Brighid — that's exactly what I want to do most in the world. To leave the stresses of life far outside these walls and just enjoy spending time together.

I've spent a lot of time hanging out with Brighid over the years. It's fun, it's comfortable, it's engaging and enjoyable in a way that nothing else but making music and being with my band brothers is. And I've had too little of it these last few years, some of that due to my own stupid ideas of what we were supposed to be to each other.

But now, today, with Brighid in my arms, and my lips, my scent, my cum all over her, marking her as mine... It's like someone took my favorite chocolate dessert and topped it with whipped cream. And I'm not sure I'll ever want chocolate mousse without that little bit extra ever again.

Maybe this new way of being with her poses a risk to the old one, but it's a risk that seems worth it when I can enjoy the comfort of having my best friend next to me and also being able to kiss her sweet lips and feel our bodies moving together, fitting so perfectly together, like we were made for each other.

Maybe she was right... maybe we had been.

As much as I want to hide away with Brighid, in her, I can't do that forever. I have commitments to the band that I am already running late for, and I have to confront Holly about her blackmail scheme before this goes any further.

I can't pretend to be with Holly when every bit of me wants to spend as much time as I can with Brighid. Maybe we can come to a compromise, with me funding some ad buys on her site or doing a few appearances with her, purely as a business deal.

Heck, I'd even let her pose as the unfairly abandoned girlfriend with the dick rockstar ex. The sympathy she'd get and the draw of people wanting to see what she says about me might even surpass the draw of her as my supposed girlfriend, especially if we timed it out with the airing of the show.

This isn't going to be a fun conversation, but it is a necessary one if I am going to pursue this thing with Brighid, which I really, really want to do. I have to get her out of Holly's range.

It's more important than ever that I do what I can to keep my best friend safe, and to keep her privacy intact. I can't expose her to the social media monster, not when this is all so new. That's a risk I can't afford to take when I want this relationship more than anything I've ever wanted before.

And speaking of social media — I've ignored my phone all day, keeping in this happy cocoon with Brighid. We ordered some amazing sushi for lunch, delivered right to her door — something you'd never have gotten here when we were growing up — and rewatched the most recent season of "Doctor Who," some of which I missed when it first aired, since we were on the road.

And we snuggled on the couch until I couldn't resist any longer and pulled down her tank top so I could suck her nipples until they were tight points and she was writhing beneath me.

I pulled her onto my lap — after about ten seconds of ridiculous debate about her being too heavy — and just made out with her, our bodies rubbing together until we were both frantically ripping the rest of our clothes off and she sank down on my cock, fucking herself on me until she came, hard, and then I fucked her from underneath as she clung to me, until I tumbled over too.

With Molly agreeing to take care of the shop alone again today, Brighid seemed content to stay in with me, though I detected a little restlessness in her until we made love again.

Nothing turns my girl's busy mind off like my touch, and it's a power I'm really coming to appreciate.

My phone beeps again. I've got a band meeting soon, and as much as I'd like to, I can't just ignore it...

Alex: *Are you with Brighid?*

Hunter: *Why do you ask?*

Alex: *You've been gone for a full day. I was going to remind you that spending time with Brighid in public means people will start speculating on what your relationship is exactly.*

Alex: *If you don't want them thinking there's something more there, you're going to have to be more careful.*

He's right, I know, and that's an issue I plan to tackle later today, after meeting with the guys and after I deal with Holly.

But Alex has always been a little nosy where everyone else's love lives are concerned. He's seemed kind of lost since Megan dumped him, before we'd even gotten signed. He said she got pissed off about Brighid staying with us and broke things off with him even though it was all innocent. Which it was with them, of course. And with me. Back then, anyway.

Considering now how not-innocent my most recent hours with Brighid have been, I kind of understand why Megan got pissed about it. But Alex has already been talking to and about Brighid, and our relationship, a little more than I like. I need more time to get us on solid ground before I let the guys in on it. I can't risk a bit of good-natured ribbing touching off her anxieties. I need to get Alex off our trail for now, the same as I need to get to where Holly and her camera crew aren't hanging over our heads.

Hunter: *Thanks for the reminder. I'd forgotten that anyone cares about who I'm having sex with. A camera crew following me around for two weeks on dates with multiple models should have been a clue.*

Alex: *You'd think. And here I am having to remind you nonetheless. You headed back soon?*

Hunter: *Yeah. I'll be there. With bells on.*

Alex: *No! You can't wear bells! I'm wearing bells! And we can't match or they'll all talk!*

Hunter: *...*

Hunter: *...*

Hunter: *I'll be there soon.*

Now I have to go, and I'm dreading it.

"Bridge — I hate to do this, but I've got a band meeting I've got to go to, and an errand or two I need to get to. Are you OK if I leave you here for a while and come back in a few hours? I can bring carryout from that nice place on the north end of the boardwalk."

"That would be nice, Hunter," she says smiling gently at me. She's still a little tentative in her new role as my lover, and I desperately want to erase that little bit of restraint she shows — ooh! Now there's an idea for later! — and help her get her bearings with me.

I briefly consider bending her over the arm of the sofa and marking her as mine again, filling her up to the hilt. But I'm going to be late if I don't get moving.

"Did you get your phone fixed?" she asks. She knows me so well.

"I got a replacement. The screen on the old one is cracked all to hell. It still works, but I needed a new one anyway. I got the basics set up on the new one. I just haven't had a chance to restore the backup from the old one."

"You mean you couldn't figure out how to restore it," she teases. And she's right.

"For such a geek, you are a total Luddite sometimes," she says, shaking her head.

"Guilty as charged."

"You want me to do it while you're out?"

She's way better with gadgets than I am. It's not the first time she'll have fixed my phone for me. I just don't have the patience for this stuff.

And now I'm asking myself again what it would have been like breaking through with the band with her by my side. She's been my partner in a lot of ways. And it's past time to acknowledge that.

"You're amazing. You know that, right?"

"You just love me for my tech-support skills."

"I do, but you're amazing overall."

"If you say so," she replies humbly. "I think you're amazing, too."

"I know," I reply with a wink.

"OK, Mr. Luddite, hand over the new phone," she says with a slight eye-roll. "I'll swap the SIM cards back, and you can use the old one until I get this done. I'll connect the new one via Wi-Fi and get it updated and restored that way, so the old one will work until we swap out the SIM cards again." And she's already lost me with her tech-speak... "Is your password still the same?"

"Of course."

I place the new phone in her hand and use the excuse to pull her hard up against me. I grope her just a little — one for the road — and I give her a slow and sensuous kiss, then let her do that card-swapping thing she talked about, before I head for the door.

"Take care of you," she says.

"As you wish," I reply with a smile.

I decide to walk back to the studio and stop in at the restaurant on the way, to put in our order for later. The boardwalk is busy, and I'm glad I've got my hat and sunglasses this time. Not to mention being sober. Drunken revelations aside, that's not a night I want to repeat. I flex my left hand and marvel again that it's only a little stiff now.

After I've put in our order and given the hostess a substantial tip — rewarding her in advance for maintaining my anonymity, at least until after I've come back to get our food in a couple hours — I head for the studio.

Alex: *You on your way yet, or are you still getting that blowjob from blondie?*

Hunter: *STFU*

Alex: *Hey, man. No need to get bent out of shape. Maybe you need to get laid worse than I thought. Bet your girl there can fix that for you. Unless you think the paps will spot your naked ass through her windows.*

I growl in frustration. He just won't lay off Brighid today.

Hunter: *I date models, Alex. Everyone knows that. The paps aren't going to be looking at some small-town girl who makes yarn and sells crystals. And I don't need anyone else when I've got four models competing to date me. I can fuck any or all of them whenever I want.*

Alex: *Hey, the girl's clearly still in love with you. You can't possibly have missed that. I'm not sure why you're putting up with the hassle of all these high-maintenance chicks when you've got Miss Puppy-Dog Eyes hanging on your every word. Easy pickings. There's no reason you shouldn't be getting laid on the regular with Brighid around.*

I really don't want the guys to know things have changed between us. Not yet. As Alex has just proven, they've formed kind of a mixed opinion about Brighid over the years. I don't think they ever understood the platonic relationship. And I know it didn't escape them that she had a thing for me that I never reciprocated. They used to tease me about it all the time, until I told them it needed to stop. If this change in our relationship came out now, they'd never let either of us hear the end of it.

She's had enough people making fun of her over the years for various things, and her thing for me was a thing we'd agreed to mostly ignore. Having the guys teasing either of us about it is a recipe for disaster. At some point, somebody was going to slip and say something she shouldn't have to hear. So I'd put my foot down then, and I can't risk reviving that habit of theirs now, not yet.

So now I need to reinforce that this topic is a no-go, or they'll be gossiping about us before I even get back to the studio. If they're not already.

Hunter: *I keep telling you — She's just a friend. I'm not attracted to her. At all. Can you imagine what they'd say on social media if I was seeing her? They'd destroy us.*

Alex: *Whatever. Get laid on your own time, or at least bring extras to share. You're late, asshole.*

Hunter: *On my way.*

There's a cluster of people ahead of me gathered around a guy with a dog, and I can see why. That thing is *huge*. Kind of shaggy, a brownish-grey color, with a head that reaches the guy's chest. Biggest dog I've ever... Seen...

Biggest dog... I've ever... Seen...

Big. Brown. Shaggy. Great big brown eyes looking up at me, at us, when I had Brighid's breasts cupped in my hands...

Oh. My. God. Gods. Whatever.

"Hey, man — what kind of dog is that?"

"Irish wolfhound. Tallest dog breed in the world. But they're gentle giants, love people — especially their person, and they usually have one they bond with above the others."

"Right. Cool. Thanks." I reply absently.

I stand there on the boardwalk, looking at my shoes but not seeing them, for the better part of five minutes.

Brighid. Shaggy brown dog. Irish wolfhound. A fireplace. A penny whistle. A spinning wheel. A big bed with warm sheets to keep us against the chilly night air along the green-edged coast.

And a white nightgown, pulled up to her knees. And then higher.

The hair's different — longer and strawberry blonde instead of ash blonde, but it's her. I know it's her. It's us.

And I start running for Brighid's house, dodging between staring people until I'm on the side street where there aren't so many of them. And then I just run flat-out.

The door's still unlocked when I hit it at full speed.

"Brighid? Brighid! Hello? Are you here?"

I'm calling for her as I'm still panting from the exertion of running all the way here. But there's no answer. I know she sometimes leaves the door unlocked when she goes for a walk on the beach and expects to come back soon.

My phone beeps in my pocket. It's Alex, asking where I am, since I'm now running really late for our meeting. This broken screen is a pain in the ass. It takes me three tries to tell him I'm on my way.

I'll have to wait to talk to Brighid about the dog. And the nightgown. And us.

But that's probably better anyway. We're going to need some time to talk this through. I don't want to be rushed while the guys are waiting for me. I need to explain this to her, and then I need her to explain it back to me, because I can't even absorb it.

I'm headed back toward Brighid's front door when I spot my replacement phone lying on the floor by the table, plugged in and charging.

"She must have gone for a walk while the phone was restoring..."

I've about had it with this broken screen. That whole conversation with Alex was painful, in more ways than one. I pick up the new phone and see I'm in luck.

"Update complete — cool!"

"Wait... What the fuck?"

At least two of those last texts showed up on this phone, too.

"Good thing Bridge went for a walk when she did. What a nightmare that would have been..."

I text Alex, just to make sure.

Hunter: *Hey — Did you get a read notification on that last text before just now?*

Alex: *No. It showed up as delivered about 10 minutes ago, not read. Why?*

Hunter: *No reason... Just checking to see if there was a delay in this phone receiving texts. It was restoring from the backup.*

Alex: *That's what was keeping you? We're waiting on your slow ass. What happened to "with bells on"?*

Hunter: *I'll be right there.*

I set off at a jog so at least the guys will know I was making an effort. I need to get this meeting done, deal with Holly and then come back to my Bridge for a nice dinner... and dessert. With whipped cream on top.

CHAPTER 25

PAYPHONE

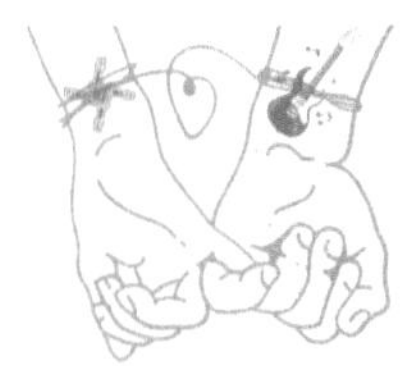

Brighid
Mere minutes before that

He loves me!
No plucking daisy petals to debate the point. He said, "As you wish."

It's not quite the same, since it's our shorthand created when things were more *challenging*, if less complicated. But that's what he meant when he said it, I'm sure. As he reluctantly walked out of my house, freshly fucked by yours truly. Who was on top this time! (Go me!)

Tentative has just rounded the corner and become cautiously optimistic. I'm restraining myself — hmm... ideas for later... — from hitting giddy. Such a small thing, such a small phrase, and yet it reshapes my whole day.

Part of which is now being spent restoring his phone from the old one to the new one. I'm currently waiting for the restore process to finish and the phone to restart. It usually takes a while, so I'm reviewing shop inventory levels on my own phone while I wait. I reordered the little polished rocks and velveteen bags before it was even done installing the updated OS to match the old one.

It's silly that I need to do this for him, but I have to admit I love it, being useful to him, caring for him. And I can do it now without feeling like a pathetic hanger-on, because we're together, and that's what you do when you're together with someone!

The important part is that Hunter seems happy with this turn of events. He could have cut out hours ago and gone back to the studio. But instead he stayed through lunch, through a whole bunch of "Doctor Who," and through two more rounds of sex. And did I mention I was on top! And he didn't complain or seem at all uncomfortable.

It's the best of best friends combined with oh-so-hot sex and sweet romance. Am I really this lucky?

The phone beeps, so the update is complete and a restart imminent. I pick it up to check. Actually, it's a message coming in over the Wi-Fi, since the SIM card is in the old phone, which is with Hunter. It's right there on the lock screen, where I can't help but see it.

Alex: *Hey, the girl's clearly still in love with you. You can't possibly have missed that. I'm not sure why you're putting up with the hassle of all these high-maintenance chicks when you've got Miss Puppy-Dog Eyes hanging on your every word. Easy pickings. There's no reason you shouldn't be getting laid with Brighid around.*

I put the phone on the table, the screen facing down. My hand is shaking as I do it.

"This is none of my business," I tell myself, giving that Nosy Nellie in my head a stern lecture. "No reading of the texts. Even if your name is mentioned. Privacy. Maintain his privacy..."

As a second restart begins on his phone, I continue my inventory review on mine, this time sitting back a few feet from Hunter's. I glance at it warily, begging the universe to just let it hurry up and finish.

The phone pings with the default notification sound again, and I debate picking it up, staring at it as if it's a rabid badger that's been teleported into my living room and is eager to eat my hand.

"It could be the notification that the restart is complete..." I reason. "That's all I'm doing with it. What are the chances he's replying in real time on the other phone when he should already be at the studio by now? Slim to none. Let's just get the new phone finished up."

I pick up the phone again, with determination.

Hunter: *I keep telling you — She's just a friend. I'm not attracted to her. At all. Can you imagine what they'd say on social media if I was seeing her? They'd destroy us.*

My heart stops, my stomach instantaneously dropping to somewhere in the vicinity of my toes. My mind freezes, with the painful, consuming blankness of the void.

"Oh."

"Ow."

"Wow..."

The phone drops from my hand, forgotten on the floor, and I find myself walking away in a daze.

"Serves me right for looking, I guess."

My tone is bitter, like acid is forcing its way up from my stomach and somehow activating my vocal cords. "At least now I know how he really feels..."

I turn and race up the stairs to my bedroom, which offers considerably less comfort than it did a mere day ago, now that I realize Holly was right, and I was just a pity fuck for him. Or maybe Alex was right about what he said in that first message, and I was just an easy lay. Convenient and willing, just like a groupie.

Obviously, that connection of ours only lets me know what Hunter's feeling when that feeling isn't about me.

I hesitate when I reach the bed and see the sheets still rumpled from multiple rounds of sex last night and this morning.

The image of another bed, warm in the firelight, overlays itself unbidden in my head, and every bit of hard-won confidence, any sense of power, of balance, or rightness, evaporates, like it had all been a dream. A dream turned nightmare.

I throw myself face-first into the bed, where I inhale our mixed scents, then exhale a sigh that becomes a sob before all the air has left my lungs. I pull a pillow over my mouth to dampen the sound, which is too sad even for my own ears.

Dear, sweet girl... I hear that familiar voice in the back of my head, like warm water in a bath, and I sense a gentle hand laid upon my back. Intangible but comforting. But not even Her healing touch can mend my broken heart. Not when it's shattered in a million pieces under the hard boot of Hunter's own words.

It seems he was right. Becoming more than friends was exactly what it took to destroy our friendship.

Chapter 26

The Fall Out

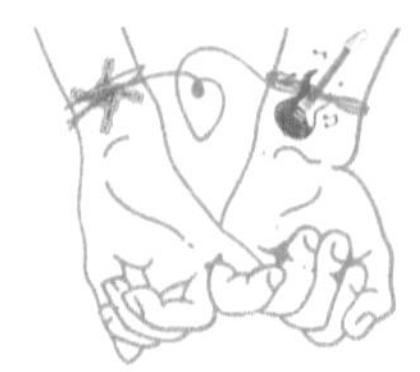

Hunter
Mere hours after that

Brighid has shut me out again. Literally.

By the time I got back to her place tonight, bags of fine food in hand, she had not only removed the Japanese goddess from the porch entirely, she had actually changed the locks on the doors.

To keypad locks. No more keys for me to find, nor to charm her neighbor into giving me. And if tomorrow she miraculously forgave whatever I did and gave me a key code, she could change it to something else an hour later.

And, yes, I tried all the key code possibilities I could think of. Including my birthdate, which has been her standard PIN since she opened her first bank account. Probably too obvious, eh?

I love that she's handy, but knowing she took the time to go out to the hardware store, buy new locks and install them, all before I picked up our dinner — that tells me that whatever set her off this time, I'm going to have to pull out all the stops to get her back.

So, no, she's not responding to my texts, calls, emails, skywriting, plane banners... The lights are *off*, and somebody *is* home. But she won't answer the fracking door! And the neighbor threatened to call the cops if I didn't stop pounding on Brighid's door and shouting her name like it was Stella instead of Brighid.

I gave the nice dragon-lady the lukewarm food, which I had been really looking forward to tasting when I got it but now had no appetite to eat, and thanked her for her patience with a heartsick man.

She clearly took pity on me, because she didn't call the police and even let me sit on her porch swing while I waited for Kier to come pick me up on the Harley he decided to test out while we're here. (And, no, I did not wrap my arms around him to keep myself on. No matter how much he begged me to.) I just couldn't face another Lyft driver right now.

To top it off, I couldn't get hold of Holly, either. Which is concerning.

I was hoping we could work out something that wouldn't result in a nuclear option raining paparazzi on my head like a flock of seagulls on a fresh batch of boardwalk fries.

And now I'm sitting here on the deck at the studio house, waiting for the other shoe to drop. I suspect it's going to be a 5-inch stiletto-heeled pump when it does, and it'll be aimed straight up my ass.

Whatever is coming, I'm prepared to take the hit, so long as Brighid doesn't get hurt.

Well... hurt worse than she is now, which seems like it might be a lot.

"Fuck!" I scream at the sky, wishing Brighid's namesake would just drop down, right here and now, and help me figure this out. "You're a healer, right? Well, why don't you mend this fucked-up, broken-ass disaster that is my life! Fuckin' hell!"

I'm not a violent guy by nature, but I have to say that I punched the side of that house pretty darn hard. It left a not-insignificant dent in the siding. And in my hand. Ow.

"Hunter! What the fuck! Have you lost your damn mind?"
Declan again.

"Maybe a little," I manage through clenched teeth.

"What did you..." His eyes go wide and then black as he sees what caused the impact that apparently got transmitted through an entire huge house.

"Oh, no. Tell me you did not just punch a house with your fretting hand. Your injured fretting hand."

"I did not just punch a house with my injured fretting hand," I mimic back to him, just as requested. "I just punched a house with my *miraculously-healed* fretting hand. Which now appears to possibly be broken."

I kind of lose track of Declan's effusive string of curses, on both the universe and my stupid ass, about five minutes in.

By then, he's gone back inside the house, still cursing, and has brought the rest of the band back with him, which yields even more cursing, just with four additional voices. If it wasn't so dissonant, I'd say we should add it to the next album.

I'm now sitting sideways on a deck chair, holding my busted hand with the not-busted one, which Declan threatened to break, too, before Kieran dragged him back inside. Rhys is calling a Lyft to take us to the hospital.

Alex took one look, shook his head and went back inside.

David's doing his quiet, pensive thing, sitting next to me on the lounge chair.

"So, what happened?"

"I yelled at a goddess and punched a house."

"I see." He pauses, absorbing what I'd said. "Was the goddess Brighid?"

"Yes." I growl. "I mean, no — not *my* Brighid. The actual Irish goddess Brighid."

"I see. And did Brighid — the goddess, not the girl — yell back?"

I know he's got to be thinking I'm nuts.

Dave's smart. Like Brighid (the girl, not the goddess, though she's probably smart, too) -level smart. He's also a year older than me and Declan, even though they were in the same grade in high school. Dave got held back one year when they were younger, and Declan's run the Carter Brothers show ever since, which meant when Declan decided not to go to college so we could do music full-time, David didn't have a lot of choice about going all-in with the band.

Don't get me wrong — Dave really loves music, like breathes it, even more than Declan and I do, and I think he'd have ended up doing the band full-time with us anyway if we'd all gone to college, just four years later. But he'd *really* wanted to go to college. I think he'd wanted to be a marine biologist or something, which is maybe why he's been spending all of his free time here surfing or sitting on the beach. It's just his natural environment. That and being behind a bass guitar.

But, bottom line, David is really smart. And logical. And I've never once since I've known him seen him get emotionally invested in a woman. I'm starting to suspect that one day he'll find a beautiful dolphin swimming next to his surfboard and declare her to be the love of his life.

So, when David asks me if a goddess yelled back at me, I have to stop and think about it for a minute.

Alright... What happens when you yell at a god? I suppose if you piss them off, they might take revenge. That's what all the myths say, at least the ones I've read, which are admittedly mostly Greek and Roman and not Irish. (And "Xena." Don't forget "Xena." Also Greek.) Anyway — I yelled at a goddess who'd just healed my hand. And a minute later that same hand is probably broken.

Oh.

"Sorry," I mouth silently at the sky, fully penitent, because — hey, man, my hand is now broken.

Yeah. Well, you are *stupid.*

It's not Mary Stuart Masterson's voice I hear saying that in my head. It's not even Brighid's — my Brighid's, anyway. The voice is warm, melodious, lilting, deeper than my girl's but decidedly feminine, and maybe even a touch amused.

No. Fucking. Way.

I look over at David to see if he's hearing it, too, and he's just looking at me expectantly. Glancing down at my hand, I realize I never answered his question.

"Yeah. I think She did yell back."

"Interesting." He's quiet for a minute. "This place is... odd," he says, like he can't quite find the word for it. "Why's it called 'Mystic Beach'?"

He knows I grew up here. It's only reasonable that I'd have some kind of answer for him.

"A lot of unexplained stuff has happened around here over the centuries," I tell him, searching my brain for details I haven't thought about in all the time I've been gone. "Shipwrecks, pirates, strange fog and lights sometimes... there was a rumor about a swamp monster... Someone once said they'd spotted a mermaid, but I think that was just made up to attract tourists... Ghosts — the B&B down the road reportedly has a haunted bathtub. Witches — like actual curse-your-ass, cackling witches, not Brighid's Pagan friends and her customers at the shop. Though she did say she's had a lot more customers the last few years..." I shrug. "Why?"

"Just wondering."

His interest seems like a little more than casual touristy curiosity. But I drop it. He isn't dropping a big butterfly net over my head for talking about a goddess and punching a house, so I'm not going to pry into his reasons for calling this town "odd." Even if it's now making *me* curious.

"So, what's up with Brighid? The girl, not the goddess. I'm assuming she's why you're punching houses and yelling at gods," he says after a while.

"I don't know, man. I thought we'd finally gotten ourselves sorted out. And then it all blew up in my face."

I break down and tell him what had happened with Brighid. All of it. Well, most of it. I didn't mention anything about brown dogs or spinning wheels, though after I admitted to yelling at a goddess, I'm not sure I can come off as any crazier. Now I know how Brighid feels...

"She's not even reading my texts. I don't know what else to do. I left there at like three, and by seven, she was shut up in there like it was a castle with a moat full of acid and a dragon guarding her in a tower with no stairs or doors. I don't know what I did, so I can't even try to fix it, even if I could get her to listen to me."

"Women are confusing."

I turn and look at him. I'm not finding that commentary any less "odd" for David than his calm acceptance of my yelling at a goddess or his curiosity about the town.

Like I said — I've never even heard of Dave dating anyone. It's been a decade of one-night stands with the occasional groupie, and nothing more. So, to hear him say women are confusing catches my attention.

"How so?"

"They act like they want you, and then they run. I can't tell if it's because they want you to chase them, or because they think you won't be interested if you don't *have to* chase them, or if they're just genuinely terrified of what would happen if you *did* catch them."

"There's something profound in there, man."

"What?"

"I'm not sure. But there is."

We're quiet for a second.

"If you want her, you're going to have to fight for her."

Now, this almost makes my jaw drop. Dave never stands up for himself, even with Declan. He hates conflict (Brighid says that's a Libra thing, and who am I to argue?), and he doesn't go out of his way to do anything that isn't just falling right into place for him.

So to hear him advising me with such certainty to fight to fix this mess with Brighid is kind of astonishing. And that makes me take it even more seriously.

"I know. I spent too many years fighting what she wanted, and now I've got to fight twice as hard for what we both want to prove to her that I really do want it."

"It took fifteen years to get you here. Are you going to wait another fifteen to fix it?"

"Fuck no."

"Then you need to do something about it. Now."

"I've tried. I can't think what else to do."

"What would prove to her that you love her? You do love her, right?"

"More than anything."

"Then act like it."

He's right. I'm just not sure how I can show Brighid anything when she won't talk to me.

"Car's here," Rhys announces from the doorway to the deck.

"Who's going with me?"

"Yeh big baby," Kier comments from behind Rhys's curly red head. "We got an XL. We're all going."

"Not me," David corrects. "I need to see a lady about a fur coat."

We all look at him like he's the one who's nuts now. It's nice to no longer be the band poster-child for strange behavior. It's the one positive point in my night. Let's just hope that it keeps getting better from here.

CHAPTER 27

DOCTOR DOCTOR

Hunter
Two hours later

"Well, it's definitely broken."

The doctor delivers that unsurprising news while looking at an X-ray image that clearly shows a crack in one of my bones.

"That's the bad news. The good news is that it's just a hairline fracture of the fourth metacarpal — the bone in your hand that leads to the ring finger.

"It's also nicely aligned, so you won't need surgery to make sure it will heal straight, and you should be able to get away with just a fitted brace for a few weeks to stabilize it so it can heal properly."

"I can't play guitar with a brace on my hand."

"No. You can't," the doctor agrees. "You can't play at all for at least three weeks, maybe four. If you do, you're likely to delay the healing, at best, and, at the worst, may exacerbate the break, which is pretty small right now. So don't do it."

Four pairs of eyes swivel to look right at me. Brighid's comments about how I handled my last injury pop into my head, because she had the same look in her eyes when she told me I was too contrary for my own good.

"OK, guys! Geez... I get it!"

"What about the sprain?

That's Declan, who's turned into a cross between a mother-hen and a cranky Rottweiler about the condition of my hand after this second incident.

"What sprain? You didn't mention a sprain, Mr. Graves. And there are no indications of any damage to the ligaments in your hand from tonight's incident. Just the break and some bruising and swelling around the knuckles. You got lucky there."

"Yeah... Lucky," Declan grouses, rolling his eyes.

The doctor is checking my records now, because I really didn't mention the sprain. I'd kind of forgotten about it, since it had been fully healed... before I punched the house.

"This was... ten days ago? Is that right?"

"Yes."

"And, as your friends have suggested, you didn't rest it afterward, as the doctor instructed at that time?"

"I did rest it. Just not as long and as much as recommended."

"I see." He's pulled down his glasses to look at me over the top of the rims. "It must not have been as severe a sprain as the doctor at that time believed," he concludes. "Because if it was, we'd still be seeing signs of ligament damage now, without your recovery instructions being followed."

The guys are all looking at me now.

I shrug.

"I don't know what to tell you, doc. I got a little work done on it by a friend the other day, and..."

"What kind of work?"

"Just a little massage in some warm water."

"That wouldn't have erased signs of a sprain like what was documented here in your chart. I'm sure the other doctor just overestimated the amount of damage. You weren't in pain — before you hit the... the house, was it?"

"Yup, doc — he punched a house," Rhys puts in helpfully.

"No, no pain, doctor. It felt fully healed."

"Then that must be what happened," he declares. Case closed. The other doctor was wrong. And I'm not telling him anything otherwise, especially not in front of the guys.

“**O**K, shithead. You want to tell the rest of us what the fuck is going on with you?”

We're back at the house now, a stiffer brace on my hand and some painkillers making their way through my system, thank however many gods and their mothers are appropriate.

The guys have corralled me on the inside corner of the big sectional in the living room, two on each side of me and the big coffee table preventing my escape. It's an intervention, aMUSEd-style.

So I'm kind of resigned to answering their questions once Declan starts things off. I've already told David most of the story, and he's off doing the thing with the lady and the... coat? Fur coat? Does anybody even make fur coats anymore, and why would David want one?

Not my oceanside circus, not my sea monkey... monkey see, monkey do... do do... de da da da...

(Yes, the painkillers are kicking in.)

They get the same story I told David, minus the yelling-at-divine-beings part. No dog, fabric-string or gloriously see-through nightie, either. I'm saving that part of the story for Bridge. If I can ever get her to talk to me again.

“Dude — you told me hours ago that you were ‘just friends’ with Brighid, despite her being all googley-eyed over you since before I met you. And, I quote, ‘I'm not attracted to her. At all.’”

Alex has a pretty good memory, it seems.

“Yeah, I said that. It was a total lie.”

“What the fuck, man? You had to lie to me about your girl, putting her down like that... and for what?”

“You all haven't exactly been her biggest fans over the years. Megan dumped you after Brighid moved in...”

“Not Brighid's fault. Megan was a jealous bitch who couldn't trust me as far as her scrawny ass could throw me. She clung to me like a barnacle on a boat. The girl was jealous of my fucking keyboards, for god's sake.”

"And how many times did Declan make fun of Brighid for being there for all of our gigs? 'She's your "*biggest*" fan!'"

"Hey — that's true. She *is* your biggest fan. Utterly devoted," Declan says in his defense.

"That wasn't a reference to her size?"

"I take offense at that, Hunt. I may be a dick, but I'm not so big of a dick that I'd make fat jokes at someone's expense. Except Rhys. All that time spent sitting on his throne, he's getting a little 'wide load' back there."

"Hey! I'm just big-boned. Really. Wanna see?" Rhys starts unbuttoning his jeans, until Alex smacks him upside the head.

"And then there was that joke at the release party about her not fitting in that got me in such hot water with her that she didn't speak to me for two years! Two fucking years, Declan!"

"OK, fine. I'll own that one. But I thought you liked her quirkiness!"

He's right — I do. And I did then, too. But I was too drunk, on fame and beer, that night to think of it that way. I'd been so nervous about Bridge finally coming to New York, how she'd be perceived, whether she'd end up on the pages of the tabloids with the haters coming for her... I'd almost decided not to invite her. I'd procrastinated about putting her on the invitation list for so long that she wasn't even on the version security had that night, even though I'd invited her a week beforehand. It might have seemed from the outside like I was embarrassed by her, that she didn't look like a model or whatever, but I just didn't want to risk her getting bullied. Not again. And especially not on that kind of scale. But I handled it badly. Not for the first time, and not for the last. She deserved better. She always had.

"It didn't seem like such an insult when I was saying it," Declan adds.

I can see how he'd say that. Declan gets stuck in his own perceptions sometimes and forgets that how he's perceived by others isn't always the same as it looks from inside his own head. I have that problem, too, sometimes. I'm just not perceived as nearly as much of a dick. Most of the time. And he wasn't even the only one who came off like a dick that night. That it was more than just Declan was what had really hurt Bridge.

"And then David joined in..."

"He's already explained that to you — he was just answering my question about how the song went. He didn't mean anything by it, and he's apologized to Brighid. But you're the one who finished it for him."

Yeah. And I paid the price for that one. Two years without Bridge. Though I can't deny now that the wake-up call she gave me as a result had made me a better person. A far better person than the one I had been turning into.

"Seriously, Hunter — Bridge is awesome!" Declan continues. "So she's a little curvier than average. Have you seen those eyes? And those boobs are a perfect handful... and—"

"Hey! That's my girlfriend you're talking about!"

"Not at the moment, she's not."

Suddenly, the painkillers aren't doing enough. It's not just my hand that's hurting.

"My man, I'm not sure why you think we don't like Brighid — she's got a great name, just to start," Kier puts in with a smile. "That Brighid's cross she wears is like a postcard from home, and the girl has her cúpla focal!"

"And she's got great taste in movies," Rhys adds. "She can quote Star Wars with the best of them, and she's a Trekkie, too. Curse your betrayal of that awesome girl, Hunt."

Was that it? Was *I* the one to betray her by letting her think the guys saw her as an unwelcome hanger-on? A bumped-up groupie I just didn't want to sleep with? Had I treated her like that, even unconsciously?

The repeated insistence that we were "just friends," the perhaps-too-quick corrections when people assumed she was my girlfriend or wife — had that undermined her self-esteem even more than the cruel comments in high school and from the grown-up mean-girl squad that included Holly?

"What I don't get, Hunter, is why you refused to go there with her," Alex says. "I mean, fine, if you're not attracted to her, fine, but I've seen the way you look at her — the way you've *always* looked at her. Like she hung the moon in the sky and then brought it down to use as a spotlight for you on stage. She's a gift, man, a treasure, and I thought you saw that. So why have you been fighting this so hard up until we got here? It's a long time to leave an amazing girl like that out in the arctic cold."

"It's not her, alright?! It's me!"

I shout that a bit louder than necessary, and in the dead silence that instantly falls across the whole room, I realize that this is the truth I should have told these chosen brothers of mine, and should have told them long ago.

"I've been trying to protect her from *me*," I say quietly. "She's been my best friend since we were 6, and I didn't want to hurt her and fuck up that one good, pure thing in my life, like my old man did with my mother. He couldn't keep his dick in his pants, and Mom knew it but still tolerated it, even when he was cruel to her. Until the day I walked in on him and his girlfriend-du-jour, and then, when she called him out on it, he tore her down so badly that, while I was hiding out at Brighid's, licking my own wounds, she killed herself."

The guys are silent. They knew my mom was dead. They knew I'd fallen out with my dad right after that. David and Declan knew some of the story, but not that Mom had killed herself and not why.

"Wow, man. That's a heavy thing to be carrying around all these years. I'm sorry..." Declan eventually says, with a chorus of nods from the others. "But I'm not sure why you think that means you and Brighid can't be together, that you'd hurt her. You're a good guy. Even when it was 'groupies galore' for us in the early days, you were pretty respectful. You didn't treat them like just a piece of ass. I can't say I've done the same," he admits, seeming for the first time since that night in the hotel in O.C. like maybe he regrets that. "And you may not have limited yourself to a single girlfriend, but you treated them like real girlfriends and not just pretty bed-warmers. That right there makes you a decent human being."

"And it seems to me like you've gone out of your way to protect Brighid, including from yourself — which I think is totally unnecessary," says Alex. "She's good for you. And you're a good guy. We've seen the way she looks at you, sure. And I may tease you both about that more than I should, but at least a little part of that is because, frankly, I'm jealous, man. You've got a good thing in your grasp, and it's something I'm not sure I'll ever have."

"Look — if you don't believe us, believe Brighid," Kier suggests. "Sure, she's not speaking to you right now, but she *has* been speaking to you for years — look back at what she's said. Read her texts to you, her emails. She wouldn't be this devoted to the guy you're afraid of becoming. Figure out why she feels that way."

"And don't just look at *her* messages — look at what you've said *about* Brighid, to us and to whoever else you've talked to about her," Alex adds.

He pulls out his phone and starts reading some of the things I've said about Bridge before today's stupid attempt to lead him astray.

"'Brighid wants to come up to visit. I miss her.'"

"'Can't go out tonight. Movie night with Brighid. We've been doing that since we were kids. I've missed too many lately.'"

"'I'll be there in an hour or two. Too tired. Need more sleep. Crashed at Brighid's and stayed up all night talking.'"

"'Do me a favor and distract Holly. I need to go call Brighid and clear my head, and Holly will just be a bitch about it.' — that should have given you a heads-up right there about who you should be with."

"Here: 'Brighid's my best friend, and always has been, and I can't lose her.' That was the other day, when you thought she was done with you the first time this week."

"Seriously man — y'all gotta get your drama down to a workable level," Rhys puts in, shaking his head. This, coming from the guy we call "The Madman." Alex smacks him on the back of the head again. "Ow! What? I was just being honest!"

"And here's where you were talking early on about not being attracted to her. How much in denial were you at that point? Idiot." Alex shakes his head at me. "The girl is hot, Hunter. So she doesn't look like Holly — we know how little appearance says about what's inside with that cankerous bitch. Brighid's solid gold, inside and out. She's good for you, and you'd be damn lucky to have her, and I told her so."

My jaw drops.

"You did what? When was this?"

"Shortly after we got here. When she was hanging around at the TV shoot and making moon eyes at you whenever your back was turned. I felt sorry for her, and I told her it was a shame that you were being such an idiot. She said it was a sore subject between the two of you and asked me not to mention it to you because she didn't want to upset you again. I agreed not to, but we've all seen how happy you are with her around, minus this drama. We all knew you had a thing for her. You were the only one denying it. And it seems like you were the only one who bought that bill of goods you were selling."

"Until now."

I take Alex's phone out of his hand to reread that message I had sent him months ago, but the messages have refreshed and only the most recent few are on the screen. But there it is again — me telling him I'm not attracted to Brighid.

It was a lie. It's always been a lie, even if today was the first time I said it that I wasn't also trying to persuade myself that it was true.

Because today I knew it wasn't true and had never been. I'd always been attracted to her. Heck, even at 13, 15, my dick knew what it wanted. It had just taken me this long to realize it, and all that went along with it.

I really *am* stupid. *Really* stupid.

I look again at today's false-ass text to Alex, and it's only then that I spot it — the "Read" time stamps on those last couple texts.

It wasn't right before I texted Alex back from my new phone to confirm they hadn't been received while Brighid was still working on the new phone. It was before that, when Brighid would almost certainly have been sitting right next to that phone to babysit the restore process.

When the messages could have displayed both on my old phone, sent via the phone network, and on my new phone, connected to Brighid's Wi-Fi and maybe right in her hand.

"Mother of twelve gods!"

CHAPTER 28

NIGHT OF THE HUNTER

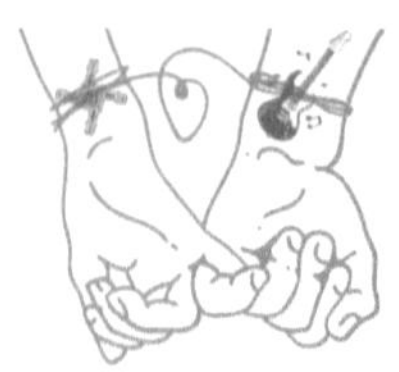

Hunter
The next day

I wanted to run out of the house and straight over to Brighid's the moment I realized what had happened — that she'd read my message to Alex saying that I wasn't attracted to her, at all.

Which I'd written not long after we'd had sex for the fifth time in twenty-four hours.

Have I said I'm an asshole? Even when I'm not trying to be, I manage it. And the guys wonder why I say I'm not good enough for her...

I say I *wanted* to go over to Brighid's. Obviously, I didn't do that.

First, I couldn't think what would have gotten her to listen to me when she'd already made it clear she wasn't hearing a word I said. Not that I blame her. After what she'd read coming from my own damn hands, she had to have been feeling used.

Especially when Alex had jokingly referred to her as "easy pickings" in his less-than-tactful effort to encourage me to give her a shot.

I could see the picture that had been formed in her head:

The guys in the band all think she's ridiculous and desperate because she's been so transparently interested in me for so long, without her feelings being requited.

Holly was cruel to her, lording it over her in public as the model girlfriend (literally), and made a huge effort to humiliate her on national television, suggesting that I was somehow out of Brighid's league.

And, worst of all, I've been ducking her affections for years, stopped telling her I loved her to avoid encouraging her, dated women who looked nothing like her, and had Alex calling her "easy" almost exactly at the point where I, the flirty rockstar, began a sexual marathon with her, which was only shortly after I'd accidentally kissed her for the first time and had gotten all kinds of hard from doing it.

Yeah. It wasn't a pretty picture. At all.

And that was just the first reason I didn't immediately go see her.

The second was that, well, I had a painfully broken hand and was on heavy painkillers. By the time I'd realized what had happened with the texts, I was already a little loopy. And within half an hour, I was unconscious to the point where, during the night, I fell off the sofa where the guys had left me to sleep, and I spent the rest of the night passed out on the floor with the brace making indentations in my forehead. I was just lucky I hadn't landed on top of it.

And, third — I still hadn't been able to get hold of Holly, and my concern about that had ramped up exponentially. I still wanted to get Holly taken care of before I went to Brighid so I could finally come clean to her about everything, clear up the misunderstandings and tell her — in just those words — that I loved her, that I was *in love* with her, and that I wasn't letting Holly, or anyone or anything, get in the way of us being together, as a couple now, not just friends.

For a woman whose entire existence revolved around trying to get people to pay attention to her, and who had my balls in a vice with her little video, Holly was being very firm about avoiding me. I had a bad feeling about this.

Which turned out to be Brighid-level prescient.

"Hunter! Hunt! Wake up! Hunt! Come on, man. Wake the fuck up!"

I had just started to open my eyes when a torrent of cold water rains down on me from above. No, I hadn't rolled out onto the deck in my drugged sleep and into the rain. Rhys had just dumped a big cup of cold water on my head.

"What the fuck, man? What the hell was that about?"

"Dude — You've gone viral!"

"What? What for? A broken hand?"

"Small potatoes, my man. No one cares about your hand. Well, except for Declan, and the rest of us, to a slightly less disturbing degree."

"Then why am I viral?"

"Someone leaked footage from your reality show — and Holly's shared it over and over again on all her channels, calling you a cheater, liar, breaker of hearts, deviant and rockstar slumming it with…"

He pauses and looks at me nervously. Totally not like Rhys.

"Spit it out, Rhys…"

"'A frumpy, fat hippie-chick Stevie Nicks-wannabe who's desperate to get a multi-millionaire rockstar between her legs and trap him with a kid that's probably not even his.' Those are Holly's words, not mine," he warns with a supplicating gesture that suggests I might hit *him* instead of the house this time.

"Let me see it."

He hands over his phone, which has Holly's Twitter feed pulled up, and he's right. That's exactly what she's said, word for word, across six tweets in the last five hours.

And my heart splits in half and drops to the floor like the petals of a dying flower.

There's no way I can get Brighid back after this. She'll never forgive me for letting Holly humiliate her with footage I'd told her had been erased, especially when she already thought I'd made a fool of her and used her for easy sex. After 25 years of being best friends.

That's it. Game over. I've lost her. I can forget building a relationship with her. She's never going to speak to me again. And I'm going to spend the rest of my life missing her friendship and knowing I'll never find another woman I can love like I do her.

Rhys looks at me, clearly uncomfortable now that the adrenaline of his find has waned.

"Sorry, man."

He takes his phone, claps me on the back in sympathy and heads off down the hallway, uncharacteristically quiet.

My phone drops out of sleep mode at that precise moment and I'm instantly deluged with notifications — Twitter,

Facebook, Instagram, TikTok (which I never even fucking use), email, texts, Messenger, calls and voicemail... if it exists and I have an account, I've got dozens... hundreds... thousands of notifications.

Crap.

The first thing I do is check to see if I have any notifications from Brighid. Anything at all. She's on my VIP list, so I can see quickly that there's nothing. Not a word.

I am unsurprised.

I check our text thread and discover that the last two texts I sent to her, before I realized that she'd seen those texts between me and Alex — they weren't even marked as delivered.

I decide to try calling her, knowing it's a long shot, and, sure enough, not only does she not answer, my call is shunted straight to voicemail.

She's blocked my number.

Things just keep getting better and better.

A new text message comes in.

Holly: *I warned you not to go near that roly-poly playmate of yours. I hope she enjoys her fifteen minutes of infamy.*

Holly: *And you make sure to enjoy your new reputation as the scumbag rocker who cheated on one of the most popular women on the internet with some small-town gold-digger who finds it easier to suck you off in public than walk across a room in heels.*

The phone beeps again. It's a photo this time. Taken from across the street from Brighid's shop, with a long lens. In it, Brighid and I are pressed together from lips to hips, lost in each other, and Brighid's hand is clearly on the button on the waistband of my shorts.

Well, there you go.

Seems I was wrong. Holly was having me watched. And I led her, and her photographer, straight to Brighid's door.

Can this day get any better?

And to answer that question, the Twitter app pings to tell me I've been tagged again.

Holly has just posted the photo to her feed.

#TheHunter caught on camera, cheating with #smalltownslut. We are #notaMUSEd!

And #smalltownslut is already trending. Well, to be fair, so am I. And Holly. And aMUSEd.

Which reminds me... I'm going to have to deal with the negative PR this is creating for the band and the label, too. Oh, boy!

Well, at least it will keep me busy so I'm not fixating on things with Brighid. Instead, it's going to be my sole mission in life to fix things *for* Brighid. And I actually have an idea how to do that.

CHAPTER 29

S.L.U.T.

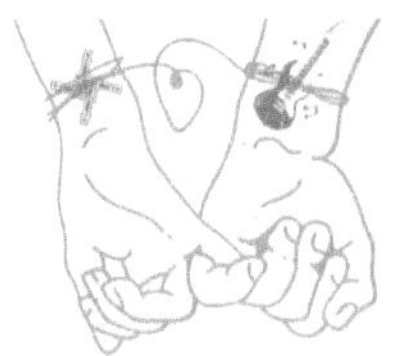

~~Brighid~~ #smalltownslut

"Thanks for stopping by, Mrs. Lowell!"

"Thank *you*! I appreciate you opening up early for me, before my Zumba class."

"Happy to be of help! And share the word — I'm going to be doing a clearance sale on my incense blends. So if people want anything specific, they should come in now, before the crowds arrive!"

Mrs. Lowell is so sweet. She reminds me of my grandma, just a little more... witchy.

"Uh, Brighid — I think the crowds have already arrived!"

"What?"

Curious, I walk over to the front door, where Mrs. Lowell is looking out through the glass with an expression of... alarm?

There's a crowd gathered on the sidewalk, and it's not the usual line running out the bakery door early on a Friday morning in the summer.

"What on earth?" I ask, incredulous, as I unlock and push open the door to see what's going on.

"Brighid! Brighid! How's it feel to be the other woman?"

"Brighid! Can you comment on that kiss?"

"Are you really pregnant? Is it Hunter's?"

I'm instantly blinded by camera flashes and nearly deafened by the cacophony of what seems like several dozen reporters?

paparazzi? locusts? shouting at me all at once. I pull the door shut and relock it before one of them can slide their foot into the doorway.

"Is that because of your young man from the other day?" Mrs. Lowell asks gently.

I heave a sigh.

"I would think so, Mrs. Lowell. I'm not sure what else it would be about."

"He's handsome, that young man of yours... what's his name? He has a nice smile."

"He's Hunter Graves, Mrs. Lowell. He grew up here."

"Oh, well, that's nice, dear. It's always nice to have old friends come home to visit."

I'm tempted to argue with her. I decide not to. No need to spread any more of my personal business around when, clearly, that's already been done for me.

"Mrs. Lowell, I'm going to let you out the back. I'll let Callie know you're coming to her kitchen door, and she'll let you out through the main entrance."

"Thank you, dear. Are you sure you don't want to come with me?"

"I'll be along shortly, Mrs. Lowell. I have to make a few calls first, though. Be safe, and I'll see you next week."

"You certainly will, Brighid, dear. Tell that handsome Hunter he needs to take better care of his friends."

"I will, Mrs. Lowell. The next time I talk to him."

I open the back door carefully, making sure there's no reporters, photographers or other reptiles lurking out there.

Mrs. Lowell hurries along toward Callie's café, while I call to ask my neighbor, and sometimes customer, to let Mrs. Lowell out where she won't be mobbed.

"Sorry for the inconvenience, Cal — I'm a little swamped over here."

"I was wondering what the crowd was about. Susie's doughnuts are good, but they're not *that* good."

I chuckle, despite the downward progression of my mood.

"I'll probably need an escape route myself shortly. I'll do the special knock on your door so you'll know it's me. I don't trust these vultures not to try to pump you for information."

"I have no interest in talking to reporters. Especially not about rockstars," she says, and the tone of her voice tells me there's a story there. I'll have to ask her later.

After I hang up, I grab a large weaving from the wall display and some packing tape and I tape the weaving up over the glass door, making sure to stay behind it the whole time. I'm not going to make this easy for them.

Then I call Molly.

"Don't come in today, Mol. We're going to be closed. I'll pay you for the time you were supposed to work."

"What's going on?"

"I need to have a pest-control company come in and remove some unwelcome guests."

"Mice? We've never had any mice in the shop."

"No. Pests of the human variety, unfortunately. Sorry about this, Mol. And if you can do me another favor — don't talk to anyone who asks about me, my personal life or the shop."

"I wouldn't anyway. But what's going on?"

"No good deed goes unpunished. Especially in the social media age."

"OK. Good luck. Let me know if there's anything I can do to help."

Next I call the Mystic Beacon.

"Aurora Carmichael, please."

"Hold just a moment."

Ten seconds later: "Aurora Carmichael — how may I help you?"

"Rory? It's Brighid down at Dream Weaver. I think I need a favor."

"I'll just bet you do, you minx, you..." she replies with a chuckle. "How long have you and the local rockstar been an item?"

"We're not," I tell her definitively. "We *were* childhood friends. Bottom line, I did someone a favor the other day, and it's come back to bite me. And not in a good way."

Rory laughs heartily. It's nice to hear. She's had a loss recently, though I don't know the details. But Lyric said it was a devastating one.

"What can I do to help you out?"

"I'm swamped with paparazzi and reporters and I don't know who else down here at the shop. I can't even get out the front door. Do you have any ideas?"

"Well, a couple, actually. One short-term and one for the longer term. Give me a few minutes. I'll call you back."

I peek around the merchandise in the front window, and the crowd is still gathered there, now chatting amongst themselves. A few latecomers are joining them, and I heave a big sigh. One of the newcomers, a photographer, answers his loudly-ringing cell phone and, just as loudly, says, "They're where? ... The one in Ocean City? She was supposed to be here at the shop. ... Headed to the conference center? ... I'll get on the road right now. Maybe I can even beat them there. Thanks for the heads-up. I could get an exclusive out of this."

He takes off back the way he came, and the other photographers and reporters rush to follow him. Two minutes later, the sidewalk in front of my shop is clear.

Well, huh. How about that...

I write a "Family Emergency, Closed until further notice" sign on a piece of paper and tape it below the regular "Closed" sign. I check the sidewalk to make sure the coast is clear. Wow. Rory's good.

My phone rings. I check to make sure it's a number I recognize — and that it's not Hunter. Then I remember that I blocked his number after yesterday's humiliation. So, no, not Hunter, regardless. At all.

It's the Mystic Beacon.

"Whatever you did, you rock, lady!"

"Happy to help. So — that's your short-term problem solved. Over the longer term, I can get the... less savory... members of my profession off your back. But it may require a bit more exposure than you'd like to have."

"What do you have in mind?

"An exclusive interview. With me. You — and your 'childhood friend,' if you can get him to cooperate."

"Hunter won't be doing any interviews with me."

"Are you sure? It's usually best to get ahead of the story, rather than letting people speculate and gossip."

"There is no story."

She sighs.

"I hear you... but I can tell you that Holly's made sure there *is* a story, whether it's true or not, whether you're actually part of it or not. The best way to deal with that kind of thing is to give the public your own take. They're more likely to believe something coming directly from the subject and published in a legitimate news source than from social media."

"I appreciate the advice. But I will not be doing any interviews with Hunter."

"OK. Will you let me interview you solo, then? Tell your side, give an official response to her allegations?"

"I haven't even seen the allegations yet. The reporters outside said something about the kiss, which I presume means the video from the reality show got leaked, even though I was promised it had been destroyed. They also asked me about being 'the other woman,' so I presume Holly's framed herself as the wronged girlfriend and me as the harlot who's stolen her rockstar?"

"In a nutshell."

"And they asked about a pregnancy, so I'm guessing Holly suggested that I'm pregnant and/or trying to trap Hunter by getting pregnant."

"You're three-for-three. Frankly, I'm pretty pissed off that Holly went straight for body-shaming and slut-shaming. The only prejudice she missed was pointing out that you're a witch."

"Not everyone knows that, so I'd like to keep it on the QT if we can. My tarot readings aren't widely advertised, and even then, it's not inherently a witchy or Pagan thing. I'm not sure Holly even realizes I'm either of those things."

"If she did, she might have reconsidered the wisdom of coming after you at all."

"Truth. She'll get what she's due on the gods' own timetable."

"If I can help out a little with the 'avenging hand-of-god' thing, let me know. My sense of honor gets bent out of shape when people use the media for their own personal vendettas and some of my 'peers' cooperate."

"No kidding. I'll let you know."

"In the meantime..."

"I can give you an interview tomorrow."

"We can do it over the phone, or I can come see you at the shop or at home."

"I'll see how things are going tomorrow and let you know. That OK?"

"Works for me. We go to press on the next print edition on Monday. But with this kind of national attention, it's probably better for both of us to get it online ASAP."

"I'll have to deal with the fallout from all of this first. But I can do the interview tomorrow."

"I'll do a quick turnaround and get it up on the website tomorrow night. Once the tabloids' potential for a first exclusive is gone, they'll start looking for something else that could be a big payday. At that point, it won't be you."

"I can only hope."

"Call my cell when you're ready to talk. On the record or off, Brighid — you've been a good friend to Lyric, and I really appreciate that. You deserve better than this invasion of your privacy."

CHAPTER 30

YOU'VE GOT TO HIDE YOUR LOVE AWAY

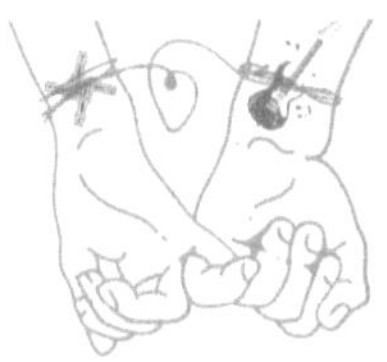

Brighid #smalltownslut

I arrive home to find three photographers in front of my house. I don't stop — I pull around the back of the block and park in my neighbor's driveway. I get permission to leave the car there and go across the back yard to my house.

I blame Hunter for this. He promised this was taken care of. Now, even though it sounds nothing like the Hunter I know, I have to wonder if he and Holly planned this all along. It certainly sounds like the kind of PR stunt she'd go for, and maybe his label... Or maybe he'd just pissed her off and he's not nearly as persuasive as he thinks he is.

Either way, my whole life has been disrupted by this tabloid nonsense, and I am not a happy witch. Especially when it's messing with my business. I can afford to close the shop for a couple days. Beyond that... I may have to move Molly to full-time and hire someone else to help her so I'm not in the shop until after this craziness dies down.

I can stay home and spin and weave, work on my incense blends, manage inventory... My tarot, counseling and other specialized clients will have to do without, though. And while I can still let the circle members gather there after-hours, I won't be able to facilitate. Amber is still recovering from her injuries and avoiding going out except to her shop, so that leaves Lyric, or maybe Siobhan, to lead in my absence. And Lyric has other responsibilities, while Siobhan is a Druid, so her rituals and perspectives are a little different from what we usually do. But we're an eclectic group. We'll figure it out.

In my head, I'm glaring at Hunter. I can't believe my best friend of 25 years has put me in this position. I can't believe he'd treat me with such disrespect as he did when he decided to sleep with me.

"Easy pickings?" Wow. I'm only easy when I've already decided I want a guy. It hasn't really worked out for me, but I'm a modern woman with a healthy libido, and I'm not going to let Alex, Hunter, Holly or anyone else label me a slut just because I fell in love with a guy at 15 and never fell out of love with him.

Until the world's worst wake-up call showed me that maybe he wasn't who I thought he was. *At all.*

That phrase is going to be stuck in my head in perpetuity.

I grab the makings of a salad and enough crackers, cheese and fruit for a decent cheese tray, and I take the whole mess upstairs, where I can sit in the dark and not have to worry about anyone knowing I'm home.

I couldn't bring myself to wash the sheets on the bed last night. I gave myself one last night with Hunter's scent around me…

Wow, even thinking of it like that hurts. How many times have we slept in the same bed since we were kids? Too many to count. Probably half the nights of my life I either slept with Hunter next to me or with his scent lingering on my sheets from the last time. Not having that ever again carves a deep hole in what little is left of my heart.

But it's time to let go of that past, as illusory as it was. So I strip the sheets off the bed and put on a clean set in my favorite shade of violet. Mom said they matched my eyes. This was the set she gave me the last Christmas I spent at home before she died.

I don't know what Mom would have thought of the pickle I've gotten myself into by trusting Hunter. She always adored him, nearly as much as I did.

I'm not going to ponder my father's opinion of Hunter. He formed that when Hunter was 15 and had lost his mother, and had all but been abandoned by his father.

I wonder now if Hunter's path was shaped by his father's in ways that he didn't even realize — if what seems now to have been his well-hidden attitude toward me was anything like what caused his father to treat his mother with such disrespect.

Hunter always said that he'd do anything to avoid being like his father, and I think he meant that. But sometimes even the patterns we set out to avoid following still leave their imprint on our lives. And those of the people around us.

I consider running a load of laundry tonight, just so I can get those sheets clean. But I don't want to risk being seen in the laundry room by the back porch. And when I think about actually sticking the sheets in the wash, I'm hit by such a wave of melancholy that I just pick them up off the floor and dump them in the back of my closet.

I consider taking a bath, or spinning, or maybe watching a movie, but all of those things now remind me of Hunter.

The one thing I haven't done is look at the social media posts that have turned my life upside down today. Thanks to Rory and the paparazzi, I already have an idea what they say. But this is a step I need to get over with if I'm going to move forward and if I'm going to be ready to answer Rory's questions tomorrow.

I check my email first, discovering a bunch of emails from addresses I've never seen before, many of them with unflattering subject lines. Great! I don't even open those. Select. Move to Junk.

Kara and Maire have both emailed from D.C. to express their outrage with Holly and ask how I'm doing. Since I can't honestly answer that until I finally check social media, that's what I do next. I start with Holly Harwood's Twitter feed, which now has 11.3 million followers. I'm pretty sure it was substantially less a few days ago.

It's a shock seeing the things she said about me, and about Hunter. I still feel that deep need to protect him, but it's even less my place now than it was a few weeks ago. I lament the meanness he's being subjected to but release my need to actively do something about it. I won't comment on her posts. I don't want my personal social media accounts going viral, so I lock down my privacy settings. Already I've had a few friend requests from total strangers. How they even found my accounts, I don't know. Maybe mutual friends.

I see Holly has the #smalltownslut hashtag trending. Cute. I'm not going to let that one bother me, though. Anyone who knows me knows I'm anything but popular with men, and, moreover,

I own my sexuality and I refuse to have myself or anyone else judged by what they do in the privacy of their bedrooms.

Oh, but wait! Holly has a photo of me and Hunter caught in the act — of me being slutty, apparently. A passionate kiss and my hand poised to unbutton his shorts. So, not the privacy of the bedroom. Nevermind that that was as far as it got there. She must have had someone with a long lens following Hunter around, and she got the goods on her boyfriend and his mistress. Good for her.

Don't read the comments. It's always good advice, and I want to follow it, but curiosity gets the better of me. It's about what I expected. Lots of her followers dragging me for my weight, my clothes, my alleged behavior.

What the hell does he see in that fat cow?

We're here for you, Hols! Stand up for what's right!

She can't even walk across the room without falling on her fat face! LOL

I thought his hand was broken, not his eyes!

That one got me shaking my head. A sprained hand that was healed days ago, but the word had already gotten out that it was broken, thanks to Holly and her misinformation machine.

Look at his face when he realized who he kissed! Priceless! ROFLMAO

I still had that particular image stuck in my head, so I can see how it made an impression. I should have listened to my instincts and just accepted that the idea of being with me horrified him. Instead, he'd felt sorry for me and decided to make up for it with sex he didn't even want to have, apparently. I wish he'd just stuck with honest horror. Pity cloaked in passion had left a bitter taste in my mouth.

I'd have his baby in a heartbeat. #cantblameabiggirlfortrying

There is a theme starting up...

That plus-sized Cinderella sure made a quick exit #biggirlsdontcry

Did the house shake when she ran for it? #biggirlrunning #thunderthighs

Did Hunter get his hand crushed under all that blubber? #whalewatching #reallydangerouscurves

Where'd he find this super-sized Stevie wannabe? #reallyheavymetal

(For the record, I prefer Lindsey Buckingham, despite my chosen clothing aesthetic and general witchiness. And Stevie's not even a witch, anyway!)

I lose count of the green-faced and puking emojis, the elephants and rhinos, cows and whales, pigs and hippos, the high heels, screams, thumbs-downs and peaches. Who knew there were so many ways to call someone fat, ugly, repulsive and a general failure to live up to the standards of modern beauty?

I see just one comment that makes me feel better.

I'd do her! #ilikebigbutts #nolie

My butt isn't particularly large, but apparently it is still a plus for someone with very specific tastes.

On that note, I'm ready to call it a night. But I realize that I never actually watched the leaked video. I take a full minute to decide whether I want to, whether I can without falling apart. There's a warm presence behind me, and the counterpart to that nasty little shove Holly gave me that day — a firm pressure forward, with an unspoken promise of support.

So I click the play button.

Whoever released this video cut down the video to show just a few moments of the other three kisses and the model-perfect women delivering them. Holly was featured more prominently, of course.

Then, the comic relief: me.

I watch myself, in uncomfortable shoes, my skirt hiked up higher than I would even in a flash flood, makeup disguising the handful of freckles across my nose and making me feel like I'm watching a stranger. I blush when the woman on the screen trips and wobbles while crossing the room.

But then I see Hunter as the camera picks up her slow path toward him. Handsome as ever, his broad shoulders filling out the suit jacket I've so rarely seen him wear, his ink hidden under its sleeves, the tie I know he hates and will take off the second the cameras stop rolling, the loafers he'll swap for Chucks or Docs, or bare feet, at the first possible moment...

His dark gold hair is tamed from its stage persona but still styled beyond how I'm used to seeing him — rumpled at 4 a.m., sticking up in odd directions as he lays his head in my lap while we watch TV, slicked back as he pops up out of the ocean after an oncoming wave makes us both dive deep, falling into his eyes as he's bent over his guitar...

Those eyes, so unbelievably green, are hidden behind the blindfold, but memory supplies their appearance in perfect detail... playful as he runs across the playground, sleepy as he crashes in my bed at 13, drowning in sorrow with the loss of his mother, begging for the comfort and understanding I'm so willing to give him when his father rejects him, scary intense as he looks in my eyes and both of us are overwhelmed with that connection, filled with joy and passion as he plays a new song, twinkling with mirth as he pretends he didn't shoot that straw wrapper at me in a restaurant...

And laced together in front of him, his strong, gentle, sensitive, callused hands, which in a smaller form held mine as I crossed the low balance beam during P.E., handed me my birthday presents for every birthday from 6 through 17, that spooned up my chocolate mousse like it was ambrosia from the gods, that wrapped around my waist as we slept peacefully together at 14 and clenched as he slept so fitfully at 15 with his mother gone, until I kissed his forehead and he settled once more into peaceful slumber.

The same hands that just three days ago had caressed my shoulders, traced the curves of my breasts and played my body, inside and out, like an instrument he was born to make sing, and sing it did.

And now, as I watch that awkward woman reach for that extraordinarily perfect man, I see the lips I'd longed to kiss for nearly two decades, sensuous and supple, capable of beatific smiles and heartbreaking frowns, sweet and innocent moments pressed to my forehead or my hair, and the far-from-innocent ones just days ago, when they sucked at my nipples, brushed across my breasts, slid up my spine, found that little spot between my neck and collarbone, smiled wickedly as they dropped from breast to belly and then below, before kissing my lower lips like they were desperately needed sustenance, sucking my clit into his mouth, eating me until I cried out in ecstasy and lapping up my juices like he'd never get enough.

I see that man respond to the most tentative kiss from that woman, and I see them both instantly come alive, feasting on each other with a need and a passion neither of them seemed to expect, electricity zapping between them in a palpable way as the cameras rolled and people watched, and yet neither of them seems aware that anyone else exists in the entire universe, because they have everything they could ever need or want right there, wrapped in their arms.

And I look as that man inhales her scent and instantly recognizes it, pulling off the blindfold. And in his bright green eyes, I see not horror, but fear.

And those eyes, full of fear, call out to me, as they always have, to provide that man with safety, shelter, comfort, ease… and love — unconditional love.

I can feel a light growing behind me, a flickering flame, warm and comforting, the light of a cozy fireplace reflected in soft brown eyes, the gentle illumination of a candle across the white sheets of a bed, the play of lantern-light on a penny whistle and of a campfire on a green guitar, of sunlight on a spinning wheel, moonlight on skin, and the light of love in that man's eyes as he looks into the eyes of that woman and smiles.

And I realize that Hunter isn't the only one who's been very, very stupid.

CHAPTER 31

SECRET OKTOBER

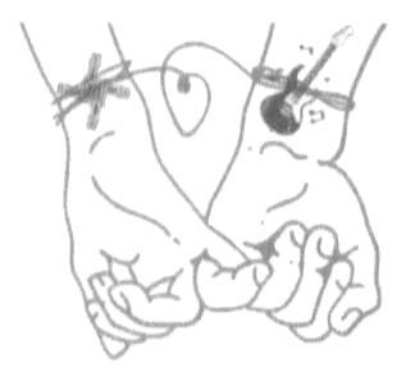

Hunter
The next day

I'm getting my cardio today by pacing back and forth in the small office off the meeting room at the local library.

Weird place for me to be getting in my 10,000 steps, right? Actually, I've probably hit 25,000 at this point.

I haven't paced nervously before a performance since I was 19 and we had our first show in front of an audience of more than 20,000 people.

But this is going to be the most important performance of my life. Today, I set the record straight on what happened that day at the shoot, my relationships with Holly and Brighid, and how it came to be that I am now reviled as a liar, a cheater and a ravisher of curvy women.

OK — that last part isn't true. Holly seems to think that one photo of Brighid with her hands on my waistband, taken from the other side of a closed door, paints Brighid as a slut. So, it's Brighid who's taken the bulk of the indignation over our little bit of not-even-semi-public foreplay.

Seriously — you see worse in a PG-13 movie airing on a broadcast network at 8 p.m. on a Friday night. I've watched more graphic sex scenes with Brighid and not even gotten hard.

OK — that's a lie, too. I totally got hard. See — I really am a liar. Just a bad one. But at least I'm not lying to myself anymore.

I really don't know how Holly has managed to stoke righteous indignation in her followers over a kiss and the placement of a hand on the outside of my clothing. Puritan revival? PMRC back from the dead and taking aim at aMUSEd? The monthly meeting of the Tight-Ass Club?

But she has.

Personally, I'm determined to think of it as me ravishing the gloriously delicious Brighid in her place of business because she is simply irresistible. (Now that I've admitted it, that's becoming one of my favorite things to say. I'm actually thinking of making it into a song.) But if anyone's slutty here, it's me, and I'll own that.

I spent most of yesterday working with Billy, the rest of the band, the bulk of the Siren's Song PR team, our hardworking aMUSEd social media staff, some of the best crisis-management consultants on the planet, and even Marina Matthews herself, to draft a strategy and a statement to fix this mess I've created.

Brighid would be proud of me.

OK, no — she'd be irritated and probably pissed at me. Because I'm being my usual contrary self. Tell me to do something and I'm likely to do the opposite just to see what happens.

The consensus from the experts was that I should make a joke about the video to lighten up the context, acknowledge that I'd broken things off with Holly and she had every right to be upset, request privacy for myself and Brighid as we explored our new relationship, and apologize for having not ensured we couldn't be seen by a paparazzo with a 600mm lens. The end.

Yeah... No.

Not doing that.

I have a long list of things I resent about this entire situation, and I'm not going to just try to put this behind us in some effort to limit the damage done to my image, and the band's.

The people at fault here are going to get what they earned. Including me.

By the time the press conference is scheduled to start, I've got more tension in me than a guitar neck with the strings tightened to the point of breaking. So, I do what I usually do when I'm feeling tense before going in front of a crowd: I turn on the Charming Hunter Graves, Rockstar, persona and come out smiling at every person in the room like they're a long-lost best friend. Which is painfully ironic today. But, hey, it works.

There's a wave of flashing light and a rush of sound as I step out to the table at the head of the little meeting room. The room is filled to capacity, which is strange to see in our little library. A lot of people came from far away to see this performance. I'd better make it good.

Showtime!

"Ladies and gentlemen, I'm Billy Neal, manager for aMUSEd, and representing the band and Mr. Hunter Graves personally in the matters that bring us here today. We're going to begin today with Mr. Graves reading a prepared statement. We ask that you hold all questions until the statement has been read."

"Good morning, folks. I apologize for dragging you away from your home environs, but I'm sure you'll find that our little slice of paradise here in Mystic Beach more than makes up for the inconvenience."

Hey — while I've got their attention, I might as well do a solid for the local tourism board, right?

"As you are aware, aMUSEd is here working on our next album and taking some well-earned time off after our sold-out tour." I glance to my left and right to acknowledge my band brothers, who could not be dissuaded from showing up to support me.

"During this time, I was also asked to take part in filming a television show that would follow me on a series of dates through which several women would be competing to be declared my official girlfriend. While I found the premise both invasive and implausible, I was asked to participate by our label, with the proviso that my appearance fees would be donated to a mental-health awareness non-profit. This is a very personal cause for me, and I wanted to use the TV program to help raise awareness, so I reluctantly agreed to participate."

Sporadic flashes of light remind me that this is going to be seen by a lot of people. It's up to me to sell my story. I take a deep breath and smile apologetically at Billy, who's going to be very unhappy with me in a minute.

"I'm going to pause for a moment here in the text of my prepared statement to say something I feel is important to say publicly, while I have your attention on this topic and while I am here in the town where I grew up," I interject. "I ask that you hold your questions until I finish."

I take a deep breath and plunge forward.

"When I was a kid, my parents didn't have the healthiest relationship. I lost count of the number of times my mother locked herself in her bedroom and cried, usually after my father berated her for minor failings and often for nothing other than just being herself. Frequently, for having just been a loving mother to me."

The guys' eyes have all gone big, and I give them a strained smile to confirm I'm wanting to do this.

"One day when I was 15, I walked in on my father... in a compromising position. I'm not going to go into details. I consider this to be a private matter. But the bottom line is that, as a result, they got into an argument in which my father hurled some painful insults at my mother — insults that I now recognize constituted emotional abuse."

The room erupts with questions I'm not going to answer. I remain silent while Billy calls for order.

"My mother suffered from clinical depression for much of her life, and she was sometimes so overwhelmed that she didn't leave her room for days. I'm certain the ongoing emotional abuse from my father contributed to this. And on this particular day, after hurling some pretty horrible insults at her, my father stormed out when my mother locked herself in her bedroom again. I wanted to do whatever I could to help her, but she insisted she would be fine and sent me over to my best friend's house to spend the night."

I close my eyes and take a couple deep breaths before I continue.

"The next morning, my mother was dead."

I'm blinded by the flashes going off, and I pause until the room quiets again.

"She had taken her own life rather than continue to face an existence in which she was subjected to near-daily verbal abuse, often about her weight and appearance. I loved my mother very much. She was a beautiful person. She was the first person — one of two, really — who truly believed in me and who gave me unconditional love, while I was often criticized by my father. Her loss was — and remains — devastating. And it was only with the love and support of a dear friend that I came through that time with my soul, and my love of music, intact."

The room is quiet now.

"I've been tremendously blessed in having my band brothers around me for more than a decade now, and we've all been blessed with tremendous success in our careers. But I owe a lot of my part of that to that same friend, who has stood by me for all these years, my biggest supporter and my constant touchstone as we carved out the success we enjoy today. In that context, I'll get back to my prepared statement...

"During the course of filming the show two weeks ago, I was informed that one of the women had fallen ill and would not take part in a 'game' in which I was to guess each of their identities based on a kiss. An additional donation to my selected charity was offered for each one I guessed correctly. So the loss of a contestant was potentially a loss for my charity. My understanding now is that the woman in question was not, in fact, ill, but had been pressured by another of the participants, Holly Harwood, to claim illness so that a substitution would be needed."

Murmuring begins as people absorb Holly's name.

"I have also since learned that, in collusion with Miss Harwood, a producer had arranged for my bandmate Alex Winters" — I nod over at Alex, who nods back — to be on set at the time so that he could be used as leverage to ensure that Miss Harwood's real intent was carried out. That intent was to set up my friend — the same friend who has been so vital in supporting me for more than 15 years, including through the death of my mother — so that she could be pressured into taking the place of the fourth contestant so that Miss Harwood could publicly humiliate her."

I now have to speak up to be heard.

"Miss Harwood's plan was carried out due to the willingness of my friend to put herself in an uncomfortable position — purely to spare *me* from being placed in an uncomfortable position with my coworker. Miss Harwood has since continued her campaign against my friend and her effort to drive her out of my life, motivated by jealousy and to build her lucrative social media presence, profiting off a campaign of bullying that reminds me very uncomfortably of the emotional abuse that drove my mother to her death."

"Quiet! Quiet, please!" Billy is shouting now.

"Miss Harwood has gone to extreme lengths to ensure that her scheme would raise her online profile. When the production company ordered the destruction of footage in which my friend appeared, Miss Harwood obtained a copy for herself and proceeded to blackmail me — her supposed boyfriend — into..." the room erupts, but I just speak louder "...into continuing to appear with her publicly, after I had made it clear that I wanted nothing further to do with her. She held my friend's reputation, and my friendship with her, hostage to a campaign of coldly calculated bullying. She demanded my silence, and she extorted my — brief — cooperation, while also having me followed by a person or persons unknown, wielding a camera with a long lens, in hopes that she could catch me in a compromising position and thereby justify her release of the footage she had illegally obtained."

"Has Holly Harwood been charged with a crime?" one of the reporters yells above the fray.

"We are currently distributing to you copies of a signed statement and videotaped confession from Miss Harwood's co-conspirator — who came forward in hopes of minimizing the professional and legal consequences of her actions. She has confirmed that the footage released yesterday is the same footage she personally gave Miss Harwood before the production's original copies were erased, per the company's orders. She is no longer an employee of that company but is cooperating in their pursuit of a copyright claim against Miss Harwood, as well as in a possible civil suit against Miss Harwood for violation of legal agreements she signed, which could result in awarding of damages to the company."

"Is the show still going to be released?" another reporter shouts.

"Any questions regarding the production will have to be directed to the production company," Billy replies.

"Local authorities have been informed about the blackmail attempt perpetrated against me by Miss Harwood," I continue. "It will be up to them to pursue criminal charges against her if they feel it merited. I have confirmed my willingness to testify should the case proceed, and I have approved the release of phone and text message records that would support those legal matters. Beyond that, I'll have to refer you to local authorities.

"On a side note, you may have noticed that I'm wearing a brace on my left hand," I raise it up and the flashes pop again. "With all the drama going on, I managed to injure myself a couple days ago. It's a very minor injury and it'll be a matter of weeks before I'm back playing. Well before we need to be laying down tracks on the new album. So, any rumors regarding the end of my musical career are as greatly exaggerated as other rumors being circulated by certain people focused on drawing attention to themselves."

I look at the remainder of my statement and sigh. Here goes nothing!

CHAPTER 32

SHE'S MY BEST FRIEND

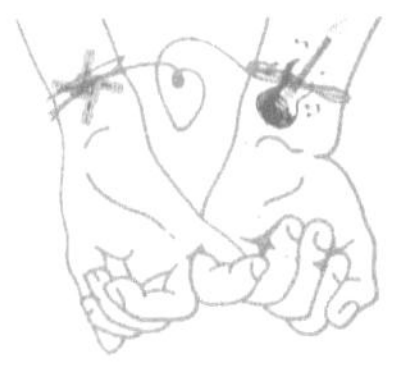

Hunter

“**I** want to correct a number of statements Miss Harwood has made in pursuit of her vendetta against me and my friend. Firstly, at no point in time before I informed Miss Harwood that I would no longer be seeing her romantically — or, if I had my way, at all — was I involved in a romantic relationship with my friend. Miss Harwood's allegations of my lying to her and 'cheating' on her are patently false and were made in an attempt to damage my reputation and that of my friend. Unfortunately, Miss Harwood has already publicly revealed my friend's first name, violating her privacy, so for ease of reference, from this point on I will refer to her by that name.”

I swallow and then continue.

“Brighid has been my best friend since we were 6 years old.”

Flashes pop once again.

“She has been there for nearly every significant event in my life, from birthdays and vacations through my mother's death and my breaking ties with my father, and most of the milestones in my career. If anything, I have failed to sufficiently convey my appreciation of her as a person and a friend, to her personally and in public. So I'd like to make up now for some of the unwelcome attention she has gotten this week.”

I look over at the guys. Kier is smiling encouragingly. Alex nods, indicating I should go ahead. David's got a far-off look on his face, but I'm going to chalk that up to this fur-coat thing of his. The important thing is that he's here. Declan is his usual confident self, leaning back with his arms crossed across his chest, telling me he knows I've got this. Rhys gives me an unabashed thumbs-up.

I'm about to disappoint them all.

"Brighid is the most beautiful woman I know, inside and out, and I'd be lucky to have her, as would any man. But we are just friends."

Along with the buzz in the room, I can hear the guys' jaws drop on either side of me. I don't have to look. And I can't if I'm going to finish this.

"I repeat — Brighid and I are just friends. We have had a platonic relationship for nearly 25 years, and it has been the most important friendship of my life. I adore her more than words can express, but she has never been my girlfriend, and — especially in the wake of this week's inexcusable violations of her privacy, and the gossip, insults, bullying, libelous accusations and abuse she has been forced to endure — I could not in good conscience ever consider subjecting her to that life."

"What about that photo of you two kissing? That wasn't part of the show!"

Holly really screwed us over with that photo. But I have to follow this through. So here's hoping I'm a better liar now than I usually am...

"The incident Miss Harwood's photographer captured took place just a few days ago. It is not evidence of me 'cheating' on anyone — especially a woman I had ceased any willing relationship with. In a misguided attempt on my part to make up for the insult delivered to Brighid in the ambush-style surprise Miss Harwood orchestrated, I did, indeed, kiss her while apologizing to her inside her place of business. She was unaware of my plan to do so, and was taken aback by it after our lengthy platonic friendship. She pulled back in surprise and began to lose her balance, grabbing instinctively for my shirt. I have to admit — I was still caught up in the kiss," I ad lib. "I mean, she's a serious bombshell — right, guys?"

There's some agreeable laughter in response.

"The photograph Miss Harwood had taken and later distributed is deceptive. The angle, the distance involved, serve to make it appear that Brighid was reaching for my pants when, in fact, it was my shirt she had reached for, and solely for balance. A moment later, and the photo would have shown me grabbing her wrist to keep her from falling backward. And contrary to Miss Harwood's ridiculous assertions, not even I can get a woman pregnant with all our clothes on and with only a brief kiss and touch on the wrist. I mean, I didn't get an A+ in biology class like Brighid did, but even I know that! I may have been stupid back then, but I'm not now."

They laugh out loud. Good. Maybe that little message of apology will slip through unnoticed by anyone but the intended recipient.

"Miss Harwood plotted to embarrass us by having photos taken without our knowledge, and she clearly selected one that would make things look like something they were not. That's the only story that photo tells, as much as she, and your editors, might like to suggest otherwise."

Some of them chuckle, joining in the joke.

"Despite my misguided effort, Brighid, rightly, has made it very clear — to Miss Harwood, to the production company, to her friends and to me — that she has no interest in pursuing a romantic relationship with me. As you wish, Bridge! And, frankly, her friendship has been so important to me that I wouldn't want to risk that to pursue anything beyond what we have had for so long. Losing her friendship would be the worst thing that has ever happened to me, and I'll do whatever it takes to ensure that never happens. I can only hope that she can forgive me for the invasion of her privacy, and I would ask you all to maintain her privacy from this point forward. I hope we can all begin to make up for the trouble we have caused her, so I ask for your cooperation as responsible members of the media.

"Some man is going to be very, very lucky to have Brighid as his life partner someday. I can only hope he'll treat her as well as she deserves."

I have felt five sets of eyeballs boring into my head during this entire monologue. Sorry, guys. It's time I took better care of my girl, even if that means she's not mine.

"I ask everyone who may see mentions of Brighid and/or our friendship online to keep in mind that she's a tremendously special person to me, and to do whatever you can to ensure that Holly's bullying campaign comes to an end. The body-shaming... Seriously, guys — and you, too, ladies — who wouldn't want to spend time with a genuine, vivacious, intelligent, gracious woman like Brighid, as friend or more? Why would you try to tear her down, unless you're seriously insecure yourself?

"The same goes for the 'slut-shaming.' I thought we'd grown past that as a society, but it seems all it takes is one hashtag and a jealous ex. In this case, the allegations are false; but the takeaway is that what people do in their private lives isn't for the rest of us to judge. Let's choose to be more gracious to our fellow humans, to build people up, not tear them down! I've seen firsthand what happens when words and bullying become weapons that wound and kill. We're better than that. I know our great aMUSEd fans will lead the way in making anti-bullying the norm. You've always been so great to us, willing to embrace us as authentic people and musicians, and I really hope you'll treat Brighid like the amazing member of the aMUSEd family that she is. She's more than earned that."

I see the guys are back on board with me, and even a few of the press are nodding in agreement.

"Finally, I want to ask everyone to keep in mind — especially in light of this week's events — that we still have a long way to go in normalizing mental health care, so if you're struggling or you know someone who is struggling, talk to someone, especially a doctor, therapist or other expert. Volunteer with or donate to organizations that increase awareness and provide support, because chances are someone you know could use that support. And, lastly, if you're being abused — physically, sexually, emotionally, whatever — or you know someone who is, please, please reach out for help. No one deserves to be treated like that, and if someone is telling you you do, they're the ones who are wrong. We've got your backs, regardless of what you're struggling with. If each and every one of us stand up to the bullies, the abusers, the shamers and haters, we all stand stronger together, like me and my brothers here.

"Thank you, everyone. We are aMUSEd."

CHAPTER 33

DIAMONDS ARE A GIRL'S BEST FRIEND

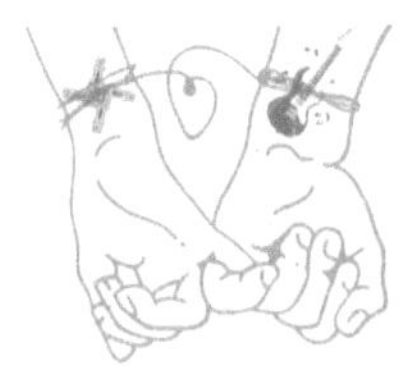

Brighid
Several hours prior

"I'm not sure you're going to need to do our interview," Rory tells me.

"Why's that?"

"The band called a press conference this morning."

I contemplate what this might mean.

"Any idea what they're going to say?"

"All they've told us — the media — is they're going to clear up some things around the reality show."

"So, nothing about me, or Hunter's private life?"

"Well, Hunter's private life and the show are kind of inextricably linked..."

"I suppose so."

"Brighid — are you OK? Do you want to do the interview after all? I can push it back to this afternoon so you can respond to whatever the guys say at the press conference."

"Can I just hope this will go away? Is that realistic?"

"Not so much."

"What do you think I should do?"

Rory is quiet for a moment.

"If it was me, I'd watch the press conference live, from home, and see exactly what they say. And if you don't like it, or you feel like you have something you need to add, then we'll do your interview and I'll get it up online this afternoon."

"Who's going to be showing it live?"

"That I don't know. Even the outlets that cover it live aren't likely to cover the entire thing. Let me call the library and see if I can fix that for you."

I'm still not sure I want to watch it. Maybe it would be best if I don't, if I don't do the interview and just give Hunter and me some space to figure out what, if anything, we want from each other going forward.

"OK, Brighid — I got them to agree to set up a videoconference on one of the library computers. They'll set it up as if they were doing a remote meeting, and you can watch the whole thing from start to finish. Sandy owed me a favor after that last fundraiser feature I did."

"I can't thank you enough, Rory."

"Don't thank me. You really got a raw deal here. Besides, if you decide to do an interview, you're giving me some pretty amazing traffic to the site. And independent journalism in a free newspaper on an ad-funded site — you could single-handedly fund a part-time reporter."

I laugh.

"I'm glad this implosion of my life could be so good for the future of independent journalism."

"You're a sweetheart, and you deserve way better than you've gotten, Brighid. Whatever happens with you and Hunter going forward, I hope he realizes how much he'd be losing if he loses you."

I've never told any of the circle girls, let alone Rory, who's one step removed, about my visions. Some things strain credibility even amongst the witchy set. It's also a very intimate thing, and sharing it more widely just feels wrong.

"To be honest, Rory, I've started to realize how much *I'd* be losing if *I* lose *him*. I think I may have misjudged his reasons for his recent actions. I'm just having a hard time separating the lifelong friend I know so well from this charming rockstar who's used to getting pretty much anything he wants."

"It's the textbook definition of 'It's complicated,'" she observes with a laugh.

But she's not wrong, and she doesn't know the half of it. The question is whether I, or we, can do anything to make it less complicated.

"Thanks, Rory — really."

"No thanks needed. Just…" She pauses and I can hear her take a deep breath and sigh. And when she speaks again, there's a tremor in her voice.

"If you have a chance to fix things with Hunter, if you can find a way forward that will give you both a shot at a happily-ever-after together — do it. Do whatever you need to do to be together, whatever that means to you. If the universe gives you something that special, you have to value every moment of it. Don't give up even a second — not in anger or fear or because playing it cool is the way you're 'supposed' to do it — because you don't know how many of those seconds you'll get. And each one is so incredibly precious."

"Are you sure you haven't been visiting my back room lately? Or Lyric's shrine at her house? Something about that advice feels familiar."

She laughs.

"No, neither. But I've been told I have a knack of knowing the right thing to say."

"Indeed you do."

It's time for the press conference to start, and I'm sitting in butterfly pose on my bed with my tablet in my lap. Appropriately, I've got a flock of butterflies in my stomach right now.

The last time I saw Hunter was when he kissed me so sweetly and walked out my front door after we'd spent a full day together, enjoying each other's company in more ways than one.

And then that misdirected text.

The more I think about it, the less sense it makes. I don't doubt for a moment that he'd said it, talking to Alex. The question is why those words and his actions were in such contrast with each other, and whether that means one was real and the other wasn't, or is it even more complicated than that?

Alex I got. He wasn't incorrect that I'd been easy pickings for Hunter once he'd decided to sleep with me — in the non-platonic sense. I hadn't exactly been subtle about my interest, even if I tended to forget that at times. And Alex's comment to me about thinking Hunter should just go ahead and be with me — it rang true with what he'd said to Hunter, even if it was more crudely said to his friend than it was to me. I chalk that up to guy talk.

But could Hunter really have had sex with me — five times! — if he wasn't attracted to me? Would pity and/or the need to make up for how badly Holly had treated me really have been enough to overcome a lack of physical attraction?

Assuming Hunter really had appreciated my friendship for so many years, would that have been enough for him to push himself into a sex-fest with me just to make me feel better? I want to think he knows me better than to believe I'd want to have sex with him when he wasn't genuinely interested in me.

I've always been fine with friends-with-benefits. It's a valid mode of expressing affection and getting mutual satisfaction. But sex out of obligation is a dead-end for any relationship, casual or committed, friendship or romance. And I can't believe Hunter would choose to send us down that path after all these years of being friends — not out of pity, or as an apology or even just to repay me for being there for him for so long.

Now it's time to see what Hunter has to say, even if he's saying it to the press and not to me. If I can take what he says today and start to make sense of what had happened between us, then maybe we can work out the rest just between the two of us.

I see the back of Rory's golden-blonde head from the webcam on the library computer. It looks like the computer is on a desk behind her. The only empty space in the room is behind the front table. A few moments later, a door opens and Hunter,

Alex, Rhys, Kieran, Declan and David file in behind the table, led by Billy. Hunter and Billy take the central seats at the table, and the other guys spread out around them.

Hunter looks tired, but full of nervous energy. It's like watching him head onstage in front of an arena full of people. I haven't been to any shows in the last handful of years, but I remember how things used to be for him — so nervous until he pulled on the rockstar charm like a cloak and made the stage his own. His left hand is back in a brace — odd, since the brace he had on three days ago is sitting in my closet, with the sheets I haven't yet brought myself to wash, and since he'd said he was feeling totally fine when he left my house that morning. Had he been wrong?

My protective instincts kick in, and I find myself wanting to climb through the screen and fix whatever has gone wrong. Instead, I focus on Hunter as he begins his statement. The Hunter Graves charm is turned up to 11 as he tries to get the media in his corner. At times like this, I marvel that the entire world doesn't fall at his feet. He's entrancing, delightful...

As he dispassionately explains the circumstances behind the reality show, I can see the reporters are following along but desperate to ask questions. Then things go off the rails. Amidst explaining his passion for the mental-health charity that benefited from his participation, Hunter is suddenly telling the world about that horrible day fifteen years ago when his parents had their last fight and he learned his mother was dead at her own hand.

Hunter has *never* talked to anyone else about that day, at least that I'm aware of. As far as I know, the only one who knows what he went through then is me. My mom is gone now, too, and even she only knew the basics of what happened. Declan and David know some of the story, but as far as I know, none of the tragic details. So to see, to hear Hunter open up and tell literally the entire world about how his mother died, why she died, and how much it impacted him... Something has happened to change him in the last few days, after fifteen years of burying this deep.

I feel an odd combination of closeness with him and distance, since after all this time as his only real confidante, I'm not sure what has motivated this huge change. I'm hoping this is cathartic for him, to share this intimate personal story and use it to motivate others to support a cause that is so important to him.

But then he's talking about how he got through that time in his life, and I'm stunned. I know I'm his closest friend. I know I'm the one who was there for him. I know that next to his mother, I'm probably the person who's loved him the most in this world. But he's crediting me, publicly, with helping get him where he is today. There's a respect there that I had wondered if I would ever get. And now it seems like I've always had it. I just didn't see it. The nods from Alex, Kieran and Declan, the smile on Rhys' face — they all say the same.

But as he begins talking about the circumstances behind that fateful on-camera kiss, I realize just how thoroughly I was manipulated. Holly and that producer used Alex, used my protectiveness of Hunter to set me up to fall. And I did. All but literally. I feel like a naive fool. Why didn't Hunter tell me this? He had to have known what they'd done when he told me the footage had been erased. And now I understand why Hunter revealed such intimate details about his mother and his past.

Holly's efforts to tear me down reminded him of how his father bullied his mother. Right to her grave.

Oh, Hunter...

I'm instantly sent back to the moment I saw Hunter remove the blindfold in the video Holly so helpfully shared, and I again realize it was *fear* that filled his eyes. It's the same emotion I see below the surface in him now. There's more here than what he's telling everyone. There's a more complicated story to be told. I don't know all of it, but now I start to understand how motivated he must have been to make it up to me that I'd been bullied as a result of my effort to protect him.

And just when I think I can't feel any more protective of him, he tells the world that Holly blackmailed him into pretending they were still together. That she threatened me to keep him under her thumb.

Holly Harwood is very lucky she is not in the same room with me right now. She would not be breathing for long. Avenging hand of god? Rory's got nothing on me when someone has done injury to my Hunter. Holly should pray to whatever divine entity she holds dear that I never get within reach of her ever again.

As it stands, the wish that people get what they deserve will serve in lieu of a curse my moral code won't let me cast. Could her scheme even have led to his comments to Alex about not being attracted to me? Had he been trying to ensure no one knew about us until after he'd dealt with Holly's threat?

As Hunter continues to lay out the details of what happened, it all starts to make sense — his ditching me for the better part of a week; the supposedly erased video footage that then resurfaced; a drunken night that resulted in a sprained hand, a dramatic visit to the ER, a territorial live-streaming "girlfriend" and a visit to my shop, where he transformed our friendship into something more.

What it doesn't explain is how his hand went from injured to healed to injured again, and with weeks of additional recovery time ahead of him. If he couldn't afford a few more days without playing, how is he going to deal with weeks out of commission? Again, I restrain myself from climbing through the screen, this time to fix his hand, again.

As Hunter sets the record straight, I'm reminded of all of those moments we've shared, from our earliest days of friendship through when his career was on the verge of exploding and I was standing there to support him. Again, he's publicly handing me credit, respect, appreciation — all the things I had long ago given up on having where the band was concerned. It wasn't something I needed, but the lack of it had undermined my confidence in ways even Holly's efforts to humiliate me had not.

That Hunter was now making such an effort to fix that... I can't help but wonder if it means he wants to repair not just our friendship but the relationship we'd just barely begun before a text message and jealous ex had blown it all to hell. With my complicity, since I hadn't even been willing to let him explain...

So, so stupid.

I owe him better. Especially if we have a chance of putting this all back together.

As I watch his band brothers' encouraging gestures my heart begins to soar. Could he really be ready for us to be more than friends?

And they look just as stunned as I feel when he once again crushes that idea under a heavy boot, and my heart with it. The thought that we'd been on our way from girl friend/boy friend to girlfriend/boyfriend just three days ago is eviscerated in an instant. We never were. We never will be. He won't have me in that part of his life.

And he explains away that first real kiss we shared, in my shop, with such brutal logic and careful clarification that I start to wonder if I dreamed the whole thing — or perhaps it was just another vision that held no more meaning for him than the others I had shared. Because it seems that even that kiss was motivated by pity, guilt and a desire to make amends for the kind of bullying that he so hated to see, since it reminded him of his mother's tragic death.

The rest is a blur, as I hear Hunter Graves confirm again on live TV that we are just friends and will only ever be friends, appeal to the public to address issues of mental health and bullying, and even tell the world how some other lucky guy will get to have me someday.

Maybe we've both been stupid. But I've clearly been dumber than I'd ever feared possible. No more.

CHAPTER 34

DEAD OR ALIVE

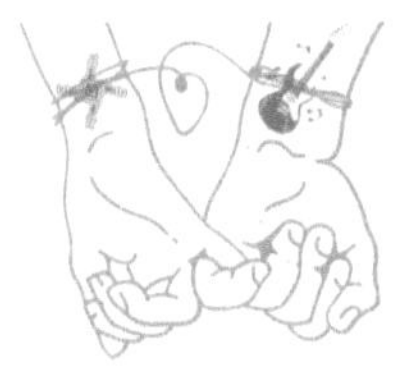

Hunter

"What the *fuck*, Hunt!"
Yeah. Declan again.
"Yeah — what the *fuck*?"
OK. That's Alex.
"*You* are a *moron*."
Rhys. Ouch.
"Feckin' eejit."
And another country is heard from. And it's Ireland.
David just looks at me and shakes his head, like he's given up all hope of my ever redeeming myself as a human being.
"What did you just *do*?"
Alex is irate.
"I had to do it, guys. You saw what happened to Brighid when she did nothing but try to protect me from what was supposedly just a production problem on a TV show she wasn't even supposed to be involved in! What would happen to her if we were together for real? If she was on the record as my girlfriend? I can't even think about it without feeling sick."
"You're sick, alright," Alex says. "Completely fucking nuts."
"Hey — didn't we just talk to like a million people about the stigma of mental illness?"
"I can't tell if he's serious or not," Rhys says.
"I'm dead serious."

"You've got that half-right. Bridge is going to fucking murder you in your sleep. And I may help her," Alex warns.

"I get why you guys are surprised. I didn't give you a heads-up that I'd decided to deviate from the plan. Sorry about that. But I knew you'd try to talk me out of it."

"Of course we'd have tried to talk you out of it! It's utter madness!" Kier retorts.

"And I can confirm that, since I'm 'The Madman,'" Rhys puts in.

I sigh. I know I'm not going to win this argument. But it doesn't matter. I get the only vote on this one, and I've made up my mind.

"How exactly do you envision this playing out?" Declan asks.

"I said it in the press conference — Bridge and I are best friends. She's always been there for me. I won't risk our friendship over a romantic relationship and I won't risk her to the media circus. Not after this."

"And you think she's going to suddenly start speaking to you again and let things go back to 'normal' just because you told the world that you're 'just friends' and shoveled out a fuck-ton of flowery shit about how she's been so valuable to you in your rise from tragic teen to rock superstar?"

Alex is incredulous.

"You lied about kissing her, when there was photographic evidence that showed exactly what happened. You told everyone she had never been and would never be your girlfriend — after you spent 24 hours fucking like bunnies, *and* after you'd accidentally told her that you don't find her attractive. 'At all.' Which you did *after* you'd spent 24 hours fucking like bunnies."

There was a ton of fucking that happened that day between the two of us. But she's clearly not wanting to continue that, since she stopped talking to me after the text thing. I can't blame her.

"You asked everyone to preserve her privacy and defend her against a bullying campaign that called her a fat slut, while simultaneously yourself calling her a 'bombshell' and inviting every man in the world to see if he can become the 'lucky guy' who'll get to keep her after *she* rejected *your* dumb ass."

OK. When Declan puts it that way, it seems a little less good.

"But I told her I was stupid before and wasn't being stupid anymore!"

"*That* is a matter of opinion, and I think you'll find that your conclusion is in the minority," David says.

"All those in favor of concluding that Hunter remains stupid, say 'Aye!'"

"Aye!"

"Aye!"

"Yup."

"Damn straight!"

"Feckin' eejit."

"No — you don't understand. We've got this thing — 'Some Kind of Wonderful' —"

"I totally get why you're always watching that movie. Mary Stuart Masterson was *so* hot!"

"Way hotter than the redhead."

"Personally, I think redheads are the hottest."

"Doesn't count, Rhys. You can't vote for yourself!"

"Arrgh! If you all have seen the movie — and you're welcome for that — you know when Watts tells Keith he's stupid that it's actually about them realizing they love each other, even though he hadn't thought of her as anything except his best friend until right before that."

"So, when you told her — or the international media — that you were stupid but you weren't being stupid anymore, you were actually telling Brighid that you love her."

"Exactly!"

"While also telling her that you only kissed her because you felt sorry for her, even though you then fucked her sideways, before accidentally telling her you didn't even want her easy ass because you don't find her attractive."

Oh.

"But I also said, 'As you wish!'"

"'Princess Bride'? You realize the bride ends up married to the evil prince, her true love ends up mostly dead and the whole point of 'As you wish' is that he never actually says the words, 'I love you' to tell her how he feels?"

"Did you also tell her, 'I know'?"

"No. Because she used to tell me all the time that she loved me and I didn't want her to think I was *in love* with her when I'd promised myself that I wouldn't risk our friendship by crossing that line, so I used to just acknowledge it when she told me she loved me by telling her I knew she did. With Star Wars flair."

"So, to summarize: you've avoided telling her for fifteen years that you were in love with her because you didn't want to risk your friendship; you've sucked up—"

"Well, sucked face, more accurately—" Declan puts in.

"Oh, I think he sucked more than that! Ow! Stop smacking me, Alex! I'm not wrong!

"—sucked up to her to make it up to her that Holly had told her she was just a 'pity fuck' to you..."

"What?! Holly told her what?! When?"

"The night you got drunk and fell off a fence, when Brighid kept calling Holly, trying to get her to help find you."

"Why didn't you tell me that?"

"Mostly because I forgot. But I also kind of figured Brighid would have told you when you kissed her, or at least by the time you fucked her."

"Oh. Crap."

"So, this is even worse than we thought it was?"

"Yeah."

"Back to the summary: You've rejected her for fifteen years. You accidentally kissed her but even though it was like liquid sex on a stick, you then acted like she had the plague, before telling her she shouldn't ever kiss you again because you only wanted to be friends.

"You then ducked her for a week while your ex-girlfriend blackmailed you. Then you got drunk and realized you wanted her after all, sprained your hand, had your blackmailing fake-girlfriend-ex call her a pity-fuck and chase her out of the hospital, at which point she was so hurt that she didn't speak to you for a week. And only then did you manage to see her, at which point you kissed her — which you later basically retconned — took her home and fucked her until your dick begged for mercy. *Then* you accidentally told her you weren't attracted to her—"

"*At all,*" the rest of them chorus.

"You punched a house—"

"And yelled at a goddess!"

"Dave! Come on, man..."

"Wait. What? I think we need to have that explained..."

"Later. And that was *before* I punched the house."

"Then you let her get humiliated on the entirety of the internet, before calling a press conference in which you ignored half the expert PR plan we all agreed to just so you could tell the girl *you love* that you don't love her, never did and never will, only kissed her because you felt guilty and only fucked her because you pitied her and not because you're attracted to her, and that you respect her immensely but will only ever be her non-sexy friend.

"When she already wasn't speaking to you because she now thinks she was a pity-fuck."

"And now you think she's going to come back and be your bestest friend and lifelong non-sexy pal/bed-warmer because you told her you'd try to be less stupid and you remember a line from a geeky—"

"Cult classic!"

"—film about a guy who waited until after he was mostly dead to make sure the girl he adored knew he loved her and wanted to spend the rest of time with her."

"Uh. I guess so?"

"You really are stupid."

CHAPTER 35

EMOTIONAL BARRIER

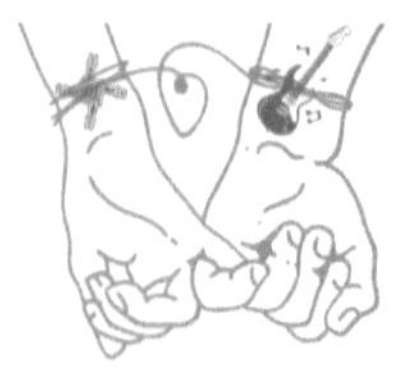

Brighid
A week later

I'm avoiding... well... everything. It doesn't matter if the paparazzi aren't gathered at the shop — it's staying closed. I can't concentrate enough to do inventory anyway. I've been crying too much to be able to smell anything, so working on incense blends is out of the question.

Spinning is a recipe for disaster right now, because I'll undoubtedly end up having a vision of Hunter and me having sex, which I will now only ever associate with pity. Half the movies I might watch I also associate with Hunter, so that's a no-go. And under no circumstances am I allowed to go online, because even if the entirety of the universe fell under Hunter's spell and is now welcoming me as the saintly bombshell of the aMUSEd family, I can't deal with the video clips from the press conference or the hashtags or the not-really-kissing photo or the video of that first kiss and my poor-man's Cinderella act.

My phone is off because it kept ringing with offers for interviews, for me and for Hunter, and friends and customers who are various degrees and combinations of curious and worried, and a number of hang-ups I figure are probably aMUSEd fans who want to ask me things but are too shy to do it when I actually answer the phone.

Likewise, I'm not answering the door. Which is why I freak out when I hear the back door pop open and smack against the wall.

"Fuck!"

"I thought you had it!"

"I thought *you* had it!"

"Ssshhh! You're going to wake her up!"

"It's 10 a.m.! She's probably been up since 6."

"Ssshhh!"

My initial panic fades as I recognize Molly's dulcet tones and a few other familiar voices.

"Bridge! It's Molly, Callie, Siobhan and Rory! Can we come up?"

I sigh. This is sounding like an intervention.

"Sure! Just be forewarned: I haven't seen a shower or hairbrush in a couple days. And I'm wearing my worn-out neon-pink yoga gear with Halloween socks!"

"Oh, you poor thing!"

I chuckle. It's pretty bad when Rory, who doesn't know me well, knows that neon pink, worn-out comfy and out-of-season witchy in any combination is a sure sign that things are very wrong with me.

Ten seconds later, I'm surrounded on my bed by four members of my self-appointed lady-squad, who have come equipped with the basic necessities of a custom post-breakup wallow follow-up. (Does this even qualify as a breakup since, according to Hunter, we were never together to begin with?)

Callie is toting pastries and ice cream, Siobhan a spa-day box full of facial and nail-care goodies, and Rory two bottles of orange juice and... sparkling cider?

"What? Lyric said you don't really drink. So this one —" Rory says, raising one of the bottles "— is orange crushes for us, straight from Callie's award-winning bartender, and these are the makings of a virgin mimosa for you." She gestures with the cider and second bottle of orange beverage. "Lyric also said if you haven't come to see her by tomorrow, she's coming over here, and she's bringing my darling godchildren! So, you probably want to get right on that..."

A half-hour later, we're all sitting around with mint-green goo on our faces, munching carefully on croissants and, for at least four of us, giggling madly under the influence of sweet, citrusy adult beverages and bitter life lessons.

"I can't believe he did that to you! He seriously retconned your entire actual first kiss, the one he gave you after like two decades of friendzoning you?" Molly's ready to string Hunter up with my nicest handspun.

"I'd be serving his balls up, sous vide, with a nice red sauce, if he'd pulled that on me!"

Callie is... well, Callie. She's all chef all the time. It's a major girl-squad emergency op if she's here during her lunch rush, leaving her restaurant in the hands of her sous chef.

"If he shows up in my shop, I'm tattooing your name on the inside of his left eyelid and a middle finger on the inside of the right one."

I'm pretty sure Siobhan wouldn't actually do that. But only pretty sure.

"It would definitely serve him right." Rory's a little quieter than the others. But she's made it clear she thinks Hunter is a major screw-up. "Have you been online in the last couple days?"

"No. I promised myself I wouldn't. Let the furor die down, see if the appeal to stop attacking me works. I can handle being offline for a couple weeks."

"You really haven't been on, have you?" Rory asks. "I wish I had that luxury — I've got to keep on top of this stuff for my job, even if I don't want to. But you're missing the best part!"

"Holly is hemorrhaging followers and sponsors," Molly jumps in. "Hunter really tore a hole in her self-important promotional balloon, and she's learning the very hard lesson that it doesn't pay to be a bully."

"I heard she'd lost her three major sponsors, and a modeling gig, and they're talking about banning her for intentionally spreading misinformation and violating copyright," Siobhan adds.

"They already made her delete the original video," Rory confirms. "It keeps popping up elsewhere, but she's not getting any algorithm boost off it anymore, no ad revenue.

"The comments..."

"I know... '#smalltownslut,' '#evilboyfriendthief,' yada-yada..." I say.

"Actually, it's kind of a mixed bag at this point," Rory clarifies. "Hunter's efforts seem to be making some headway. Every time one of Holly's minions calls you fat or slutty, they get instantly pounded down by three other people for bullying."

"They've pushed #wevegotyourback and #aMUSEdgotyourback to the top of the trending list. They've even taken over the '#wearenotaMUSEd' hashtag — it's not Holly and her mean-girls using it to tear you down — it's aMUSEd fans condemning *them* instead," says Siobhan.

"And I saw a couple really positive comments on the aMUSEd posts, with people saying how much they admired the friendship you two have had, and praising Hunter for being so brave about telling his story and standing up to support people like his mom and you, who've had to deal with this kind of thing," Rory adds.

Callie is quiet.

"I don't do social media," she says. "Especially not musicians."

O...K... (There's definitely a story here... But I can bide my time until she's ready to share.)

"I assume you haven't talked to Hunter, right? I mean, his anti-bullying efforts aside, why would you want to after that gaslighting he gave about what you two had been up to..." she adds, clearly hostile.

It's a stark contrast from Rory, who seems hesitant to condemn him.

Unfortunately, I'm having a hard time getting any angrier with him than she seems to be. Her pre-press-conference pep talk — urging me to do whatever I needed to do for Hunter and me to be together, to not waste a moment — is weighing heavily on both our minds, I think.

And, if I'm honest, the person I'm most angry with is myself. I may not have planned it that way, nor even thought of it that way, but I basically waited the better part of fifteen years for Hunter.

I've tried dating other people. I didn't hold on to my virginity, waiting for Hunter. Not for long, anyway. I've looked for anyone who put the kind of joy and love in my heart that Hunter always has, who's felt like home. There is really no one who does that for me, at least not like he does.

I don't know if I'm just not most guys' cup of tea, or if I give off some kind of "her heart is taken, guys — don't bother" vibe, but other guys generally don't seem to want me, and I don't really want them, not like I always have Hunter.

What is wrong with me?

No, I mean that. Really. If you have the answer to that question, let me know. Just not via social media, because I won't be checking that...

And I also mean it in the sense of not being able to figure out why I'm so stuck on Hunter.

Is it the visions of us in the past, which I believe but can't prove to him are real?

Is it just that we've been so close for so long that I know I can never be that intimate — emotionally or otherwise — with anyone else?

Or am I some kind of emotional procrastinator, waiting around for someone to drop in my lap who's going to sweep me away, and unwilling to make whatever effort it would take to go out and find that man myself? Instead, maybe I just stay in the safe confines of my feelings for Hunter.

I haven't wanted to date in a long time. I've got a business to run, clients to take care of, the small joys of watching favorite shows and listening to favorite music, and I have a deep devotion to Herself that is fulfilling beyond measure.

What else do I really need? A little regular "self-care" goes a long way toward addressing the one remaining need. So, do I need something more than a platonic best friend and a handful of supportive girl-friends? I'm not sure I do.

So why am I tearing myself apart, why am I putting that one key friendship in my life at risk just to try to find something with him that he's made clear he doesn't actually want?

So, yeah, I'm mad at myself for having waited around for him for fifteen years, and I'm mad at myself for putting my own desires ahead of our friendship.

And to top it all off, I'm the one who got us in this mess. If I hadn't been, on some level, desperately waiting for an excuse to kiss Hunter, would I have been so easily persuaded to jump in when Marcia — and Holly — pushed me to "fill in"? I let them use me to ambush Hunter, just the same as if I'd stood back and let Alex fill in. Just because we don't work together doesn't make it less awkward. Just because I'm female and Hunter is straight doesn't make it less problematic. If he'd wanted to kiss me before now, he would have. It's not like I ran away screaming at the idea...

No, I did that afterward, when I realized that he still didn't want what he'd been telling me for years that he didn't want.

"Brighid? Earth to Brighid?"

I've zoned out while I puzzled all of this out, and they've been talking to me for who knows how long.

"Ladies — let me pose a hypothetical... You have a guy friend who asked you out at one point, and you said no. But he keeps letting you know he's still interested. How do you feel about that?"

"A little creeped out," Molly says.

"Pissed off."

Callie's got a temper as fiery as her big-ass commercial stove, and I've never known her to date. Ever. She's never told me her story, but I know there has to be one. And based on that answer, I'm guessing it involves a guy.

"I don't know..." Siobhan says. "I like guys. I like sex. And I've had guy friends who I've had sex with. Some of them more than once. I mean, as long as he's not stalking me or making me uncomfortable about it, I don't mind a little bit of innuendo, and if his proposition hits me at the right time, maybe I go for it. No strings attached, of course."

"Of course," I acknowledge.

Siobhan has a *lot* of male clients. And she not infrequently has her hands on parts of the human body that your average business owner never touches. She's not intimidated by anyone, and she's probably the most at ease with her own sexuality of any of my friends. Which is probably a good thing. She's gorgeous, especially if you like edgy — 5-foot-10, athletic build, pierced nose and eyebrow, plentiful ink and white-blonde hair down past her hips, full of little braids. Part of me wants to be like her when I grow up.

I suspect she's an outlier in my little survey, but it's a perspective I appreciate.

"If I'm not interested, I make it clear," Rory puts in. But I can tell she's thinking deeply about something. "Brighid — I get the feeling there's more to your question than just a hypothetical friendzone issue. What are you thinking?"

"I'm thinking this is all my fault."

CHAPTER 36

DON'T DREAM IT'S OVER

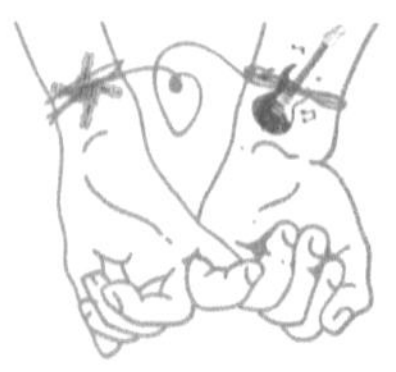

Brighid

Oh, what a mess.

Hunter, my best friend — he stuck with me when I didn't give up this idea of us together even after he'd told me no. And when I got myself played, he felt like he had to make it up to me, and did something no woman I know would have done.

Fine, it was pity sex. I should be disappointed that he wasn't honest with me, that he didn't feel like he could be, even after all these years together — not pissed off that he'd cared so much about my feelings that he'd probably spent 24 hours with some lingerie model's face plastered to the inside of his eyeballs just to pull it off.

And now I feel like total shit.

I can't even chalk it up to mutually satisfying sex that maybe happened for a reason it shouldn't have. I also can't imagine how Hunter is feeling, having done that for me. No wonder he's ready to openly declare us "just friends" and chalk it all up to a mistake.

The question is whether Hunter, after all that I put him through, is really wanting me back in his life as a friend. I wouldn't blame him if he doesn't, and I would totally understand the PR effort to put a positive spin on it. I've made a mess of his life, and the least I owe him is letting him have back what we had before — now without the pressure, spoken or not, to make it something more.

It doesn't matter what images I have stuck in my head. Hunter has said he doesn't want it, here and now, and I'm going to go forward with that as the only option that exists.

The girls argued with me when I told them I'd realized I'd been the one in the wrong, and that it was on me to fix it.

Molly, Siobhan, and especially Callie, said it was Hunter who'd made the real mistakes in denying what had happened between us. They didn't want me to "let him off the hook" for that, or at least not to do it without making him grovel just to get our friendship back.

Rory had had other concerns.

"Brighid, I'm not saying he didn't make some major mistakes — the least of which was trying to pretend you two had never been together. But I don't think taking all the blame on yourself is fair to you, either. This seems like a case of expectations that were set too high to begin with and things that progressed too fast, without you all really taking the time to communicate with each other."

She pauses for a minute.

"Hunter never talked to you about how he felt about that first kiss, except to say it couldn't happen again. And he didn't tell you about the blackmail. If he really was just trying to make it up to you that he'd freaked out about the kiss and that you were hurt by the way Holly treated you and the internet morass... Brighid — he should have talked to you about that, and been honest. From what you've said, you were close enough that you deserved that kind of honesty, to go into whatever he proposed with your eyes open and on solid ground. It was wrong of him not to give you that, to let you be blindsided by everything that came after. So, even if you share some of the blame, that doesn't remove the need for the two of you to really talk this out and figure out what you both want now that all of this has happened."

I get what she's saying. The problem is that Hunter has already told me — told the world — what he wants. And that's just my friendship. Nothing more.

"I can't put any more pressure on him for something more. I should have listened to him the first time he said he didn't want to cross that line with me, and I should have just dropped it. All the fallout here is because I didn't do that. I let myself get caught up in this idea of what we could be, and I stopped treating our friendship like it was the blessing it has been. That stops now."

"So what are you going to do?" Molly asks, despite her stated reservations. "Call him and apologize? Show up at the studio house and try to make amends? Surprise him at a gig?"

"He can't play right now — so no gigs," Rory points out. "They were supposed to have a gig tonight, and I confirmed with their manager that that's not happening. No gigs for at least a month, he said. They're going to be working in the studio only."

I'm still wondering what the heck happened to Hunter's hand that he's now not able to play for even longer than he'd been *before* his hand was healed. Is this my fault, too? Did I ill-wish him without meaning to? I've got to fix this.

"I'm going to put on my big-girl panties — and *keep them on* this time—" Molly giggles, while Siobhan raises a pierced eyebrow "— and invite him to come here and talk. I don't want to put him on the spot by showing up there. This has to be his choice. And I'll do what I would have done if all this craziness hadn't happened. I'll order dinner from that restaurant we were supposed to try, and I'll put his orange soda on ice and add 'Return of the Jedi' to my streaming queue. And I'll hope he meant it when he said he wanted our friendship back."

I don't think anyone in the room is thrilled with this plan. But it's my plan. It feels right. I'm going to ask Brighid for her blessing, to heal what was broken between Hunter and me. And I'm going to move on, asking Hunter for nothing but his friendship. And hope against hope that he can see his way to giving me back that precious gift I had really taken for granted.

So I unblock Hunter's number. And I change the door lock code. And I order the food to be delivered around 7:30, which was our usual time to eat dinner when he wasn't on the road. I make sure I have his orange Fanta in the fridge. I update my video streaming queue. And I send Hunter a text.

Brighid: *1006 — 7:30*

Here goes nothing.

When six o'clock arrives, I get out my favorite sundress, lay it on the bed, brush out my hair and run a bath. Sea salt, and lavender, lemon verbena, heather and cedarwood — my Brighid blend — straight into the bath. And me straight after. And then I clear my mind and turn my focus inward.

"Blessed Lady, grant your priestess forgiveness for foisting her notion of what should be upon the world and my dear friend. I have realized my error and can only hope that you, and he, can forgive me.

"Let the healing waters of your sacred cauldron clear the way between us and repair what has been broken. Make our friendship once again strong and true, and grant us the blessing of understanding as deep as your sacred well.

"You, who with your nineteen priestesses tend the eternal fire that gives spark to creativity, grant me that my words convey my deep penitence and my acceptance of what is willingly given.

"Lady who shapes steel into sword and silver into starshine, grant us the strength to withstand the fires of your forge and emerge in our truest and highest form, beautiful and truly tempered as a result of your skilled crafting.

"With your blessing and your benediction, Go raibh sé amhlaidh."

I'm still working on my Irish. It's far from perfect, but it's a language almost no one on the entire Delmarva peninsula speaks, even though it's a required course in Irish schools now, which is why I knew Kieran would likely speak at least some. I've had to make do with apps and remote classes. I've made it up to Irish 105 in my DCU course online, and it's finally making sense to my brain. Hopefully, She appreciates the effort, even if the results still need work.

Hair washed and conditioned, I dab on my custom perfume blend and slip on the sundress. I check my phone — no reply from Hunter. It's seven now. Hopefully, he's just busy and will give me a chance to talk things out with him. Sending him the new door code feels like a good peace offering, as many times as I've locked him out — literally and figuratively — lately.

I'm too nervous to watch TV, and spinning or weaving right now seems like a bad idea. I need to keep my feet, and my head, in the here and now. I do a quick check of the house, putting away anything that's not in its place, setting the little table in the kitchen with two place settings. We usually eat on the sofa in front of the TV, but if we're going to talk and work things out, it's probably better than we do it facing each other, without Jedi distracting us.

I pick up my crochet magazine and lose myself in it — only checking my watch every two or three minutes — until the doorbell rings. I'm strung so tight I jump. I take a deep breath and answer the door.

My heart skips a beat when I see the long blonde hair tucked under the cap. Then he turns around.

"Delivery!"

Distracted, I take the food from Not-Hunter and absently hand him a tip.

"Thanks!" he says effusively, and I blink, only then realizing that I just handed him a 50-dollar tip on a hundred dollars' worth of food, and not the 20-dollar tip I had meant to give him. Oh, well. He earned it with a timely delivery, I guess.

I can't say the same for Hunter's arrival. The text I'd sent earlier with the door code was marked as read just before five. I'd hoped he was just too busy to reply. Now I'm starting to worry that he's not coming, that he doesn't want to see me and can't even bring himself to acknowledge my message.

Well, it won't be the first time I've made a fool of myself with Hunter. And after the ordeal of trying to make me feel better by doing... what he did... I can see why he wouldn't want to see me, especially not at the scene of the crime.

I'm trying really hard not to cry. I know it's only 7:55, but it feels like our friendship is slipping through my fingers with every tick of the clock, every grain of sand passing through the hourglass...

I know what I need to do. I can't make Hunter come talk to me. I can't force him to be my friend again. But I can appreciate and accept the friendship we have had and let it be what it has been. Even if it's all in the past.

I slip off my shoes and take my hair down, letting it flow loosely over my shoulders. I take a deep breath as the clock passes through eight. My breath catches along the way, but determination keeps me breathing.

I make sure the front door is locked and head back into the kitchen. I stop to look at the table laid out for two. And I put the food in the fridge. Then I do my best to put a smile on my face. I don't buy it, but I give myself credit for the effort. Fake it 'til you make it! And I walk out the back door, down the short path to the beach, where I find a secluded spot away from the boardwalk and sit directly on the sand.

I look out over the ocean, and I find a hint of a genuine smile when I see the near-full moon reflecting on the water out past the breaking waves. The sound is soothing, its rhythmic quality a reminder to breathe in and out, no matter what is, or isn't, going on around me. It's a lesson I'm going to need, moving forward without my best friend.

I offer a silent thank-you, to Her, and to him, for having been given that gift so many years ago... that green-eyed boy who stood up for me and held my hand; waited for me on the playground; held me tight after my mother died; pummeled me with straw wrappers; made me smile with his geeky humor and his limitless charm; who met my eyes with a connection so strong it was tangible; who played music that filled my soul; and wrapped himself around my body and my heart so thoroughly that I sometimes couldn't tell where I left off and he began.

I'll always treasure that. And him.

CHAPTER 37

KNOCK THREE TIMES

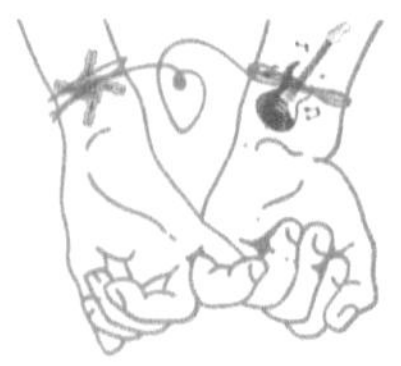

Hunter

Mother of twelve gods!

I cannot believe that Brighid finally unblocks me, invites me back to her house — I mean, what else could my birthdate mean at a time like this when it's her favorite PIN code! — and she's waiting for me, for a reply, something, anything, and I'm stuck on a fracking plane!

I had gotten a text right as I got on the plane back from New York, and being the last passenger boarding after I rushed to the airport from my orthopedic consult, I no sooner sat down than the plane was backing away from the gate.

I pulled my phone out to see who had messaged me, and about jumped out of my seat when I saw it was Bridge! Maybe my hastily executed plan at the press conference actually worked!

I started to reply, only to get the hairy eyeball from the flight attendant, who was at that exact moment in the middle of her "stow your shit and turn off your phones" spiel.

When I moved the phone under my arm to unlock it and reply on the downlow, she gave me a look that reminded me of Mrs. Taylor when I tried to confiscate the five remaining servings of Brighid's chocolate mousse — for scientific comparison. Yeah.

I did my best Hunter Graves, Rockstar™, impression, but she wasn't buying it, not even with the little twinkles in the corners of my sparkling green eyes. She held her hand out and gestured for me to give her the phone. I thought about arguing, but I wasn't sure that wouldn't result in her confiscating it until the end of the school year.

So much for my legendary flirting skills.

Two hours later, I'm on the ground in Salisbury, with nearly an hour's drive ahead of me to get back to Mystic Beach, once I get to my rental car.

I finally get a chance to unlock my phone and reply, only to find out that my battery is dead and I brought the wrong damn charging cord with me on my brief trip. And the only shop in this little airport is closed.

The universe is just fucking with me today.

At this point, I don't want to waste any more time getting back to Mystic Beach, and I aim to make it back to the house in record time — only, eight miles an hour over the speed limit is apparently a bridge too far today, and I'm pulled over and issued a speeding ticket. I do not attempt to flirt with the state trooper. The way things have been going, I'd end up charged with solicitation and be stuck in jail overnight... My otherwise clean driving record weeps, which I'm about ready to do myself if I can't get to Brighid very, very soon.

It's another half-hour before I make it to Bridge's house. I barely take the time to close the car door, sprinting up her front porch and punching in the keycode she gave me. Ooh! That's a good sound! I like the little green light. No more big X-buzzes and red lights to tell me I'm not welcome here. Awesome!

I turn the door handle and push it inward, only to discover that she's got the security latch on.

Maybe she gave up on me and went to bed already? Possible, but not likely. Maybe she went out with her girlfriends to get drunk and forget my stupid ass? Highly unlikely. My girl hasn't been a drinker since college, though she might want to be forgetting stupid-assed me.

Maybe she's decided she hates my guts because I've left her hanging all day, and she's barricaded in her bedroom, sticking pins in fabric-string dollies that bear a striking resemblance to yours truly? Considering how my luck's been going, this is a genuine possibility, if an unlikely one. Brighid has a temper, but she's a gentle soul, a healer at heart, and I honestly think that even if she decided she hated my guts, she couldn't so much as wish me a hangnail. I would have earned it, though.

Which leaves the only likely option. She's not home.
She's not home!
She's been waiting for me for who knows how long, so she's probably upset, one way or another, and where would my girl be if she was upset?

I run around the back of the house. The back door comes right open when I put in my code. Woot! I resist the impulse to do a celebratory dance, if only because someone would inevitably be looking out their window and record the crazy rockstar's less-than-smooth moves on their phone, and I'll be a TikTok phenom within an hour. And not in a good way.

Not doing that again. At least not this week.

I let myself in the house, calling her name, just in case she *is* here. No answer. I see the kitchen table set for an intimate dinner for two, and bags that clearly contained takeout boxes from the restaurant we were supposed to have food from the night I fucked up and accidentally told her I wasn't attracted to her.

Audience participation segment (All together now!): *At all.*

Yup. Stupid. But I'm going to fix it. And I'm going to fix it right now.

If Bridge isn't in the house... if she got dinner and waited for me and I didn't show... There's only one place she's going to be.

Ripping off my shoes, I run full-speed out the back door, down the path to the beach. As soon as I clear the top of the dune, I see her, sitting on the sand off to the side, away from the boardwalk, her flaxen hair spread out around her shoulders and down her back. Those amazing shoulders — strong from her spinning and weaving, capable of bearing up under tremendous pressure, but soft and sensuous, like the rest of her.

The moon is shining on the calm ocean in front of her, and I know instantly why she was drawn here tonight, after the disappointment she's suffered.

"The earth is our mother. The ocean is her blood. The moon shines upon her, gazing longingly with love."

I can't count how many times I've heard her say that over the years. She was an ocean girl before she was a weaver, a mermaid before she was called to serve the flame. If she's not spinning or sitting at her altar, here's where she'd come for solace.

I approach her quietly from behind, not wanting to startle her out of her reverie.

"I know you're there," she says out of nowhere. "I always know."

I sit down beside her on the sand, both of us looking out on the ocean, and not at each other.

"I know you do. You knew I was hurt when I fell and sprained my hand. I probably would have been there for hours if you hadn't kept on the guys to find me. They're a little spooked about that, actually."

"Not the first time."

"Probably not."

"It's a shame it doesn't work where you and I are concerned. We'd have all been spared a lot of pain and humiliation if I'd actually known how you felt about me all these years."

"Yeah... We need to talk about that..."

"Not necessary. I've been doing a lot of thinking, and I realize now that where we went wrong was when I pushed you for something more than friendship. And I'm sorry about that."

She turns to me and grabs my right hand in hers.

"It was disrespectful and I'm sure you were uncomfortable with me continuing to talk about my crazy dreams and fate and whatever else seemed like it was all rolled into that. And, honestly, I've had time now to rethink all of it, and I've concluded I was wrong."

What now?

"What? What do you mean?"

"It was a silly teenage girl thing. I deluded myself into believing that what my mind showed me in my sleep was something more than a stupid crush playing itself out in my subconscious. And I pushed that on you, tried to push us into that mold, which didn't come close to fitting. You felt it all along, and I just didn't listen."

"Bridge — I wanted to talk to you about that. About the visions."

"I really don't want to think about it anymore, Hunter. I just want to put it all behind us. It's done nothing but cause us both trouble and pain, and if there was really anything there, this wouldn't all have been so hard on both of us."

"Wait... I need to tell you..."

"I know, Hunter — I saw the press conference. Rory made sure I could see it all. And you made things very clear. To everyone. It was a wakeup call that I needed after fifteen years. And I've had time now to absorb it all, get some clear perspective — and I've decided to move on."

No!

"We've been far better friends than we've made lovers, and I'm actually a little heartsick at the idea that you forced yourself to try to make things up to me — things that weren't even in your control. It actually makes me ill to think about us being together when I think about how it happened."

I feel everything I wanted, everything I thought I had a chance to get back, to build, slipping away from me. And I'd been warned. Marina Matthews had warned me to take care of her, to listen to her before it was too late. And now it's too late. I start to see how Brighid must have felt when I called us being together a mistake. And now she says thinking about us together makes her feel sick...

"It does?"

"Really. Yeah. You were right. It was all a mistake. It was a mistake fifteen years in the making, and I have to own that. It's my fault I pushed us beyond what we were supposed to be, and even worse that I did it after you told me for so long that you didn't want that with me. I feel kind of creepy about it now, actually."

"Wow. I wasn't expecting you to say that."

"I know. I've been hard-headed about it. Unreasonable. Selfish. You've got this amazing, glamorous life, and I just don't fit. I'm sorry Holly felt so unnecessarily threatened that she decided to blackmail you. That's kind of my fault, too."

"No, Bridge. You *do* fit. You'll always fit. And it's not your fault. Holly is the only one responsible for that whole thing."

"Maybe. But that doesn't change the fact that it was my going along with her little charade that set all of this in motion. And I can't think about that moment without connecting all this fallout to it, and I own the blame for that, because it was me wanting that one thing you'd told me all these years that you didn't want that got us here, where we almost lost each other entirely."

She's wrong about so much of what she's said tonight, but there she's right.

"I mean... I said 'almost,' but I will totally understand if you want to cut your losses right here and call it quits, permanently. We've had an amazing friendship, and I'd much rather remember it how it was before I messed things up. I haven't deserved you, and even then I took it all for granted. So you'd be entirely reasonable to say this is it for us."

"No. No, no, no. Bridge! That's not what I want. At all."

I cringe at those two words that came tumbling out of my mouth, and she looks away. I can see the tears welling in her eyes. I can see how much I've hurt her. And I owe it to her to stop doing that. Right now.

CHAPTER 38

WAITING ON A FRIEND

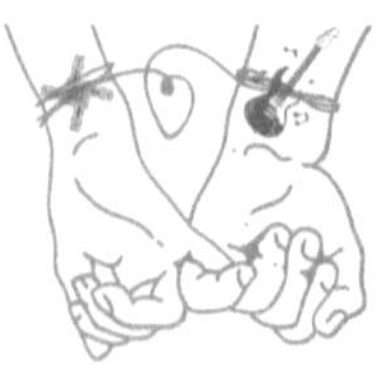

Hunter

I just can't do it. No matter what I want now. I can't ask her to change her mind again and give us a chance. She's taken the time to think through what happened, and she's concluded us being together as more than friends was a mistake. Just like I'd told the world.

And, again, I now know how she must have felt hearing those words from my own lips. And I can't blame her in the least for wanting to just put it all behind her. I'm kind of surprised that she's the one asking *me* if *I* still want to be friends.

I grab her hands back, kissing them as I hold them in my good one.

"Bridge — you are the most important person in my life. Period. Maybe ever," I add, acknowledging that Mom got me through fifteen years and gave me the guitar that started this odyssey, but Brighid was the one who made sure I survived losing her and that I got my music back. She was the one who had been there for me, from the moment we met, until now, almost a quarter-century later.

"I meant what I said in the press conference about how important you've been to me, and to the band." In fact, it was one of the few things I said about us that was entirely true and not me trying to take the heat off of her. "I know you feel like you've been looked down on and mostly tolerated by the guys, but we've talked about this a lot in the last week, and you need to know that they all love you. They all respect you. Even when Declan's being a dick."

She smiles her amusement at that. It's just plain good to see her smile, about anything.

"Which would be most of the time."

"Totally," I agree with a laugh.

"You're really important to all of us. I mean, you basically gave the band our name."

"No, I didn't. I just reminded you of your own words. You ran with it, and Declan was the one who snatched it out of the ethers, like it was meant to be."

"Maybe. But that doesn't change the fact that you're the one person who's been there with us all along. You're the one who got me down to the beach that day, at that time, when David and Declan just happened to be walking by, and you're the one who ensured I was playing the guitar that I hadn't touched in weeks. That's all you. You've been a guiding light for this band from Day 1, whether you knew it or not, whether *we* realized it or not. But we all realize that now, Bridge, and the guys have been pretty fucking angry with me over how I let things get out of control. At this point, I think they might want to teach you how to play guitar just so you can replace me."

I wink to let her know I'm just joking. She smacks me on the shoulder. Too much? Maybe. But she's earned that praise, and so much more.

"Are things OK with you all? The media, your reputation, PR? And the guys?"

"Yeah, they are. I went off-script a bit, and that pissed them all off. But things have not only settled down in terms of our reputation — we've actually had a nice bump in positive impressions since I pushed the anti-bullying message."

"About that..." she says. "I'm sorry you felt like you had to tell the world your story because of me. You've avoided that for so long, and you really had every right to keep it private. But I know it must have really hurt to see that happening to anyone."

"It did. Especially since it was you. But, honestly — I should have told the guys the whole story years ago, maybe from the start. And I think what we're seeing now is the impact of telling my story. It seems to be helping people connect personally with these issues, so it's doing even more to get people help. Including me. I've got an appointment scheduled with a therapist next week."

She blinks and gives me a small smile.

"I'm glad about that, then. For your sake and anyone else who will get help now."

"And you get credit there, too, Bridge. Not because it took someone targeting you to make it happen, but because knowing you had my back for all those years, from the moment I found out what happened to now — that's what gave me the strength to go ahead and put it out there, and now to get some real help. You gave me that strength."

"But I haven't been strong, Hunter. I've run away from things more times than I can count. I can't seem to stop running."

"Well, you can always run to me, Bridge."

I grab her around her shoulders with one arm and give her a strong hug, kissing the top of her beautiful head. This conversation hasn't turned out at all like I expected, and certainly not like I hoped. And I'm not sure my heart is ever going to recover from knowing I lost her love because of my own stupid words.

"I love you, Bridge." Her eyes widen in surprise. "You're my best friend." I have to let her believe that's the only love I feel for her. "And I'll always be here for you. I've got a lot to make up for, and I'm going to do just that."

"I love you, too, Hunter. And I'm glad we can move forward as friends. It would have been so hard to have lost you. Painful... Oh! Speaking of painful..."

"What?"

"Your hand! What happened to your hand? It was better, wasn't it? Didn't we heal the sprain?"

"Yes. You did. Both of you. And then I broke it."

"So it really *is* broken? What did you *do*?"

I'm really reluctant to admit this. But she's my best friend, so I kind of have to.

"I punched a house."

She stares at me in disbelief.

"You *punched* a *house*."

"Yes, I punched a house."

"With your freshly healed fretting hand."

"Yup. You're starting to sound like Declan here."

"I am not a dick."

"No, you are not. You are a wonderful, caring, gentle healer-person who happens to be best friends with a raving lunatic."

"Now, wait a minute. You shouldn't talk about Rhys like that!" We both laugh.

"I meant yours truly. Because I've been doing some crazy stuff since I got here. Is there something in the water that I've been missing while I was gone? David said Mystic Beach is 'odd.'"

"He's not wrong. Things have gotten decidedly weirder here in recent years. But it's mostly seemed to mean more business for me, so as long as it stays *safely* odd, I guess it's OK. So, why did you punch the house? Really."

"I was upset because I thought I'd lost you. And then I lost my temper. For like the first time ever," I add with a chuckle. "No — correction... Second time ever. There was that door at the frat house..." I recall, suddenly noticing the common element. "You see how important you are to me?"

"I don't want you hurting yourself over me," she replies quietly, like she's feeling guilty about it.

"It's just a hairline fracture in one bone. And it was totally on me. Well, on me and Brighid, kind of."

"What do you mean 'Brighid, kind of'?"

"I kind of yelled at Her."

"You yelled at Her. Not at me, Brighid? At Herself?"

"I did. And, as David put it, She yelled back. I apologized after I realized what I'd done."

"I guess that's good. But it's not like Her to undo a healing, let alone let someone get injured just because they yelled at her. She's not the kind of god you read about in some of the myths..."

"Now, that was what *I* said. But She told me I was stupid. I got the impression I'd asked for it."

"Wait. She *told* you you were stupid. Like actually spoke to you?"

"Yup. I heard a voice in my head — see, your best friend is crazy! — and it wasn't you and it wasn't Watts, but it was warm and female and... amused? I'm not sure if that's ironic or not. And David was sitting right next to me and didn't hear a thing. So, I know it was just in my head." That and a lot of stuff these days...

"Wow. That's pretty extraordinary. I don't even know what to think about that. I mean, I told you She liked you, the whole poet/musician thing. But speaking to you? Now do you understand what I mean when I say She talks to me?"

"I know exactly what you mean. I just wish I hadn't been rude to Her, because I kind of need my hand."

"That still doesn't make any sense."

"Maybe I need to do some penance."

"She's Irish, but she's not Catholic. Well, the goddess isn't. The saint, on the other hand... No. It's not like Herself. I'm kind of baffled on this one. I'm sure there's a reason, but I can't think what it would be."

"Do you think I'd be pressing my luck if we tried the healing thing again?"

"Hmm... I don't think so. If She doesn't want to help, She won't."

"Too late to try it tonight?"

"Sorry, yes. I'm exhausted. I haven't slept well for a few days, for obvious reasons. And the emotional toll... I need at least a good night's sleep to recover."

"Well, my hand isn't going anywhere. Speaking of which..."

"Yes?"

"Would it be totally out of line if I stayed over tonight? Like the old days?"

"Cuddled up in the same bed, like a pile of puppies?" she asks with a laugh.

"Yeah, together."

She seems to give it some thought before answering.

"I guess that would be OK."

"You don't sound sure."

"Well, I'm not sure how much sleep I'll get."

"Just friends, Bridge. I promise I won't make any moves on you."

"No — I mean I'm not sure how much sleep I'll get with you hogging the bed like you usually do." She smiles and pokes me in the ribs.

I give her another hug, brushing my lips across her hair.

"I promise to behave. You can fend me off with pillows if you need to."

"I'll hold you to that. Remember — no sleep for me, no healing for you!"

"Can't have that! I *really* need my hand!"

"Next time, don't yell at divine beings, even the relatively understanding ones."

"That is a lesson I have learned. Painfully well."

"Well, let's see what we can do about that."

CHAPTER 39

SOME KIND OF WONDERFUL

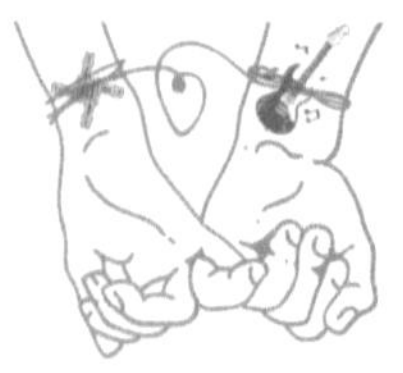

Hunter

This isn't how I wanted this to work out, but it's the next best thing. And the moment that thought runs through my brain, I realize that, all these years, since we were 15, that's what Brighid's been settling for — the next best thing to what she wanted. Has she been satisfied with that? Sometimes it's seemed like she was. But it's already feeling pretty bittersweet to me, thinking of what we had so briefly and that she doesn't want that with me anymore. But I cannot lose her as a friend, and I'll do whatever I have to to keep her. I've kind of earned feeling this way, after all I've put her through.

"Hungry?" she asks as we enter the kitchen from the back door.

"Always," I joke. I'm not sure if it's a double entendre on either of our parts. Probably not on hers. But it's true either way.

"Why am I not surprised?" She chuckles. "The food will survive reheating. We just can't give them any reviews after waiting so long to eat."

"Sorry about that... I tried to get here as soon as I could. But there was a plane, and a flight attendant with a ruler, and then a state trooper..."

"What?" Her eyebrows shoot up.

"I was coming back from New York from my orthopedic consult when I got your text. And the flight attendant was very adamant about the whole 'plane mode' thing. She actually *confiscated* my phone! And then the Maryland state trooper thought I was in a little too much of a hurry on the way back from the airport."

"No private jet straight from New York to Georgetown this time?"

I laugh.

"No, only for official band business, which this kind of was, but they don't bring a jet out just for me."

"Oh, the hardships of the rockstar life!"

"You have no idea," I joke.

"The little taste I got was more than enough for me," she says, chuckling wryly. I take a deep breath.

"I'm really sorry about that, Bridge. I never wanted you to have to deal with that kind of thing."

"Not your fault, Hunter. I stepped into a trap, and I got a little beat up as a result. But I'm fine."

"The shop back to normal?"

"Not yet. I took some time off. I'll probably go back tomorrow — actually, the day after, since we have plans for tomorrow now. Molly said the coast has been clear."

"That's good."

"Mrs. Lowell likes you."

"She does? She looked kind of skeptical when she was leaving the other day, like she wondered if I was a cad."

Brighid roars with laughter.

"Will you ever live that down? I can't believe Dottie and company called you a cad, even though you weren't a big-name rockstar yet. You were always a nice guy. But they were a little overprotective."

"No kidding. They threatened to impale my posterior with knitting implements."

"They didn't!" she exclaims in disbelief.

"They did."

"You never told me that."

"I didn't want you living in fear for my ass."

Now we're both laughing, and it starts to feel like old times again. We enjoy a nice (reheated) meal, but it's a little weird eating at the little kitchen table set for two. Especially when I keep thinking that I'd much rather have had a romantic candlelit dinner for two with her instead. The conversation lags a little —

too much going unsaid, probably on both our parts, but mostly on mine, even if they're things I can't tell her now.

"You know... We're overdue for a little Keith and Watts..." I say.

"We just watched it a couple weeks ago," she says skeptically. "You just want to see Mary Stuart Masterson on the drums again."

"Guilty. Watts is hot."

She laughs.

"I'll take your word for it. I will concede that she's definitely cute. And I always wanted those gloves... Eric Stoltz is *still* hot," she adds as an afterthought.

"You always had a thing for redheads."

"I did," she admits. "But not only redheads." She blushes a little, and my heart leaps for this tiny thread of hope. Could there still be something there?

"Rhys will be very sad to hear that."

"He will have to remain sad. My heart is taken..."

I'm waiting with bated breath.

"By Eric Stoltz."

"Oh, ha ha ha," I retort. "I'll go put on the movie, if you want to watch it again."

"No popcorn this time, since we just ate, but let me put the plates in the dishwasher, and then I'll grab drinks."

"Sounds good."

I head out to the living room, cue up the movie and arrange the throw pillows on the sofa for our movie party for two. The blanket is ready and waiting. But my cell phone buzzes.

Rhys: *You've gone viral again!*

Hunter: *What the heck! What did Holly do now?*

Rhys: *Not Holly. You and Brighid. Have you been offline all day? Somebody did a video remix of your big kiss and uploaded it to TikTok. It's gone viral. And it's sparked a craze.*

Hunter: *Do I want to know?*

Rhys: *Everybody is making videos declaring their love for their best friends! Some look kinda like they're more than friends, if you know what I mean, but it's all kinds of friends.*

He sends me a link.

Someone's cut the video Holly released down to just me and Brighid kissing. They've added a snippet of Queen's "You're My Best Friend" as a soundtrack, and dotted hearts and kisses and hashtags all over what is down to less than a minute of just that kiss. It seems cut to emphasize the most intense moments, which are repeated throughout.

The hashtags include #BestFriendBoyfriendsRock and #BestFriendGirlfriendsRock, #JustFriendsNot, #ExtremeHeatWarning, #BestFriendsBestLovers, #BlindsidedByLove and #BestFriendLove.

And Rhys is right — it's gone viral, with those hashtags spawning even more videos. There are videos with that kiss cut together with other kisses, some from movies — "The Notebook," "Spider-Man," "Casablanca," "My Girl," "From Here to Eternity," "Ghost" — and some from what looks like the videomakers and their friends? Partners?

Some of these people are definitely not "just friends," unless they're just giving each other a friendly tonsillectomy.

I click through one that has a familiar-looking thumbnail image: Watts and Keith from "Some Kind of Wonderful." Sure enough, someone's cut me and Bridge kissing together with Keith and Watts engaged in that "test" kiss.

"You watching it on your phone while you're waiting for me?" Brighid suggests with a laugh as she walks into the living room. I quickly turn off my phone and set it face down on the coffee table.

"Just trying to remember what color Watts' gloves were, since you mentioned them."

"They're red."

"See — you remember. I should have just asked you!" I joke.

We settle down on the couch, just like we did a couple weeks ago when we last watched this — my arm around Brighid, her head tucked into my shoulder.

My *mind*, meanwhile, is stuck in TikTok — something I never, ever thought I'd say — and on that kiss between Brighid and me, the thing that woke me up about how I really felt about her. In my head, it's now mixed together with all those romantic, sweet, hot kisses from films of many eras. I marvel at how inspired other people were by our kiss.

We haven't even gotten to that big kiss in the movie, and I'm already shifting around, trying to settle my dick down in my pants before it becomes obvious to Bridge that I'm aroused as I sit here holding her, picturing us kissing, and then what came afterward — her riding me on this very couch, or her lips wrapped around me, the unforgettable look on her face as she came with my tongue inside her.

And then, I'm remembering that other house, that other bed, the fire, pressing her facedown into the bedding and sliding home inside her, a perfect fit, a perfect match, driving me crazy as I do the same to her.

"You OK?"

"Huh? Oh — yeah, fine."

"You just looked... far away," Brighid says.

"Just a little tired from all the traveling, I guess."

"You can go lie down if you want. We don't have to finish the movie."

"You're the one who should go lie down. You already said you were tired."

"I am, but I have a couple things I need to do before I go back into the shop, and we're going to be busy at least part of the day tomorrow."

"True. I'll go ahead on up to bed now, if that's OK."

If nothing else, a little distance will, hopefully, calm things down down below.

"Sure! I'll be up soon. *No hogging the bed*!"

"I know not of what you speak."

She bops me on the head with a throw pillow. I stick my tongue out at her, and she laughs, but all I can think of is how I'd much rather be using my tongue for other things where she's concerned.

I grab my phone and head up the stairs, reveling in Brighid's scent on the sheets as soon as my head hits the pillow and dozing off with less-than-pure thoughts of the last time I was in this bed.

CHAPTER 40

TIK TOK

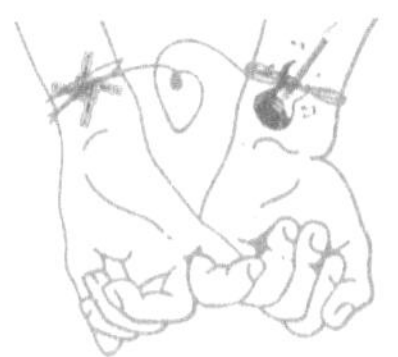

Brighid

I shouldn't be so happy at the thought of Hunter in my bed again. I'm putting behind me what happened there the last time we were together. I have to. But as he walks up to my bedroom, I find myself smiling, and with more than anticipation of sleeping comfortably in his arms, as we've done so many times.

Stop! No. Bad girl! Heel! Sit!

I listen to at least one of those commands and sit back down on the sofa. I've got to pull myself back together. Maybe this emotional whirlwind of thinking he wasn't coming, that he didn't want to be friends anymore, then having him find me on the beach and want to give our friendship another chance... Maybe that's just pushed me off-balance.

I can do this. Even if I slipped earlier in reminding him that I've also always had a thing for one particular blonde.

No — comfy friendship. That's where we go from here.

I wasn't exaggerating how I feel about what happened, with him pushing himself to make things up to me with sex. I want to think he enjoyed it, even if it was just about getting off. But "I'm not attracted to her. At all," keeps repeating in my head, and, yeah, I'm feeling a little nauseated. Actually, nauseous, too.

I shake my head. I need to get my mind off all of that. No more warm-fuzzies of the non-platonic variety, no more lusty feelings or thinking about Hunter during a "self-care" session, and definitely no more sex. Nope.

My phone is in the kitchen, where I left it before I headed down to the beach. I bring it back out in the living room and run quickly through a handful of text messages from the lady-squad, all asking what happened with Hunter and really adamantly wanting to know how I'm doing. I'll send them all an update in the morning, when I've had time to absorb it all.

Work comes next. I've been gone from the shop for the better part of a week. I need to confirm inventory levels and put in some orders. Mrs. Lowell now wants some moldavite. Once I'm caught up with the shop tasks, I check my personal email and I've got several. One from Maire, asking how I'm doing. One from Kara, also asking how I'm doing. Another from Lyric, which I open immediately since, as I suspected, she's reminding me of the threat Rory passed along — that she'd bring the kids over tomorrow if I don't come see her.

She and the kids are off for the summer, her from her job as a music teacher at the elementary school, and the kids from school. Along with mom duties, she'll be spending her summer writing poetry, which she is brilliant at. Brighid — the goddess, not me — has given her that gift in spades, and she's hoping a fellowship might be in her future. It would enable her to take a year or so and spend more time with her own kids while she writes.

The kids... Despite the threat, I adore those two! Her youngest is 7, a beautiful little girl full of fire and imagination and stories she wants to turn into books. The elder is a 10-year-old boy, and one of the reasons she really needs more time off. He's autistic, non-verbal, developmentally closer to his sister's age than his own. And completely obsessed with drumming, like his late father.

She's done an amazing job on her own, but I know she wants to spend some time focusing on his needs and working on his communication and social skills, without having to shortchange her daughter on time or attention. Together the two of them are a whirlwind of energy, and Lyric and I joke about her leaving the kids, boxes of sugary cereal and sodas, and Auntie Bridge, all alone together. I'd manage. She's skeptical. But she deserves a spa day or something. Soon.

I let Lyric know I'm fine and will stop by to see her in a couple days and update her in the morning, along with the rest of the ladies, so she doesn't feel compelled to pack the kids up in the car and bring them over tomorrow. When I'm going to be a little busy trying to fix Hunter's hand. Again.

There's now a second email from Maire, with the subject line of "UREGENT!" (Maire doesn't like autocorrect and her typing is lousy when she's in a rush.) That's concerning.

Bridge — if yu haven't already cked social media this afternoon, you may not want 2. Or maybe you do. I dont know. There's a thing you should see. I think. Maybe. I can't list al the hashtags, but start w/ #JustFriendsNot.

Call me if you need to talk! Love u!

I've been here before. Social media hasn't been my friend of late. I'm not sure I even want to know. Curiosity killed the cat and made Brighid very sad. But I can't go back to work if Holly's stirred up the press again.

I open up Twitter and type in the #JustFriendsNot hashtag.

What I see is a slew of video thumbnails, mostly linked from TikTok. Some of them are of other people kissing, but I don't have to scroll very far before I recognize the images of me kissing a blindfolded Hunter.

I do that thing you should not ever do, and I look at a few of the comments. If there's an uproar happening, it's going to be in the comments. It's been more than a couple days, but the tide of the comments and hashtags seems to have turned.

Instead of people calling me a fat slut, it's things like that #JustFriendsNot hashtag, or #DangerousCurvesAhead. There's a few more admirers of my moderately ample butt, which I'll admit is decently shaped, but #NotMyKink. Hey, more power to them if that's their thing, though. No kink-shaming from me.

I'm a little taken aback by the prevalence of #IdDoHer, #ShesHotHotHot, #BrighidSoHot, #BountifulBeauty, #BlondeBombshell (thanks for that one, Hunter!), #RockAndASoftPlace, #SmartIsSexy and even #HighHeelsSuck.

Then there's also #BestFriendBoyfriendsRock and #BestFriendGirlfriendsRock and #REALLYBestFriends. I'm starting to think people are going overboard when I get to #BestKissEver, #HotHotHot, #SpeakingInTongues, #SuckMyKiss (apologies to the Chili Peppers — I know my ass in a short skirt was not what you were expecting to see) and #Thunderstruck (yeah, sorry about that, too, AC/DC).

Wondering what all the renewed fuss is about when the video has clearly been all over the place this week, I click on the one that seems to be most popular.

The familiar melody of Hunter's designated ringtone sounds, but it's not an incoming call — it's the background music for the video. "You're My Best Friend" always makes me feel warm inside, because I associate it with Hunter. But what's on the screen doesn't make me feel warm... It's way beyond warm.

"HotHotHot" is stamped over the video, and that seems pretty accurate, since whoever made this video cut together the steamiest parts of that kiss, over and over again. And the telltale #JustFriendsNot hashtag seems to pretty clearly indicate the maker's take on Hunter's declaration that we are just friends and nothing more.

Is it possible to have both chills and hot flashes at the same time? My body can't make up its mind between terror that this will be out there embarrassing Hunter all over again and a visceral reaction to seeing that heated scene between the two of us, over and over. My core instantly goes liquid, and I'm caught up in the kiss once more.

Now, with Hunter's reaction trimmed from the video, I'm not seeing a passionate kiss cut short with his fearful eyes on me. Instead, I'm seeing the unvarnished electrical connection between two people who haven't ever kissed or had sex before, but who have a sexual chemistry that is undeniable.

And it smacks me in the face, because here I am having decided that that chemistry has to be denied. Because Hunter isn't attracted to me. At all.

But that's not what it looks like on the screen. And that's not what it looked like when he was eating me like his favorite chocolate mousse or plunging into me in this exact spot a week ago.

That's also not what it looked like fifteen years ago, when I saw that other Hunter and that other Brighid lying spent in each other's arms, his seed pouring out from between her legs. And it's not what it looked like last week, when he slid slowly inside me and rocked his hips sensuously before taking my mouth with his, his eyes full of passion and... what seemed like... something more?

Forced to look back at that moment, caught on video, before everything was colored by that one text, I realize there was no fear in his eyes *last week*. Determination, maybe. There was no revulsion or even the distance that might suggest he was picturing some other woman while he was having sex with me.

I'm seeing the same thing in this first, accidental kiss that I saw the last time he was in my bed. A man who wanted me. Badly.

Could I really have been wrong about this again? His words to Alex had made no sense considering what we'd spent the prior day, and night, doing. They'd never really made sense at all, except to the Brighid who'd been so often wounded by the words of others and by his repeated rejections over the years.

But the Hunter who'd been here last week, the Brighid who'd thrown caution to the wind and risked everything for that dream he held out to her... They weren't caught up in rules and complications and appearances and pain. They were tied together with passion, mutual attraction and, yes... maybe even love.

But if that's true, why didn't he argue with me when I told him I couldn't be more than friends with him anymore? Why didn't he stop me when I told him I didn't want to put him in the position of feeling like he had to have pity sex with me?

"Pity sex" — those were Holly's words, put in my head as she sought to knock me down and keep Hunter for herself. Something she was so desperate to do that she'd blackmailed him.

Was it possible? Had he really wanted me when we made love the first time? Had he been misleading me, and the world, when he insisted we were just friends? The internet clearly thought so. Hunter never lies to me, except when he thinks it's for my own good. And sometimes, he's wrong about that. Had he done it again with that press conference? Had he done it tonight in accepting my determination not to ever again pressure him for something more than friendship?

Acceptance. Yes. But he *had* argued with me. Or at least he'd started to try. I think. Hadn't he? And I'd shut him down, told him I didn't want to hear any more about it. This same man who had sung my praises in front of the world, from calling me a "bombshell" to telling every man on the planet that they'd be lucky to have me.

Suddenly, nothing is clear anymore. My certainty that I knew how he felt, how things had to be between us going forward — it's gone. And the certain knowledge that he'd forced himself to sleep with me is no longer fact but a very questionable conclusion based largely on Holly's spite, my insecurities and Hunter's inexplicable words to his friend in a text I was never meant to see.

We have to talk about this. Now.

I rush up the stairs, ready to wake Hunter's ass up so we can clear the air about this. Until I see him sleeping soundly on one side of my bed. (And just the one side, not the middle!)

The blankets are down around his waist, showing off the solid planes of his chest and the strong muscles of his arms, images embodying his guitars (and thereby his mother), his music, his band, engraved there in permanent ink. His blonde hair is scattered across the pillow, drifting into his eyes, which are closed but convey a sense of peace and comfort that I'm loathe to disturb after the long day he's had. The long day *I've* had.

I can't bring myself to wake him up. Especially knowing what we have ahead of us tomorrow. It's going to take a lot out of both of us, and I can't justify cutting short his sleep for a long-overdue, and likely lengthy, conversation fifteen years in the making.

We'll have time tomorrow to sort this all out. And this time, I'm not going to stop him from telling me what's on his mind, what's in his heart. Whatever that is, good or bad.

It's tempting to put this revelation of mine to the test by climbing into bed naked. But only for a moment. We need to get ourselves on solid ground before moving ahead, wherever that takes us. So I head into the bathroom to change.

I crawl gently beneath the blankets, careful not to wake Hunter from his sweet slumber. I turn over on my side, facing away from him, to remove the temptation to lie there and watch him sleep. The movement rouses him, and I'm prepared for him to wake up. Instead, he, too, turns on his side, wrapping his good arm around my waist and pulling my back tight against his front.

I take a deep breath and absorb the feeling of his hard body against my softer one, the firmness of his grip on my waist. He mumbles into my shoulder. It sounds like "Love you," but maybe he's still asleep. I want to turn to see if he's actually awake, but I don't want to wake him if he *is* asleep. His lips brush against my shoulder, and I sigh. Is his subconscious telling us both the answers to the questions I now need to ask? And will his wakening answers agree with the ones he seems to be giving now?

I settle into his arms for another among our countless nights together. We have a lot of things to do tomorrow. And trying to mend his broken hand could be the least among them. Even with divine intervention, healing a broken heart, or two, could be the tallest order of all.

CHAPTER 41

WHITE FLAG

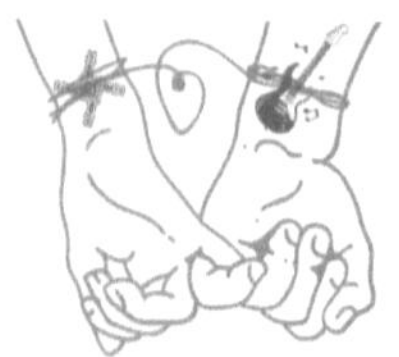

Hunter

When I wake up, the sunlight is drifting in over Brighid's spinning wheel.

Brighid!

She's lying snuggled up against me, with my good arm around her waist, her hair draped across my shoulder and such a sweet, peaceful expression on her face. It's one of the most wonderful things I've ever seen in my life. It makes me smile.

My dick is also extraordinarily happy to see her snuggled up so close, and he'd be happy to show her exactly how excited he is about that, except...

Our discussion last night comes roaring back, and I fight not to lose my smile entirely, while junior's just going to have to get over his disappointment. But just friends, or more, we're together again, and I remind myself of that. Whatever we've been through, whatever we have going forward, I know our friendship is safe. And that makes me smile again.

I lift the blanket gently so as not to disturb my favorite sleeping beauty. I slide out of bed and lay the blanket back down. I slept in my boxer-briefs, because I'd promised Bridge I wouldn't put the moves on her. I'd kept that promise. Brighid's tank top and clingy yoga pants don't leave much more to the imagination than my own choice of sleepwear, and I'm pretty sure I'm going to have to go take a shower before I do anything else, whether a cold and uncomfortable one, or a hot one with a side of relief.

I head off to the bathroom, where I'm again confronted by the naked-lady wallpaper, which I find both amusing and arousing. While the shower warms up — yeah, not going to torture myself any more than needed this morning — I look into the increasingly foggy mirror over the sink, and the guy looking back at me looks about as unsettled as I feel.

His eyes are a little haunted, his mouth torn between a neutral smile and a wry frown, like any minute something could change and surprise him, for better or worse. And he's dreading it and desperately wanting it, all at the same time. Yeah — I've got more to talk to the therapist about than my past trauma.

A couple extra days' growth of beard means I'll need to tidy it up today... well, tomorrow, because I'm not going anywhere today. I'm not sure I can even bring myself to leave Brighid's side except to shower. And I'm definitely wishing I could bring her in there with me. That'd sure take care of my other big reason for showering this morning.

Yeah, my dick is very fond of that idea, even if Brighid's still sleeping and safely out of reach of his lascivious intentions. I carefully remove the brace from my hand, strip out of my underwear and climb in the spacious walk-in shower — Brighid's concession to the big crow-foot bathtub that takes up much of the space in the bathroom.

I think half the reason she bought this old house was for that bathtub, and I don't even make it under the showerhead before I'm picturing her in it, up to her neck in warm water, blonde locks piled up messily on top of her head, with that delicious scent that's pure Brighid perfuming the air, and her breasts peeking up through some very lucky bubbles.

I'll chastise myself later, but for now, that image comes with me into the glass-walled shower, which is quickly steaming up from her really excellent hot-water supply. I grab Brighid's shampoo, skipping over the bottle of my brand that she always has, and I pour some into my right hand, working it up into a lather with some careful help from the broken one.

The scent of her hair, which was just moments ago laid across my shoulder, envelops me. It's like walking up behind her and inhaling the essence of her soft skin and sensuous curves. My hand drops to my cock, which was already hard and standing at full attention, just from picturing her in her bath. I stroke it once, twice... carefully, because I'm already too close to going over, and any time I'm thinking of her, I want to enjoy it, not just get it over with.

And now I'm lost in images of her from last week. Has it really been a week? Has it really been *just* a week? My memory pulls forth the expression on her face as I looked up from between her thighs, my hand pressing her hips to the bed as she thrashed under my mouth. Sensuous. Glorious. So close to losing control, and taking me right there with her.

Two fingers inside of her, and she's grasping them like she'd grasped my cock with her hand just hours before, firm and soft, gentle and determined.

And now I'm remembering what came after she got her hands on me... Her beautiful cupid's bow lips wrapping around my tip, her tongue licking along the head, sliding into the slit, which is already weeping in anticipation of her... any of her... whatever she wanted to do to me. Hands, mouth, pussy, breasts. I just wanted her all over me and me all over her.

Never before have I wanted to mark a woman as mine. It was a surprise that the urge was so strong with Brighid. And her gods must have looked down upon us with favor that I'd been tested recently and she was on birth control. Because I wanted to paint her, inside and out, with my cum, and I wanted to leave behind love marks where anyone who saw her would see that she was claimed — by me.

Mine. Only mine.

Brighid's soft lips running along my cock, from balls to head. Her tongue licking me like the best ice cream cone she'd ever had. I'd seen the girl eat ice cream cones all my life, and I'd never let myself think even once about what it would be like to have her lick me like that, and now it's all I can see.

Brighid in the summer sunshine, her shoulders glazed with salt from the ocean water drying on them, her hair full of beachy waves, blindingly bright as it reflected the sun's rays back at the world, the sparkle in her violet eyes as she looked at me. And I see there the love I tried so hard to ignore for so many years, and now it just lifts me to heights I've never felt before — not before the biggest concert audiences and not with the biggest names in rock congratulating me and my bandmates for a well-deserved award.

And she licks that ice cream, dipping her tongue into the soft, sweet custard like she dips it into the slit in my cock, swirling it around to catch the drips, eating me just like I'm the best thing she's ever tasted.

My hand wraps harder around my cock as the water and steam bring Brighid's scent into my nostrils, and I stroke it with the same touch and pace as she did with her tongue, wishing she was here to complete this erotic daydream and make it real. I'm so close now, just remembering the touch of her hands, of her tongue, her lips as she slides up and down my shaft.

It's an exquisite torment, riding just below the crest of this wave, and I moan, knowing the peak is nearly here and that any moment I'll be sliding down this liquid mountain of pleasure. Her face fills my vision, her eyes turned up to me, full of love, and adoration that extends not just to my cock but to all of me, as she takes in my expression of wonder and delight, pulling me over that peak and into ecstasy as she swallows me down, swallows me whole, consumes me utterly and completely, and makes me hers forever.

I spurt against the wall of her shower, riding the exquisite sensations of her mouth in my memory alone, my head resting against the smooth tile and my heart pounding with my release.

There's a gasp from behind me, and the sounds of a frantic retreat back out into the hallway. I'm instantly aroused again, thinking about her watching me jerk off in the shower, surely having no idea that I was thinking of her the entire time, but watching just the same. Maybe even enjoying it? Aroused herself by what she saw? Can I hope? Just a little?

I sigh and quickly wash my hair one-handed, rinsing off and then grabbing one of her big fluffy towels to wrap around my waist.

I'm going to have to fix this. She and I agreed that it was just friends going forward, and I don't want her to think I'm creeping on her, jacking off to thoughts of her, even if I am.

"Bridge?" I call tentatively toward the bedroom.

There's a moment of silence.

"Yeeesss?" she replies hesitantly.

I can't help but crack a smile. She got caught watching me, got caught watching me come all over her shower, and she has no idea that was all for her.

She's reverted right back to my childhood friend, tentative with sex, hungry for it but uncertain. I have no idea how that innocent girl became the sexpot I fucked over and over again last week. Natural instinct maybe? How many of those erotic dreams? visions? about us together had she had over the years?

I have no idea how she's going to absorb what she just saw, even after having me inside her so many times in that one day a week ago. This is almost worse than having her walk in on me fucking that groupie in the dressing room all those years back. And I'm still chuckling. Sorry, Bridge...

"You OK?"

"Yeeesss?"

"Was that a statement or a question?"

"I don't know."

"I'm coming in. I'm not naked."

"OK."

I walk through the bedroom door, hair still dripping down my chest and back, and my hand holding the knot in the towel that's all that's keeping her from getting another eyeful.

"Uh... That's still pretty naked." She observes, shielding her eyes with a hand. A hand whose splayed fingers aren't hiding nearly as much from her view as she might want me to think.

"You're not seeing anything you haven't seen a hundred times. And even if I dropped the towel, you wouldn't be seeing anything you haven't seen up-close and personal in the very recent past."

"I know?"

"Was that a statement or a question?"

"I don't know that, either."

"Alright... What *do* you know?"

"I heard something in the bathroom, and I thought maybe your hand was bothering you, and if you were trying to shower, you might need some help... You know — washing your hair or something."

"Washing my hair. I see... So, were you going to jump in the shower with me and wash my hair?"

"I really don't know."

I'm trying really hard now not to crack up, because I don't want her to be embarrassed by what happened. But it's so fucking funny, after all we've done together, and she's so unnecessarily out-of-sorts.

"Did you want me to come help *you* wash *your* hair?" I ask, hoping she'll realize that if I was "washing my hair" at that moment, that I'm not talking about giving those long blonde locks of hers a shampoo.

She's turning phaser-fodder red and has executed a classic Picard facepalm maneuver.

"Bridge?"

"*I* don't have a broken hand."

"No, you don't. But I'd still help if you wanted me to..." I can't keep myself from hitting her with a good-natured leer.

"Hunter!" she exclaims, with much less outrage than she might have wanted.

"If nothing else, Bridge, having slept together should make what little remaining self-consciousness and modesty we had between us entirely nonexistent. You can laugh about it. I am."

"I'm *so* sorry, Hunter! I should have never gone in."

"What are you doing?"

"Apologizing?"

"Are you asking me or telling me?"

"Oh, stop! I'm just trying to be considerate, respectful..."

"And you're doing Cirque de Soleil-level contortions just trying to accomplish it," I joke.

"OK — enough. I surrender."

"Do you really? Because I've got this nice white flag here, and I could wave it and offer my own surrender." I start to loosen the knot on the towel around my waist.

"*No!*" she shrieks.

"Is the idea of seeing me naked again really *that* scary?"

"Yes... No. I don't know."

"You seem like you're confused again."

"Very."

I look at her, and I realize there's more going on behind her eyes than just embarrassment over walking in on me jacking off in her shower. I don't prompt her this time, though. I wait.

"Hunter... uh... I... um..." Moments tick by.

"You were the one who got the A-plus in English, right? Along with biology?" I waggle my eyebrows at her. I am a very, very bad boy. I'm totally breaking my promise not to hit on her, even if she probably doesn't realize it's more than just friendly teasing.

"Aaarrgggh!" she exclaims in frustration, jumping off the bed and stomping past me and down the stairs.

"I'll be down in a minute," I call down after her. "We need to talk."

"That's what *I* was going to tell *you*!" she yells back.

Oh? Now I'm the one who's confused.

CHAPTER 42

THREE CHORDS & THE TRUTH

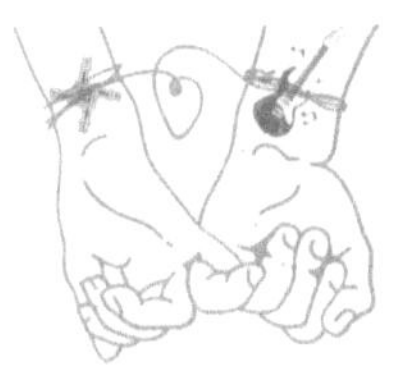

Brighid

O h. My. Gods.
Seriously.
All of them. Like three, or 12, or 450.
And their mothers.
I cannot believe that just happened. I am utterly mortified.
And now I can't get the entire scene out of my head... That moaning sound as I got out of bed and wondered where Hunter had gone, since rarely is he up before me. And wondering about his hand, afraid that he was in pain and had maybe made things worse before we could even try to heal it again... Rushing into the bathroom to see if he needed help... And...
Wow.
It's been a week since I'd last seen him naked. And even then, it was a whole lot of touching and doing and not so much just looking. And today I was, honestly, just dumbstruck by the glory that is that man's rear view.
I don't like objectifying people. It feels disrespectful. But I've always had a hard time not looking at Hunter and having my mouth water just a little, at least since we were teens. My hands automatically move to touch, and I have to restrain them from doing it. Thankfully, I was so stunned by what I was seeing in the bathroom that I didn't have to smack my own fingers back into proper behavior.

But it did leave me frozen in place in the doorway, staring at Hunter's shoulders, back and, yes… ass… with the overtly sexual movements he was making, the little noises of high arousal that instantly had my nipples tight under my tank top, and my pussy as liquid as my watering mouth.

Instinct did tell me to go help the man out. I mean, that's kind of how I'm built — I help Hunter out with whatever he needs done. So, it's an unconscious and instinctive battle in my head — don't touch because he doesn't want me, or he didn't, or… — See! Confused! — or touch because instinct says to touch, and then keep touching, *and* because my sex drive is now in full gear without me touching a thing.

Aaarrggghhh! And all the teasing… He hasn't ever teased me like that. He knows I avoided talking about sex with him after the first five or six rejections. He and I never got into the details of what happened when I walked in on him and that girl, or the other one, nor when I almost lost my virginity at that party when I'd had too much to drink and he intercepted the would-be cherry-picker before anything really happened. And I'd refused to indulge his prying where Mace was concerned, or even when he asked about "Tyler."

It's not that I didn't want to talk to him about that stuff. My libido is probably just as strong as his. I just never let it loose. And I didn't want things to be uncomfortable between the two of us when he'd ruled out anything sexual between us.

And no matter how many long showers he had in my bathroom, from his teens all the way up until last week, I had never let myself think about what he was doing in there (OK — maybe once)… never let myself picture his hands on his cock… his mouth open with pleasure… water and soap slicking his palm… his eyes rolled back into his head as he coated the shower wall…

And I think I'll stop now. If he comes down here anytime soon, there'll be no hiding the headlights operating at "peak" efficiency.

"You OK there, Bridge?"

I jump.

Stealth-mode Hunter has snuck up behind me, having descended the stairs with the silent prowling prowess of a panther.

I wrap my arms across my chest to hide the telltale pinpoints that just thinking of him has created, and I turn around to face him. And my jaw drops.

He's right. It's not like I haven't seen this all before. Mostly in a nominally platonic context, but we had a very productive 24 hours of mutual sexual exploration.

And still I'm stunned by the overtly sexual energy that radiates off him as he stands there in just his jeans. Bare feet, bare chest, his damp hair starting to curl around his neck. I can tell from here that he's just gotten out of the shower, because he smells incredible... like that favorite shampoo of his, mixed with sex, even though he just showered, and... is that my shampoo I smell a trace of?

I lift my jaw back up in some semblance of not drooling, and I raise an eyebrow and study him skeptically.

"Did you use my shampoo?"

"Is that a problem?"

"I'm not sure..."

"You don't seem to be sure of a lot of things this morning, Bridge," he replies with a chuckle.

"OK... What is going on here?" I ask, gesturing frenetically back and forth across the several feet of space between us.

"What do you mean?"

"I thought we'd agreed that this was 'just friends' from now on. I mean, you told literally the entire planet that there was nothing else between us."

"I lied."

"You *lied*? You seemed pretty adamant about there being nothing between us. I thought maybe you were embarrassed about me. You even had me questioning whether I'd lost touch with reality. Besides — you're a shitty liar, Hunter. Everyone knows that."

"I was motivated."

"By what?"

"Wanting to fix the mess I'd made out of your life."

"This last week... this was you *fixing* the mess?"

"Well, I tried."

"I repeat — you're a shitty liar."

"Hey — most of them believed me!"

"Have you seen TikTok today? Believe me — most of them *didn't* believe you."

"Oh, you saw that..."

"I saw plenty."

"Including that video clip?"

"Which one? The original, or the fan cut? Is there a Snyder cut of it that I missed?"

He laughs. You can always rely on Hunter to get the geeky joke.

"Either. Both. All. If there's a Snyder cut, I need to see that one," he adds with a leer, before his expression gets serious.

"What did you see?" he asks earnestly.

"The same thing I saw when I watched it the first time: a very awkward me, kissing a very blindfolded and unaware you, until you recognized my scent... — you really should work as a perfumer, you know? — until you recognized my scent and ripped off the blindfold, looking as upset as I've seen you in a long time."

"You didn't see the kiss?"

"Well, yes, I did. I just said that."

"Did you watch the kiss, Bridge? Just the kiss. Before I realized they'd set us up."

I know what he's trying to get at, and I'm being purposefully obtuse. I wasn't ready to have this conversation on the heels of this morning's little watery escapade. Everything I'd planned to say last night was driven entirely from my head by thoughts of... Yeah. But he's standing there, with no shirt on, just waiting for me to reply. I don't think I have much choice here.

"I did."

"And what did you see, Brighid? What did you see when you *really, really* looked at it, looked at us kissing each other?"

I turn off my well-worn filter and plunge ahead with the truth.

"Sex. Chemistry. Passion. An electric current running between the two of us... Until..."

"No — no 'until.' What did you see in that recording of you," he closes the distance between us and grabs my hand with his good one, "of *you, Brighid*, and *me, Hunter*, kissing each other? Not like little kids with a quick smooch or like friends with a little peck on the cheek. Like grown-ass adults who know what sex is, what chemistry is, what feels good, what feels *right*. What did you see between those two people? If they had come to you afterward and asked you whether they should be together, just on the basis of that one kiss, what would you have told them? Be honest."

I swallow and force myself to answer truthfully, bravely.

"That they were meant to be together. That they fit perfectly together, like two puzzle pieces, like an electrical connection that just snaps into place, like sex on a stick, like everything — like, together, they're everything."

"And why are you doubting that, what you concluded using your own eyes, watching from the outside?"

"Because I didn't just see that kiss that day. I saw the look in your eyes. And it seemed like horror, and then I looked deeper and it felt like fear, and that's not how you look at someone you're meant to be with."

"That's *exactly* how you look at someone you're meant to be with, when you're terrified of failing her, of hurting her, of breaking your promise to yourself that you'd never let yourself be with her because you knew you'd end up failing her and hurting her, and you couldn't ever risk losing her. Not if you had any say in the matter."

"What are you talking about, Hunter? You haven't failed me. And the only way you've hurt me is in denying what we are to each other."

"I know that now. But I didn't then. I really, honestly, thought I was protecting you."

"From you? From my best friend? From the man who I've loved basically my entire life?"

"From the rockstar who can't limit himself to just one girl, even if I don't fuck random groupies anymore. But, more importantly, from a man who could easily turn out like his father, sticking his dick in everything with a vagina and in the process obliterating the woman he was supposed to love."

"You are not your father, Hunter! Sure, you've had more than your fair share of sex, more than your fair share of partners, but you've treated them with respect — every single one that I've seen, anyway. You are a rockstar. You are *not* a cad!"

That makes him smile.

"You could *never* be like your father," I tell him, laying my hand along his jaw. "You have too much of your sweet, caring, loving mother in you. You have too much of *me* in you, after all these years, just like I have a lot of you in me..."

"Less now than I'd like..." he mutters.

I laugh.

"Is that where we are now in this conversation? The time for the truth to be told and the cards to be put on the table, where they should have been all along between two best friends?"

"I need to hear it, Bridge. I don't think I was the only one trying to protect someone here. I saw that fire in you, in that kiss, in every kiss we've shared since. You've wanted me a long time, and I have been an utter idiot in resisting it, but I don't think you really want to be just friends. I don't think you ever really did."

I sigh. Cards. On the table.

"I never really did. I was honest with you, Hunter — it made me sick thinking that you had sex with me out of pity or remorse, when you're not attracted to me..."

"Whoa! Wait a minute! Who said I wasn't attracted to you?"

"You did! In that text to Alex..." I break off, realizing that I've just admitted to reading his private texts, even if I didn't really mean to.

"A-ha! J'accuse! And I don't even speak French!"

I cringe. I have been caught red-handed. I look at my feet, because I can't look at him right now.

"I shouldn't have looked. I'm sorry. But I was working on your phone, and Alex's text came up, and I tried to ignore it, and I thought then that the update had finished, so I looked again, and there it was. And it just hurt so much, Hunter..."

He grabs me to him tightly and strokes my hair, looking directly into my eyes, our faces just inches apart.

"Bridge — it was a lie. It was a lie I told Alex, and even myself for a while, when I was doing whatever I could to avoid breaking my promise to myself to just be your friend. And I repeated that lie that afternoon because I needed to figure out where we were going, what you wanted, how we were going to make this — us — work, before I told the guys and had to deal with the inevitable teasing about how stupid I'd been not to have been with you all along, and whatever stupid shit they might say to you after all this time.

"And because I needed to defang Holly and her threat against you, against us, before I could do any of that. I had a plan. I was just too late. She'd already seen us together, and she was already lighting the fuse of her nuclear option. And then everything turned into utter chaos."

"Because I refused to let you explain. And not for the last time."

"Yeah, you do that sometimes. That whole running thing you do? It involves a lot of 'La-la-la-la I can't hear you!' when you're hurting and you can't face whatever hurt you."

"Guilty," I admit. "And I'm sorry about that. I can only promise to try to do better. But this thing between us... I said it that first night we were together — it scares me. You were scared of hurting me, and I was scared of damaging us, our friendship, by asking something of you that you could not give."

"The only reason I couldn't give you want you wanted, Bridge — what on some level you always knew was right — was because I was scared of hurting you, and, yes, of damaging or destroying what we already had. I'm the one who should have been braver there. Because if I'd told you why I was holding back, why — stupid teenage Hunter — I was screwing half the cheerleading squad, and then random groupies, and then Holly's bitch-squad... We could have avoided all of this."

He's quiet for a minute.

"I can't tell you how many times in the last few weeks I've wondered to myself what things could have been like for us if I'd kept you close by my side during this crazy ride that's been my career. Things would have been different, but I can't think of any way in which it wouldn't have been better. And I'm sorry I didn't give you, give us, that chance."

"You did what you thought was best, Hunter. Which you do sometimes even when you're wrong. I think we'll find that if we try to work these things out together, honestly and openly, we'll do the wrong thing a lot less often, hurt each other a lot less often. For two best friends, we have been absolutely horrible at communicating these last few weeks, and for a while before that."

"Agreed. I should have been honest and open, probably even with the press conference, and I should have let you make your own decisions about what you wanted and whether it felt safe to try for it."

"And I should have let you explain, rather than letting your well-intentioned lies — really, don't do that anymore — and Holly's jealous ravings creep into my heart and prevent me from seeing the Hunter I know and love."

"Speaking of which — let me be extremely clear about this: I am *not* embarrassed by you. And you were never a 'pity fuck.'"

I cringe.

"I would never have done that to you, as eager as I was to make up for my mistakes and all the hate that had been directed at you solely because you were my friend. And I had no idea Holly had said anything like that to you, until after the press conference. If I'd known, I would have knocked down your fucking door — new locks and all — and held you down until you believed me when I told you I'd fucked you because I wanted you, because I was ridiculously, irresistibly attracted to you, and that I made love to you because you're the most beautiful woman I've ever known..."

I roll my eyes at him.

"Stop that! I mean it! If you don't believe me, if you don't believe all those #IdDoHer hashtags..."

Now I laugh.

"Which, I have to say, I can't decide if I should show up on those guys' doorsteps and beat them up, or take them out for a drink because they have amazing taste!"

He sighs.

"Bridge, if you don't believe my words, believe this."

He pulls my hand straight to his crotch and cups my palm over what is a very not-insignificant erection.

My eyes go wide in surprise.

"What — *who* — do you think I was thinking of when I was up there jacking off in your shower, with your shampoo all over my hand and my dick?"

"Mary Stuart Masterson?" I can't keep a straight face, and neither can he. We both crack up.

"*You*, stupid," he says, putting his hand on my cheek and caressing it. "I had your gorgeous face, your joyful eyes, your sensuous mouth, your perfect breasts, your strong thighs, your elegant shoulders, your graceful hands, your perfectly curvaceous ass, your glorious hips and belly, and the chocolate mousse with whipped cream on top that is that magic pussy of yours — I had that all in my head when I was getting off. Which I had to do because your inexpressibly sexy self, in those yoga pants and tank top, had me so horny I couldn't even consider going on about our day without at least taking the edge off my desire. My desire for you.

"I made love to you, Brighid, because you are, truly, the most beautiful woman I've ever known. And because that's how you show the woman you love that you love her."

My eyes well… My throat goes dry. There's no hedging here, no code, no caveats. He said he loves me. He's looking straight into my eyes, no hesitation. And he bends down to kiss me sweetly, firmly, promising more…

"If you had really wanted to just be friends going forward," he admits, "I would have gone along with it. Because you, with very rare exceptions, went along with me for all these years when I insisted we were only going to be friends, if wonderful ones. And because I felt I owed you that if it was what you really wanted, after all you've been through.

"But I'd be lying — and badly — if I told you I didn't want more. Because the moment I finally woke up to what we have between us, I was lost to it. I'd have lived the rest of my life feeling like I was living half a life."

I look away from him for a moment.

"Bridge — I understand now what it must have been like for you all these years, knowing you had this amazing life within your grasp and being told you weren't allowed to even reach for it. Even just the last day, the last week, feeling that way, it about drove me nuts. The guys are seriously concerned for my sanity. And my hand."

"Speaking of which… Have we cleared the air between us? Gotten everything said that needs to be said, that should be said, that we want to say?"

"I'm sure I could think of another fifteen or twenty ways to tell you you're off-the-charts sexy and at least a hundred more ways to tell you I love you," he allows. "But that's all I've got at the moment. I'm sure I'll find time for all the rest of them later. And a few non-verbal ways…"

I'm starting to really like this eyebrow-waggling he does when he's hitting on me. (He's hitting on me! Hunter's hitting on me! And he loves me!)

"We need to get set up to work another healing on your hand. Your fretting hand. With which you punched a house."

He looks up and mouths, "Sorry," and I chuckle.

"I think She knows you understand now that you messed up. Let's focus on seeing if She'll step in and help us fix it."

"We were supposed to have a gig next week. I'm pretty sure Billy canceled it. The orthopedist agreed with the ER doc that I need another three weeks, at least, with the brace on and no playing. It's going to be a month or more before I can perform or record. The guys are not happy about that. The label isn't happy about that. Anything we can do to even shorten that time will be a huge help."

"Well, let's see what She's got in store for us."

"Go get your shower, before I give in to the temptation to join you..."

He smacks me on the ass, snatching a kiss before pushing me toward the stairs. If we didn't have serious business to attend to first... there's nothing that would have stopped me from having him do just that. But I've got healer's work to do.

CHAPTER 43

WHEN THE LEVEE BREAKS

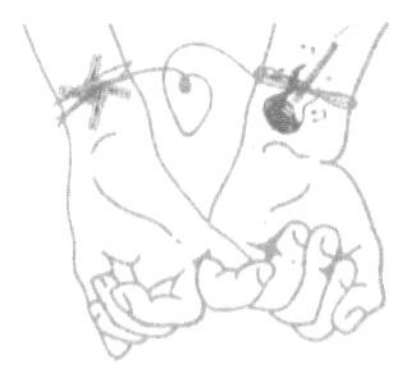

Hunter

I'm pacing again. But it's not pre-show nerves that's got me doing it this time. The relief of knowing Brighid and I are finally on the same page should have left the most happy, relaxed guy on the planet. Nope. I'm wound up, wired, almost anxious, because that sultry-sweet seductress is finally within my grasp and I just let her run upstairs to take a shower. Without me.

It's fine. It's OK. She wants to hold off until we get some important business taken care of. I can wait until later to finally claim her completely, with no secrets left between us, no denials.

OK. Shirt. I need a shirt. Bridge will have a T-shirt I can borrow... Yes, borrow. She'll get it back. Eventually.

I get up to the top of the steps, and I'm drawn to the sound of cascading water.

Shirt. Get a shirt. Put it on. Behave yourself until we can focus on us.

I can see the empty bathtub through the partially open door, and I'm remembering my earlier daydream of Bridge in that tub, bubbles barely covering her nipples, sensuous shoulders traced with moisture, hair damp at her nape as she leans her head back, dripping water down her neck.

Shirt? Fuck the shirt. And fuck behaving.

I shuck my jeans back off again, cock already rising as I push the bathroom door open. I drop my brace on the floor as I pace across the room, taking in the most glorious thing I've ever seen. Brighid. *My* Brighid. Naked as the day she was born, long blonde hair drenched and reaching down past the soft curves of her hips, veiling her tattoo, as her loose waves are pulled straight. She turns under the warm water raining down upon her, eyes closed, reaching up to wash her breasts, and my hands long to be the ones touching her, caressing her curves, brushing across her taut nipples...

Nope. Not waiting.

I pull open the glass door and her eyes pop open, startled. She looks ready to chastise me for having not followed the plan to let her shower, until she takes in my expression, which I know is pure hunger. I haven't had my girl in a week, after having her for only a precious single day. A busy day, but just one — not enough to work off pent-up need, and I'd spent the better part of the week before that wanting her. Fifteen years of wanting her and not letting myself feel it, let alone indulge it. It was a bottomless well of want, and I'm not sure I can ever have enough of her to sate it.

"Hunter... We can't..." she warns, stepping away from me, holding her hand up between us to fend me off. "We've got to work on your hand..."

"I've got something better for you to work on," I tell her, pushing her up against the shower wall and pulling her hand to my cock while crushing my mouth to hers, water all around us, liquid fire inside. She moans into my mouth, wrapping her arms around my back and returning my kiss with ardor.

I drop down to my knees in front of her, using my face to press her back against the tile and sucking her clit straight into my mouth.

"Oh, gods..." she moans, pulling me against her. "Hunter... Gods above and below... We... Oh!" My tongue distracts her from whatever admonishment she'd been about to give me. I slide two fingers inside of her, stroking and caressing her walls. I want to learn this woman's body, inside and out, and I haven't had nearly enough time with her to do that yet.

"Time..." she mutters, once again seeming to be directly connected to my mind. "No time." Or not. I lick her from opening to apex, hoping to once again shut off that sharp brain of hers, get her to lose herself in feeling alone.

"Hunter," she says more firmly, and I look up to find her eyes open, her face disapproving but with reluctance also clearly displayed. "Come here," she says, gesturing for me to stand up. I do as she asks, but I press myself up against her again, making sure she can feel my cock pressing into her belly.

"You never follow instructions, do you?" she chuckles, stroking my jaw, and I can see that affection in her smile, that deep love for me that she's always had and that I spent so long ignoring and avoiding.

Her hand wraps around my cock, stroking, and I rock into it, hoping she's changed her mind and decided we can make time for this. I slide my fingers up through her slit, causing her hips to spasm and press both of our hands between us.

"Bad, bad boy..." she says, shaking her head. "And now your contrariness is going to teach you a lesson," she says. I'm not liking the slightly sadistic smile on her face.

She pushes me away from her, and I'm wondering if she's changed her mind entirely, if she's decided she's pissed enough about what I put her through that she's going to call a halt to all of it. But then she drags her fingertips up my cock and my arousal starts to rise once again.

She walks around me and out of the shower, grabbing a robe from the back of the bathroom door and a second from a shelf. She tosses the second one at me. I grab it with my good hand, wondering what she's got in mind. She bends down to snatch my brace off the floor, and I relish the view, her ass tipped up in the air, breasts tipped forward. My breath catches. She approaches me slowly, hips swaying, and shoves the brace in my hand, leaning in close and whispering in my ear, "Put them on."

With that, she turns on her heel and walks out of the bathroom, shrugging her own robe on over her shoulders.

Whoa.

I follow her into the bedroom, sliding on the robe and fastening the brace on my hand again.

"Lesson, Bridge? What kind of *lesson* are you going to teach me?" I leer at her.

"The intersection of sex and magic," she says, an imperious eyebrow cocked at me.

"Sounds like fun."

"Depends... Today's lesson is on how sexual tension can offer an energy boost to ritual. So long as it goes unspent."

"Unspent... Oh. You mean..."

"No orgasm for you, boyo," she says with a chuckle, reaching out to again stroke my cock through the opening in the robe. "Or for me. At least until afterward... I told you we should get the healing ritual done first thing. You didn't listen. And now we're both horny as Hel and it'll have to fuel the work, because if I come now, I'll be too loosey-goosey grounded to do it. So, we're going to have to wait."

I really have to learn to follow instructions.

Brighid has brought me into one of the guest bedrooms upstairs, only this one contains not a bed but her altar table, with her Brighid statue on it, surrounded by candles, a cauldron, her woven cross, a heavy carved hammer and more. On the walls are three of her weavings in the Soul series — the mysteriously returned Ireland, as well as Hunter and Inspiration — and images of flame, red-haired women, a well, an anvil... This is one of the few rooms in the house I've never been in, though I've seen some of these items in her living spaces over the years.

She takes some of the candles from the altar and places them at spots around the room. She pulls a pack of matches from a pocket on her robe and starts to light them, one by one.

"See — no lighting them with my mind, nor with a snap of my fingers," she explains with a wink.

"Sit," she orders, pointing at the floor, which is covered in the center by a thin rug. When I'm seated, she returns to her altar, repeating the steps she had performed in her shop just over a week ago. Herbs spooned into the cauldron — this one slightly larger — and water from a pair of jars on the altar, one heated and poured over the herbs and a second splashed in afterward to cool it down. She places the cauldron on the floor in front of me, pausing to run her finger down my nose with an affectionate expression.

She turns back to the altar, bending her head to the Brighid statue before lifting a thin cloth from around the statue's shoulders and starting some music playing. I recognize the softly percussive rhythm of a spinning wheel, hypnotic as it carries under the melody of the song.

"Irish?" I ask her, as the sound of the language seems familiar from when I've heard her speak it with Kier.

"Scots Gaelic, actually. But it's a spinning song," she explains, sitting down on the floor opposite me. "Mary Jane Lamond, Canadian artist from Cape Breton, where there's a large Scots population. Many of them still speak it. And it's close enough to Irish that I can read it almost as well as my little bit of Irish, though it's harder for me to understand it spoken."

She takes the cloth and wraps it loosely around my injured hand, much as before.

"There's a line in one of her other songs..." She pauses, seeming thoughtful, looking at my cloth-wrapped hand. "Basically, it works out as, 'I won't say it, but I have loved you since I was a child.'" She looks up at me hesitantly, as if afraid of what she'll see.

I grab her around the back of her neck and pull her to me across the cauldron, claiming her lips once again. Mine. I look into her eyes. So much there unspoken, but no need, because we understand each other now, again, nothing hidden, no subterfuge... But one thing does need to be spoken.

"I love you, Brighid."

She gasps. And I hate that it comes as such a shock to her when I say it openly now, meaning it just as she has meant it when she's said to me for so many years.

"I love you," I tell her again, letting it sink in for her as I run my thumb across her bottom lip and give her my eyes, wide open and awake, and filled with what I feel for her. A small, sweet smile graces her face, and she's instantly the most beautiful that I've ever seen her. No makeup, her hair in a messy bun atop her head, wearing only a fluffy white robe, and just literally stunning, the most beautiful woman in the world, made even more so because she finally knows I love her.

She sighs.

"Time to mend things."

And as the sound of the spinning wheel continues around us, carrying the words of a song I do not understand, Brighid caresses my hand in the warm waters of her cauldron, muttering softly in Irish, her eyes closed and her focus within. I close my eyes, too, trying to find that feeling I had after I broke my hand in the first place, of something other, something more, something divine.

After a minute, the music drops away, though the sound of the wheel continues, and I open my eyes, finding Brighid —*my* Brighid — sitting in front of me, spinning as I have seen her so often, and I smile at this beautiful woman, my beautiful Brighid, my wife, focused upon her work. And I lift the penny whistle to my mouth, playing her a little more of that tune I've written for her, gifted to her. Her eyes lift from her spinning, and her smile lights up her face, far more than the firelight from our hearth. She lifts her hand to me, and I take it, placing a kiss on the back before pulling her toward me, out of her chair.

This time, I do not pull her hard to me to claim her in passion. That will wait. Now, I lead her past my shaggy friend and his spot at the foot of our bed, outside, onto the side of our hill overlooking the sea, the full moon lighting up the water and the night. And I wrap her in my arms, her head leaning back into my shoulder and her hands pressed over mine where I embrace her. It's a comfortable silence, both of us content to simply stand and watch the world around us, so long as we are together. I lose track of how long we stand there, only noting that Brighid is now speaking, murmuring quietly to herself as she so often does, her eyes closed in the safety of my arms.

There's a light growing in front of me, and I first think we've managed to stand here all night, with the sun now rising over the horizon, but instead I see a bright figure in front of us, hair all the colors of fire combined, a pale blue cloak over her shoulders, and she smiles at me. It's a reflection of the smile that lights my Brighid's face, and she holds her hand out to me, beckoning me to come to her. I look down at Brighid, still immersed in her own prayers, and the lady smiles, letting me know she will be safe where she stands.

I let her loose and walk to this brilliant apparition, taking her proffered hand and walking up close to her. Her eyes are emeralds, lit with flame from within, and I'm transfixed and stunned all at once, my knees beginning to bend, whether in weakness or prostration I do not know. Her hand grasps harder to mine, and I stand solid in her gaze. Again, the smile that reminds me so much of my Brighid.

Let what has been broken be mended. I hear the words, but her lips do not move, still smiling as she pulls my hand to her face and places a kiss on the back of it, between my thumb and forefinger. There's a sensation of heat and flame, as if I had momentarily traced my hand through a candle flame and just escaped being singed. I hear a melody in my head that I recognize as my own, and I glance back up at the Lady's face, now nodding in benediction as She lets loose my hand. I look behind me to make sure all is well with my Brighid. She stands much as I left her, eyes closed and murmuring, and I look back at this bright light made manifest in front of my eyes, only to find that She is gone.

I look down at my hand, unsure whether I have dreamed all of this, the imaginings of a crafter of songs lost in his own thoughts, and am stunned to find emblazoned upon the back, in the very space she applied that fiery kiss, the image of a woven reed cross, four equal arms stretching out like the reflection of the rising sun on the ocean before me.

I turn back to my beloved wife, standing on the hill before our little cottage, and her eyes are open now, shining as surely as the loving smile on her face as she looks at me. She holds out her hand to me, and I rejoin her. She presses a sweet kiss to the back of my hand, and I press a more passionate one to her lips, a promise of things to come.

She caresses my hand, and I look up at her, opening my eyes to meet her violet ones.

"Hunter? How's it feel?" she asks as I become once more aware of the room around us, music playing, candles burning, my hand immersed in warm, scented water, held in Brighid's own as her fingertips trace across my skin, now unwrapped from the cloth.

She's waiting for my answer, and I flex my hand, grimacing when the pain I'd felt before makes itself known again.

"No? Not any better?"

"I don't think so," I reply, feeling both confused and disappointed.

She frowns slightly before taking a small towel and drying it. She places the brace back on my hand, dropping a kiss to the back of it.

"Give it some time. We didn't notice the improvement until the next day last time, and it's a more significant injury," she says.

"That, or She's no longer willing to heal me."

"Don't draw any conclusions. These things often work in mysterious ways. We just have to be patient and see if something else doesn't come along. And, if not, you're no worse off than you were this morning."

No, but infinitely more confused. What the heck was that?

CHAPTER 44

OFF THE GROUND

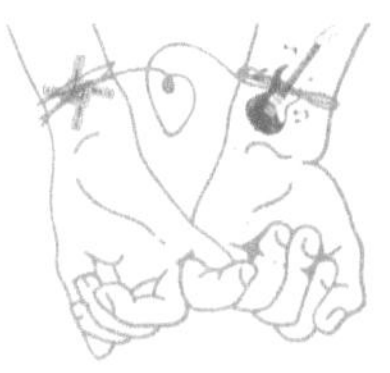

Brighid

What was *that?*
      I had slipped into a vision once more. That's not new,
nor is it unusual to have it happen during ritual, whether a
modestly more formal one like this one today or just sitting
at my spinning wheel. But this wasn't just another vision of
then-Hunter and then-Brighid. She was there with us. She drew
him to her and placed a kiss upon his hand.

It felt like something had happened, or should have happened,
or... I don't know. I honestly expected, after that, for Hunter's
hand to be fully healed when I came back from the vision.
Healing is rarely that instantaneous or patently miraculous. The
only time I've seen it happen like that was with the sprain he'd
had before. Was healing a broken bone too much to expect
when any healing was already miraculous? Had we asked too
much? Had he truly offended Her and she had withheld Her
healing?

I'm at a loss. Hunter appears at a loss. I'm not sure if I got his
hopes up too high. He barely credits any of this stuff as being
real. Did I just undo every bit of credence he'd given it?

"It's OK, Bridge. It was a longshot, I know."

He stands up and holds his good hand out to me, to help
me up off the floor. I stop to snuff the candle flames and
turn off the music, laying the mantle cloth out to dry and

transferring the contents of the cauldron to a bucket I'll use later to water my plants. He stands, watching me do all of this. It's the first time he's even observed me at my rituals, excepting the spinning-wheel invocation that produced "Fire in the Head." It's another thing for him to decide whether he can accept, especially considering the lack of an immediate result.

I'm still feeling floaty, which happens often after ritual, especially when a vision results. I need to ground myself back in the here and now, in my physical body. That means mental effort, or a shortcut, with food, salt... Hunter's hand sweeps up my back... Or sex... that'll do it, too.

He steps up close behind me, wrapping his arms around me and leaning his head down onto my shoulder.

"Did you want to finish what we started earlier?" he purrs in my ear, pulling gently at the tie of my robe. I throw my head back against his shoulder. "Are you still wet? And I don't mean from the shower," he adds, sliding his hand between my legs, under the robe. I shudder. "Yes, you are, aren't you? Wet for me." He runs his fingers up my slit, carefully avoiding that one spot. I nearly growl in frustration.

"I've been wet for you for years, Hunter," I tell him, turning in his arms so that I can wrap him in my own. I attack his mouth, relishing the fact that I have tacit permission to do this now. So many times I wanted even to just touch his lips, and now they're mine. He's mine.

"Mmm... Sounds like we've got some lost time to make up for... Want to see if we can break our record from the last time?" Eyebrow waggles galore from this man. He grabs my hand and rushes me down the short hallway, back into my bedroom.

"Fast and hard this time, Bridge, O.K.? I don't think I can hold on long enough for anything else. Want you too much," he says, sliding my hand down to his cock, which is definitely ready to go after the earlier interruption and this little bit of verbal foreplay. He kisses me hard, mouths open and feeding on each other, and then gives me a solid push back onto the bed. He climbs up right after me, pulling me up in reach of the headboard and yanking open my robe, baring me to him in one movement.

It's a hungry look he gives me now, like he's soaking up every nuance of what he sees. I force myself to relax, to enjoy it, being appreciated as he seems to be doing right now.

"Sexiest creature alive, Bridge. Never doubt it."

He dives for my pussy, sticking his tongue straight in my opening before sliding it upward, through my slit, up my belly, around my bellybutton, across my chest, where he pauses to nip sharply at each nipple before continuing his mouth's journey up to mine, by way of my shoulder and neck, which he bares, pulling the robe down off my shoulders and tossing it behind him with his own.

"Do you believe me now? Do you believe this to your core? That I love you, that I want you, that I am endlessly attracted to you, just as you are?"

He looks me straight in the eyes, probing, and there's again no discomfort in it, just earnestness and connection, and, yes, love.

"I do, Hunter. But you mentioned some non-verbal ways earlier..." I tease.

"Oh, I am so going to prove it to you, with and without words. Starting right now."

He places his tip at my opening, caressing my clit as he moves his hand away. His eyes carry lust, as well as love, now. And that electric connection between us is made solid once again, tangibly physical as he thrusts into my center. I moan with it, as the emotional, physical and mental connections between us all meld into one. Hunter groans as well as he seats his cock fully within me.

He takes a beat, his eyes closed, seeming to savor the feeling of me wrapped around him.

"Yeah, Bridge — this is going to be fast. This first time. Next time slow, then fun, then hot, then nasty, then making love until we lose track of where each of us stops and the other begins. You're free until tomorrow, right?" he adds with a laugh. "Because I intend to keep you in this bed for at least 24 hours."

"Is that a threat or a promise?" I ask, laughing with him.

"Oh, it's definitely a promise. One I'm going to do everything I need to to fulfill. Even if I have to tie you down to do it," he adds. "I've had to exercise a lot of restraint these last few weeks. It's past time I exercised it on you."

I shudder.

"Oh, you glorious sexy thing you... just perfect... built for me."

"Yes, Hunter, built for you... always have been."

"And now I've woken up to that fact. Finally. And I'm never going back."

Could he mean…? Could he really understand what is between us, finally, and have woken up to it? I want to explore this more, but as he pulls back within me, I lose any real ability to think. I know what's coming, and I'm already ready to explode.

"Hold on, Bridge. I'm coming home…"

He begins thrusting into me, hard and fast, as promised, and the heat inside me ramps up so fast that I'm almost instantly ready to roll over that hill of ecstasy. I wrap my thighs around his hips, pulling him to me and deepening his angle, and there it is… that one spot, stroked and strummed as masterfully as his fingers do his guitar.

He reaches his head down and gives a sharp bite to one of my nipples before sucking it into his mouth, and that's all she wrote… I'm flying high, my muscles clamping onto him in time with his continued thrusts before he lets loose with an ever-increasing pace, slamming home over and over again, the two of us locked together there and in our heads, a continuous connection running between our eyes as he, too, tips over the peak and spends himself inside me.

We both lie there panting for a moment, until he slides out of me and off to the side. He looks over at me as I look over at him, and we're both instantly grinning from ear to ear.

"I love you, Brighid. I really, really do."

"I love you, Hunter. Welcome home."

CHAPTER 45

EVERY TIME

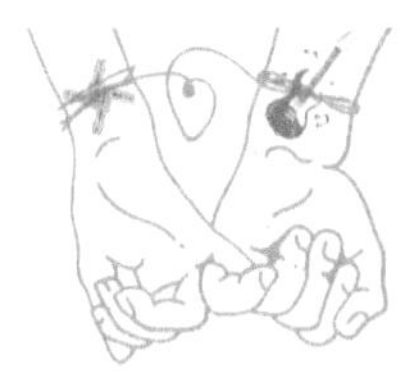

Hunter
The next day

I know, I know — I should have told her about what I'd seen during the ritual. I still hadn't told her what I'd seen a week ago, with the dog and the white nightgown... Amidst all of the craziness, I'd nearly forgotten I'd seen that at all.

I told myself I needed to cocoon myself in Brighid's bed with her, just for a day, without anything else complicating things or getting in the way. I needed to solidify this new element of our connection — something I hadn't gotten a chance to do last week — with sex and closeness and telling her I loved her so many times that she'd never again question it. And I feel like I've done that, or at least gotten a good start.

I still have years of rejection to make up for, and I'm ready to spend the rest of my life doing that, if need be. But Brighid had promised her friend Lyric she'd come see her today, so I was already going to be at loose ends. And I needed to spend some time trying to figure out what had happened during that ritual, what I'd seen and what it meant.

So I'm sitting on the beach. Out of all the places I've been here, other than Brighid's house, this is where I feel most at home. While many things in Mystic Beach have changed in the last decade or so, the coastline hasn't. The sand still feels the same under my feet as it did those days Bridge and I played here as kids. The ocean still looks the same — a modest surf at the edge of endless deep blue water. The air smells the same — salty and clean, with just a hint of boardwalk fries when the wind comes from the north.

Other than Brighid, this is home for me. And no fancy apartment in New York, no tricked-out tour bus, no luxury hotel room could compare to either. I am more myself now than I've been in years, more at peace than maybe any time in my life. Brighid did that for me, and being here cements that feeling. I should have come back more often, and sooner. There are *a lot* of things I should have done differently in my life. But I'm going to do everything I can to set those things to rights now.

I flex my busted hand, still contained within the brace, and I wince. I'd really hoped Brighid — the girl, not the goddess — had been right that I hadn't offended Brighid — the goddess, not the girl — so badly that She'd refuse to help. But Bridge had said not to worry about it, that there could be any number of reasons why my hand was still broken, not the least of which was that it simply needed more time.

And time...

I have no time to waste getting my hand healed. But I also have a lifetime of memories to discover and assimilate, if the two visions I've now had myself are to be believed. Because I don't know what else to call them. Bridge had been right all along. We were inextricably connected to each other and had been since before we were born.

No wonder we'd bonded so quickly as kids, and stayed so close through our teens and onward, until my career had pulled me away from her, until I'd let fame and ego and getting lost in distractions derail me from the path I should have been on and take me away from the person I should have become. Bridge saw it. She called me on it. A couple of times, to be honest, though the real wake-up call had been her cutting me out of her life for two years. I'd worked pretty hard to find the old Hunter during that time we'd been apart, and I think I'd mostly gotten back to him, aside from my bullheaded determination to never even attempt a committed relationship.

In hindsight, Bridge was also right about what she'd told me that summer she moved in with me and Alex for a while. I should have been talking to someone about what had happened with my mom, and with my dad. The only one I'd ever talked to about it at all was Brighid herself, and then only very superficially. I have a sneaking suspicion the therapist is going to want to see me more often than once a week after that initial appointment here in a few days. I have a lot of lost time to make up for, both with Brighid and with teenage Hunter. Both of them deserved better than I gave them. Really, I robbed them both of the potential life I could have had with Brighid. Now all I can do is try to make the most of this second chance.

God, I love that woman. Gods. However many I need to swear that to in order to ensure I can spend the rest of my life — lives — with her. We'd been *married*. Not just lovers or passing acquaintances. Husband and wife. And that now feels more natural to me than any other way of living.

I'd come down to Mystic Beach refusing to even pick a single girlfriend, and then, having been tricked into kissing my best friend, I'd woken up to the reality that she was that and so much more, including the woman I would gladly commit myself to from this moment onward. And that feels like exactly what I should do.

I pull from my memory that vision image of the bright lady made of flame, so much like my Brighid, then and now, but with the flaming hair and those emerald eyes full of fire. Fire embodied in a kiss that marked my hand without burning. I pull off my brace, half expecting to see the woven cross still emblazoned there. It's not there, of course, and somehow that feels wrong.

"Did you make it up to her?"

A tall woman with white-blonde hair down past her hips and a pierced nose and eyebrow plops down on the sand next to me. She's striking. But she's not my Bridge. I take in the tattoos that cover most of her arms. It's beautiful work. As good as any I've had, maybe better. If anything, it reminds me of that first tattoo, my green PRS and the band's muse logo.

"Sorry?"

"Did you make it up to her? Brighid? For lying to everyone about loving her?"

"Do I know you?"

"No. But *she* does. And I know your music. I've drawn your music before, put it into people's skin. I know what 'Fire in the Head' is about. *Who* it's about."

"Who do you think it's about?"

"It's about Brighid, of course. She's your muse. Always has been. Longer than you'd realized. Longer by far. There's a melody in you waiting to get out, and you're almost ready for it..." she says cryptically.

"You're one of her witches, aren't you? One of the circle?"

"No, and yes. Siobhan," she says, offering me her hand, which I notice now is entwined in Celtic knotwork. I shake it. "Brighid's barely a witch herself, as I think you know. She's a priestess, healer, weaver."

"And you?"

"Druid, artist, tattooist," she says, giving me a nod that just says, "At your service" without speaking a word. "My shop's a couple doors down from Brighid's. I did the priestess piece on her back."

And suddenly I have an idea. Or rather, I've been given an idea, inspiration.

"Are you busy right now?"

"Depends."

"On what?"

"You ready to start letting that song out of your head?"

I order dinner from the restaurant on the boardwalk again. Third time's the charm!

And by the time Brighid comes back from Lyric's, I have a full candlelit dinner set up at the table in the kitchen, food piping hot, "Return of the Jedi" queued up for later.

"Welcome home, my dear!" I tell her as she walks in the door.

Her jaw drops.

"Are you playing house-husband today?"

Her expression falters as she seems to realize what she said. *Husband.* It's not going to be a painless transition, I can see. She's still self-conscious, a little insecure about our future. But it's my job now to make her feel secure, even if I can't yet talk to her about why I'm able to do that.

"Yes, dear," I tell her, giving her a sweet kiss on the lips. "How was your day?" I intone dutifully.

She's staring at me now with a slightly skeptical expression.

"Hunter? Are you feeling OK?"

"I'm feeling wonderful, my darling. Never been happier," I declare. "Except maybe when I'm inside you..." I purr into her ear.

She blushes.

"And there he is," she says, chuckling.

"Tonight," I tell her, gesturing to the spread on the table, "we have, for your epicurean delight, crab-and-corn bisque and crispy brussels to start, then seared tuna with asparagus and black lentil salad for you, and oven-roasted chicken with fingerling potatoes and haricot verts for me, and, for dessert..." I mimic a drumroll.

"Chocolate mousse topped with whipped cream!"

She raises an eyebrow.

"Actual chocolate mousse with actual whipped cream, to be followed by the chocolate mousse with whipped cream that is your magic pussy."

She cracks up.

"I see..."

"After 'Jedi.' Unless my 'sweet-tooth' is in such high gear that I can't wait for that second helping."

"Why do I suspect your sweet-tooth was in high gear before I walked through that door?"

"Because you know me so well."

I walk up to her, wrapping my hands around her waist.

"Better than anyone, ever. Even myself sometimes."

And I claim that mouth, that sweetly sexy mouth, for my own.

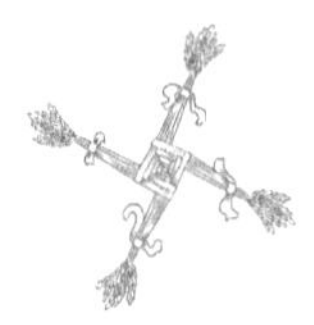

The next morning

"**H**unter, what are you doing? It's not even light outside."

"Gotta hit the studio with the guys today."

"But you can't play!" she points out, as if I'd forgotten the brace still encasing my hand. "What are you going to do, dictate chords to Kieran?"

"That's actually a really good idea! You're brilliant, Bridge — a real genius. Literally. Thanks for the suggestion."

I kiss her forehead.

"I'll be back in time for dinner. You were working today, right?"

"Yes. I'm taking the early shift. Molly will cover the evening and close up."

"Awesome! I'll get some of that risotto with dayboat scallops that you liked, from that place in O.C., and bring it for dinner."

"I can cook, you know."

"Indeed you can, and well, but you are a hard-working entrepreneur and my job is to ensure your life is as easy as possible."

"Hunt? You're a rockstar. Literally. It's not your job to ensure I don't have to cook."

"Sure it is! It's my job to take care of you, just like you've always taken care of me."

She looks confused, so I take advantage and devour her lips, getting her focused on that one thing.

"Love you, Bridge. I'll see you later!" I tell her cheerily as I head down the stairs.

"Love you, too, Hunt!" she calls down after me a few seconds later.

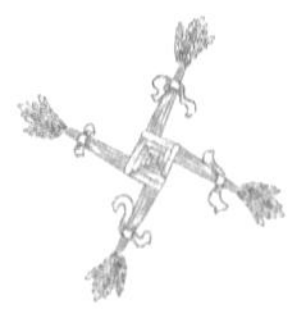

Brighid
Five days later

Hunter is acting oddly. It's nothing I can really call him out on, since it's mostly just him being sweet and caring and devoted, and maybe this is just how he is when he's infatuated with someone? I don't think either of us knows, since I don't think he's ever actually been in love before.

But he's out of bed just after dawn every morning, and always home by dinner time, bringing me some of my favorites from local restaurants, without me even suggesting them. He's... chipper? I'd chalk it up to therapy doing him a world of good if this shift in his mood hadn't started even before he went to see the therapist for the first time the other day. And he came home from that just like I expected he would — somewhat pensive and a little tired, but seeming lighter, like a little weight had been lifted off his shoulders. Within hours, though, he was back to... well, whatever this new mood of his is. It's just enough different from the normal Hunter that it's set off warning bells in the back of my mind.

It's the height of the summer, and the shop is busy nearly every day. I'm giving myself one day a week off right now. I'm going to have to hire some additional help at this rate. I've had a handful of people in just the last few days who've asked to buy my sample weavings. They offered amounts well above prices I'd normally charge for my gallery pieces. Something is up. I just have no idea what it is.

My phone rings.

"Hi, Rory! How's it going?"

"I should be asking you that. I'm hearing rumors that there's been a trending hashtag — #brighidweaver — that leads directly to your woven work at a D.C. gallery. I didn't realize you had gallery pieces."

"I had a handful listed with Case Galleries. I haven't talked to Sheila Case in a month or so, with everything that's going on. I haven't even returned a lot of the calls I've gotten in the last couple weeks."

"Well, based on their website, it looks like they've sold all of your work that they had. I had no idea fiber pieces went for that much! Ten thousand dollars? Wow!"

"Wait. What? Ten thousand, you said? The top price I had for those pieces was four thousand."

"Well, they're all marked as sold, ranging from seven thousand to ten thousand."

"I'll have to give Sheila a call and see what's going on. But that would explain why I've had so much walk-in traffic and people offering exorbitant sums for my store samples. This is the Hunter effect, isn't it? Be honest."

"It may be that Sheila Case is cashing in on your newfound name recognition, yes. But according to their artist info, your work has sold for those kinds of prices before. What's your agreement with the gallery say about pricing?"

"I'd have to check. I think there was some flexibility if she deemed higher prices were suitable based on the market."

"Then that explains it. I'd go ahead and call her, but it sounds like your work is having an increase in demand. Which is part of the reason I called... I'd like to do a piece on the shop and your work."

"I don't know, Rory... Hunter and I just finally got things to a stable point. I definitely don't want to connect this to the reality show or the blackmail scheme or the social media notoriety from that."

"This would just be a standard business story, plus the angle of your work as a noted artist, which I don't think has ever been covered in the local media."

I'm hesitant to agree to it, but I owe Rory a lot, especially after she encouraged me to give Hunter another chance.

"No Hunter angle? You promise?"

"You know you can trust me."

"I do. O.K. When and where did you want to meet?"

"I'll have to get my photographer over to the shop in the next day or so. I was hoping you might be able meet me for dinner tonight. I've got another story I'm working on, and I've got to go out for that tonight, but I'll be spending some of that time just waiting. I figured it'd be a good time for us to catch up and grab dinner, and we can knock out the interview at the same time. What do you say?"

I definitely owe Rory, and it would be nice to spend some time outside of the house and work...

"O.K. — let me check with Hunter, let him know I won't be home for dinner."

"That sounds very domestic."

I smile.

"It has started to get that way."

"Good. Just send me a text if you can make it. I'll send you back the address."

"Will do!"

Brighid: *One of the girls asked me to go out to dinner tonight. Are you OK if I miss dinner? I shouldn't be out too late.*

Hunter: *I was actually just getting ready to call you. The guys want to get this song sorted out tonight. I may not be back until late. So if you want to go out, tonight's perfect for that.*

Brighid: *Oh! Perfect timing! Have fun! Love you!*

Hunter: *You have a great night. I'll see you soon. Love you!*

CHAPTER 46

SYLVAN SONG

Brighid

Rory failed to mention that her other interview was at the Pirate's Cove, the same bayfront restaurant and bar where aMUSEd had originally been set to perform tonight.

"Thanks for coming out, Brighid," she says, gesturing to the chair opposite her at a two-top by the stage, where she's got a perfect vantage point for the performance. I don't expect to stay that long, though. "I've got to talk to these guys tonight if I'm going to get a preview of their next show published in time. But I'll have to wait until after their set, so it's perfect timing for our interview."

"'Tattletale Signals'? Are they some kind of Telltale Signs tribute group?"

"Something like that."

"Aedan would be amused."

"Aedan Mason? You know him?"

"A bit. The guys opened for them twice early in their careers. He and I hit it off."

"'Hit it off'? Should Hunter be worried?"

I laugh hard at that idea.

"Rhys used to tease Hunter about that all the time. But my heart's always belonged to Hunter."

"Even back then?"

"Always. Literally. Since the moment we met, at age 6. Sometimes seems longer," I add, feeling like the before-time should not be ignored, even if I haven't persuaded Hunter that it was real.

We order drinks and food, and Rory puts on her (figurative) reporter hat to ask me about how I learned to spin and weave, and how my work came to be in such demand.

"You went to Ireland and came back inspired?"

"I really did. I put everything into those first few weavings. And then the next series sold almost as well. Honestly, I haven't done much weaving since I opened the shop. I usually send something to the galley every few months. That's about it."

"And you're still spinning your own yarn? From Irish wool?"

"Most of what I spin I sell for my customers' use. That's been the case since before I sold my first pieces. I do prefer Irish wool. But I'll spin silk, domestic wool. I've got a farmer down the road who sells me her carded wool, and another who provides me with alpaca fleece."

Rory has enough questions to last until our food is gone and Tattletale Signals comes on stage.

They jump straight into a ballad before I've even gotten my chair turned around. It's an odd choice for an opening song.

And then I hear it. That little melody Hunter played for me, on his guitar that first night he played again at 15 and on the penny whistle in the vision I first had that night while he played.

I nearly knock my chair over in my effort to get turned around. When I'm finally facing the stage, Hunter is right there, in his usual spot with aMUSEd, but all the way at the front of the stage. He's playing his green guitar, just like he was that night...

Mother of twelve gods! Hunter is playing guitar!

I'm ready to march straight up on that stage and make him stop, but Rory touches my arm and gestures for me to wait. And when I look back at him, I can see he seems to be playing without pain, though his brace seems to limit his movement a bit.

And now he's singing, too, over a more stripped-down sound than I'm used to hearing from the band.

Hunter never sings lead vocals on aMUSEd's originals. Even when he's written the lyrics. It's always Declan. I've heard him sing, of course, and he's got a great voice. But Declan is a natural-born lead singer. There's no denying that, and I think

Hunter prefers it that way. He likes doing backing vocals. But this is different...

The words he's singing finally sink into my head as the rest of the band joins in, with Declan singing harmonies behind Hunter. I'm frozen in my seat, because Hunter's singing about green hills and blue seas and a little cottage with a spinning wheel by a hearthfire and a shaggy dog who hates the rain.

It's a wonderful ode to a domestic life. It's also, without question, describing our life together — then-Hunter and then-Brighid — as if he had been there or... seen it. Seen it!

The white chemise. He *had* seen it. I'd dismissed it, not believing that he could have understood what he was seeing, if he'd actually seen anything at all. And I'd resolved not to bring it up unless he did first.

But this song isn't just a man wondering about a dream with a white chemise. He had seen it all. It's us, made into a song that hung from that little melody that had carried me into that first vision of us together, unleashing all that came afterward, up to and including this last week of domestic bliss with my newfound "house-husband." Who never even blinked when I called him that. Because... he knew. He believed!

Kieran takes center stage now with a guitar solo that hints at bagpipes and fiddles, and rather than just stepping back until he's done, Hunter puts down his guitar and steps off the stage, walking up to me and offering me his good hand. Tears are welling in my eyes, my brain still slow, still trying to process what seems to have happened.

Hunter pulls me from my chair and guides me to the middle of the dance floor, where he wraps me in his arms and pulls me into slow dance that fits perfectly with the song — and yet this is nothing aMUSEd has ever done before. An actual ballad. As the extended solo winds to an end, Hunter releases me with a kiss to my hand, jumping back up on the stage, where he slides his guitar back on and approaches the mic.

But before he starts the next verse of the song, he holds up his broken hand, which I still cringe at him using to play this soon. And he takes off the brace. I shake my head vigorously at him, imploring him not to try playing without it. The man never listens!

He wraps his hand around the neck of the guitar, and then I see it. A small woven reed cross marked in green on the back of his hand, and it's still red around the edges — the sign of a fresh tattoo. My hand goes to my mouth in shock. He's gotten Her symbol tattooed permanently on his hand, where it's plainly visible as he plays guitar, which he's now doing unencumbered. Like his hand had never been broken...

I grasp the Brighid's cross pendant around my neck and send Her my deepest gratitude. Hunter is singing again, of days spent tending sheep and weaving, nights together by the fire, songs played on a penny whistle and a woman with hair like flame and eyes of emerald green.

And I can feel Her, Her hand on my shoulder, standing behind me, with a smile on Her face as Hunter looks at me with an expression of such deep love that I wonder if this is how I've looked at him for all these years, my heart in my eyes and every bit of my being broadcasting that this man was the center of my world. His eyes drift above my head, seeming to focus behind me, where he directs a smile and a nod as he brings to a close the story of us. Then-us. Because our story here and now is only just beginning.

The audience erupts into applause, standing as one as Hunter gives a slight bow and then gestures for me to join him. I shake my head, but he won't take no for an answer.

"Ladies and gentlemen, I need to bring up a very special person in my life, who is the inspiration for that song — which we're calling 'Shepherd Me Home' — and an inspiration for me in every moment of my life. Brighid, come up here! Let's give her some encouragement folks, because I'm not moving on until she gets up here."

His five bandmates are now all standing behind him, joining in the extortionate applause. I'm turning beet-red, but I recognize that they won't take no for an answer either.

I finally take his proffered hand — his left hand — and step up on the stage next to him.

"I lack the words to tell Brighid how much she means to me, but I'm hoping that this song — the second I've written with her as my muse — will at least come close," he says.

Now the tears are flowing freely down my face. His muse?

He reaches over to pull me close, and gives me a torrid kiss that has the guys, and the audience, hooting. I'm not sure my face could get any redder. But I kiss him back, just as fiercely. And in that instant, I'm transported back to that moment when my lips first touched his and our connection and our chemistry made themselves known — to both of us, and to the world. Suddenly, the applause and cheering fade away and we're the only two people left in the world.

Until something cool and moist brushes my hand, and I look down to see an Irish wolfhound licking my fingers. He's not the exact same color as the dog in my vision, but he's beautiful.

"I need to introduce another member of our family... this big guy here is Crógan, and he's ours, if Brighid will have us."

My eyes go wide, my hand to my mouth.

"I never told you the dog's name," I whisper into Hunter's ear.

"You didn't have to," he says. "I was there."

Crying freely now, I throw myself at him, wrapping my arms around him and pulling him as tightly against me as I can manage. Our mouths feast on each other, and I'm lost in him again. Until a cold, wet nose nuzzles into my hand, and we both start laughing.

"You look good wearing my past, and my future," I tell him, tracing around the mark on the back of his hand and picturing another pair of best friends who finally found each other and found love.

Hunter cradles my cheek in his hand and kisses me once more.

"Uh... Guys — we love all the feels, but we've still got a show to do here..." Rhys interrupts over his mic. "Or I could do a six-minute drum solo..."

"No!" the rest of the band yells.

So Crógan and I go sit with Rory, to whom I give a big hug of thanks and some serious side-eye for her subterfuge. We sit back to enjoy the new music that aMUSEd has created. Even with Hunter hampered for a few weeks with his injuries, what they've created already stands with their best work and could well exceed it. It's emotional and intense, joyous and dark, personal and yet speaks to universal truths that their fans have always found in their music. It's a hit in the making.

As the last notes of Declan's vocal rise, Crógan decides to sing us the song of his people. Hunter's the first to crack up, and from there it's contagious, infecting the entire band except Declan himself. He glares at Crógan, who takes the opportunity to pull free of my hand and hop up on the stage, standing up on his hind legs to put himself at well over six feet tall and giving Declan a big slobbery kiss on the mouth. Then even Declan joins in on the laughter.

CHAPTER 47

DOUBLE VISION

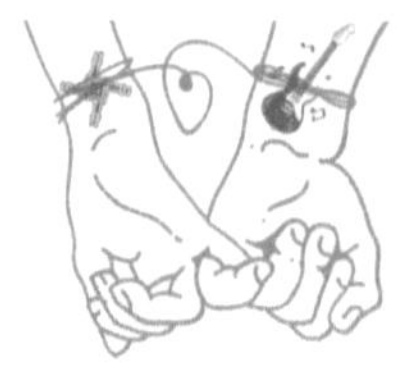

Brighid
An hour later

Hunter pins me up against the inside of my front door, just as he did that night we made love for the first time, his hips pressing into mine, his hard cock to my center. He grabs my hands and lifts them over my head, holding them in place with his left hand while his right starts sliding up the outside of my thigh, taking my skirt with it.

"Is it really healed?" I ask him, looking up at the hand now wrapped around my wrists.

"Good as new. No X-ray to prove it, because I've already risked freaking out one doctor. But, yes, it feels like it was never broken."

"But how? Were we just too impatient?"

"No. I don't think it was that. I think it was the tattoo. When we did the second healing ritual, She gave me a task to do. I just didn't understand that at first. She sent along a second messenger to make it clear."

"Who?"

"Your friend Siobhan. She said something about tattooing the inside of my eyelids and that I was lucky I'd finally gotten my head out of my ass..." I smirk at this, and he gives me a knowing smile. "Then she told me her fee was one new song. She etched that cross into my hand while I sang her a song of the luckiest man alive, who lived on an Irish sheep farm by the sea with his dog and his beautiful, talented, sexy wife. And when the tattoo was done, so was the song. All it took was making the commitment, to my muse," he explains, letting my hands go to caress my cheek.

"It was fixed right then? Instantly? I mean, Siobhan's astonishingly good, but that's beyond anything I've ever seen."

"It was sore that night — the one when we had the candlelight dinner — but I'm not sure how much of that was the tattoo and how much was the broken bone. And I wasn't sure why I'd been told to get it done. But the next morning, when I took the brace off to check the tattoo, my hand felt normal, like it hadn't even been sprained, let alone broken. So I went to see the guys and we started working on 'Shepherd Me Home.'"

"I don't like that you hid it from me, but I can't say I object to the surprise. It was wonderful!"

I hear movement behind Hunter and peek around him to see my entire sofa blanketed in steel-gray dog. I chuckle.

"And speaking of hiding — where was this big guy hiding, or did he just arrive?"

"The rescue group brought him in a few days ago. They wanted to check the house before they finalized the adoption anyway. I had them over while you were at the shop. He's been hanging out with the guys at the studio for the last few days."

"Is that why he was doing harmonies with Declan?" I ask with a chuckle.

"Actually, yes. We're getting ready to start laying down tracks on some of the new songs, so Declan's been practicing constantly, ironing out his delivery. Crógan's gotten in the habit of joining in. But, weirdly, never when anyone's in the live room."

"So, what you're telling me is you got me a shop dog, and he's become a studio dog instead," I tell him with a raised eyebrow.

"He can do both! He's flexible."

There's a massive snore from the sofa, and I look over to find Crógan sprawled on his back.

"I can see that. And a big couch potato, too, apparently."

"He is. Molly said he spent all afternoon on the sofa."

"So, he was with her today?"

"He was. He's got a giant dog bed and a raised feeding station in the kitchen. The rescue said that was important. And I've got a guy coming in tomorrow to install a fence in the back yard. They said a sight-hound can take off if they see something to chase, so a fence is best."

"I think he proved that when he decided to give Declan a taste of something besides groupie."

Hunter chuckles.

"I've never seen anything like it. He seems to sense when Declan's being his most diva-ish and tries to take him down a peg every time."

"Good boy," I tell our fuzzy kid. He sneezes and goes back to sleep.

"And now that he's settled in..." he grabs my hands back up, rolling his hips against me, and his hardness has me instantly wet. "I'd like to make love to my girl."

"I could be persuaded..." I drawl.

"And what will it take to do that?"

"How about you go check the dog bowls so I know he's settled for a while? I've had enough of dogs watching us make love to last me a lifetime..."

We both laugh, and I realize we both remember that.

He plants a slow, sweet kiss on my lips and releases my hands.

"You run upstairs and I'll meet you up there. And be quick, or I'll catch you before you reach the bed and take you where you stand..." he warns. I shudder, and then duck around him, but not before he gets in a smack on my ass. "Run! Because I'll do it!"

I take off up the stairs as he heads into the kitchen, a smirk on his face.

Five minutes later, he's got my legs up on his shoulders and he's pushing slowly in and out of me, our hands entwined between us. He's set a tortuously slow pace for us, and time feels like it has stretched out, every movement taking longer than it seems it possibly could, and yet all of it delightful and hot, increasing the tension to an excruciating degree. I want it to go on forever, and I also want to come right now, want to see him let loose and come inside me this instant, and also want him to always be part of me like this.

As slowly as we're moving together, we're both covered in sweat simply from wanting each other so badly and struggling to hold back. Hunter finally moves to rub his thumb against that swollen nub between my legs, and my arousal jumps up another notch, pushing me to the brink.

I pull his other thumb to my mouth and suck it inside, laving it with my tongue in time to his slow thrusts within me. And as I speed up my pace, so does he, finally setting us loose to collide feverishly, flesh slapping against flesh, both of us panting, the tension building to the breaking point. And then we do. It's the crash of a wave on the beach, hard and punishing, soft and sensual, all at the same time.

He drops my legs to the bed beside him and climbs up next to me, snuggling me under his arm. It's a familiar position for us, so often experienced clothed and at least nominally platonically in the nearly twenty-five years we've known each other. Now it has new meaning, because we're closer than we've ever been, no need for anything to come between us, naked both physically and emotionally, and it's all the more delightful for that.

After a few minutes lying quietly together, I'm thinking back to tonight's surprise and Hunter's new song, which I already suspect will be the standout hit of the next album, especially since it will be their only ballad across four albums. But that little melody has stuck in my head, as it has so often in the past, before I could explain to Hunter what it meant.

"Hunter?"

"Hmmm?"

"Would you play that song for me again? The one you played that night you first started playing again?"

"Anything for you, beautiful. That's an easy request to grant. Let me go get my guitar."

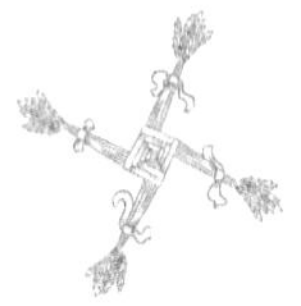

Hunter

I put my boxer briefs back on and head downstairs again, finding Crógan still asleep on the sofa. I take my guitar out of the case and head back up to Brighid. I find her sitting at her spinning wheel, wearing that little blue chemise she had on the first night we were together as lovers — the one that wasn't the long white gown I'd seen in that before-time. She's spinning some ivory yarn now, focused, as always, on her task.

She doesn't seem to notice I'm back until I pick up that melody that is so much her, so much us, and begin playing it. She turns to watch, but something in me misses that sound of the spinning wheel. It's like this simple arrangement of the song, without the band, needs that soft percussive rhythm underneath it. It seems like it needs to be there. I stop playing.

"Keep going, Brighid," I urge her. "I like how the melody rests on top of the sound of the wheel when it's just the guitar."

She nods, resuming her work... the left, right, left, right movement of the pedals, the shifting of her hands across the roving, all in time with our sweet melody as I play it on the strings of my guitar, plucking and strumming and then humming along with the piping notes of the penny whistle. Crógan whines, and I put down the whistle to go let him out, but Brighid has also risen to her feet, and I offer her my hand.

We go together to open the door for Crógan, and he shoots off toward the beach. Brighid and I wander outside, hand in hand, both of us looking up in wonder at a stunning night sky, which is velvety midnight blue and clear, with bright stars spread across it, more numerous than I can remember having seen. There's a flickering, shifting light coming from the beach, and without words we walk toward it.

At the foot of the dune is a bonfire, blazing brightly against the ivory seafoam of the surf and the deep blue of the sea behind it. Crógan sits quietly nearby, getting his head scratched by a woman who has the hood of her pale blue cloak pulled up over her head. As we approach, she turns her face to us, and it's alive with the shifting hues of the firelight, which is reflected in her deep green eyes. She looks down at our joined hands and smiles, beckoning us to her.

What was broken has been mended.

Her lips don't move, but I hear the words nonetheless. I look to Brighid, and she smiles back, seeming to have received the same message. The lady holds her hand out to me, and I offer Her my own. Her touch is the warmth of the hearthfire as She traces the mark on the back of my hand, and again She smiles, giving a nod of approval.

She gestures for Brighid's hand as well, and then She joins our hands together once more, clasped inside Her own. She looks to Brighid, an unspoken question on Her shining face. Brighid smiles and glances toward me, and then nods decisively. The lady turns to me, again a question on Her face. I look deep into those flame-touched emerald eyes.

Shall what has been mended be forged anew?

And I know instinctively that She's asking me whether I wish to commit myself to Brighid once again, now that we are together and whole. I look to Brighid, whose bright smile lights up her face as she looks at me with those violet eyes of hers, and it's the easiest question I've ever answered.

I nod.

The lady pulls at the sleeve hem of Her mantle where it lays across Her wrist and a thread comes loose, illuminated from within, like the light around the wick of the candle. She unwinds a length of the glowing thread from Her mantle before smiling at both of us.

There's a feeling of rightness, of eager joy, like the first blossoms bursting from the frozen ground in spring. It's warmth and hope and promises of wonderful things to come, and it wraps itself around us as the lady winds the thread around our joined wrists. She places Her hand atop our hands, Her fingertips on the bright thread, and the light begins to grow, spreading out from our hands until Brighid and I are the only thing in the world, surrounded by that light.

It glows within her and within me as our eyes connect and our lips come together, alive with flame and threaded with the sound of a penny whistle, joining us together as one, a new whole, born fresh in this moment, tempered and tested and ready for whatever is to come.

I hear a gentle susurration as my fingers trail along the neck of my guitar, like the brush of my callused fingertips across the wound metal of the strings, but rhythmic. My fingers fall from the guitar and my eyes fall open as the susurration begins to wane. Brighid makes a slight gasp from her place at the spinning wheel, and our eyes lock onto each other as she turns to me.

"What was that?" I ask, hoping she will know, because as much as I think I know, I'm really not sure.

"I think we just got married. Again."

CHAPTER 48

BE CAREFUL WHAT YOU WISH FOR

Brighid
The next day

"Uh... Hunter? Why are there check marks on the dog bowls?"

"Last night, you told me to check the dog bowls. I checked the dog bowls."

I'm torn between groaning and laughing so hard that I fall to the floor.

Hunter arrives in the kitchen, looking very proud of himself.

"You didn't."

"I did," he confirms with a smirk.

I walk over to him and give him a little peck on the lips.

"Clever twit."

"Thank you," he says, with a flourishing bow.

"Bridge?"

"Hmm?"

"What do you think I should do with that brace? How sentimental are you feeling about it, given everything that has come to pass?"

"What do you think?"

"I think I'd like to stick it in a box to show our grandkids someday," he says in my ear, wrapping his arms around me from behind.

"Gotta have kids before you can have grandkids…" I point out.

"I think we can safely say we won't have to go to any extra effort for that," he says, running his hands up my sides and squeezing my breasts. My breath halts. "I'm going to enjoy filling you up with me, over and over again." My knees threaten to go out from under me.

"You really ready for kids?" I ask him before we can get carried away and miss having what seems like a pretty important conversation. "We just got a dog. And you haven't officially moved down here yet. We're not even legally married."

"We can fix that," he says, licking a trail up my neck to my ear.

"Which part?"

"Both. I already told my landlord I won't be renewing my lease. I'm not sure I even want to go back to the apartment. I may just hire movers to bring my stuff here, minus the furniture. You know — my mom told my dad that you'd make a great mother. I think she was right."

That stops me in my tracks. When would she have said that? And why? Did she have a feeling we'd end up together?

Regardless, practical matters need to be addressed.

"We haven't talked about touring, either, Hunter. You're going to be on the road a lot. I can take care of a dog by myself, even if he thinks he's mostly yours," I point out to him, shaking my head. "What would you do if we had kids?"

"Shorter tour legs, longer breaks, buy a damn jet so I can fly into Georgetown anytime I want… or a bigger, better tour bus so you — and our amazing hypothetical kids — can come on the road with me."

"You'd really want to do that? Bring kids on the road?"

"Why not? Lots of people do. Nannies, tutors, educational side trips, seeing the country — the world — all before they're old enough to even start school."

"What about the shop?"

"You tell me. Would you want to hire a manager, more help, and spend some time on the road? You can bring your spinning wheel, your loom. I'll make sure the bus is big enough. You can send your work back to the shop, to the gallery…"

"Which reminds me — apparently Case Galleries has discovered there's a hot market for Brighid Weaver weavings. They hiked the prices up considerably — some of them more than double. I could support myself solely off a handful of weavings a year if those prices hold. Wherever I might choose to make them. It's just odd timing, with all that happened."

"The benefits of internet notoriety? It'd be nice to actually get some kind of positive out of what we've been through this summer."

"True. Sheila said she's got one buyer who bought all of what she has at the gallery right now. A repeat buyer, she said. I wonder if it was the same person who bought the first two. I really need to find out who that was and get 'Spirit of Ireland' back to them."

"I can make some inquiries through the band's security contractor, if you like."

"Maybe... Let me think about that."

"Meanwhile... You never did say what you thought of the idea of kids."

"I'm not getting a goat," I deadpan.

"And I'm not buying you a llama, despite Rhys' insistence. Kids, Bridge," he says, drawing my eyes back to meet his. "Do you want kids with me?"

"I've wanted kids with you since I was 15, Hunter."

"Then we should probably get working on that," he says with a purr, claiming my mouth.

"We can't right now. We'd get distracted for hours, and you've got to leave soon to get set up for that private gig Billy booked for you tonight."

"Party-pooper."

"Voice of reason. I'll make it up to you later."

"I'm going to go ahead and stick that brace in the bedroom closet."

"With the other one?"

"Did you keep the other brace, too?"

"I might have," I tell him coyly.

"Sentimentalist."

"Guilty."

He's headed for the stairs when a thought occurs to me.

"Hey, Hunt..."

He stops and stands in the kitchen doorway, looking expectant.

"Bridge?" he asks when I don't immediately respond.

"Seeing you with that brace got me thinking... What exactly did you say to Herself when you yelled at Her — exactly?"

He ponders for a minute, trying to recall.

"I think I said something like, if She was a healer She should come help me mend the broken-ass disaster that was my life."

"And then you punched a house."

"Yeah."

"With your freshly divinely-healed previously-sprained fretting hand."

"Yeah."

"Goddess bless..." I say, shaking my head.

"What?"

"Hunter, you asked a goddess of healing to mend your broken life. And then you broke the hand She'd just healed."

"Yeah... Not getting it Bridge..."

"Would you be here now, talking to me about moving in and having kids, having seen the things you've seen of us from that time before — would you be committed to the idea of us, if you hadn't broken your hand?"

His face shifts from confused to concerned.

"Are you saying She broke my hand to mend my life? Not because I'd yelled at Her? But because that's what I had asked Her for?"

"She told you you were stupid, didn't She? Like immediately after that? Like Watts' line from the movie, where Keith had finally woken up and realized how oblivious he'd been to what was between him and Watts?"

"Yeah."

"I knew it sounded out of character for Her..." I say, half to myself, with a wry chuckle. "That wasn't revenge wrought by an angry goddess, Hunter. It was a wake-up call. You asked for help fixing your life, and She fixed it. In a roundabout fashion, but She fixed it. And once it was fixed, She gave us a path forward, together."

"Mother of twelve gods!"

I crack up.

"When did you start saying that?"

"After we kissed for the first time. Accidentally," he adds with a look of embarrassment. "The kiss, not the gods-mom thing."

"Well, it's entirely apt, considering the massive drama domino collapse that kiss set off."

"You think I'm going full Pagan on you?" he asks, sounding mildly concerned.

"Nah. I think you just have a goddess who's fond of you. Fond enough to break your hand to fix your life."

"And to give me the best gift I ever could have wanted — one I would never have realized I should've asked for," he says, pulling me up against him.

"She gave you that gift when we were 15, Hunter, or perhaps long before. It just took you that long to unwrap it."

"Sounds like a plan," he says, sliding his hand under my shirt and dragging it off over my head before I can say another word.

"Hunter — we don't have time."

"That first day we made love…"

"The one where you told Alex you weren't attracted to me — *at all* — after having had sex with me five times?" He pulls my breasts out of my chemise to play with my nipples.

"That conversation never happened. Beside the point."

"So what's the point?" I moan as he tweaks both nipples to a point with his fingers.

"Besides these?"

He nuzzles in my neck runs his tongue up and over the shell of my ear. I shudder.

"I wanted nothing more when I walked out the door that day than to bend you over the sofa and fuck you fast and hard, fill you up with my cock and my cum, and leave you marked, claimed as mine."

My core goes molten.

"I think I should do that right now," he growls, turning me around to suck a nipple into his mouth. He steers a moaning me backward past a snoozing wolfhound and into the living room, where he flips me around and pushes me down across the arm of the sofa, my ass in the air. He runs his hand up my spine, pressing me down into the cushions, and my back bows under the sensation. He tosses the back of my skirt up above my waist and slides my panties down in one quick move. He presses his hips against my ass, letting me feel how hard he is now.

"I'm going to fuck you, Bridge. I'm going to sink myself into you so far that I'll be part of you forever, and I'm going to leave pieces of me behind so you'll always know you're mine."

I moan, wriggling against him. How does he know what this does to me? Does he just know me that well? I feel him undo his jeans and pull out his cock, and just when I'm so eaten up by anticipation that I'm ready to turn around and look, he slams home inside me. It's fast and hard and rough and completely wild, almost feral, and it's wonderful. He reaches around my hips, right next to where he's pounding into me and slides his fingers up to the top of my slit, where he starts circling my clit.

"Come for me, Bridge. Make that magic pussy of yours suck me dry, take all of it." And I want that, badly.

He's striking home inside me, over and over again, and within moments, I fly free, screaming his name as my inner walls clamp down on his cock. His frenzied movements lose any sense of control as he continues to slam into me, so deep, so good. And the tension within me builds so fast and so high, and I roll over the top again.

"Yeah! There's my girl. Gonna fill you with my cum and leave you dripping!"

And then he does just that, exploding within me, his seed erupting to fill all of me while my pussy continues to throb with echoes of my own orgasm.

He goes still, panting for a moment, and then lays himself down across my back, nuzzling into the side of my neck before sucking the sensitive skin there inside his mouth and bruising it against his teeth.

"Mine," he says. "Inside and out."

I shudder.

He pulls out of me, and I can feel our arousal dripping down the inside of my thighs. He grabs my hand, pulling it to his cock, still coated with me and with him.

"Yours. All yours," he says.

He slides my panties back into place and turns me around to face him, placing my hand on his cock once more.

"Do you understand? Do you believe that in your soul? I am all yours. Only yours."

I look up into his eyes and see the intensity in them. He means this, and he needs me to know that whatever has gone before, it is a universal truth.

"I do, Hunter. I'm yours and you're mine. Always."

He takes my lips hard, pushing his tongue inside my mouth as I gasp with pleasure. His hand traces up across the front of my panties, which are soaked.

"Leave those on. Don't clean up. I want me all over you tonight."

Whoa. Who would have thought even two months ago that it would be like this between me and Hunter?

"And now we can go," he says with a self-satisfied smile, tucking himself back into his pants and moving to pack up his gear for the ride to the venue.

He's a rockstar. My rockstar.

CHAPTER 49

AGAIN

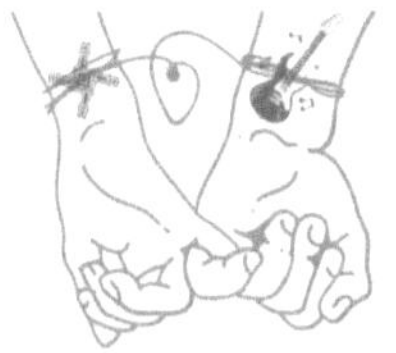

Brighid

"Where's this private party? You didn't tell me."

"Oh, it's at the same place as last night's gig. Someone asked for a more intimate gig, and they were willing to cover the cost of the band and closing down the restaurant and bar to the public. We were already here and the gear was already going to be mostly setup from last night, so Billy jumped at it. It'll say 'Private Event' on the marquee, so we can actually just do our thing tonight with no pretense that we're not aMUSEd." He chuckles. "I still love that, by the way, all these years later. I'm giving you total credit for it."

"Well, I'm not accepting it. And Declan needs it. So let him have it. And you're sure they were OK with Crógan being there? We've still got some work to do on his manners when he's in public. He can't go around French-kissing multi-millionaires at will," I add with a chuckle.

"It was the most emotional connection Declan's had in a kiss in years."

"Oh, be nice. Someday, Declan will find a sweet, down-to-earth girl to keep him steady and will settle down."

"Just like I'm doing?" He lifts my hand to his lips and kisses it gently.

"You really are a romantic under there, aren't you?"

"For the right lady, most definitely."

I look over at him and smile, then pull into the Pirate Cove's parking lot, which is only partly full, unlike a normal Friday night. It must have taken a chunk of change to buy it out for the night. Not to mention aMUSEd's appearance fee. But if they welcome a giant hound at their expensive shindig, they have to be good people.

"I've got my gear. Why don't you go and get Crógan situated? I'll be right behind you," Hunter says.

So I wind my way to the bayside deck, pleased that Crógan isn't pulling on his leash.

"You be a good boy tonight, eh, Crógan? Let's not make them regret issuing you an invitation."

Most of the tables are taken, and I look for a two-top, so I can keep Crógan from bothering anyone during the show. I instantly see that the one Rory and I sat at last night is free and make a beeline for it. I turn around to see if Hunter's got his gear sorted and...

"Surprise!" comes roaring at me from all around.

And I start to process all the faces that had been attached to the backs of the heads I saw when I first came in. Rory, Molly, Siobhan, Callie, Lyric and her kids, Alex, Rhys, Kieran, Declan sitting off to the side, uncharacteristically quiet, and David, again seeming preoccupied. And there's Billy... Mrs. Lowell? Kara and Maire? I recognize a handful or so of aMUSEd's road crew. Amber's sitting quietly in the back, near Callie, and that she's here at all astonishes me. I don't think she's gone anywhere but her house and her shop since the accident. I see a few more faces that are vaguely familiar and must be attached to the band. The house sound engineer is the only other person here besides the waitstaff and bartender.

"What is this? It's not my birthday! What is going on here?" I ask, flabbergasted and confused.

Molly comes up to hug me and takes Crógan's leash.

I turn around when I hear a noise, and I see Hunter up on the stage.

"Hunter, what is this? This clearly isn't a private party."

"Well, my dear, it actually *is* a private party. It's just *our* private party."

"For what?"

"Well, I could say 'just because,' because we've earned a 'just because' after all we've been through. But I'm hoping that a celebration will be in order tonight."

I just look at him, confused.

He holds his tattooed hand out to me, pulling me up on the stage next to him for the second time in two nights. He keeps hold of my hand, turning me to catch my eyes with his own, eagerness painted atop those deep green irises. *What is this?*

"I want to welcome and thank all of our friends, our chosen families, for coming out tonight on relatively short notice to share this occasion with us. It looks like we have successfully surprised my brilliant Brighid."

"You have. You also haven't yet explained why we're here, Hunter," I remind him, arching an eyebrow.

"Patience, my dear. Patience..." he admonishes me before becoming serious.

"Bridge, you really have had such patience with me for all of these years... for the nearly 25 years we've known each other and the nearly 15 years since stupid Hunter decided that a committed relationship was not in the cards for him and blindly rejected the greatest gift he could ever have asked for. You stuck by me and cared for me, got me through the hardest times of my life and helped me reach for the stars. You are the one person in my life who stood behind me to help me make my dream real, even when I wasn't exactly at my best nor the best at supporting *your* dreams. And that I will always regret, because you were right."

"Write that down, dear! You hear it so rarely in a relationship!" Mrs. Lowell shouts, lightening the moment as everyone laughs.

"I readily admit it today, because I have accepted the truth of us in my heart and my soul."

"And his pants!" Rhys adds from behind us, netting some chuckles and a glare from Hunter. It's Rhys. I just shake my head and smile.

"And that truth is that we belong together. We have always belonged together. Best friends, childhood friends become a two-person family, partners-in-crime..."

"Not literally!" Rory adds. "That's how rumors get started!" There's some chuckling, but we all know she's right.

"And now lovers," Hunter continues.

Alex wolf-whistles, and Rhys, Kieran, David and Declan join in for some catcalls. Rhys manages to get in a "Bow chicka wow wow" before Alex smacks him on the back of the head. Hunter rolls his eyes and plunges onward, with me still perplexed as to where this is headed. Are we really here to celebrate publicly that we're officially sleeping together?

"The two of us have always belonged to each other, in every way that mattered, and I know now that we always will." He takes a deep breath and looks around at the gathered friends and family before catching my other hand in his and looking deep into my eyes.

"They say you should marry your best friend..." *Wait. What?*

"I am *not* marrying Kier! Ow! Alex — stop fucking hitting me!"

"Let me try this again..."

He takes a deep breath.

"They say you should marry your best friend... I would have to be stupid not to follow that advice, and as we have now established, I am not stupid *anymore.*"

Everyone laughs.

"So..."

He gets down on one knee, and I am suddenly wondering if this is just another vision, but of a thing that has never happened. He can't be... Can he?

"My beautiful, wonderful best friend... my soulmate... Will you marry me? Again?"

Everyone is looking around at each other, confused, hoping someone can explain.

"Again?" Rhys asks, the only one willing, apparently, to put voice to their confusion.

I'm just looking at Hunter, down on one knee in front of me, holding my hands like I've wanted him to for so long, smiling so bright, a light in his eyes that is so familiar and yet so new, and that I hope I'll get to see every day for the rest of my life, and all the ones after.

"As you wish," I reply with a gentle chuckle.

He pulls the rings from my left ring finger and drops them into his pocket, and he slides on a new ring — an Irish claddagh ring with an emerald for the heart, a flame emblazoned upon the crown and a Brighid's cross atop one hand, just like the one he now has permanently etched upon his own. I know instantly that it's Amber's work, unique and made specially for us.

"I love you, Brighid Weaver."

"I know."

Our friends are apparently geeky enough to get that one, chuckling at the shoe having been put on the other foot, finally. But I won't leave Hunter hanging.

"Yes, Hunter, my best friend, my soulmate — I love you, and I will gladly, joyfully, happily marry you."

"Again," I whisper into his ear as he rises up and claims my mouth the way I'd always dreamed he would do, and then I claim his in return. He is mine and I am his, as has always been and always will be.

Epilogue

Callie

I love Brighid dearly, but she is asking for a world of pain committing herself to a relationship with a rockstar.

And I speak from experience.

I couldn't miss her party, though. She's been so generous with me since I came back to Mystic Beach, helping me source rare herbs for my dishes, and offering support when things had been tough in the early days after first opening the café. We're business neighbors, and I consider her a friend, of which I have precious few, so I value them all the more for that.

I tried to be supportive when her beloved Hunter was being an asshat, but I'm completely out of the loop with pop culture, gossip, social media and music. I avoid it all like the plague. I don't have the time or energy for it, and I think Brighid's experience this summer proved that's the right call.

Besides, any mention of musicians, let alone famous ones, is enough to turn my stomach, which automatically sets me up for a bad day in the kitchen.

Castalia is a true labor of love. The only thing I've wanted since even before I'd turned 18. I'd spent hard years in culinary school, followed by hard years working my way up through some of the best kitchens in New York, from salad prep all the way up through sous chef, never taking the time or energy away from my goal for anything else. But it worked, and I was successful enough that I'd decided to come home to Mystic Beach a few years ago and make my own landmark on the Culinary Coastline, as they're now calling it.

Distractions are something I can't afford. My customers rely on me putting my passion into my food every day, and I won't sabotage that with even secondhand contact with a rocker. So I've had to make an exception for Brighid in order to be here tonight. And sitting in the very back of the bar area, far away from the stage and Hunter's bandmates, is about as good as I could manage. Amber is probably here just as grudgingly, since she so rarely leaves her home these days unless it's to go to her shop. And she, too, is sitting back here away from everyone else.

Brighid comes in with that big dog of hers that Molly told me Hunter just got her, and I'm automatically on high alert. Because I know her rockstar will be coming out at any moment, and I've built my defenses high against anything having to do with those kinds of people. When he comes out, I acknowledge that Hunter is objectively attractive, with his long, shaggy blonde hair and casual confidence. Even with an audience full of friends, he takes control of the room as soon as he steps on stage.

I shudder. I've seen that kind of charisma before. I understand why it might appeal to Brighid, but for me it's a giant alarm bell ringing at full volume. I just hope the fact that she and Hunter have known each other so well and so long means she's going into this relationship with her eyes open. I didn't know either of them when we were kids, though she and I have mutual friends these days. I just hope for her sake that they'll be happy, despite his occupation.

There's no doubt that when Hunter gets down on one knee she's going to say yes. I'm lost with some of the apparent inside jokes, but she seems very happy and he does, too. More power to them. I'll offer her my congratulations whenever she's in the shop next.

I did pull together a quick celebration cake this morning, after our friend Siobhan called to invite me. It felt like the only thing I could do other than just show up. So, while I'd like to just make my excuses and go back to the restaurant to help with the dinner rush, I trust my sous to run the kitchen, and I want to see how the cake is received.

But now that she's accepted and congratulations have been offered, Hunter and his bandmates are getting up on the stage, apparently planning on actually putting on a show. That's my cue to leave. I'm digging for my car keys when the first notes of their song begin. I feel slightly nauseated. It's definitely time to go.

And then I hear it. A feral growl that transforms itself into a gut-wrenching wail, becoming the focal point for the song and everyone who's here. Including me. Because, as impossible as it is, I know that voice, know it as well as I know my own. And as my eyes are drawn unwillingly to that little stage, I want to blot out the image from my brain, because I know that face. I've seen it so many times, and it always made me smile. Until the time it didn't. That last time.

He's older, but he seems to have grown into that lush beauty he had all those years ago. Inarguably masculine, but with a richness that treads the fine line between handsome and pretty. His hair, the color of dark chocolate, falling into his eyes and tracing around his jaw as he moves, prowling the stage like a caged panther looking for his prey, ready to spring. I remember those eyes, too, almost as well as my own. Intensely blue, like a clear lake in the sunshine...

No. No. I have to get out of here.

I knock over my barstool as I scramble to get away. The sound draws the attention of most of the small audience and the band, despite the blaring noise from the stage, and the instant our eyes meet I'm in a full run, halfway to my car.

"Callie!" I hear him cry from behind me, as if my name or the sight of me could somehow wound him, this man who nearly destroyed me, who changed me forever. I have my key in my hand before I reach the car, and I'm pulling out of the parking lot when I see him careen around the corner, pushing through the waitstaff who'd gathered for the show.

"Callie!" comes the wail again, penetrating even the closed windows of my car. I don't look back. I've had enough looking back to last me a lifetime, and I'm not giving Declan Carter another second of my life. He's stolen too many from me already.

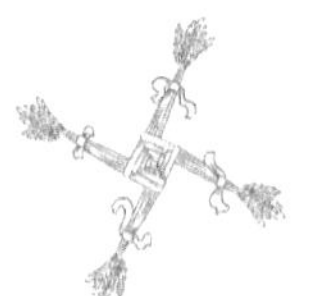

Epilogue, Part 2

David

Only a handful of people know my brother's secret — that he broke his own heart when he was just 17 and never even tried to put it back together. Would he be as big of a dick now if he'd found himself a girl to help him put it back together, or — better yet — if he'd found a way to make things up to the girl he'd loved enough to want to marry her? Probably. Based on past experience, I think his dickishness comes naturally. But he'd probably be less of a dick. I think.

"How is she even still here? I've got to find her."

Declan slams back a double shot of Jameson. I find myself glad we never rented a car to use down here. I'm not sure what Declan would do right now if he had the means to try to chase down Callie.

He's right — what are the odds she'd still be here, after all these years? And at Hunter and Brighid's surprise engagement party?

Brighid's surrounded by her friends now, beaming on Hunter's arm. She glances over at the bar, frowning slightly at Declan. I share her concern. Dec's always been a little bitter, a little angry under the surface, ever since that day he woke up and realized he'd cheated on his girl. I've seen him with countless women, always a different one after every gig, and often two. But there was always an element of self-destructiveness to it, like he was still punishing himself, from first flirtatious glance through the moment he sent each girl on her way. It's kind of sad. But it's become part of who Declan is.

A giant fuzzy head lands in his lap. Hunt and Brighid's massive wolfhound has taken a liking to Declan, if you can call his doggie duets and unwelcome kisses that. And even though she seems annoyed with Declan, Brighid has literally released the hound, letting him drag his leash behind him so he could go to my brother. He's all dog now — sticking his nose in Declan's palm, insisting on being petted, despite Declan's sour mood. And not even Declan can resist Crógan's efforts to comfort him.

There's a round of nervous/curious glances from the circle around Brighid — her friends, Hunt, our bandmates. It seems like Declan's secret is out, or soon will be, thanks to that dramatic display.

My secret — well, the new one, the big one — rests in a pair of big brown eyes. And not Crógan's. No, these eyes belong not to a giant dog, but to a petite brunette girl. The secret's hers, too, really. It was hers first, and now it's ours, and despite that, she's dodging me.

"Don't do anything stupid, OK?"

Declan glares at me. "When have I ever..."

"Just about every night since things went haywire with Callie."

He looks ready to argue with me, but he appears to consider it and stays silent instead.

Call me a romantic — I am, despite my persistent solo status until this point in my life — but even though he looks miserable right now, maybe this little turn of events is exactly what Declan needed.

I feel eyes on me, and I already know exactly who it is. I turn and spot her leaning up against the side of the restaurant, her iPad still in hand, as if she's waiting to see whether we're going to go back on stage. She's hired for the night, so she can't run away from me. Not this time. Not if she wants to keep *this* job, and I know better than anyone how determined she is to keep *this* job, especially when her other one is already hanging by a thread. Though that's on me, which is half the reason she's dodging me.

I walk over and I lean up against the wall next to her.

"Are you going to be playing more?" she asks after a minute.

"Probably. I don't know."

She heaves a frustrated sigh.

"No one here is going to report back to Steve that you were talking to me."

"It's a bad idea nonetheless."

"Piper..."

I give a frustrated sigh of my own. Then I grab her hand and pull her behind me to the other side of the corner, out of view of everyone at this little private party. And then I push her up against the wall, my hands going to her face, my mouth within inches of the temptation of her lips.

"You don't have to do this. I'll fix it. I can still fix this."

"It's better this way, David. For both of us. You'll be leaving soon, and I can't leave Mystic Beach. And I can't live with the risks involved. *You* can't live with the risks involved."

My fingers trace up the side of her neck.

"It's worth it to me."

I brush my lips across hers, and I can feel her melt, her mouth opening to me, eyes sliding closed. My hips press into her. There's a clatter as the tablet slips from her grasp.

She pushes me away, grabbing for the iPad and frantically examining it. Though it appears undamaged, damage is still done — she pushes me away.

"It's not worth it to me, David. I won't risk it. I can't."

She scoots out from between me and the wall and walks away, taking my heart with her.

We're a sorry pair tonight, the Carter brothers. It's going to take a miracle for either of us to get a happy ending out of this.

"Smoke on the Water"

David

All I wanted from this working vacation was some time on the beach — a little sun, sand, surf and maybe a seal-sighting or two. We've got an album to record, sure, but Mystic Beach means vacation to me. It's where my family spent summers when I was a kid. Now that there's a recording studio in this quiet little resort town, it's basically my definition of paradise. The only thing missing is someone to share it with. But finding that kind of connection is a dream I gave up on long ago.

Piper

Ever since I arrived in Mystic Beach, all I've wanted to do was make my mark in the music industry, as a sound engineer. I managed to get an internship at the new studio here, but that's been less fulfilling than I expected, since it seems my boss thinks girls are better at making coffee than making music. Everyone at home is counting on me to make this work, especially given all that's changed in the last year. So I struck out on my own, moonlighting at a part-time job running live sound. And that's where things get even more complicated, because one of my clients — we just connected. But I've got secrets that he'll never believe, and if he did... it could destroy lives — mine, his and more.

A rockstar who has given up on finding the magical connection he's always wanted. A sound engineer struggling with sexism and anxiety on one hand, and secrets and tragedy on the other. His passion has always been reserved for his music and the ocean. Music has become not just her passion, but a lifeline for the people depending on her. What neither of them ever expected was finding each other, and a connection stronger than anything they've known before. But when her secrets threaten to destroy them and everything they hold dear, could that connection be the one thing that saves them?

Stay tuned for the fourth book in the Mystic Beach rockstar romance series, "Remind Me."

When Declan and his band, aMUSEd, return to his childhood vacation spot to record their fourth album, he's looking forward to the working vacation. But he never expects to bump into the local girl he fell for in their teens and dumped when his career as a lead singer took off.

Running her own restaurant has been Callie's sole passion since getting her heart broken, and in the decade since, she's put every bit of herself into her food, with truly magical results.

They once thought they'd be together forever. Will more than a decade apart have been enough time for her to forgive him, or will their soul-deep ties have been severed for good?

Are you wondering what actually happened between Brighid and Aedan "Mace" Mason all those years ago? "Down to the Sea" reveals the secret story of Brighid's brush with a rock superstar before Hunter had even made his first album. (Warning: Ireland is cool, but Mace is hot. Pack for summer heat! — and if you want to remain blissfully in the dark, skip this one. You won't miss a bit of the Mystic Beach arc for aMUSEd. Just pick up with the next in the series, "Smoke on the Water," David's story.)

BACKGROUND NOTES

Glossary & Translations (Irish/Gaeilge):
Go raibh sé amhlaidh — This is the equivalent of the standard "So mote it be" often used by Wiccans, Pagans and other magical types to conclude a prayer or spell.

Cúpla focal — Literally, a couple words, or the smattering to basic level of Irish vocabulary a beginning Irish-speaker might have.

A note on the many names of Herself:
There are literally entire videos devoted to the many variations of the names for the goddess (and saint) Brighid. Some are regional or more common to a period of time, others used as they seem appropriate to whoever is using them. Except to differentiate between the saint (Naomh Bríd) and the goddess, they're largely interchangeable. In Irish, Brighid and Bríd are pronounced pretty much the same — that H aspirates the G, leaving the I the only sound in the middle of the word that is pronounced — like "Breed." Brigid, on the other hand, is an Anglicized form and is pronounced like most English speakers pronounce the name. But, as you may have noticed, Hunter calls our Brighid "Bridge" for short. Brighid didn't start learning Irish

until after she started exploring the legends around Herself, so she uses the Anglicized pronunciation, and that's what Hunter and everyone else use thereafter. Now that she knows some Irish, she uses the Irish pronunciation when speaking Irish and the Anglicized version when speaking English.

A note on Herself herself:

The veneration of Brighid, as both goddess and saint, is on the rise, both inside and outside of Ireland. As a recent New York Times article notes, even while the influence of the Catholic Church has waned in Ireland, veneration of Brighid — as both goddess and saint — has only increased. That's affirmed by the 2022 addition of an official government holiday honoring Brighid, observed on or around Feb. 1 each year, on the saint's feast day, which was itself aligned with the older spring holiday of Imbolc, or Brighnassadh, as I prefer to call it. The Brigidine sisters in Kildare seem to have greeted this phenomenon with open arms, welcoming Christians and non-Christians alike. It has seemed to me to be a hallmark of Brighid's devotees that they generally accept each other very freely. She has a pragmatic reputation in both her forms, so this is not unexpected. You do what needs to get done, with the tools at hand. If you're curious, there are numerous groups and websites online that offer further insight into Brighid in both her forms.

Suggested Playlist

Many books these days have their own playlists, especially rockstar romances, because what is a book about amazing musicians without amazing music to go with it?

You'll find this playlist informed by my own... eclectic ... tastes in music. There are only a couple genres I don't listen to, and everything else runs the gamut from classic rock to world music to metal to folk and beyond. And maybe you'll even discover a new favorite in here amongst the many 1980s "new classics."

An important note: When I set out to make a playlist for this book, and the first book of this duet, "Once Upon a Dream," I had two separate lists to pull from: (1) the song-title-based chapter titles that I'd decided on a whim to try to use, which I was selecting to at least nominally match the content and, ideally, the feel of each chapter; and (2) songs for reading (or writing) the book.

But a strange thing happened when I started pulling songs to fit those criteria — songs I hadn't even known existed turned out to, nearly perfectly, fit the chapter with those tentative chapter titles; and songs I pulled for listening, or to give me a mental musical image/feel of a performance or songwriting scene, they just magically (spookily at times) fit perfectly thematically or lyrically with the chapter I was writing.

There's a lot of synchronicity (seemingly related things happening by actual inexplicable coincidence) in this book, to the point where it is openly declared that there is no coincidence, only fate. But in the writing of the book there has been exactly that — coincidence that defies the odds of being explainable. An inexplicable amount of it.

So, while not every song on this playlist fits perfectly with the chapter that bears its title (and some aren't songs at all), in listening to the playlist and in reading the book, understand that much of what you're reading, and hearing, came straight out of the ethers, as if it was being handed to me by a muse, or perhaps by a goddess of poets and the creative spark — the "fire in the head."

"Dream Weaver" Playlist
  Call Me — Blondie
  Lovefool — The Cardigans
  Alive — Pearl Jam
  Fat Bottomed Girls — Queen
  Brick House — The Commodores
  Higher Ground — Stevie Wonder
  Higher Ground — Red Hot Chili Peppers
  Dark Necessities — Red Hot Chili Peppers
  Crave and Wonder — Arc Angels
  I Go Crazy — Flesh for Lulu
  Saved By Zero — The Fixx
  Up To Me — Seven Nations
  No Excuses — Alice in Chains (cover by Al Cook, https://soundcloud.com/amcook1971/no-excuses-aic-cover)
  You're My Best Friend — Queen
  Kiss Me Deadly — Lita Ford
  A Kiss Before Dying — Candlebox
  Wake Me Up — Red Hot Chilli Pipers
  Rock and a Hard Place — The Rolling Stones
  New York Minute — Don Henley
  Broken Wings — Mr. Mister
  Learning To Fly — Tom Petty & The Heartbreakers
  Meeting Of The Waters — In Tua Nua
  Bach Suite For Solo Cello — Yo-yo Ma

If You Could Only See — Tonic
Deja Voodoo — Kenny Wayne Shepherd
Black Dog — Led Zeppelin
The Fall Out — Slide Show Baby
Herne — Clannad
Secret Oktober — Duran Duran
Sparkling Diamonds — Moulin Rouge soundtrack
Shadowboxer — Fiona Apple
Emotional Barier — In Tua Nua
Don't Dream It's Over — Crowded House
Waiting On a Friend — The Rolling Stones
Some Kind of Wonderful — Zydecosis
Tik Tok — KeSha
When the Levee Breaks — Led Zeppelin
Off the Ground — The Record Company
Time — Pink Floyd
Time In A Bottle — Jim Croce
Sylvan Song/Dream of the Archer — Heart
Double Vision — Foreigner
Be Careful What You Wish For — Erasure
Again — Lenny Kravitz
Song for You — Alexi Murdoch
Waltz For Crystele — Seven Nations
Read Between the Lines — The Fixx

A Note from the Author

I admit it: I've put Brighid and Hunter through a lot in these books. But I'd never throw so many challenges at characters who weren't going to get their happily-ever-after. I'm a sucker for a happily-ever-after. I turn off movies with sad endings while the characters are still happy (I'm looking at you, "The Notebook."). So while I left these two at a rough spot with a cliffhanger at the end of "Once Upon a Dream," there was never any question that they'd end up together, happy and feeling like they'd earned that happy ending. They're soulmates, after all.

And that's the thing about soulmates — it's not just a pair of people who belong together. It's two people who force each other to look at themselves in the mirror and decide whether they really like what they see, and whether they're going to try to change the parts they don't like. In Hunter's case, it's his unhealthy response to his trauma that Brighid forces him to look at, and eventually, he realizes if he wants to be the person she sees in him, he's going to have to finally deal with that trauma in a healthy way. He has a terrible time getting out of his own way even after he realizes that, but she knows that about him and accepts it. It's her gift of unconditional love.

For her part, she's loyal to a fault. But in her mind, that's justified, because she knows he's worth it, even if it doesn't seem that way to everyone else. In the end, he proves her right, just as she knew he would, even if there were points that even she questioned it. He challenges her belief in herself, her intuition and in the two of them, and in the end, she holds up to that challenge, even if she falters a bit here and there. Hunter also forces her to confront her lingering insecurities, even if the way it happens was far from what he intended. And, in the end, he succeeds in proving to her that she, too, is worthy of unconditional love, and that she had it all along, even if took him way too long to tell her that and a bunch of painful missteps along the way.

Wise Lady Maire once told Brighid that people collect the pieces of themselves along their path, and that sometimes things don't fall fully into place for someone until all those pieces are present and the time is right for them to be put into place. When that happens for Brighid and for Hunter, they both end up exactly where they were supposed to be, together.

Acknowledgments

Once again, I'll start off by emphasizing that this is a work of fiction, and despite the apparent strong resemblance to a number of real-life people, the situations and characters here-in are fictional and any resemblance is purely coincidental. Yes, indeed.

And, once again, the biggest chunk of credit for this book goes to my best friend, Al, who was the inspiration for a lot of Hunter, as well as aspects of several of the other characters in this series. A full-time professional musician and sound engineer himself, Al's a big part of the reason this series even exists, including giving me his insight as a working musician and tolerating me being the hanger-on at so many of his own gigs, as well as having brought me into work as a live sound engineer in my own right. Al was also the first one who really said, "You're a very good writer, and what you've written is good." And he said that after having read the work, despite it not being at all his usual type of thing. He then defused the near-daily author freak-outs and tolerated my discussing fictional people like they were people he should know and remember.

In "Dream Weaver," as with its prequel, "Once Upon a Dream," what carries across most in Hunter is Al's sense of humor, which has kept everyone who knows him cracking up, rolling their eyes and/or grinning from ear to ear, to the point where they sometimes forget he's got a genius-level IQ and more musical talent in that once-busted hand of his (in his case, because he's also a klutz) than is fair for any ten people combined to have in their entire bodies. Once again, snippets of real-life have been pulled as inspiration for some of the elements of this story, though the outcomes are different, and the names have been changed and the credit dispersed to protect the guilty and confuse the innocent.

I again have to thank two people who've been vital in keeping my new-author anxiety in check so that I could actually finish this book. Jill and Sandy, you two got me through weeks of fretting about reviews and sales and page reads, with some hope that what I've written will stand up and serve as a solid basis for this series and my writing going forward, that people are really enjoying it and will continue to. You also ensured that my last-minute course correction for the flow of these first three books took things where they should have gone all along, so thank you. In addition to Jill (who went so far above and beyond) and Sandy (who ensured I listened to Jill), I also need to thank Heather and Lisa and all the other members of my writer's group who, despite being busy with their own lives and releases, always took a moment to give me a Like or a Care, or offer a word of support or advice.

Next, I have to thank Julia, who stopped in the middle of reading "Once" to tell me how much she was enjoying it (and Hunter) and instantly defused a mini author freak-out, even leaving me with a smile, and from there eagerly dove into every bit of writing I threw at her. Jaime also gave me a much-needed boost, despite coming onto my ARC team last-minute for "Once." And then Kara came through with a last-minute bit of tough-love, for me and for Brighid. Thanks also goes out to the Rockstar Romance Book Lovers group on Facebook, who have made me feel so welcome, both as a new author and as a fellow lover of the genre, even though my series is cross-genre. Thanks are also again due to Audrey Nickel, author of "The Irish Gaelic Tattoo Handbook: Authentic Words and Phrases in the Celtic Language of Ireland," who checked my Irish for me early in the process of publishing these first few books in the series.

Thanks once again to my co-workers who have ignored my endless rambling about release dates and rankings and marketing, etc., etc., etc., and have in some cases even bought a book. (I promise, I warned them all this was steamy stuff. I just hope none of them gave that warning too little weight.) And the same goes for my other non-writer friends who've been so tolerant of my focus on the series as I get these first few books finished and released. Your patience is appreciated. Once again, my spawn gets kudos for showing that he really has acquired some serious graphics skills, pulling off some wizardry that was beyond my own abilities. And my dear friend and soul-sister Melissa gets extra-special recognition here, too, for offering me a glimpse, a flicker of insight, that sparked so much in my mind's eye.

Al's wife — yes, ladies, (and you, too, fellas), he's taken — gets the credit for incorporating into the book the real-life checking of the dog bowls. (I may or may not have photographic evidence to prove that actually happened...) Al approved of me borrowing liberally from real life (he's married to a writer, so he knows how it works), but he gets the credit for the inspiration.

But Hunter is not Al, so don't draw any conclusions about Al from the content of this book or about Hunter from... well, Al... (Al actually stole my Eagles tour T-shirt, not my Fleetwood Mac shirt. He keeps promising to return it. Usually when it's soaked with sweat from load-in.)

I also have to acknowledge Al's real-life bandmates, the legendary Ocean City, Md., classic rock band Tranzfusion, going on 40 years of rocking peoples' socks off, for which Al has been around for nearly a decade of that. My personal "guitar hero," Hank, offered some insight on his beloved PRS guitars that helped me properly equip Hunter (Al helped there, too), and there may be a few conversations and scenarios herein that were inspired by real-life interactions with the band members, their families and fans. All of whom are wonderful. I promise. Come out and see them sometime. Tell Al he's extra-famous now! (But don't let him flirt with you! He really is incorrigible. And watch out for those flying straw wrappers!)

I promise you, not all of our model girlfriend posse members are inspired by Al's real-life exes. Just one. Maybe. But really not. And she wasn't a model anyway.

I want to again thank all my friends who supported me in adding professional fiction writer to my professional journalist identity. From serving as alpha readers and editors to just plain encouraging me to keep at it — 12 years after an app glitch ate most of my notes for the first Aurora Carmichael/Mystic Beach novel — you made things a lot easier, and I appreciate it. I have to thank my family, both by blood and otherwise, for getting me where I am today, that I could start writing about these characters with whom I've fallen totally in love.

Don't take some of my characters' dysfunctional relationships with their families as indicative of my own. All in all, I had a pretty normal childhood that gave me the leeway to do things I'm good at and enjoy, and I'm grateful for that. We lost my dad in early 2021 to COVID-19, and while as I write this I'm still grappling with that loss and its impacts on me and my family, I know we are not alone and I hope you all have someone to support you through your losses as beautifully as Hunter did in Brighid and vice-versa.

Hunter's mom's illness and her fate also hit close to home for me, as I have struggled with clinical depression for most of my life and know very well how challenging it can be just to get out of bed in the morning and make dinner at night. I haven't always managed it, though I've done the best I could at any given time. And I want to express my deepest love for those among "my people" who have had to help take up the slack or deal with the impact of that slack on their lives, and who have done so so gracefully and lovingly. None of us are perfect, but you make it a lot easier to keep trying.

For anyone who's feeling like just one more thing going wrong, one more harsh word or slight, will be too much to bear, I ask you, please, to talk to someone — especially a professional. You have no idea how many people value your presence in this world nor how many of them would happily give you a hand to hold you above water until you can swim on your own again. Give them the chance to do that for you and give yourself the grace to let them.

Once again, I have to note how many times Chris Cornell's voice served as inspiration while I wrote this book (if you want to know what aMUSEd sounds like in my head, Temple of the Dog and Soundgarden are in the neighborhood), and I continue to lament that he's not still with us today, writing incredible music and letting us enjoy one of the greatest voices ever in rock.

No matter who you are, there's somebody who would desperately want you back if you were gone. Never think otherwise. Give people the chance to help.

If you or someone you know is in an emergency, call the National Suicide Prevention Lifeline at 1-800-273-TALK (8255) or call 911 immediately. If you're uncomfortable talking on the phone, you can also text NAMI to 741-741 to be connected to a free, trained crisis counselor on the Crisis Text Line.

Finally, I add here my thanks to Herself, who has kept pushing me along on this journey, even when I was plagued by doubt and second-guessing us both. She knows I've appreciated it, but it feels important to publicly acknowledge Her role in this work coming to life.

About the Author

Aislinn Archer is an award-winning journalist, columnist and photographer, music and tech journalist, and editor, as well as a semi-retired live sound engineer.

She is in the process of writing two interconnected series spanning the urban fantasy and rockstar romance genres, set in her personal stomping grounds in Coastal Delaware. She is a member of Mensa and the Order of Bards, Ovates & Druids.

In her free time, Aislinn is an Irish language learner, persistent advanced-beginner guitar and bass guitar player, photographer, foodie, gadget guru, jewelrymaker and lampwork glass artist. She is a voracious reader of the urban fantasy, fantasy and rockstar romance genres, and dedicated music fan across many genres. Aislinn also loves visiting Disney World with her teenage son and her best friend, attending concerts and spending time on the beach.

For release updates, freebies, sneak peeks and inside details, sign up for her newsletter on her website at AislinnArcher.com, and follow Aislinn Archer on social media, at https://www.facebook.com/AislinnArcher; on Twitter @AislinnArcher; and on Instagram and TikTok @aislinnarcher. Visit her websites at AislinnArcher.com and MysticBeachRocks.com.